T0357574

THE LOLLIPOP MAN

Also by Daniel Sellers

The Lollipop Man

The Devil's Smile

THE LOLLIPOP MAN

DANIEL SELLERS

Allison & Busby Limited
11 Wardour Mews
London W1F 8AN
allisonandbusby.com

First published in Great Britain by Allison & Busby in 2025.

A CIP catalogue record for this book is available from
the British Library.

First Edition

ISBN 978-0-7490-3261-6

Typeset in 11.5/16 pt Adobe Garamond Pro by
Allison & Busby Ltd.

By choosing this product, you help take care of the world's forests.
Learn more: www.fsc.org.

Printed and bound in the UK using 100% Renewable Electricity at
CPI Group (UK) Ltd, Croydon, CR0 4YY

For Laura

1

Wednesday 6th April, 1994

The call came while Adrian was eating Scampi Fries and waiting for Nige to finish his third pint in the Golden Lion. His satchel burst into a bleeping version of 'Whistle While You Work', bringing gawps of disgust from the old men hunched about the bar. He dived for the exit, wiping his orange-stained fingers on his jeans, and pulled out the phone's stumpy aerial.

'Adrian?'

'Hi, Linda. Just a sec.' The signal was dodgy so he moved to the edge of the pavement, as if that might help. It was raining hard and he hunched against it.

'Are you still in Halifax?' There was a note of stress in the newspaper editor's voice.

'Yeah, we're still here.'

'Is Nige with you?'

'He's – erm, he's . . .'

'In the pub, is he?' A sigh. 'Adrian, you don't need to cover for him. Just go get him, will you? Then head over to Toller

7

Bridge. Police have found a young girl's clothes by the canal.'

'Right,' he said, momentarily stunned.

'A place called Gorton Lane.'

His fingers began to tingle.

'It's behind the old cinema. You might need to look it up.'

He didn't need to look it up. He knew Gorton Lane all right.

'They're going to give a statement at the scene . . . Adrian? Are you still there?'

'Yeah, I'm here.' Rain clouded the insides of his specs and his hair was dripping. He pushed it behind his ears. 'That's fine, Linda. I'll go get Nige.'

'I'm sending Kev to meet you there. Can you ask Nige to take *general* photos: cars, crowds, but at a respectful distance. The girl's mum's likely to be there, and we are not the *Daily Star*.'

She rang off.

Gorton Lane. Of all places.

Back in the pub, Nige was rolling another cigarette and staring contentedly into space.

'Linda wants us to go to Toller Bridge,' Adrian said, and told him why.

'Blimey,' Nige said, and downed his pint.

Gorton Lane was a cobbled street running alongside a section of the Rochdale canal in the middle of Toller Bridge. Today the cobbles were crowded with vehicles, including police cars. People gathered at the far end – a mix of police and locals, by the look of it. Adrian parked the Fiesta in the first spot he found, by the gable end of a terrace.

'You could get a bit closer to the kerb,' Nige muttered, readying his camera.

It was rich coming from Nige, who'd lost his licence for driving drunk. Adrian had started temping as an admin assistant at the *Calder Valley Advertiser* in November; when he passed his driving test in the February, just after his eighteenth birthday, Linda had quickly added photographer's chauffeur to his list of duties. Since then he'd spent part of every day ferrying Nige about the local area to take snaps, but he often had his own tasks to perform as well. Today they'd been at a clothing outlet, so Nige could take snaps of some of the summer fashions. Adrian had taken down some details using standard questions and would type these up so one of the reporters could produce an article. The clothing place was paying for a double-page advert, so it was an important task and he took it seriously.

'Should have reversed in, really,' the photographer complained now.

Adrian bit his tongue. Besides, he had plenty of other stuff on his mind.

He got out of the car and stood on the cobbles, breathing in the cold air, smelling the faint, bready smell of the canal, and waited to feel . . . anything.

But apart from a sense of unease, there was nothing. Possibly because the street looked different to how he remembered it. Shorter. Narrower. And of course it was daytime now.

But he was still unsettled.

Act normal, he told himself.

Nige hurried across the road to take some wide-angle snaps while Adrian headed towards the crowd, curious in spite of himself to know what exactly had been found. The girl had lived only a few streets away from here, in a red-brick terraced house that was now familiar from TV news reports.

He passed a huddle of women, whispering to each other.

Another woman joined them, saying loudly, 'He's gone and drowned the poor kid, hasn't he? She'll be lying at the bottom in the reeds.'

Adrian looked towards the half-hidden canal, its oily surface gleaming between the overgrown vegetation. He doubted there were many reeds growing in there.

'What's your business here, young man?' an oldish policeman said, stepping in his way, frowning at his wet hair and, no doubt, Adrian's youth.

'*Calder Valley Advertiser*,' Adrian said, holding out his press pass. 'I've brought our photographer.' He cleared his throat. 'Who's in charge, please?'

'That would be DCI Struthers.'

Adrian followed the man's gaze and recognised the detective from the TV news, with his peak of red hair and blue raincoat, busy talking to a group of locals.

'Thanks,' Adrian said, moving to loiter discreetly at the edge of the crowd, from where he could watch proceedings. He had a talent for going unnoticed, being short, a bit unkempt with his longish hair, and bookish in his square specs. To many people he was 'just some kid' and generally no one paid him much attention – which suited him fine.

'Awright, Gaydrian!' cried a familiar voice, merry as anything. 'New coat? Leprechaun green, eh?'

He glanced down at the green jacket. It had cost thirty quid in the Corn Exchange in Leeds.

'Tosser,' he muttered, and Kev cackled, drawing appalled looks from two women standing nearby.

Kev Simpson was the newspaper's trainee reporter. He was three years older than Adrian and had his sights set on a career with one of the tabloids. He was skinny and lithe, with bristly dark ginger hair and a narrow face. He made no secret of his opinion that he was wasting his time training at a local rag, writing up committee meetings and village fêtes. For the past twelve days Kev's glee at eleven-year-old Sarah Barrett's disappearance had stunk out the newsroom like a fart. Linda had lost her temper with him more than once.

'DCI Struthers is in charge,' Adrian told him.

'Already spoke to him,' Kev said smartly. 'Early bird, an' all that. Where's Nige?'

Adrian nodded to where Nige was taking photos further along the road.

'Nige!' Kev yelled, waving. 'All right, fella?'

'Linda said not to intrude,' Adrian hissed.

'Bollocks to Linda. Oh, oh – look who's here.' He nodded towards a blue sports car that had just parked. 'Only the flaming Queen of Sheba.'

A stout woman with a silver-blonde bob and a fuzzy dark blue shawl over her shoulders was easing herself out of the car. Adrian recognised her at once and a sense of dread made his muscles lock round his bones. He felt faint. Panicky too. Mouth dry, he glanced along Gorton Lane to the police cordon at the main road, beside the old cinema, and tried to think of an excuse to get away.

'So she wants in on the act, does she?' Kev said. 'Always has to make it about herself. Look at her – all simpering smiles for the community.' He barked out a laugh.

The woman was Sheila Hargreaves, familiar to Adrian, and to everyone else it seemed, as the anchor of *Yorkshire Tonight*, Yorkshire TV's magazine programme, broadcast on weeknights apart from Wednesdays. Soft and motherly in appearance and demeanour, she was often called 'Yorkshire's auntie'. She had a reputation for laying it on thick with her emotional style of interviewing.

Adrian had met her once, years ago, and he didn't want to see her again – now or any time. Unlikely though it was that she'd recognise him, he turned and stepped in behind Kev.

Sheila took herself in the direction of DCI Struthers. People watched, excitedly craning their necks.

'Good afternoon, everybody,' she said, sparing sad-but-warm smiles for the observers.

'Was it Sarah Barrett's clothes?' Adrian asked Kev quietly once she'd passed by.

'Sounds like it.' Kev licked his lips. 'Some lad found them draped on the brambles over there, plain as day. A jacket, a top and some jeans. Realised what he was looking at and told his mum and dad. I'd like to get the lad's name.'

Along the lane Sheila Hargreaves had finished speaking to Struthers and was returning their way, sad-eyed and pensive.

'How's tricks, Sheila?' Kev bellowed to her, making Adrian shrink miserably back so he was almost touching the nearest gable end.

She stopped and turned. 'Ah, Kevin,' she said distastefully. 'And how are you?'

The two had had a run-in, Adrian recalled, when Sheila was opening a village fête and Kev was there to write about it for the paper.

'Surprised to see you here,' Kev said. 'Thought you were all celebrity memoirs and cooking demos these days.'

She came close, her bright green eyes blazing. Not so soft and motherly now. Adrian sensed the crowd watching them. 'I am here to meet Sarah's mother Irene,' Sheila told Kev quietly. 'To do what I can to help.'

'Mother Teresa in person, eh?' Kev said, with a snort.

Adrian held onto the cold brick behind him and willed himself to become invisible.

'Might I suggest, Kevin,' Sheila whispered tersely, 'that if you can't say anything pleasant or sympathetic, then you've no business being here.'

'Steady on, Sheila,' Kev said, miffed.

And then she spotted Adrian.

'Have we met?' she said, peering close.

'I'm—I'm just the driver,' Adrian stammered.

'And your name . . . ?'

She flashed her familiar smile, all antagonism gone. But there was an avid interest in her shrewd emerald eyes. Kev was observing his reaction curiously.

'Adrian,' he managed.

'Adrian?' Her eyes narrowed. 'Right. Yes . . .'

She'd recognised him all right, but looked as if she couldn't place him. 'Well, it's very nice to meet you, Adrian.' Less pleasantly she added, 'Goodbye, Kevin.'

Her gaze lingered on Adrian, then she stepped away and began to talk to a group of women standing nearby.

''Sup with you?' Kev demanded when they were alone. 'Starstruck or summat?'

'No!' He felt himself redden.

'Sheila's a has-been,' Kev snorted. 'Except she's the only one who hasn't realised it.'

A new murmuring from the onlookers. Heads turned. A female police officer was coming carefully along the cobbles, guiding another woman gently by the arm. There was no mistaking the skeletal figure of Irene Barrett. Her face had been all over the TV news for the past week and a half. She looked scared to death. She was sallow with big dark eyes.

Sheila Hargreaves swept over the cobbles to meet her and snatched up Irene Barrett's unoffered hand in both of hers. Suddenly she was embracing the woman, and the two of them were crying.

Nige appeared at Kev and Adrian's side.

'Go for it, Nige,' Kev ordered quietly.

Nige looked embarrassed, but pointed his camera and began to snap away.

Sheila Hargreaves and the policewoman led Irene Barrett to meet DCI Struthers. Adrian stayed put while Kev trailed after them, listening out for quotes that Linda would never let him use.

Adrian felt sick. This was a circus. He took himself back to the car to wait for Nige. He didn't get in, but stood outside and smoked the last of his menthol cigarettes.

A crowd of onlookers had gathered behind the police cordon at the end of Gorton Lane. People stood grimly silent, eyes on the police activity. But one of them, an old woman with curly dyed-black hair, seemed much more interested in Adrian than in everything else that was going on. She eyed him intently, her lips moving as if speaking a curse.

He turned his back and finished his cigarette.

2

He told Kev he had a migraine and asked him to give Nige a lift back to the newspaper office, saying he'd collect the Fiesta from Gorton Lane later.

'You better be at Barry's thing later,' Kev warned him, car keys in hand.

'I'll do my best.'

'I mean it, Gay-boy. I need someone to take the piss out of.'

Barry Tillotson, the deputy foreman of the printworks, was a racist, pot-bellied pig of a man, and Adrian had no intention of going to his retirement do at the Irish Club.

Excuses made, he hurried in the direction of Toller Bridge's main street and phoned his pal Gav from a call box, and an hour later they were in the King's Head. Gav was a connoisseur of old man's pubs and this was his choice. They weren't the pub's typical clientele – Adrian resembling a grungy student, Gav strikingly gothic with his Russian trench coat, backcombed black hair and eyeliner – but no one bothered them.

'Decision's made,' Gav said, lighting a roll-up then picking tobacco off his lower lip. 'I'm gonna leave Sunderland. I hate my course. Hate my course mates. *Really* fucking hate the people in my halls. I told my mums when I got back last night.'

'Right. What did they say?'

Gav shrugged and beamed. 'That it's my choice and they'll support me. I'll apply to start at Leeds in autumn. You and me can rent together.'

Gav beamed and clinked his pint of Guinness against Adrian's glass of Coke.

Nearly all Adrian's school friends had gone to university the previous autumn, leaving him at home to resit the two A-Levels he'd messed up while his mum was ill. He missed his pals, Gav most of all. Gav was Adrian's only friend from school who knew he was gay, though he still struggled to understand Adrian's home life. But then their lives were very different. Gav had grown up with two mums in Hebden Bridge, the lesbian epicentre of Britain. His home was a place of acceptance and empathy. It was ironic that Gav was as straight as they came, while Adrian found himself gay and having to hide it. His mum, he suspected, would be fine after she got over the shock. His dad, less so.

But he was resigned to his situation, focusing on his future away from home, away from High Calder. Away from his past.

And things were coming together. He was on track for better grades and a place at Leeds University starting in the autumn. He imagined himself and Gav sharing a house. One of the shabby red-brick terraces around Hyde Park. Leeds would suit Gav. It was bigger, with a thriving goth scene. No one in Leeds batted an eyelid at eyebrow piercings or dyed hair on a man – even make-up. The thought of living there with his pal conjured up an idyll of freedom; a complete displacement from stress and shame. He found himself unexpectedly welling up.

'You OK, man?' Gav said, eyeing him.

'Yeah.'

Gav drew him into a patchouli-smelling embrace.

Pulling away, Adrian wiped his face on his sleeve.

'Here,' Gav said, and pushed a rollie across the table.

He lit it inexpertly, inflaming half the cigarette and having to blow it out, making them both laugh.

'They think it's him, then?' Gav asked. 'The Lollipop Man?'

'Linda does. And Kev's in his element, the wanker.'

'After all this time? How long has it been?'

'Seven years, four months.'

Gav eyed him. 'Sorry. Guess I should know that.'

'Why should you?' Adrian said. 'It's my business, isn't it? I'd love it if everyone else forgot.'

Gav drank some of his pint.

'Why would he start again? I mean, where's he been?'

'Fuck knows.' He sank deeper into the soft leather of the bench and shut his eyes. He'd lied when he told Kev he had a headache, but now one was starting, high in his shoulders and neck.

Just over eight years ago, Samantha Joseph, age eleven, had gone missing from Halifax, four miles from here. Four months later, in the July, ten-year-old Jenny Parker vanished from Wyke, near Bradford. This time there were two witnesses, who had seen Jenny being walked across a road by a man they assumed was a lollipop man. He'd worn a white coat and carried the familiar 'Stop – Children' sign that resembled a giant lollipop. Then, in the October, eleven-year-old Paula Sykes vanished in a suburb of High Calder. None of the children were seen again, though items of clothing identified as theirs were found near the places they'd vanished from within a couple of weeks, stained with blood. Then in the December, a fourth child was taken, a boy this time – Matthew Spivey, age ten. He was taken away in a van from behind the old cinema at the end of Gorton Lane in Toller Bridge – but released after two hours. No one knew why he'd been let go, certainly not the boy. After that there were no more kidnappings. Just three families left with their grief and communities left with their fear. And a fourth family left traumatised but mostly ignored.

Now, just over seven years later, eleven-year-old Sarah Barrett had gone missing and items of her clothing had been found – at Gorton Lane.

It was only a matter of time before the community, the police and the media ran to ground the boy who'd spent time in the Lollipop Man's company and might recognise him again: for instance, the crime reporter-turned-TV-presenter who'd interviewed the boy at the time.

'The truth is, I don't remember a lot about it,' Adrian said. 'I didn't remember much at the time. They said it was shock. I tried to give them a description, but the photofit looked like Mr Potato Head.'

'So let them ask,' Gav said, blowing smoke. 'Tell them you're sorry but you can't help.'

Adrian looked at his hands.

'What?' Gav demanded.

'It's best no one knows.'

'Best for who?'

'For me. For my mum and dad.'

Gav nodded but looked unconvinced.

'My mum's in pieces every time she hears Sarah Barrett's

name on the news. And my dad . . .'

Gav watched him, as if sensing more was coming.

'He didn't cope at the time,' Adrian said quietly, making Gav frown. 'It's best if . . . it's best if I just keep out of it. And hopefully no one will make the connection – after all, I've got a different name now.'

He checked his watch. 'I'd better go. Walk with me back to the car and I'll drop you at the station.'

3

Sheila Hargreaves emerged from Irene Barrett's overheated terraced house to find a small group of women huddled on the pavement outside. They'd been chattering away in low voices but clammed up when they saw her.

'Good afternoon,' she said, managing a smile but avoiding eye contact.

'How's Irene, Sheila?' one of the women called to her.

'She's very brave.' She turned quickly away to hurry down the hill towards Gorton Lane where she'd left her car.

She heard the excited chattering pick up again in her wake and felt a wave of anger. The vultures pretended concern, perhaps even told themselves they had Irene's best interests at heart, but in reality, this was a feeding frenzy.

Sheila had been a crime reporter at one time, and considered herself battle-hardened, but the encounter with the missing girl's mother had shaken her badly. Sitting in the tiny living room, dark because of the closed blinds, she'd felt as if she was in the presence of an almost malignant misery. She'd spoken words of support and comfort, all the time wanting nothing more than to escape the room, the house, and get away.

But running away wasn't the answer. She had to do something. To stop this if she could.

Gorton Lane was still busy with police and onlookers. She felt eyes watching her and heard excited whispers as she passed. She wondered if anyone would have the gall to request a signed photograph – and what she might say to them if they did.

She looked for Malcolm Struthers but didn't see him.

'DCI Struthers left ten minutes ago,' a young, male uniformed officer told her.

'That's quite all right,' she told him. 'I have his number.'

Back in the car she opened her address book and dialled on her mobile phone.

'Malcolm, it's me, Sheila. Is now a good time?'

'Hello, Sheila.' He sounded weary. 'Finished with Irene Barrett, have you?'

'I've just left her place. That poor woman. She's *haunted*. We have to do something to help her, Malcolm. What I mean to say is, I'll help you. I'll help you catch him.'

'Will you, now?'

She hunkered down in the low seat of her MG, eyes scanning the bleak lane, taking in the little groups of people here and there, the blue-and-white tape flickering over by the canal.

'It is him again, isn't it?' she said. 'It is the Lollipop Man?'

'We don't know that yet.'

'Oh, come on, that's what everybody's saying.'

'I thought you'd given up the investigative stuff,' he said. 'You're all local worthies and phone-in competitions now, aren't you?'

'You're right,' she said. She shifted uncomfortably in her seat. 'I want to help, that's all.'

'Really? You're a journalist at heart, Sheila. I suppose you were grilling poor Irene Barrett for a story.'

'I wasn't, actually.' She took a breath, already anticipating his reaction, and admitted, 'I asked her to come on the show tomorrow night.'

'You did what?'

'She said yes.'

'Sheila—'

'It's a free country, Malcolm. She's within her rights. She wants to make an appeal directly to my viewers. I have a platform, so let's use it!'

She could hear him breathing fast and shallow, enraged no doubt.

'Four nights a week I talk to an audience of nearly half a million people across this county – they listen to me. They *trust* me.'

'And what if Irene Barrett decides to trust you instead of us? What if she tells you something that doesn't seem significant but which one of my officers is trained to spot? An anomaly. You're right that I can't stop her, but I'll be talking to her and making a very strong case to keep out of the public view and to talk *only to us.*'

'Right.' She heard a tremor in her voice and saw Irene Barrett's face again, wet and blotchy, her eyes like dark holes: wells down to an underworld of horror. 'And what about her little girl?'

'What's this all about, Sheila?' Malcolm said. 'You're acting like the angel of bloody mercy—'

'You think this is about my ego?' Her voice was calm again, thank God. Cold. 'I'm part of this community, too, remember. I don't *ever* want to live through anything like that again.'

'No. Of course not.' He sounded sheepish. 'I'm sorry, love.'

He thought he'd upset her because he'd questioned her motives. Her integrity. He hadn't. He'd called her out for playing an angel of mercy, and thus reminded her, unknowingly, of a time she'd been the exact opposite. She could tell him about it. But he would no doubt tell her to get over it, not to make mountains out of molehills, and she didn't think she could bear it.

'It is the Lollipop Man, isn't it? It must be. The way he left the clothes . . .'

'We're not ruling anything out,' he said. 'We're not ruling anything in, either.'

'The very idea that it could happen all over again . . . Let me help you, Malcolm. Surely there's a better chance of catching him this time. Think about it. He took three children in the space of six months, then nothing else for more than *seven years*? Why the gap? I know there were theories at the time and afterwards: did he get frightened and go to ground? Did he move away? Did he get sent to prison for something else? You could check, couldn't you?'

'We looked at all of that when he went quiet. A case like this is never truly cold, especially when the bodies are still undiscovered. Even so . . .'

She listened hard to the silence down the line.

'There's something you're not telling me, isn't there, Malcolm?'

He took his time, then said, 'It's not clear-cut.'

'Oh?'

'Sheila, I'm busy right now,' he said. 'Tell me when you're home and I'll pop by.'

4

'Awright, Gay-boy,' Kev called when Adrian returned to the newsroom in the centre of High Calder, four miles from Toller Bridge. 'Got over your brush with fame?'

'Piss off.' Adrian slung his bag onto the back of his chair at the corner desk.

'Language, *please*!' Linda said, making him jump. The editor was on her way back from the little kitchen, coffee in hand.

'Sorry,' he muttered, feeling himself redden while Kev chuckled.

'Adrian, can I have a word?' Linda said, tone kinder now. 'It'll only take five minutes.'

He followed her meekly into her office overlooking the market square, then sat and waited while Linda readied herself. She looked tired and harassed. She wasn't forty yet, but looked like she'd had a hard life. Kev said it was because her kids were bastards. The oldest of the three was always in trouble and Linda was forever being called in to see the school.

'Kevin told me what happened,' Linda said. She leant over her desk. 'Are you all right?'

He stared and felt a flutter of panic in his chest. 'Yeah. Yeah. I'm fine. What did . . . What did Kev say?'

'That you got a bit upset.'

He groaned to himself and balled his fists in his lap.

'I should have thought before I asked you to take Nige there,' Linda went on. 'It's a horrible thing. How are you feeling now?'

'I'm fine. Honest!'

'You told him you had a headache. Maybe you just needed some time.'

'I did have a headache,' he said, avoiding her peering gaze. 'That's why I said it. I had a headache so I went to Boots.'

She gave a little nod and a half-smile, as if happy to play along with the fiction.

'Can I go?'

'Of course.'

He got up.

'Oh, and I nearly forgot,' Linda said. 'Your mum called. She wants you to ring her at work.'

'Right.' He took a deep breath. 'Thanks.'

'She called twice. It sounded important.'

Back in the main office, Kev was on the phone. 'Nice one, mate,' he said and hung up, then leant back in his chair so that it creaked. 'Good news, Gay-boy: Barry and the lads are finishing at four and heading out for beers. Get tanked up for tonight. You know what that means. We'll be knocking off early.'

'I have to go into college,' Adrian said.

'You have to go to fucking college?'

'I'm getting an essay back—'

'And that'll take, what, about twenty minutes?'

'It's important!'

'You're not gonna come. I knew it!'

'I'll come for a couple.'

'Jonno's booked a stripper,' Kev said now. 'He's asked for Big Tina.'

'That's a disgrace,' Linda said, appearing in her doorway.

'Not your party, Linda, love.'

'Leave him alone, Kev,' Linda said.

'Well, if college is tonight you can come for a few at the Bridge at four.'

'I'll see.'

Adrian typed up the shorthand notes he'd taken at the clothing outlet in Halifax. He didn't need shorthand in his admin role, but he'd shown an interest so Yvonne, Linda's deputy, had begun teaching him. His notes weren't perfect but he managed to decipher them, then went downstairs to the little meeting room and rang his mum at the carer's agency she managed in Huddersfield. She answered quickly, then fired off questions about his welfare and when he'd be home.

'Mum, I'm fine.'

'It's all over the news,' she said in a rush, her voice rising with stress. 'It's him again, that's what everyone's saying. He's taken this little girl and – oh, God, *her poor mother!*'

She was sobbing now. He held on to the receiver and closed his eyes.

'They don't know anything for sure,' he tried uselessly.

'*Of course it's him!*' Cross now. 'And her mother will never see her again.'

He did his best to mollify her, then reminded her he had

a work do tonight, so would be late home. It was a lie, but a white one. To reassure, not deceive.

'I need to go, Mum,' he said. 'Try not to worry.'

He was crossing the cobbled market square, heading for the bus station, when he realised he was being watched from under one of the arches.

It was the stocky old woman he'd seen at the end of Gorton Lane, the one with the jet-black perm. She was eyeing him beadily, her lips working away.

He hunched his shoulders and hurried on, only to hear quick footsteps behind him.

'Oi, you,' she growled. 'Wait!'

He turned and stared as she approached. She was shorter than him and peered up, nodding in satisfaction to herself.

'Adrian Brown, isn't it? Don't lie.'

'Do I know you?' he demanded, recoiling.

'Thought it was you,' she said, half to herself. 'Said to myself when I seen you earlier, *that's him*. Knew your name and remembered where I'd seen you. Nowt gets past me.' She smiled unpleasantly.

She had an aggressive face, with a snub nose, heavy chin and small black eyes. She had a single gold earring and her tightly permed, dyed-black mullet combined with the leather jacket made her look like an old rocker.

'Who are you?' he said, heart racing.

'Name's Wormley,' she said and hitched the strap of her big leather handbag higher onto her shoulder. 'Edna Wormley. Reckon I get called all sorts besides.'

Wormley. Yes, he'd heard Linda and Yvonne complaining about her, with Kev chipping in the occasional rude remark.

She was a troublemaker, he recalled, forever writing semi-literate letters to the *Advertiser* and ringing up, demanding to speak to Linda.

'What do you want?'

'Just a little chat.' She smiled. He detected a meaty smell off her, possibly from the leather jacket.

'I haven't got time,' he said. He turned to go.

'Not so fast,' she snapped, stepping in front of him with remarkable nimbleness. He made to go round her. 'I know *everything*, young man. I know your name – your *real* name, I mean. And I know your mam's called Margaret. Works at Hardaker's in Huddersfield.'

He stopped and gawped at her, feeling as if the blood had left his face.

'I've got something I thought you might be interested in,' she said.

He tried to appear nonchalant. He glanced about. The square wasn't busy, but he might be seen – including by Kev from the office window behind him.

'Then again, maybe you wouldn't . . .' she went on. 'Might be wasting my time.' Her voice hardened. 'It's about Sarah Barrett.'

Adrian was aware of a woman in a bright blue coat and holding an umbrella glancing his way as she passed. She looked vaguely familiar.

'Not here,' he hissed at the old woman. 'Follow me.'

He led her into the shadows under one of the arches where there was a bench, though neither of them sat. Pigeons cooed unseen under the roof. The shelter smelt of their droppings.

'What about Sarah Barrett?' Adrian demanded now.

'She's with the angels now.' Mrs Wormley smiled sadly through the gloom.

He could smell alcohol on her breath, its sweet sharpness mixed with the meaty smell from her jacket.

'Is she?'

'She is,' she said, her voice breaking a little, 'the poor mite.' She pulled a tissue from her sleeve to wipe her nose. 'And I know who took her,' she added, her voice hard again.

His stomach churned. 'Who?'

She narrowed her eyes.

'Like to know, wouldn't you?'

'If you're telling the truth.'

'Don't believe me? Oh, well, I've better things to be doing.' She looked about her, as if about to take her leave.

'If you know something about Sarah Barrett, you should tell the police,' he said.

'Talk to them buggers? Ha.'

'Well, OK. Tell me, and I'll talk to them.'

'I want it on the front page of your newspaper,' she said. 'My picture with it. You can organise that, can't you?'

'I'm just the administrator. I could ask Linda. She's the editor—'

'I know who she is, lovey, and we don't need her.' As if in preparation for the anticipated photo shoot, she took a lipstick and compact mirror from a pocket in her jacket and touched up her lips. 'You and me, Adrian Brown,' she said when she was done, 'we know what this is about. Folk think I'm mad.' She tilted her head, eyeballing him. 'I hear them. "There she goes, the old loony."' She chuckled. 'Must think I'm deaf and all.'

She went on, making the case for how she, and *only* she, saw things for what they were. How all her life she'd exposed lies and been proven right, time after time.

'They'll say it on Judgment Day. They'll say, "Here she

is – Edna Wormley – she saw through them. She had it right." That's what they'll say – the angels.'

She rambled on, mentioning John Major then Boris Yeltsin. Adrian recalled Kev saying she had an obsession with Russians.

'Gorbachev,' she said now. 'He's another one.'

He wondered if she'd ever get to the point and itched to check his watch.

'Sitting there, horrible furniture, leather everywhere, grinning away. Her waiting on him, hand and foot. Gold teeth shining but dead inside—'

He didn't know if she was now referring to Gorbachev, Yeltsin or someone else.

'Anyway, it's all in here,' she said, appearing suddenly to come to the point and rooting in her bag.

He waited, muscles locked with tension, and was taken aback when she drew out a deck of playing cards. Big ones with red backs. She gave them a shuffle.

'Choose one,' she said, holding the fanned deck towards him. 'Not scared, are you?'

He met her mocking gaze and took a card.

'Don't show me.' She studied him. 'It's the Tower, bet you anything. Go on. Take a look.'

He did so, and the Tower it was. A cartoonish image of lightning striking a black spire, cracking it in two so that the top half had begun to topple. People in medieval garb tumbled from the crack, mouths open in horror.

'Worst card in the deck,' she said. 'Knew you'd pick it. There's shame and death hanging over you like a black shroud, Adrian Brown.'

He stared, speechless, as she grabbed the card off him and dropped it and the rest of the deck back into her bag.

'Watch your step, young man,' she said.

'Look—'

'Hold your horses,' she snapped, then drew a long, dirty-looking envelope out of her bag. Slowly, like a magician. 'Here it is.'

'What is?'

'Not as if he ever *confessed*, is it?' she said, flapping the envelope about, taunting him. 'I mean, he's a bad one – always was – but he's not a bloody idiot. Neither is she.'

He reached for the envelope.

'Ah-*ah*! Hands off!'

She lifted the flap and teased out a single sheet of paper. A letter, with handwriting on both sides. Nice, curly, old-fashioned handwriting. Mrs Wormley took a pair of dirty-looking glasses from inside her jacket and set them on her nose.

'Can I see?' he said.

'No, it's mine!' she snapped. 'Is now, at any rate.'

She was playing him. Had been since the start, when she'd spoken his name in that snide way and mentioned his mum.

'I don't have time for games,' he said, annoyed at himself for putting up with her for this long.

'You've time for this,' she said. 'That little kiddie won't be the last. Now, it's time for you to make me a promise.'

'A prom—'

'I want to be on the front page. You with me – the boy who survived and the lady who worked it all out. And I want paying,' she added with a smirk. 'Don't see why I should do all this for free.'

He felt suddenly ice-cold.

'No,' he said.

'What?'

'I said, no. Take your letter to the police. I'm not doing this.'

He pushed past her and stalked out from under the archway, feeling immediate relief at putting distance between the two of them.

'Idiot!' she yelled after him.

5

'The thing is, Sheila,' Malcolm Struthers said, face to face across a kitchen table this time. 'We've got a witness this time, too.'

'A witness?'

They were in the vast modern kitchen of Sheila's house, a converted barn just off the A-road that crossed Widdop Moor – about as high and remote as you could get in this part of the Pennines. He'd asked to come here for privacy, but said he couldn't stay long. Alex, Sheila's husband, was keeping out of the way, hunched over his gardening magazines in the living room, no doubt.

'She's a young girl, mid-teens. Sensible kind of kid.'

'And?' Sheila could hardly breathe.

'It wasn't the Lollipop Man,' Malcolm said.

'But how does she know? Appearances change—'

'It was a woman, Sheila. A woman took Sarah.'

Sheila stared, horrified.

'A thin woman with bleach-blonde hair,' he said.

'My God,' she said after a moment, hands going to her mouth. 'Oh, my God. Another Myra . . .'

'Oh, don't say that.'

'That's what the tabloids will say. No one ever suggested a woman was involved before.'

'So now you understand my dilemma.'

No wonder he looked haunted. Exhausted, too. She'd noticed at Gorton Lane that there was a lot of grey in his copper hair. He was only a year or two her senior – not yet fifty – but he looked ready to drop.

She got up from the table and moved to the window, and gazed out across the paddock towards the black, looming moors under a pall of leaden clouds. The views from here were spectacular, but you could feel very exposed at times.

'You can't withhold this kind of information, Malcolm,' she said, returning to the table. 'People trust women, in spite of Hindley. Most children would trust a nice, friendly lady . . . You have to warn them. Warn the parents!'

'We will. Tomorrow probably. We're planning for a press conference in the afternoon.'

'Come on my programme tomorrow evening, then,' she said, quickly. Her producer wouldn't like it, but Sheila could deal with that. 'You can do your press conference in the afternoon, then a couple of hours later it'll be you and me on the sofa. We can reassure people, but make sure they're taking steps to keep their children safe. People are so innocent. So *trusting*. I was reading some of that book that was published a year or two after it happened. The one by Dee Thompson. There are things I'd forgotten.'

'*You* might have forgotten them,' Malcolm said. 'I was a new sergeant. I worked on that investigation.'

'One of the things,' she went on, 'was that there were two sightings of the man who took the second girl, Jenny Parker. *Two*. And yet it led to nothing. How could that be? One witness was a retired police officer. He didn't think anything of it at the time, because—'

'Because the little girl was holding hands with a lollipop man, and she seemed happy as anything as they crossed the road.'

'That's right,' she said. 'The other witness actually *knew* Jenny. She was a primary school teacher and had taught her the year before. She sat there at the head of the line of traffic, and they crossed right in front of her.'

'They didn't see his face, only the uniform.'

'But this was *after 5 p.m.* School crossings were all over by 3.45 p.m. Yet no one thought to question it.'

'Innocent times.'

'Naive times,' she said. 'Though God knows why, after Hindley and Brady a few miles up the road.'

'Things changed fairly sharpish,' Malcolm said. 'Especially after the third girl was taken.'

'I remember. They made genuine lollipop people wear ID badges. Then there were the vigilantes. Gangs of men walking the streets with baseball bats. There was nearly a fourth victim, as well, except the child got away.'

'We didn't count that attempt as part of the series,' Malcolm said. 'It was a boy. Also, the man didn't wear a lollipop uniform – the lad thought he looked like an "ambulance man". Anyway, it was a decision made by people more important than me – they didn't want to count the boy,' he said. 'Sheila, the lad was lucky. The girls who disappeared are the ones who matter. They're the ones who need justice.'

'Come on the programme, Malcolm. At least think about it.'

He watched her as she spoke, as if deciding whether to trust her.

She reached across the table for his hand, but he drew away and rose.

She saw him to the door and they said their goodbyes with nothing agreed, then she went to the fridge for a half-full bottle of Chardonnay. She filled a glass then took one mouthful before realising she didn't want it.

'Everything all right, darling?'

She looked up. Alex was standing slightly stooped in the kitchen doorway, his clothes crumpled and his grey hair tousled, as though he'd just woken up. His reading glasses were on top of his head, which meant he'd probably fallen asleep reading one of his gardening magazines.

'Yes,' she said stiffly, as though she'd been caught in the act. 'Malcolm's just left.'

'Oh, yes,' he mused, distractedly. 'All right, is he?' A yawn.

'He's . . . I think he's struggling. It can't be easy. Here, I poured this but I don't want it.' She held the glass out to him.

He came into the room and took it from her. He sniffed then tasted it dubiously. 'The bottle's been open a while,' he murmured, putting the glass down on the counter. 'What's for dinner?'

'Chicken casserole,' she said. 'I defrosted it. Shouldn't take long.'

Alex retreated, sloth-like, to the living room. He'd be asleep again in minutes, she realised, suddenly irritated. Alex was often dopey at this time of day, but tonight his yawning distractedness seemed almost offensive.

For a few minutes she stood at the sink, deliberating. She'd told Malcolm she wanted to help by giving him a slot on her show. But she needed to do more than that. She needed to help stop this monster in his tracks. Him and the woman working with him. And she knew where to start: with the failed kidnap attempt. The boy who got away.

She went into her study, where Alex wouldn't hear her, and lifted the phone.

'Jeanette?' she said. 'It's Sheila. Are you on duty tonight? Oh, good. Only, I need a favour.'

6

The Jester, like many gay pubs in Adrian's experience, was in the seediest part of town, beyond the train station, down by the canal, surrounded by abandoned buildings. It sat right on the towpath, at the point where the water vanished into the mouth of a pitch-black tunnel.

He felt jumpy walking along the towpath, especially after dark, and started at the sound of a kicked stone behind him.

'Hello?' he called and peered into the shadows.

No answer. Only silence.

A high laugh from the direction of the pub. A group of older women stood about outside, holding pints, enjoying some joke or other. He hurried their way.

The pub was like a sanctuary, garish but cosy. The Jester may be Victorian, complete with leaded windows and wood panelling, but it was the opposite of quaint. Fairy lights framed the bar. Neon cardboard stars were stuck up behind, advertising special offers in black felt-tip: *Bacardi double £1.50, Taboo £1.* A dusty mirrorball turned over a dance floor – a square of grubby laminate next to the pool table – sending silver spots flying to the sounds of the jukebox. The landlady favoured seventies love songs: the Carpenters and anything Motown. If you wanted other music, you had to pay, feeding pound coins into the jukebox. Right now the speakers were blaring Ace of Base.

He spotted his pal Debbie in her usual corner, nursing a half-drunk pint of purple liquid.

'Hiya. Do you want another one?' he asked.

'If you're paying.' Debbie beamed.

Debbie was unemployed and surviving on benefits. They'd been in the same year at school, but had never had a lot to do with each other. He'd left with nearly the right grades to go to the university of his choice, while she'd scraped a single E and left with no idea what to do next. Most of her time seemed to be taken up caring for her granddad, whom she'd lived with since her alcoholic mum booted her out a week after her seventeenth birthday. Adrian felt sorry for her. She didn't take very good care of herself, smoking too much and existing on Pot Noodles, chips and fried chicken.

'Everything all right?' the landlady Bev said when he approached the bar.

'Yeah, why?' He knew he sounded defensive and gave her a smile.

She raised a sceptical eyebrow. 'Look a bit harassed, that's all. What'll it be?'

'Pint of Carlsberg and a pint of Snakebite and black, please. Oh, and two packets of Scampi Fries.'

He carried the drinks and crisps over to Debbie. His nerves had been on edge since the call to Gorton Lane and they'd worsened following the encounter with Mrs Wormley. Her claims to have knowledge about who had taken Sarah Barrett had preyed on his mind. At college, waiting his turn to talk to his tutor, he'd noted down everything he recalled her saying in his amateurish shorthand at the back of an A4 pad. He wasn't sure what he could do with the information, but it seemed important to at least record it.

'What's up with you?' Debbie said, eyeing him with a frown.

'Nothing!' he snapped and shrugged off his jacket. 'Why does everyone keep asking me that?' He saw her recoil at his tone. 'Sorry. Been busy, that's all. I was at college to get my essay mark just now.'

'Oh? How did you do?'

'OK.'

He'd got an A in his latest essay on *King Lear* and the tutor had written congratulatory remarks at the bottom, but he wasn't about to tell Debbie, who'd be embarrassed about her own lack of achievement.

'You're so brainy,' she said glumly.

'I'm not. If I was I wouldn't be doing resits.'

'That wasn't exactly your fault, though, was it.'

His last year at school had been a nightmare after his mum's cancer diagnosis. His exam results weren't good enough to get into Leeds by several points. He had offers of university places elsewhere, but he was fixed on studying English at Leeds. Two weeks after he got his results, his mum got the all-clear, and he signed up to retake two of his courses at night school.

'If I was brainy then I could get away from here too,' Debbie said.

'Think positive,' he said. 'Decide what you want to do and go study for it, and don't give up.'

'But what about my granddad?'

'The council could send carers in,' he said. 'That's what my mum's agency's for.'

She looked gloomily into her purple pint, then took a sip. 'Ta for this.'

'Is Elaine in tonight?' he asked her now, to cheer her up.

'Starts at eight.' A small smile.

'Any progress?'

'Maybe.' The smile became a grin.

Debbie had formed an attachment to Elaine, who worked a few hours a week behind the bar. Elaine was training to be a paramedic, and was the reason Debbie spent so much time in the pub – and why she was taking more care of her appearance lately, washing and straightening her hair, even wearing make-up.

'Hiya,' a voice said, and Debbie's pal Little Phil landed on a stool beside them.

'I thought you'd left,' Debbie said to him.

'Nowhere to go to,' Little Phil said, then turned a winsome smile on Adrian. 'And then I heard Adey was here.'

Little Phil had a crush on Adrian and didn't try to hide the fact. He had bleach-blond hair and piercings in his ears, nose and bottom lip. He lived in a hostel for care leavers and augmented his dole money by selling all manner of knock-off goods here at the pub, from cigarettes to CDs – to which Bev turned a blind eye.

The music on the jukebox changed to Haddaway's 'What Is Love?'.

'Rozzers were in earlier,' Little Phil told Adrian.

'The rozzers?' The police rarely came anywhere near the Jester. 'What did they want?'

'To put up a poster of that missing kid,' Debbie said. 'It's on the board.'

Adrian craned his neck to look at the noticeboard by the bar. It was drawing-pinned among the posters advertising a pop trivia quiz and Demi's Dragalicious Karaoke Night, and the one he'd pinned up for his mum's agency. The poster showed Sarah Barrett in her school uniform grinning for the camera.

'Horrible, isn't it?' Debbie said.

'I saw her mum today,' Adrian said, chest tightening uncomfortably at the memory. 'I had to take Nige to where they found her coat.'

'Do you think she's dead?' Little Phil asked him.

'Yeah, of course.' They fell into a gloomy silence.

Mrs Wormley had thought so. What had she said – that Sarah was 'with the angels now'? Something morbid like that.

Debbie said, 'Do you remember when those kids went missing before?'

'Kind of,' he said, employing his usual strategy of vague evasion. Neither Debbie nor Little Phil had any idea what had happened to him.

'The Lollipop Man,' Debbie said. 'What if it's him again, Adey?'

As if on cue to distract her, the pub door opened and Elaine came in for her shift. She shrugged off her leather jacket and gave the two of them a little nod.

'Hiya,' waved Debbie, all girly now.

Elaine was in her early twenties, slim and boyish with short fair hair. She nodded a hello to Adrian, then headed behind the bar, where she fell into hushed conversation with Bev. Debbie stared after her, transfixed.

The women who'd been drinking outside had come in and bagged a table. The place grew steadily busier but at last Elaine came over. She picked up Debbie's finished glass and the two empty crisp packets.

'Careful when you're walking home,' Elaine said, her grey eyes wide and wary.

'What makes you think I'm going anywhere?' Debbie said.

'What do you mean?' Adrian asked Elaine.

'Some creep along the towpath just now,' Elaine said, 'hanging about in the shadows.'

'Whereabouts?' Adrian asked, feeling the blood leave his face as he recalled that skittering sound.

'Near the steps. Under one of the archways. I told Bev.' She glanced over at the bar, where Bev was busy pulling a pint. 'She said not to call the police in case it puts the punters off.'

'Druggy?' Little Phil asked.

'Dunno.'

'Everyone's so jumpy,' Debbie said to Adrian when Elaine had gone back to the bar.

'Yeah, they are,' he said quietly.

'Adey . . . ? Are you sure you're all right?'

'Yeah, 'course! I'm gonna get another drink. Do you two want anything?'

As often happened, he stayed in the pub longer than he meant to. By ten he'd drunk five pints and his head was spinning.

'Might ring Ste,' he said to Debbie now Little Phil had left them.

She raised an amused eyebrow. 'On a school night?'

He rang Ste's house from the payphone at the bar, a finger in his other ear to deaden the sound of the music. Ste's mum answered. 'Do you know what time it is, young man?' she demanded. Ste came on the line, sounding shifty and gruff as he always did when Adrian called.

43

'Wondered what you were up to,' Adrian yelled over the noise in the pub.

'Not a lot. Might watch a movie with some beers. Wanna come over?'

'Might do,' Adrian said.

Lads. Making a lads' arrangement. Ste's mum never suspected a thing.

Leaving the pub, he tripped and fell into the door frame.

'Steady,' a woman by the door said, frowning with mock disapproval at his drunkenness.

On the towpath it was dark now and half the streetlights were out. The ravine between the buildings was full of shadows. He sprang along, singing merrily, having quite forgotten Elaine's warning. If he was quick he could get a bus just after half ten from outside the station that went up to Ste's fancy housing estate. By ten to eleven he'd be up in Ste's attic room – lads hanging out in a lad's bedroom. They'd play their wordless, encircling game, choosing a place to sit, maybe the two of them on Ste's bed, maybe on Ste's floor, edging steadily closer until their arms or feet touched . . . And then, inevitably, Adrian would be yanking open Ste's belt buckle, or pulling at the elastic waist of his tracksuit bottoms, while Ste lay there, nonchalant, eyes still on the TV, as if nothing unusual was happening. Adrian put his hands in his pockets to disguise the bulge in his jeans, not that there was anyone around to—

He tripped and stumbled, striking his shoulder against the wall.

'*Fuck!*'

He righted himself, hand gripping his throbbing shoulder, and tried to work out what had happened – then realised he'd walked into something on the towpath.

He moved in closer, discerning something blacker than the darkness around it. He poked at it with a foot. It was big but soft, like a sack of grain.

What was it? And how had it got there? Had it fallen from one of the buildings? He slowed his thoughts, realising he needed to prevent anyone else tripping over it and risking injury.

He bent and touched it – and his fingers met something cold and rubbery, but with a hard, almost sharp, ridge underneath – lips. *Teeth!* He yelped and recoiled, nearly tripping again, this time backwards so that he was perilously near the canal's edge.

He looked around, panting. His eyes were adapting to the darkness. He bent in again. Not as close this time.

He should feel for a wrist, he knew. For a pulse. Except . . . the lips had felt wrong.

He looked in the direction of the pub. He could go back there. Ask Bev to ring an ambulance. The police too. But then they'd want to question him. To take a statement. And he'd be a witness.

He made himself breathe slower. To stand for a moment and think . . .

If he made a statement, he might have to appear in some kind of coroner's court. It might get reported in his own newspaper. By Kev! And there was no way he could stop his poor, exhausted mum finding out that he hadn't been at a work do after all, but in a completely different part of town. A dodgy bit, near the town's only gay pub . . . And then she'd know everything, and worry all the more – because now she'd know he was a liar. It would destroy her.

But he couldn't just leave the body . . .

He went into his bag for the work mobile phone. He turned it on. Waited, breathless, for it to glow green. HELLO, the screen said.

But there was no signal. Why would there be down here, hemmed in by the cliffs of old buildings? He thought of another possibility. There were phone boxes by the station. He could ring 999 from one of those. Do it anonymously.

That would be OK, wouldn't it? He was simply being . . . discreet.

He was about to drop the phone back into his bag and make for the steps up into town when he realised he might be able to use the glow of its screen as a torch, to take a closer look at the body.

The thought of looking into a green-lit dead face made him shudder. But he did it anyway, bending and passing the phone's screen over the figure—

And looked into the face of Edna Wormley.

Time seemed to stop. His heart with it.

Mrs Wormley's eyes were open but filmy. There was blood all over her forehead.

Oh God . . .

It came to him in a flash: the letter. This was because of the letter.

He crouched and felt about, trying not to think about what he was touching. At last he found her handbag.

He unzipped it and peered inside. But the light from the phone wasn't strong enough. He took it along the path, into the dirty orange glow of the next working streetlight. He found her purse. A scarf. A torn paper bag of what looked and smelt like Kola Kubes. He searched the main part of the bag then any pockets he could find, though he was sure she'd stuffed the letter back into the main section. The tarot cards were there, loose but contained in a side pocket. A couple had come away. Both showed the Tower, the card signifying disaster. He lifted out the deck and riffled through it. The Tower, the Tower, the Tower – every card was the same.

He nearly laughed at the malicious trick.

He put the cards back and hunted further. But there was no doubt about it: the letter wasn't there.

A sudden sound behind him. A scuffing step. Stones spilling over dirt. He looked frantically about.

Whoever had done this was still here.

Adrenalin fired through him.

'Who's there?' he yelled furiously into the darkness, unable to stop himself. 'Show yourself, you *fucker*!'

Another sound. Quieter. He peered hard into the blackness of an archway.

He dropped Mrs Wormley's bag, leapt over her body and threw himself towards the archway, arms out, ready to land on whoever it was with full force.

He cried out as his head collided with metal. Bounced off. He staggered, righted himself, and realised the mouth of the archway was barred by some kind of grille. Dazed, he stepped back, looking around but seeing no one.

He had to get away, and fast.

He ran.

'I need an ambulance – and the police.'

'Where are you, caller?'

He must slow down. He put his forehead against the glass pane of the phone box. It was grimy but cool. He gave details to the woman, trying not to sound mental, though it was hard. A woman was dead. *Murdered.*

'It's an old lady called Mrs Wormley,' he said, now putting on an accent that was anything but his own, and sounding vaguely

Welsh. 'Edna Wormley.' He spelt it out, shutting his eyes to visualise the letters.

'And what's your name?' the woman said.

'I — I don't want to say.'

'Why is that, caller?'

'Because . . . well . . . that's OK isn't it? I don't *have to* give it?'

'Did you hurt this lady, caller?'

'What? *No!* Of course not!'

He hung up. He was drunk and not thinking straight and needed to get a grip. He leant for a moment against the wall outside the station, panting.

Time was short – the police and paramedics might be there any minute – but there was one last thing he had to do.

He went back into the phone box and called directory enquiries. He memorised the number read by the automated voice, then put a twenty-pence piece into the machine and dialled the Jester.

Bev answered, shouting over the racket in the pub.

'Someone's been attacked,' he said, making his voice high and feminine. His accent had morphed into Scottish.

'*Pardon?*' Shrill. Uncomprehending.

'There's been an attack on the towpath. You need to tell people *to be careful.* Do not go out alone.' He hung up. Stood breathing hard, and sweating.

A minute later he made his way round to the front of the station, faking a casual air.

He half-fell into the first taxi in the queue.

There was only one thing to do now – just one game in town. And the name of the game was *alibi.*

He said breathlessly to the driver, 'Irish Club, please.'

7

'I could get shot for this,' Jeanette Dinsdale said, her pointed little nose twitching. She hurried ahead of Sheila into the lift and pressed B for basement.

'I know,' Sheila said. 'I'm very grateful.'

'It's not like I don't owe you, is it? Remember how you got me an interview with the bloke who saw Peter Sutcliffe in Headingley? That scoop got me my first promotion.'

Jeanette Dinsdale, Sheila's old friend and colleague, happened to be the chief reporter on duty at the *Yorkshire Evening Press* this evening. It was her job to respond to breaking stories and write them up fast for the next edition. She was a natural journalist, with a foxlike instinct for a story. There was something foxlike about her, too, though her hair was mousy instead of red. Her face was sharp and her nose quivered as she spoke. Her dark little eyes were always beadily on the move. She hadn't hesitated when Sheila asked for access to the archives, making Sheila jump for joy.

Yes, the old fire was still there; there was no use denying it.

The lift doors opened on the dark basement and Jeanette scurried out, tugging a cord that hung from the ceiling. Strip lights flickered awake, lighting the path between the stacks.

'It smells exactly how I remember,' Sheila said.

'Why wouldn't it? Right, morning editions along this side.' Her friend forged ahead, pointing. 'Stacks A to T, going back to 1974. All in binders. Years and months are labelled on the ends. Evening editions in Double-A to AJ on this side, back to 1987. Is it mornings or evenings you're after?'

'Both,' Sheila said.

'Why don't you start with evening editions from 1986. You'll need to use the microfiche.'

'OK. Can you remind me how to use the machine?'

Ten minutes later, Jeanette had warmed up a microfiche monitor and shown Sheila the cabinet for the 1986 reels. She was good to go.

'Well, enjoy yourself. And when you're ready, maybe you'll tell me what it is you're looking for.' Her dark eyes glinted. 'I assume it's about Sarah Barrett . . .'

'This isn't about a story, Jeanette. Honest, it's not.'

'Right . . . well, I'll pop down in an hour or so, will I?' Jeanette said. 'Bring you a cuppa.'

Sheila found what she was looking for well within that time. She'd calculated that it must have happened in the third week of December of 1986. And here, in grainy black and white, backlit on the huge monitor, was her own name heading a story that began on the front page of the evening edition of the *Press* from Friday 19th December 1986, and continued on pages four and five. She read it, wincing slightly at the sensational phrasing in her own copy:

50

Matthew is ten-years-old, though he looks and acts younger. Today his big, blue eyes are wide with alarm. As are those of his loving mummy, who never lets him out of her arms.

She skimmed the piece, beginning to recall the interview itself, when she'd sat in the family's front room and spoken to the boy who very nearly became the Lollipop Man's fourth victim. Her mouth went dry as she remembered the palpable fear – the *trauma* – in that room.

Matthew Spivey had gone to the cinema with his parents and a friend from his street that evening to see the film *Labyrinth*. Toller Bridge's plush little picture house – now closed down – had been jam-packed. Leaving the building through a side entrance, Matthew and his friend became separated. Matthew's dad Peter went back inside to try to find the friend. When Peter didn't come back after five minutes, Matthew's mum went in to help, telling Matthew to stay just inside the doorway. But when Mrs Spivey and her husband returned with the friend in tow, Matthew was gone.

Panic rose as the minutes ground by with no sign. The cinema manager organised a search of the building, then bowed to Peter Spivey's demands to call the police. Panic became a frenzy teetering on chaos, with members of the public joining three police officers in the search, making activity and noise everywhere. Police officers from Bradford and Leeds arrived, and a systematic search got underway. Someone was coordinating the media, and urgent calls for information – and for vigilance – went out over local radio and on the TV news.

Time ticked painfully by, minutes becoming hours. Then, just after 10.30 p.m., a woman's screams filled the night:

'He's here! I've got him!'

51

Margaret Spivey ran to meet the woman and the boy, and drew the child into her arms.

The WPC knelt and spoke quietly to Matthew, while another constable listened in.

They took him to hospital to be examined by a police surgeon, who concluded the boy was uninjured and, apparently, unmolested.

Back home, the police interviewed Matthew late into the night. The boy seemed frightened, but otherwise unfazed, with few signs of shock.

The WPC who'd taken charge of Matthew at the scene had been there during Sheila's visit, she remembered now. She'd eyed Sheila suspiciously, and almost intervened when Sheila asked the boy's mother, 'What were Matthew's first words to you when he came back?'

Mrs Spivey gazed at her son, who looked back at her with mild confusion. She stroked his hair. 'He said . . . "It's only for ever."'

The words were from the film they'd been to see. Sheila had put it in her piece, and of course it got picked up by the nationals – even BBC News.

The police released more information the next day. Matthew recalled being outside the fire door when a big man with grey hair, wearing what he described as 'an ambulance uniform', came in to say his mummy wanted the man to take Matthew to her. Matthew went. He began to feel scared when they reached a white van and the man opened the back doors. Then the man gave him a drink of Ribena from a cup and said to drink it down, or he'd get a smack. He did – and then felt very sleepy, waking up in darkness. And that was all he remembered, until he was being led quickly through the streets by a woman. And then he saw his mum, and people were screaming and crying everywhere around him.

In due course, a photofit was published, but it wasn't very good: a generic fat man with grey hair and a squashed nose who could have been aged anywhere between fifty and seventy.

She tried to conjure up the boy's face. No photo of him had appeared in the newspaper, so she had to rely entirely on memory. It was his eyes she saw in her mind: a vivid, sparkling dark blue; those and the bright red baseball cap he wore, its peak turned to one side like a kid in a Spielberg film.

She made some quick notes on her pad, and scrolled through the microfiche again, looking for follow-up articles. And here was one published a week after the first, between Christmas and New Year. It contained a new nugget of information. The boy's full name. Not just his surname, but his middle name too.

Matthew Adrian Spivey.

Not definite, but a strong indication . . .

Just then the lift doors opened at the far end of the room and Jeanette was hurrying towards her. There was no sign of the promised tea.

'What's wrong?' Sheila called, rising from her chair.

'One of my police contacts just called,' Jeanette told her briskly. 'I need to go. That means you have to leave too. I'm sorry.'

'What's happened?' Sheila said.

'They've found a shrine, up on the moors. Newspaper cuttings and a cross, just like before. Oh, God, Sheila. It's happening again.'

8

Jeanette filled her in as they rode the lift up from the basement. A farmer had spotted it as he turned off the main road into his driveway: a makeshift, waist-high wooden cross erected at the corner of one of his fields, by a low wall. He'd got out of his lorry to take a closer look and seen there were newspaper cuttings attached to the upright. A glance at just one of the cuttings and he knew what it signified and called the police.

'It's just above Halifax,' Jeanette said, leading them from the lift into the vast reception area. 'Place called Exley's Farm, on Widdop Moor.'

'Exley's Farm?' Sheila stopped walking. 'It's a mile from my house.'

Jeanette turned. 'Blimey. That's—'

'Close to home?' She felt quite breathless, but pulled herself quickly together.

'Come with me,' Jeanette said. 'I'd appreciate the moral support.'

'OK.'

'You go first in your car and I'll follow.'

Forty minutes later, Sheila bumped her MG carefully onto a grass verge and waited until the headlights of Jeanette's Renault came up behind her then dimmed. Sheila climbed out and waited while Jeanette got herself together. It was a cold and clear spring night, with stars glinting against the blackness of space, and a bone-white blade of moon lying low to the south. A sharp wind cut across the moor, making the wires of the pylons moan, and carrying a smell of rotting earth.

Ahead, blue lights flashed and floodlights illuminated an area by the roadside. There were vehicles everywhere and yet the place felt empty. Hostile in a way she'd never sensed before. She shivered but not from the cold.

'That's my place down there,' Sheila told Jeanette, when the other woman joined her. 'You can see the security light.' She wished for all the world she could go there now. Lock the door, put the kettle on. Except she'd still know what was happening a stone's throw away in the dark . . .

'Come on,' Jeanette said, hand on Sheila's back. 'Think of it like the old days. You and me, Yorkshire's answer to *Cagney & Lacey.*'

'More like *Juliet Bravo*,' Sheila said, relieved to make light. 'All moors and everyone miserable as sin.'

'*Juliet Bravo* was in Lancashire, so it figures.'

But neither of them laughed. They walked along the edge of the road, eyes fixed on the blue flickering lights.

'It's apt, don't you think?' Jeanette said. 'Up here on the moors. If it was a woman that took Sarah Barrett, I mean.'

'A woman?' Sheila said, feigning surprise.

'Yes. Hadn't you heard? They've got a witness. A kid, but

reliable. Shocking, isn't it? There's some talk about it not being the Lollipop Man at all but some kind of copycat. But I tell you this, if it is a woman, then there must be a man too. Women don't *steal kids*. Not without some nutcase like Ian Brady lurking in the background.'

'It's so awful,' Sheila said.

'It's evil.'

The road was uneven where it met the verge and slimy with mud from the moors. Sheila concentrated on not slipping, while Jeanette talked.

'Why did you give it up, Sheila? You were a good journalist.'

'I fancied a change,' Sheila said.

'Rubbish. Look at you this evening. You're all over this.'

'It's . . . a personal thing,' Sheila said, irritated.

'Oh?'

'It's something I have to do.'

'Sounds grand, if you ask me.'

'It's just . . . with it happening again. I mean, it *is* happening again, isn't it? And it must be the same man, whatever people are saying. The Lollipop Man *must* be behind it, even if someone's helping him.'

Jeanette stopped in her tracks. 'You know something, don't you?'

'No. Well, not really.' Sheila kept walking again.

Jeanette ran to catch up. 'I'm not letting you do this to me, Sheila. We go too far back, you and me.'

Sheila could have laughed. It was the same line she'd used on Malcolm Struthers earlier in the day. 'I just wanted to take another look at what happened in '86. At the mistakes that were made. The opportunities that were missed.'

'What are you talking about?'

'The witnesses, for a start,' Sheila said. '*Two* separate witnesses saw one of the girls being taken across a road by someone they assumed was a lollipop man. Yet *nothing came of it.*'

'OK . . . But you said it was personal, too.'

'Because one of the mistakes,' she said, 'one of the terrible things that happened—' *Oh, what the hell.* 'It was my fault.'

'Your fault? Sheila, what are you talking about?'

She didn't reply but walked on while Jeanette scurried close after her.

'Honestly,' her friend said. 'I haven't the faintest idea what you're talking about.'

A car approached from behind them and slowed. A window came down.

'Sheila,' Malcolm Struthers said coldly. 'Fancy seeing you here.'

9

Adrian let himself into the kitchen a little after 1 a.m. to find his dad standing in the doorway to the hall, fists on hips and wearing an expression of disgust. As usual there was no eye contact.

'Hiya . . .' Adrian said and closed the door behind him.

His dad shook his head and retreated, muttering, into the living room. Adrian could hear the sound of late-night TV.

His mum came down the stairs, worry pinching her already thin face. Her curly hair was tied back but coming loose.

'Sorry I'm late,' he mumbled. 'Lost track of time, then I missed the bus.'

It was true. He'd run for it, then stood, panting as its red lights shrank into the night. Unwilling to pay for a cab, he'd walked the four miles home, most of which were uphill.

His mum pulled him into a silent hug, then called through to the living room, 'Come to bed, Peter.'

'In a bit,' was his dad's sullen reply.

Adrian followed his mum up the stairs.

At the top, on the landing, she turned to him, eyes now meeting his.

'They've found a shrine on the moors,' she said, voice rising to a sob. 'Fiona from next door came round. Her sister rang – her husband's in the police.'

He didn't know how to answer.

'The poor tiny thing.' She covered her face with both hands. Then she burst out: 'Oh, my lovely boy,' and pulled him into a sudden, strong embrace. 'When I think what could have happened . . .'

'It's OK, Mum,' he said, embarrassed, but hugging her back. She was so slight. All bones.

'It's all I think about,' she sobbed into his ear.

'But nothing did happen, Mum, did it? There's nothing to worry about.'

She sagged a little. Nodded. Then turned and went into her bedroom. Adrian went into his own room, shut the door and breathed out a juddering sigh.

10

Thursday 7th April, 1994

Head splitting, Adrian bought a bacon roll and a Coke from the greasy spoon in the market square and had them in the shelter of one of the arches while the rain battered the cobbles. It wasn't the same arch where he'd listened to Mrs Wormley.

Only a few hours after she'd collared him here she was dead, and yet there'd been nothing on the local radio news about it. He'd listened in the shower, then on his Walkman radio on the bus into town. The only story any channel was reporting was the discovery of the cross and newspaper cuttings found up on the moors.

He began to feel sick again and trod the half-smoked cigarette underfoot, then saw from the clock in the square that it was time to go.

Yvonne Sharkey, Linda's deputy, was already at her desk and leafing through the week's new edition, which would be delivered into 16,000 homes across the area during the course of the day.

'Bloody hell, Adrian, you look proper rough,' she said, peering over the top of the paper. Yvonne was a fierce Scouser and her fashion sense leant towards the gothic. Her black hair had a vinyl sheen to it and she was wearing her new red plastic specs. They matched her lipstick and contributed to a vampiric effect. 'Is that a bruise on your forehead?'

'Banged it at Barry's thing last night,' he lied, and fell into his chair.

'Linda said you weren't gonna go.'

'Changed my mind.' He reached to turn on the StarWriter and groaned at a fresh flash of pain.

'I'm glad to see the back of that Barry,' Yvonne said now. 'Racist prat.'

Yvonne wore her principles with pride. Adrian was in awe of the fearless way she confronted bad behaviour. She regularly shouted down Kev for his chauvinistic, homophobic bullshit, and often challenged Linda when she felt the *Advertiser* wasn't playing fair.

'Did you have a nice holiday?' Adrian asked her now.

'It was great. My sister's new fella's a dick, but we had a laugh.'

The StarWriter was still warming up. He closed his eyes for a moment. A mistake – because it took all his effort to open them again. He was so tired. The prospect of having to get through a whole eight hours of work felt overwhelming.

'Morning, Adrian,' Linda said, drifting out of her room. She was holding her MUM mug and looked worse than he felt, which was a shame given she hadn't even been at the do the night before. 'Have you heard the terrible news?' she said.

'About the shrine?'

'It's so awful.' He saw, to his dismay, that she was teary.

Kev came in, with a grey face and yellow eyes.

'Awright, Gay-boy,' he croaked, then spotted Yvonne and looked sheepish.

'No show without Punch . . .' Yvonne said, pursing her lips.

'Leave me alone,' Kev said.

'Baby got a headache?' she asked.

'Something I ate.' He threw his bag down on his desk. 'There's two pigs sitting in a car down there. They coming to see us?'

'If you mean the bizzies, they're probably here to see me,' Yvonne said, rising and peering out of the window, down into the street.

'About the dead kid?'

'Well they're not here because I ran a red light, are they?'

'I'll meet them with you, if you like,' Kev said.

'I can manage perfectly well on my own. If I need a big boy to come and hold my hand I'll ask Adrian here.'

She winked across at him as the doorbell went.

Yvonne took the plain-clothes officers, a woman and a man, into Linda's room. Linda, left officeless, pulled up a chair beside Kev and began to talk him through edits she'd made to one of his pieces. Kev, usually combative, seemed to take the criticism relatively well.

Adrian rang Nige at home and talked him through his afternoon appointments, then arranged to collect him at one. The photographer's slurred responses suggested he was still drunk. Adrian repeated the pick-up time twice, to make sure it had gone in, feeling like Nige's mother.

He made himself a black coffee and heaped sugar into it, then settled down to deal with a mountain of filing.

Behind him, Kev was becoming loud as he argued a point

with Linda. Adrian put his headphones on and turned his Walkman to long-wave radio. A few minutes later he realised Yvonne had left her meeting with the police and was speaking to Linda. Linda got up from her chair and looked his way, frowning. He took his earphones out again.

'Adrian, the police want to talk to you,' she said diffidently. 'I'll come in with you.'

Linda went ahead of him into the room.

'Please have a seat,' the female officer said. She introduced herself as Detective Sergeant Claire Sanders and her colleague as Detective Constable Jamie Clark.

Adrian's face was burning and tight, and he was convinced they'd notice and want to know why. He hadn't felt this mix of terror and dread since being caught smoking at school aged thirteen. He kept his eyes firmly on Linda, who looked merely tired and concerned.

'Yesterday afternoon,' DS Sanders began, eyes boring into his, 'you spoke to an elderly lady in the market square, just outside here.'

'Yeah,' he said, squirming, and swallowed so hard it clicked. 'What about it?' He sensed Linda looking at him but didn't turn to her.

'Did she approach you or did you approach her?'

'Erm . . . she stopped me in the square. I'd never seen her before.'

'Can we ask what you talked about, please?'

'I . . . I can't remember. Why?'

'But you remember talking to her?'

He nodded, unable to think what to say. His head was still hurting, and it made his brain foggy. His heart raced and his breathing was shallow.

'Officer—' Linda began, but the woman put up a hand.

'How long did you talk to her for?' she pressed Adrian.

'I don't know. I mean, she did most of the talking.'

'For how long?'

'These questions seem very unusual,' Linda put in. 'It might help if you explain what this is about.'

'In a minute,' Sanders said to her tartly, then returned her gaze to Adrian. 'How long would you say she talked to you?'

'A few minutes.' He shrugged. 'I wasn't really listening.'

The officer narrowed her eyes. 'You remember nothing at all?'

'She talked about the Russians.'

'"About the Russians"?' DC Clark asked, incredulously. He was handsome in a squarish sort of way, but his yellow-green serpent's eyes made Adrian feel limp and scared.

'Yes . . .' Adrian said. A dribble of sweat left his right armpit and trickled unpleasantly down his side.

He turned to see Linda frowning at him.

'She told me her name was Mrs Wormley,' he said in a rush. 'She said she knew who'd taken Sarah Barrett.'

The officers' eyebrows went up in surprise.

'I didn't believe her. She said she wanted to be in the newspaper and could I help her.'

'Edna Wormley is a local troublemaker,' Linda explained to the officers. 'She's often in touch with us about everything from the bins to the nuclear threat. She's well known. I'm surprised you haven't heard of her.'

'We know of her,' DS Sanders said blandly.

'Then I don't understand why you're asking Adrian these questions. Are you about to tell us Mrs Wormley does know something about Sarah Barrett? Because quite frankly I'd find that very hard to believe.'

'Did Mrs Wormley tell you where she was going after she left you?' DS Sanders asked.

He shook his head.

'Then we'll need a statement from you.'

'A *statement*?' Linda said.

'Edna Wormley was found dead last night,' the woman said. 'From what we know, Mr Brown here was the last person to see her alive.'

11

Sheila's producer, Grace Makinde, wasn't happy. '*Yorkshire Tonight* is not *Crimewatch*,' she said.

'A little girl is probably dead, Grace,' Sheila said, barely containing her anger. She'd anticipated this pushback from her producer and had wound herself into a state of high dudgeon.

They were sitting opposite one another on the black leather settees in Sheila's office. Grace put down her clipboard, folded her hands calmly in her lap and tilted her head. She watched Sheila for what felt like an age. Sheila watched her back, feeling mutinous.

'The girl's mother has been on the news several times,' Grace said. 'She isn't relying on us to tell her story.' She saw the look on Sheila's face. 'Look, it's tragic. It's awful. The worst thing. No one is saying it isn't.'

Sheila's lip trembled and she bit down on it. Grace leant across from her seat and took Sheila in an embrace. Sheila could smell the Liz Claiborne perfume she'd given Grace for her birthday the month before. It softened her.

She dug in her bag for a hanky. 'This has happened in the heart of our community.' *I was there*, she wanted to add. *I was there last night – where they found the shrine.* 'People will expect us to acknowledge it, Grace. It's . . . it's still very raw for people here. Especially with the other murders that happened—'

'You mean the Ripper?'

'No, I don't mean him at all.' Sheila watched the confusion in Grace's face. 'Oh, but you're not from here, of course.'

Grace lifted a finely drawn eyebrow.

'You came here from London. You won't have heard of the Lollipop Man.'

'"The Lollipop Man"?'

'I've always hated the nickname. Like something from a fairy tale. He took three young girls in 1986 – tried to take a boy as well. He had a very particular *modus operandi*. He'd take the child right off the street, then there'd be nothing – no contact, no clues – for about two weeks. Then someone would find items of children's clothing: a jumper and a coat maybe. They'd be left somewhere close to where the kidnap happened, and they had . . . they had blood on them. Then, a day or two later, a makeshift cross would appear, usually in a beauty spot or by a roadside, and it would have newspaper cuttings relating to the disappearance tied on to it with string. Like a shrine.'

'That's horrible.' Grace put a hand to her mouth.

'Not one of the children's bodies was ever found. Imagine – knowing your child has been taken but never knowing what's happened to her, or where she is. Never being able to hold her again, or lay her to rest.'

Grace looked sick. Sheila wondered if she was thinking of her own little girl, Emmie, who'd just turned seven.

'He got the moniker "the Lollipop Man" because when he took the second girl, he was seen. The two of them were seen, *together*. A retired policeman saw the child being taken across the street by a man in a white coat and peaked hat, holding a lollipop – you know, a "Stop – Children" sign? The idea is that he must have whisked her across the road and straight into a van or something.'

'My God.'

'It all happened in the space of a few months,' she went on. 'Then, in the December, he tried to take a boy. After that, nothing. The Lollipop Man disappeared. Went to ground, moved away, died . . . nobody knows. So, if there's even a slight possibility that this is him again, then don't you see why it's so devastating? So important?'

'Sheila . . .' Grace began. She sighed. 'Look, I still have my reservations, but . . . OK, let's go for it.'

'Thank you,' said Sheila, and smiled, though inside she still coddled an ember of resentment. 'I'll make the calls. Let's talk again in an hour.'

When Grace had left her office, Sheila went to the floor-to-ceiling window and gazed out across the city centre. Her office was on the eighth floor of Bradford's tallest building. Below were offices and, on the lower floors, a film and TV museum along with an IMAX cinema. The *Yorkshire Tonight* studio was in a section of the museum, and a source of endless fascination to visitors. The views from all the rooms on this level were spectacular, looking west towards Haworth and the hills that marked the Lancashire border. She looked to the south-west, using the looming black Wainhouse Tower as a landmark. Higher up on the moors beyond the tower lay her own house, invisible from this distance. She recalled Jeanette's words, 'close to home' and her stomach did a somersault.

Malcolm Struthers would have been within his rights to tell her and Jeanette to get lost when they turned up at the moors last night.

'I was at home,' Sheila had said. 'Jeanette was over for coffee. We saw the commotion and came to see what was wrong.'

'Late for a coffee,' he said, looking from Sheila's pleading face to Jeanette's.

'It's a cross with cuttings about Sarah, isn't it?' Sheila asked.

Malcolm adopted his poker face.

'That's a yes, is it?'

'No comment,' he'd said firmly, then added, 'Now, please, the pair of you – *hop it.*'

Jeanette had insisted on getting as close as she could and Sheila stayed with her for twenty minutes, until it was clear they weren't going to get through the cordon that had been put across the road. Neither were they about to learn anything, not from any of the officers there. Jeanette had given up around one o'clock, saying she'd have more luck from her contact.

Sheila rang Malcolm on his mobile now, ready for another telling-off. He sounded harassed but not unhappy to hear from her.

'I'm on my way,' he told her. 'I'll be a few minutes. Pre-recorded or live, I don't mind – just point the camera and ask me your questions. We're doing our press conference at three, so word'll be out by this evening in any case.'

'Thank you, Malcolm,' she said.

'No need to thank me. We need to stop this man. Him and his missus. You were right yesterday. We do need all the help we can get.'

Hanging up, feeling oddly cheered, she turned her Rolodex.

Then she lifted the phone once more.

'Oh, yes, hello,' she said, putting on a high-class tone. 'My name is Mrs Osgood.' It was only half a lie, Osgood being Alex's name. 'Yes, that's right. I wonder . . . might I speak to Adrian Brown?'

12

DS Sanders had left, and Linda had gone to speak to Kev in the main office, Adrian having assured her he didn't need her. Adrian was alone with the handsome but dead-eyed DC Clark.

'Who saw me?' he asked now.

'I'm sorry?'

'Who saw me talking to the old woman?'

'The lady from the post office in the square. She knew Mrs Wormley and she recognised you from this place. She heard on the grapevine what had happened to Mrs Wormley and came in to see us.'

He nodded sheepishly. The woman in the bright blue coat who'd passed him and Mrs Wormley in the square. She'd seemed familiar but he'd quickly forgotten her.

'What happened?' Adrian asked now.

'We don't know yet,' DC Clark said smoothly. 'At this time we're treating Mrs Wormley's death as "unexplained".'

He sat very still and held his breath. The truth was, he thought he might be about to vomit.

'I want you to tell me exactly what Mrs Wormley said to you,' Clark said now.

'I can't remember much off the top of my head, but . . . I made some notes afterwards.'

'You wrote notes?' Clark looked amazed.

'Yeah. I thought it might be important. I mean, at the time I didn't take her seriously. I just wanted her to leave me alone, but afterwards I thought there might have been something in what she was saying, so . . .'

Clark seemed to buy it. 'And where are these notes now?'

'In my bag.'

Clark said to fetch them, so Adrian ducked briefly out of Linda's room.

'Everything all right?' Yvonne asked him, while Kev rocked back in his chair, eyes agog.

'Yeah.' He retrieved his pad from his bag, feeling his face burning under his colleagues' scrutiny. He felt swimmy-headed and grim.

Back in Linda's room he flicked to the back of his notepad to the scribbled shorthand notes and scanned quickly through them.

'She said Sarah was "with the angels now",' he said and wiped cold sweat from his forehead.

'She thought Sarah was dead?'

'Yeah. Sounded like it.'

The DC wrote something down. Adrian put his hand to his mouth to catch a hot, acidic belch.

'She said she wouldn't be speaking to you,' he said, eyes further down the page. 'To the police, I mean. She called you "them buggers".' He kept his expression impassive.

'Anything else?' Clark said, with a raised eyebrow.

'She said she had a letter,' he said.

'A letter?'

'Yes. She called it "proof of a kind".'

'Proof of what?'

'The identity of the person who took Sarah Barrett. And the others.'

'What others?'

'The three girls – the ones who were kidnapped in 1986. Oh—' Another wave of nausea swelled in him. 'Sorry . . .'

'Are you all right?'

He nodded and took a deep breath. 'She said something about gold teeth,' he managed, focusing back on his notes. He heard the old woman's malicious voice again as he read. 'I don't know who she was talking about, I'm sorry.'

DC Clark made a grumbling noise and shook his head.

'I didn't take her very seriously,' he protested. 'I mean, she's mad. *Was* mad. I wasn't paying that much attention. I was just humouring her.'

'Did she show you this letter?'

'She wouldn't let me touch it. She put it back in the envelope then stuffed it back in her bag. She was doing my head in and I just wanted her to go.'

'You said she stopped you in the square.'

He nodded.

'Why did she do that?'

'I don't know. She knew I worked here. She said she wanted her face on the front of the newspaper. She wanted the credit for finding Sarah's killer.'

'And she asked *you?*'

'Maybe she thought I was more important than I am.'

He felt himself flushing again. Another, bigger wave of nausea this time. He groaned. Linda's office was boiling and he wondered about asking to open the window.

'I'm not a reporter,' he said, feeling feeble. 'I'm just temping here. I answer the phone and drive the photographer between shoots.'

The DC wrote in his pad for a couple of minutes.

More questions followed: Did Mrs Wormley say where she was going? What did she have with her? What was she wearing? Did she mention any people she might be going to see?

And then it was over.

'We'll be in touch if we need to talk to you again,' Clark said.

Adrian rose. Relief washed through him.

'What was she doing down by the canal, anyway?' he asked, reaching for the door.

DC Clark stared at him, eyes widening.

'I mean, she lived up by the high school, didn't she, on the High Estate?'

The DC tilted his head. He said, 'Can I ask, sir, how you came to know where Mrs Wormley's body was found?'

Adrian froze as a bubble of hot vomit flooded his mouth. He swallowed hard, then coughed explosively.

Clark waited, his dead eyes never leaving Adrian's face.

'Sorry . . .' he gasped, regaining his composure and trying not to breathe. His throat was on fire with the acid reflux. 'Sorry.'

'Can you answer my question?' Clark said.

He nodded, while still trying to think. To weigh the risk of telling the constable everything and facing the consequences of that – or of keeping schtum, only to be found out later. He opened his mouth, but nothing came out.

'Mr Brown?'

'Someone told me,' he croaked. 'A friend. She said someone got attacked by the canal last night. I put two and two together, that's all.'

'What's your friend's name?'

'I—' He stopped. 'I don't have to tell you that, do I?'

The policeman's top lip curled into a cold sneer of disbelief. 'Yes, Mr Brown. You have to tell me.'

He shut his mouth. Words threatened to spill out, but he swallowed them, the way he'd swallowed his own sick.

'I think I'll ask her if she minds first,' he said, 'if it's all the same to you.'

'Mr Brown,' the constable said. 'If this *is* in fact a murder inquiry, then you will be required to assist us and any refusal to do so will mean you're hindering an investigation, for which—'

'I said I'll ask her,' Adrian said, anger rising. 'Please,' he said, breathing hard, 'don't bully me.'

Clark curled his lip but appeared to let it go. Adrian reached for the door.

'You don't look very well, Ade,' Yvonne said when the detective constable had left and Adrian was back at his desk, breathing steadily to calm the nausea.

'I'm OK.'

He felt Kev's eyes boring into the side of his head.

'Did he give you a rough time or something?' Yvonne said.

'Ooh, er,' Kev sniggered.

'Shut it, Kev,' Yvonne snapped.

'Word is DC Clark's on the same bus as our Adrian, here.'

'Meaning what, exactly?' Yvonne demanded.

'PC Plod's a bumboy, isn't he?'

Adrian swore silently and turned to his StarWriter.

'I tell you, Kev,' Yvonne said. 'I'm not going to tolerate that kind of language. It's fucking disrespectful. Adrian's sexuality is none of your business, and *I* find it offensive. And remember who's responsible for signing off your training reports.'

Adrian watched out of the corner of his eye as Kev shrank into his seat.

But Yvonne wasn't done. 'Apologise to Adrian,' she said, making Adrian wince.

'Do it!' Yvonne yelled.

'Sorry,' Kev muttered, but mouthed, 'Gay-boy.' He dropped a wink.

'It doesn't matter,' Adrian muttered crossly.

Yvonne meant well, but her gay rights campaign on his behalf wasn't welcome. He wanted to tell her so.

Yvonne said, 'So what happened in there?'

'I got a shock, that's all,' Adrian said. 'I thought they were here to talk about Sarah Barrett. I didn't know about Mrs Wormley. It . . . took me by surprise, that's all.'

'Mad old bat,' Kev said. 'Her fella probably did her in.'

'Her husband died years ago,' Yvonne said. 'There's a daughter who's a hairdresser. Got a salon up on the High Estate. Hard as nails. I mean *proper* rough.'

'If *you* think she's rough, Yvonne,' Kev said, 'then she must be *proper fucking* rough.'

'What did they say about Sarah Barrett?' Adrian said, changing the subject.

'There was a shrine for her on the moors,' Yvonne said. 'A cross and a load of news cuttings. The utter bastard.'

'Bitch, you mean,' Kev said.

'Women can be bastards too, Kev. Fucking misogynist.'

'A woman?' Adrian said. 'Is that who they—?'

'Yeah, they've got a witness,' Yvonne said.

'Blonde woman,' Kev said, rocking back in his seat so that the plastic creaked. 'Shoulda seen Linda's face when I suggested putting a big picture of Myra on the front page, saying "Look Who's Back" and three exclamation marks.'

Adrian reeled. *A woman?* But that meant . . .

'Adrian?' Yvonne was saying. 'You look really unwell, babe . . .'

'I'm fine.' He glanced at the phone on his desk. Wondered if he should ring his mum. Tell her it wasn't the Lollipop Man, after all. But . . . what if Kev was wrong?

There was a pink Post-it by the phone, the colour Kev always used for messages he took for Adrian, to his amusement. *Call Mrs Osgood*, it said, followed by a Bradford number. *ASAP.*

'Who's Mrs Osgood?' he called across to Kev.

'Posh older bird,' Kev said. 'Sounded keen, anyway. Nice experienced lady for you, Gay-boy.'

'Knobhead,' Adrian said. He hadn't meant to say it aloud. Kev yowled in mock outrage. Yvonne guffawed with delight as Adrian reached for the phone.

'Hello?' a businesslike voice said.

'Can I speak to Mrs Osgood, please?'

A pause, then a bright: 'Yes! *Yes*, that's me. And who is speaking please?'

'It's Adrian Brown, at the *Calder Valley Advertiser*. I think you left me a message.'

'That's right,' the woman said in a twittery, oddly familiar voice. 'How good of you to call me back.'

'What can I do for you?' He'd written the name *Osgood* on his pad in shorthand. It was a horrible outline. The *Os* didn't link well to the *g* of *good* at all. It irritated him a bit.

'I . . . well, what I *really* wanted to know was . . . whether you might be free to meet me? I have a *little* time later on today. I can come to you. I know where you are. I really don't mind . . . we can be discreet. There's a little place I know—'

'What's it about?' he said, trying not to sound alarmed, and all too conscious that Kev was earwigging. 'Only I'm a bit busy, so . . .'

He heard a disappointed sigh at the end of the line. Sensed it was by design, to manipulate. He held the receiver a little tighter, stiffening with defiance.

'Oh, that is a shame,' the voice said. 'Because, you see . . . well, yesterday, when I saw you. I recognised you. I know exactly what happened. And my real name isn't Osgood.'

Oh, God . . .

'My name is—'

Adrian slammed down the phone.

'Adrian . . . ?' Yvonne started.

'I don't feel well. Sorry!'

And he bolted for the door.

13

'Sheila?' Grace Makinde said from the doorway of the office.

'What is it, Grace?' Sheila turned to her producer with forced cheeriness. She was still holding the phone receiver and made herself place it back in its cradle.

'DCI Struthers is in reception,' the producer said. 'He's ready when we are . . .'

'I'd like to talk to him alone first, if you don't mind, Grace. Would you have him brought up? And maybe someone could see about coffee. Malcolm takes his black, one sugar—'

Grace lifted an enquiring eyebrow.

'I seem to remember . . .' She averted her eyes. 'I'll call when we're ready to talk through the questions.'

Gemma, Sheila's sullen dungarees-wearing PA – a less-than-satisfactory replacement for Zainab, who was currently on maternity leave – brought Malcolm to Sheila's office and deposited him with an absence of niceties.

He gazed blankly from the window.

'How are you, Malcolm?'

He didn't answer. He didn't have to – he looked dreadful.

'Sit down,' she said, indicating the comfy chairs. 'Coffee's on its way.'

He sank into a chair without taking his coat off.

'Did you get any sleep last night?' she asked.

'Not really.'

'You'll need an extra layer of make-up, or the cameras'll make you look like death warmed up,' she said, immediately regretting the turn of phrase.

A knock at the door. Gemma was back with coffee in paper cups.

'Thank you so much,' Sheila said. Gemma scowled.

'Grace is going to join us with the running order,' she told Malcolm, 'and we'll go over the questions. I don't think there'll be any surprises. The show goes out at seven, so we'll spend the first fifteen minutes on this. Grace wants us to do a brief pre-record. Just a couple of minutes: the facts, an appeal, reassurance that you and your colleagues are all over it. If the rain stays off, Grace thinks it might be good to film up on the roof garden, with the moors in the distance.'

He nodded, looking weary as anything.

'I'm worried about you, Malcolm. I can't imagine the toll something like this must take.'

He frowned. 'It's what they pay me for, Sheila, love.'

'Before we bring Grace in,' Sheila said, 'well, I've been doing a bit of research. And there are one or two things I wanted to ask you about.'

He gave her a tired look. 'Go on . . .'

'I've been rereading Dee Thompson's book about the Lollipop Man. It's not very good. Lots of vagueness, and a bit deranged in places. But she talks about three possible suspects and names two of them.'

'What names?'

'Raymond Clitheroe,' she said. 'A convicted paedophile. Served six years for assaulting two boys in a care unit in Huddersfield. Released end of '85, and went to live in a halfway house in Manningham. Subject of a vigilante attack in December '86. He was considered a suspect—'

'Clitheroe's dead. Hanged himself in 1990.'

'Did he? That doesn't mean—'

'He *was* a suspect – but only briefly. He had alibis for two of the kidnaps, one of them provided by his probation officer.'

'OK.' She took a deep breath. 'Dee's other name was Norman Waite. A lorry driver—'

'He fitted the description. The MO was on the money, but like Clitheroe he had alibis for two of the kidnaps. Solid ones.'

'Dee wanted to name a third person,' she said, holding her nerve. 'But she couldn't because he hadn't been convicted of anything. She called him "the third individual".'

'It was nonsense, Sheila, believe me.'

'Really? How can you dismiss it so—'

'Nothing was dismissed,' he said, firmly, coldly. 'Nothing and nobody. I spoke to Dee Thompson myself when she was writing the book. I know who she meant by the "third individual". We looked into it.'

'Who was he, Malcolm?'

'Sheila, please.'

She sat back, accepting temporary defeat.

He glanced at his watch. 'I don't have a lot of time, so . . .'

She nodded. 'I'll tell Grace we're ready.'

14

Gav was waiting for him at the end of the platform at Hebden
Bridge, looking exotic even for this eccentric town, with his
Russian army coat, eyeliner and voluminous black hair. He'd
painted his fingernails black since yesterday.

'You look wrung out, man.'

'I am.' Adrian stalked ahead out of the station.

'In a hurry too,' Gav called, jogging to keep up.

Adrian stopped in the car park and turned round. 'I found
a dead body,' he said in a rush. 'And the police probably think I
killed her.'

Gav stared as he processed the news, then shrugged as if it
were nothing. 'Have one of these,' he said, and handed Adrian a
tightly rolled ciggy.

'Thanks.'

Gav lit it for him and thick tobacco smoke filled his lungs,
making him cough.

'It was late last night,' he said, when they came to the main road. 'I tripped over her on the towpath near the Jester. Someone hit her on the head, or something. Either way she was dead.'

'Are you being serious?'

'It's true. I know how it sounds.'

'Jesus. Who was she?'

'Local troublemaker. Edna Wormley.'

'You knew her?'

'She collared me as I was leaving work yesterday afternoon. Said she knew who I was – and that she knew who took Sarah Barrett.'

'*What?*

He explained, keeping his voice down, including about looking for the letter in the old woman's handbag.

'I was pissed, Gav. Anyway, the letter wasn't there.'

Gav's mouth hung open.

'So I reckon someone killed her for it,' he went on.

'I take it you called the police.'

'Kind of.'

'Oh, man . . .'

'I did it anonymously. I don't want to have to go to court and explain to the world why I was coming out of a gay bar at 10 p.m. on a Wednesday night.'

'Not this shit again . . .'

Adrian gave him a look and Gav shut up.

'Was she definitely dead? The old woman?' Gav lowered his voice as a lady came their way with a poodle. 'Do you know that for sure?'

'Oh, yeah.' He told him about the police turning up at his work.

'Fuck, man. Look, do you want to go for a pint or something?'

He looked at his watch. 'Mind if we go to yours instead?

Only Sheila Hargreaves is doing a special about Sarah Barrett tonight. I want to see if they mention the old woman.'

'Why would they?'

'Because her death's connected to the kid going missing. Because of the letter, see? Jesus, keep up!'

Gav whistled. Looked at his watch. 'It's ten to,' he said. 'We better hurry.'

He realised Adrian hadn't moved. 'What?'

'There's something else,' he said.

'Oh, God, what?'

He took a breath. 'I think someone saw me. Some woman – a Mrs Osgood. She rang me at work and said she knew what had happened.'

'Oh . . .'

He'd run from the office after speaking to the woman, phoning Yvonne from a payphone when he'd calmed down and telling her he was ill and was going home. She'd begun to ask concerned questions, but he'd made excuses and hung up.

He said to Gav, 'So now I've got the police suspicious of me *and* a witness to a crime I didn't commit! I need you to help me.'

'Help you how?'

'I don't know yet.'

Gav eyed him and seemed to give it some thought, before saying, 'All right. Anything for a mate.'

Denise and Sandra owned a three-storey Victorian mid-terrace house on a hill above the town. Adrian said quick hellos to the two women, who were cooking together, then clambered up the stairs after Gav into his gothy attic bedroom. *Yorkshire Tonight* had already begun. Gav turned up the volume on the tiny TV, then they lit a couple of Adrian's menthol cigarettes and sat, cross-legged on the floor, to watch.

Sheila Hargreaves, in a sombre navy-blue suit, was laying it on thick with Sarah Barrett's mum, the pair of them in tears and hugging at one point.

'Earlier,' Sheila Hargreaves said into the camera a few minutes later, 'I spoke to Detective Chief Inspector Malcolm Struthers of West Yorkshire CID about what we know at this stage.'

The programme cut to a breezy scene filmed high above the city, perhaps on the roof of the TV studios. DCI Struthers, the copper-haired detective who'd presided at Gorton Lane yesterday, relayed the facts of Sarah's disappearance: when she was taken and the fact that items of her clothing had been found in Toller Bridge the day before, followed by a makeshift shrine on Widdop Moor that night.

'The clothes bore evidence that violence had taken place,' Struthers said.

'What does he mean?' Gav asked, exhaling minty smoke.

'They've got blood on them,' Adrian said.

'Jesus.'

'Many of our viewers will find these details distressingly familiar,' Sheila Hargreaves commented while the camera remained on Struthers.

'I'm sure they will,' Struthers answered. 'It is true that several aspects of Sarah's disappearance mirror the disappearances of three children from the local area in 1986.'

'Disappearances that were never solved,' Sheila prompted.

'That is correct.'

'But which were said to be the work of an individual who came to be called "the Lollipop Man".'

'It's important not to make any assumptions but to keep open minds. That's exactly what we are doing.'

'In fact,' Sheila Hargreaves said, 'at the press conference today, you are revealing an important new piece of information provided by a young witness.'

'Correct.'

Struthers explained that a witness claimed to have seen Sarah taken by a woman.

'Holy fuck!' Gav gasped.

'We have a fairly good description of this person,' Struthers was saying. 'She was of medium height and thin, wearing trousers and a black knee-length coat with a turned-up collar. She had blonde hair, shoulder-length but bushy and piled up on her head. The witness did not see the woman's face.'

'Did you know it was a woman they're looking for?' Gav asked him, sounding outraged.

Adrian nodded. 'Police told us earlier when they came to the newsroom.'

'It's evil.'

'Why?' Adrian asked sharply, hearing Yvonne's voice in his head. 'I mean, why is it more evil for a woman to do that than a man? Call yourself a feminist.'

They were back in the studio now, Sheila perched at one end of her settee, Struthers in an armchair. Irene Barrett was no longer present.

'Should parents worry?' Sheila Hargreaves asked Struthers now, in a low voice, to signal this was the root of the matter.

'What we are asking for is a proportionate response,' Struthers said.

He talked of communities pulling together, and repeated his reassurances about police action. Helpline numbers appeared on the screen.

'What can people do to help right now?' Sheila asked.

'We need information,' Struthers began, and reeled off a number of questions, reminding the audience of the day and date that Sarah disappeared, and the time. He gave out the phone number of the incident room, and it appeared on screen.

Sheila Hargreaves said her thank-yous, including to Irene Barrett for her bravery in speaking on live television.

'We're going to take a break now,' she said and the camera zoomed in on her face. 'And when we come back, we'll be talking about less upsetting things. Join us again in a few minutes.'

The studio lights dimmed. Sheila and her guest became black shapes against windows looking over Bradford's floodlit City Hall.

'Nothing about Mrs Wormley,' Gav said as he turned down the volume for the adverts.

'No,' Adrian murmured. 'So, what do we do now?'

Gav became quiet for a few minutes, playing with his lighter.

'What are you thinking about?' Adrian asked him.

'Ethics,' his friend said. 'It was a whole module on my course. Pretty interesting, actually.'

Adrian waited.

Another minute passed, then Gav said, 'So . . . nobody knows where this Mrs Wormley was in the time between meeting you and turning up dead?'

'Seems like it.'

'And what time did she leave you?'

'Three-thirty, give or take.'

'And you found her dead when?'

'Um . . . Ten-twenty. Something like that.'

'Did she say she was going anywhere?'

'No. But she had lipstick on. She touched it up while she was talking to me.'

'Not for your benefit, surely,' Gav said.

'Hardly.' Adrian gave him a look.

'Maybe she was going to meet a man. Someone she wanted to impress, anyway.'

Adrian wrinkled his nose, unconvinced.

'How did she know who you were?' Gav asked now.

'Not just me, remember – my mum too. She'll have seen Mum and me in the papers at the time and . . . just kept track. She made it her business because she was a nosy old cow.'

'Maybe you should be more open about it, man. Might make things feel less . . . I don't know, taboo.'

'No thanks. It'd only lead to more questions, and that'd upset my folks. You know about it. Mum and Dad, obviously. Grandma. Nobody else.'

'Mrs Wormley knew,' Gav said.

'Yeah.' They fell into a thoughtful silence.

'You're probably traumatised,' Gav said, matter-of-fact. 'These things go deep, you know? That kind of incident – it can fuck you up badly.'

'I don't think I'm fucked up.'

'No, 'course.' Gav looked sheepish. 'Do you want a drink? Help loosen up the brain cells.' And he produced a bottle of vodka from a satchel.

Gav handed Adrian a green plastic beaker. 'Give it a blow if it's dusty,' he said.

Adrian tipped a fossilised spider out of his, blew hard into the beaker, then held it out for Gav to fill. The vodka tasted good, like syrupy fire.

He closed his eyes and, for the first time since the call to Gorton Lane the day before, began to relax.

15

'You did a wonderful job, Sheila,' Grace said, coming into the office, pen and notepad in hand. 'The way you handled the mum – respectfully but with love – it was masterful.'

'You did have your doubts,' Sheila reminded her pointedly.

'I did. I still do. So does Max. He's been on the phone.'

'That man worries too much.'

Max Warner was the chairman of the channel. An old-school control freak. Grace sat on one of the settees and waved to Sheila to join her.

Grace said, 'He's worried about the resource implications of turning the programme into what he calls "a kind of Yorkshire *Crimewatch*".'

'That's not what we're doing. I hope you told him that.'

'The switchboard's going mad. Despite the police giving out their helpline number, we're still getting calls from viewers. We'll pass messages on, but we can't become a call centre for the investigation. We don't have the capacity.' She gave Sheila a meaningful look.

'Fine,' Sheila said, more sharply than she intended.

'Max wants reassurance, that's all. He suggests we open tomorrow's show by assuring viewers tonight was a one-off for very particular reasons.'

Sheila nodded, then crossed her legs and glared out at the dark city, and at her reflection in the glass.

'A few of the callers are asking to speak to you personally,' Grace went on. 'A few of the usual "committed fans". But also a self-styled "psychic medium" called Rosa Laycock. Sounds not all there, if I'm honest. There are a couple of sane-sounding callers, too. Three men, one woman, all saying they have information.'

'Oh?'

'Who I would advise you not to talk to. Remember, DCI Struthers expressly asked us not to engage with potential witnesses. We need to direct them straight to him and his team.'

'And risk missing something someone prefers to confide in me rather than the police? Tell me who's called.'

Grace consulted her notepad.

'First: a man who didn't want to give his name. Sounded Australian. Said he might have information but that he needed to speak to someone first. Wouldn't leave a name or number. Then there was—' She turned a leaf on her pad. 'Oh, yes. Brian Quigley. Says his late father Arthur ran a vigilante outfit called "the Bradford Angels" back in 1986, who tried "to do the work of the police for them", because, quote: "the police didn't know what the eff they were doing".'

'Quigley . . . it rings a bell.'

'He says he's setting up a new group and wants you to endorse it and have them on the show.'

'That's a definite no,' Sheila said, adding with dark amusement, 'Can you imagine?'

Grace looked relieved. Her eyes went back to her pad.

'Then there was a Deirdre – Dee – Thompson. Says she wrote a book—'

'She did,' Sheila said. 'I've read it. It's the closest thing we have to a documentary record.'

'She wants to talk to you.'

'Does she?' She thought about it. "The third individual",' she murmured to herself.

'Sorry?'

'Do you have her number?'

'Yes.'

'Write it on here for me, would you?' Sheila handed Grace her pad.

Grace wrote, eyebrows raised in mild disapproval.

'Who else?' Sheila said.

'A Colin Joseph,' Grace read. 'Says he's the older brother of the first girl who went missing in — Sheila, is something wrong?'

'No.' She uncrossed her legs, straightened her back. 'If he calls again, say I'm too busy.'

'Right, but—'

'But nothing,' she snapped. 'Now, is that all?'

16

The alcohol had tranquillised him, and he felt fatalistic in a mellow way. Gav had put The Cure on, and it made a beautiful melancholy backdrop. Whatever was going to happen, the wheels were already in motion. There was little he could do except weather the storm, own up to what he'd done, and refute what he hadn't – and hope to emerge on the other side unscathed and undamaged.

Unfucked up, to coin a phrase.

Was he fucked up? He didn't think so, but who was he to judge? A terrible thing had happened to him – a thing that could have turned out infinitely worse. But he'd survived. Bounced back in the resilient way kids had. He had no lasting trauma or anxiety following the event, no depression, agoraphobia or panic attacks. Not even bad dreams. He remembered being confused, excited, tired and frightened. But it hadn't *damaged* him.

As for his mum and dad, though . . . They were fucked

up, no question. His dad most of all, with his rages, his silent depressions, his drinking, the fact he hadn't worked for years.

All because of what happened during the space of two hours, one night before a long-ago Christmas.

He remembered very little of the actual kidnap, and what he did recall was unreliable, reconstructed from fragments of memory and from snatches of overheard conversation, with bits no doubt filled in by his imagination.

In his mind he saw lights and faces taut with horror. He heard voices, a tumult of chatter, rising to screams, men's shouts, a lady telling him off for being so naughty, women's tears, police sirens. Then more images: friendly policewomen, men with cameras.

And, of course, the man. Lumbering, pulling him along a cobbled street he later learnt was Gorton Lane, talking in a low rumble of words now lost to him for ever, until they reached the van.

And later, at home, only it didn't feel like home that night. It was too full of people. Family, including Grandma and an old auntie. Strangers, too. Police. Women and men, talking to him, being nice to him. Hands all over him – but comforting ones.

Some lad, eh?

That's one brave boy!

And then, after they'd all gone, the empty house. Lights on everywhere. Darkness pressing hard against the windows. His mum screaming at his dad. And the expression on his dad's face when he looked at Adrian (though he was still Matthew then), an expression of sheer . . . *disgust.*

It must have been in the early hours of the morning that his dad dragged him up the stairs and locked himself and Adrian in the bathroom. His mum wept outside the door until it was over. Until his dad was panting, sobbing on his knees, wringing his hands, repeating over and over: *What will they think? What will people say?*

'Want some of this?' Gav said, stretching across from his beanbag, a lighted spliff in hand.

'No, ta. I want to keep a clear head.'

'Understandable . . . Oh, oh—' He sat up. 'News!'

Gav turned up the volume on his TV and killed the music.

A female newsreader was giving the headlines. The first, as expected, related to the ongoing investigation into Sarah Barrett's disappearance and the discovery of her clothes and the shrine, the second to a lorry smash with a fatality on the M62, and the third to a call for help in relation to the unexplained death of an elderly woman in High Calder the evening before.

'Oh, God,' Adrian said, feeling cold fingers on the back of his neck.

'No, it's good!' Gav said. 'It's better to know what they're saying.'

'First we go to Toller Bridge,' the newsreader said, 'where police are stepping up their enquiries into the disappearance of eleven-year-old Sarah Barrett—'

Gav turned the volume down. 'Right,' he said, matter-of-fact. 'I reckon I know what we need to do.'

'Oh?'

'For starters, we don't know what the police are thinking, who they suspect or what they're going to do about it.'

'Ah . . .'

'What?'

'It's just . . . that's not strictly true.' He explained about his faux pas in front of DC Clark earlier. 'It was horrible – like he could see right through me.'

'Fuck, man.'

He glanced at the silent TV. They were onto another story now. Behind the newsreader was an image of a motorway and a bad pile-up.

'I told him I'd heard a rumour from a friend that there'd been an attack. I *think* he bought it.'

'That's how they catch you, man. They get you to relax, then you let something slip because you're so relieved and you forget to lie. I've seen it in films.'

'TV!' Adrian said sharply.

Gav reached over to turn up the volume. 'That her?' he said.

'Yeah.'

The screen showed a photo of a tipsy-looking Edna Wormley, grinning and showing yellow teeth. She was wearing a blue sparkly top as if she was at some kind of party.

His skin crawled.

'Police are keen to understand more about Mrs Wormley's movements in the late afternoon and evening,' the newsreader said, 'and are appealing for one particular witness to get back in touch.'

The broadcast cut to the handsome but dead-eyed detective constable with the text: *DC Jamie Clark, West Yorkshire Police.* 'At ten twenty-five last night,' said DC Clark, 'emergency operators received a call from an anonymous male witness, who claimed to have found an injured woman on the canal towpath near the Jester public house in High Calder. The caller gave us the woman's name. It is crucial that we speak to this caller as soon as possible, in relation to what we are now treating as murder. We are also calling for assistance from anyone who might have met or talked to Mrs Wormley between half past three yesterday afternoon and 10 p.m. last night.' He gave the number of the High Calder police station.

The scene changed. A large blonde woman with an orange face stood in front of a parade of shops. The caption read: *Sharon Wormley, victim's daughter*.

'Mam wouldn't hurt a fly,' the woman said in a gravelly voice. 'She were kindness itself.' A big sniff, and a talon-like nail scraped a tear from the corner of a mascaraed eye. She sobbed, then gasped out: 'There weren't no one ever had a bad word to say about her.'

Back to the studio. The newsreader, backed by Mrs Wormley's leering face, said, 'Police believe the motive for the attack might have been theft, because her handbag had been tampered with. However, the bag was found to contain a purse with a hundred pounds in cash, but the money was untouched.'

'Fuck,' Adrian said when Gav had turned the volume down.

'You need to tell them it was you who found her, man,' Gav said gravely. 'This is serious.'

'I can't.' He folded his arms.

'Ade—'

'No!'

He took a few moments to breathe, then held out his beaker for a top-up of vodka.

'They didn't mention the call I made to the Jester,' Adrian said after a swig.

'Maybe they don't know about it.'

'Maybe.' He'd suspected at the time that Bev hadn't heard his hysterical warning. If that was the case, good. It meant less evidence against him; and at the same time he could reassure himself he'd at least tried to warn Bev and her regulars that there was an attacker about.

'All right,' he said, calmer now and more resigned, 'what do we do?'

'Ethically? We shouldn't hinder the police, or justice. That includes not doing anything that sends the police in the wrong direction.'

'Meaning?'

'We need to tell them about the handbag. Tell them why it was moved, but that you took nothing from it.'

He groaned. 'How, though, without giving away that I was looking for the letter? If I mention the letter, that'll lead them straight back to me. I've already told them she waved it in my face.'

'You need to ring the police again,' Gav said.

'Do I?' His mouth was dry.

'Just call them anonymously from any payphone. Tell them you're the one who found Mrs Wormley and that you went through her handbag trying to find out who she was. That's all.'

'I did tell them her name,' Adrian said, liking the idea, 'so that makes sense. But they'll still wonder why I won't say who I am. That's suspicious in itself.'

'So be honest,' Gav said. 'Say you're gay but not out. Tough if they don't like it.'

'It won't work,' he said dismally. 'They'll go to the Jester and talk to people and work out it was me. Someone will tell them who left about that time. They might even think I killed her.'

'Tell them it's none of their business why you were there. Tell them you looked in her bag because you wanted to help, then hang up. It's their choice to believe you or not.'

'I don't know. My mum says, don't go halfway to meet trouble. I reckon I'm already a quarter of the way.'

'It's the right thing to do, man. It's *ethical*. It gives them the facts they need and stops them wasting time looking for the mystery caller, i.e. *you*.'

He tried to envisage making the call. But what if it went wrong? What if he froze on the call? Started sobbing? Gabbled out who he was and made everything worse? For himself, for the police investigation. For his mum . . .

'Look, don't do anything tonight. Let's hang out tomorrow afternoon. We can write a script for the call.'

'Yeah, maybe.' He looked at his watch. It was, indeed, getting late. 'I need to watch the time,' he said. 'My last train's in forty minutes.'

'You can stay here,' Gav said. 'Ring your mum.'

'Nah. Mum's in a bad place,' he said glumly. 'The Sarah Barrett thing's upset her. Last night I turned up after midnight and she was in bits.'

'We'll meet tomorrow,' Gav said. 'We can go to the Jester if you like. Might help you focus.'

''Kay.'

'I wonder what did happen to the letter,' Gav said now. 'If we could find it, we could work out whether the old woman was talking rubbish or not. We could send it to the police anonymously.'

'Nice idea,' Adrian said, dismally.

'She must have said stuff to you when she was talking about the letter.'

'She said a *lot* of stuff. I made some shorthand notes afterwards, in case she was telling the truth. But it was just words here and there. There's a couple of pages of stuff, but I don't think it's significant. She was going on about Boris Yeltsin at one point.'

'Have you still got the notes?'

'Yeah, they're at home. I'd need to transcribe them, but it shouldn't take me long . . .'

'You never know, man. You might have written down a clue.'

'A clue?' he said.

'Yeah,' Gav said quietly. 'To the identity of the Lollipop Man.'

17

Friday 8th April, 1994

'These are for you,' Adrian said, and passed three ten-pound notes across the breakfast table.

'Oh!' His mum looked momentarily taken aback. 'Thank you . . . but I don't need it till Monday,' she said, gazing with something like distress at the precious notes. 'If you—'

'I got it out of the machine yesterday,' he said. 'If you don't take it, I'll only spend it.'

'You're so good, Adrian.' She stood and kissed him.

He scraped margarine across his toast, and breathed again.

He gave her money every week, though she'd never asked for it. He knew it was needed – and welcome. His mum made a decent wage, but it didn't go far, what with ever-rising interest rates on the mortgage. His dad, currently still in bed, hadn't worked in almost three years. He spent his days sleeping late, or preoccupied by daytime TV and quizzes on Teletext. The fact his teenage son was paying for food would only make Peter wretched with humiliation, and all the more angry.

The money, then, was their secret.

'Sorry about the other night,' he said, swivelling his knife to marshal black ribbons of Marmite. 'They didn't want me to leave.'

'I'm glad you had a nice time,' his mum said. 'You work so hard.'

'So do you, Mum,' he said, a little choked.

He hated lying to her, but he did it all the time.

His mum was a little brighter today. She'd seen Sheila Hargreaves' programme the evening before. Had greeted him, almost excitedly, when he got back from Hebden Bridge with the news that the police were looking for a woman. 'It's not him,' she'd told him. 'Thank God it's not him.'

'Doesn't really help Sarah Barrett, does it?' he'd replied.

'Yes. I know that, but . . .' She'd sagged a little, standing there in the hallway. Then words came in a tearful rush: 'The idea that he could still be out there. The idea of it happening again. Going on for years, just like Sutcliffe. The police making mistakes time and time again. The mess they made over that tape . . .'

'I'm going to bed,' he'd said gently, and hugged her goodnight.

'We're going to be short-staffed again next week,' she said now, putting down her coffee mug. 'I don't know how I'm going to do it. I think I'll need to go into the office this weekend. I might have to do a couple of overnight care shifts myself.'

His mum managed a branch of a care agency with offices all over Yorkshire and Lancashire. The carers got peanuts and his mum seemed to spend all her time despairing over the difficulty of finding and keeping staff.

'Do you need me to help out?' he said, without enthusiasm.

She watched him. 'Maybe you could help me in the office.

I need to do another mailshot, so you could help with that. I'd pay you.'

'I can come in with you tomorrow morning if you like,' he offered.

'Do you . . . do you think your friend might want to do some care shifts? Deborah, isn't it?'

'Debbie,' Adrian said. He cleared his throat. 'Maybe.'

'She cooks for her granddad, doesn't she?'

He'd suggested Debbie a couple of months back when his mum was struggling badly. In an ideal world his mum and Debbie would never cross paths, and he'd keep his gay life as far away from home as he could.

'If she could do meals for the ladies in the sheltered flats a couple of evenings, it would be a great help. I can pay her four pounds an hour.'

'I'll ask her,' he said, but suspected a few hours of work would mess up Debbie's income support.

'Could you ask her today? Only—'

'I'll ring her later.'

She reached for his fingers and squeezed them. 'Let me know what she says, won't you?' Her face changed. 'I'll need to look sharp. I told Fiona I'd help with Rachel.'

'What . . . ? Oh, *Mum* . . .'

Fiona was their neighbour, a seemingly fragile single mum with a little girl. In Adrian's view she was feckless and manipulative. He wondered briefly, and not for the first time, if he ought to confront her. Tell her a thing or two.

'I said I'd take her for an hour here and there.'

'You shouldn't have done that.'

'There's no one else, and she's needing to visit her sister who's ill. Poor little girl. It's not her fault.'

'I thought she went to her grandma's most days.'

'Not at the moment,' his mum said. 'The old lady's not very sharp. If something were to happen . . . she might take her eye off her when she was playing outside.' She shuddered. 'I couldn't live with myself.'

'Did Fiona suggest it, or did you offer?'

She avoided making eye contact.

'Mum, you already work full-time!'

'I can take her into the office. Rachel's very good really.'

Adrian wasn't convinced. He found the child watchful and devious.

'You're looking after another woman's kid *for the whole day*?'

She didn't reply. Her face had paled a little. He realised, uncomfortably, that he'd sounded like his dad. It was all there in the tone: the disappointment, the scorn.

He shut up and ate his toast.

'There just aren't enough people,' she said now, with a sigh. 'That old woman came in looking for work, and I turned her away. Now she's dead.'

He swallowed. 'What old woman?'

'Her name was Edna Wormley,' she said. 'It was on the news.'

Adrenalin sparked in his chest. He said carefully, 'What happened to her?'

'She got attacked – a couple of nights ago, down by the canal. Mugged, I expect. Though what she was doing down there . . . The kinds of people you find in these places.'

His cheeks burnt.

'She asked you for work?'

'She came in wanting to register last week but I turned her away.'

'Oh?'

'Not a nice person,' his mum said. 'She gave me her CV but I told her I wasn't interested. Still, you don't like to think of her being killed . . .'

What did she say to you? he wanted to ask.

A little knock at the back door.

'That'll be Fiona with Rachel.' She got up.

'I've got to go,' Adrian said, rising too. He had no desire to see the neighbour.

'You will take care won't you, baby?'

'Yeah, Mum.'

'And let me know if you're going to be late.' She smiled a pleading smile.

'Yeah.'

'Love you.'

'You too.'

He groaned to himself. Sometimes her love wounded him, and he resented it.

18

'I saw your programme,' Jeanette said when Sheila answered the phone in her kitchen. 'You did well, love. The stuff with the mum? Wow.'

'I don't know if it'll make any difference,' Sheila said, receiver in one hand, coffee cup in the other. From where she stood she could see out across the garden, up to the empty moor, brown and brooding under a threatening sky of low clouds. 'Malcolm came across well, didn't he? And he agrees it was the right thing to do.'

'So why do you sound so glum?'

'I'm tired.'

'Too tired for a curry after tonight's show?'

She thought quickly. 'Actually that would be very nice. Come to the studio about eight-fifteen but be prepared to wait if need be.'

'Good . . . That'll be good.'

'Jeanette?' she said, detecting something in her friend's tone. 'What is it?'

'Had a tip-off,' Jeanette said, excitedly. 'Something the police are keeping up their sleeves to weed out the cranks.'

'What?'

'Tell you later. Meanwhile, talking of cranks . . .'

'What about them?'

'You put yourself in the spotlight last night, Sheila. There's a lot of strange people out there. Watch yourself. Careful where you park, keep your keys in your hand – you know the drill.'

'I do – but thanks for the reminder. See you tonight.'

19

The Jester was depressing in the daytime. The mirrorball hung still and the fairy lights around the bar barely seemed to glow. You could see the grime and fag burns on the carpet.

Adrian and Gav had arrived via the steps next to the tunnel entrance, the usual route being cordoned off with police tape. A man was just leaving the table beside the fruit machine, shrugging on his jacket. Adrian didn't recognise him. He had dark hair and a pale, pretty elfin face, and his eyes looked red from crying. He was also painfully thin.

Illness here – even a suggestion of it – was unsettling. A reminder of a different kind of danger than that posed by Mrs Wormley's killer, or by the Lollipop Man. A silent danger, invisible and insidious, and just as deadly – but one that took its time.

'By the window?' Gav asked.

'Yeah, I'll get the drinks. You can start looking at these.'

He went into his satchel, found his transcribed shorthand

notes and handed them over.

A woman was ahead of him at the bar, in a green-and-black lumberjack shirt and boots, waiting patiently for someone to appear and serve her. He'd seen her here plenty of times before. She was older – over forty, even – and for some reason he thought she was a nurse and that her name was Mary.

'Hiya,' he said, and tipped his money onto the bar to count it, calculating quickly that he had enough to keep him and his friends in drinks for a couple of hours. He might even spend a few quid on the jukebox.

'Damien's changing a barrel,' Maybe Mary said and gave him a good once-over.

She looked over to where Gav sat, poring intently over his transcribed notes, then appraised him again. Something in her eyes troubled him.

'Quiet today,' he muttered, feeling the need to say something. Anything.

'Maybe it's to do with what happened the other night.' Her eyes didn't move from his face.

'The other night?' he said, innocently.

'You were here on Wednesday evening, weren't you?' she asked. 'Lateish?'

He pretended to think about it, and felt himself reddening under her scrutiny. 'Wednesday? Yeah. Yeah, I was.'

'A woman was killed,' she said, almost conversationally. 'Out there, on the towpath, just before the steps. Surely you've heard about it.'

'Oh, that . . .' he said stiffly. 'Yeah. That was bad.'

'I reckon you left not long before it happened,' she said. 'Maybe you saw something.'

'No, nothing.'

'Only the police are wanting to talk to anyone who might be able to help.'

'Don't think I can,' he said feebly.

Damien, the part-time barman, appeared and cried, 'A throng awaits! A thousand apologies! Who's first?'

Adrian pointed at Maybe Mary.

'Two halves of bitter, please, Damien,' she said.

She took her drinks and Adrian watched her install herself alone at a table by the loos, clearly waiting for someone to join her. She caught him looking and nodded, giving him a smile that didn't go near her eyes.

Adrian's pal Debbie came in just as he was handing Gav his Coke.

'Back in a sec,' he said to Gav.

'What's up, Adey?' Debbie said.

'Nothing,' he said, defensively.

But she seemed more interested in scanning the bar – doubtless for Elaine.

Little Phil appeared through the door behind her, beaming when he spotted Adrian. After some chat, he headed for his favourite perch, the stool at the end of the bar, where he could be spotted and bought drinks.

'Mum asked if you might be interested in some shifts,' he said to Debbie. 'Sounds like it's just warming up food for some of the oldies.'

'Yeah, maybe. I could borrow the Smurfette.' This was Debbie's nickname for her auntie's Fiat Panda. 'Is it cash in hand?'

'Doubt it.'

'Oh . . . Only, it's tricky with the dole.'

'Mum's desperate.'

'Is she?' She looked uncomfortable. 'I'll think about it.'

'Thanks. Do you want a drink?'

Her face lit up. 'Usual please, Adey.'

'You buying, Adey?' Little Phil called from his perch.

'Yeah, go on then. What do you want?'

'Same as Debs. Thanks.' A winsome smile.

'Starting to think you've robbed a bank,' Damien said to him as he began to make the snakebites.

'Maybe I should,' Adrian said, eyes on his dwindling cash.

'No one'd ever suspect you if you did – handsome lad like you.'

He winked and Adrian felt himself blush. Damien wasn't his type at all. Skinny and blond, he spent so much time on his skincare routine that he looked permanently shiny. Every second Sunday he doubled up as Demi Whore, drag queen karaoke MC. Demi Whore shared Damien's dour outlook, making cutting remarks and rolling her eyes at the audience as successive drunk singers attempted Mariah Carey or Queen numbers.

He took Debbie and Little Phil their drinks, then returned to the table where Gav was poring over the A4 sheets.

'What do you think?' Adrian asked.

'If this is a good record of what the old woman said, then she was fucking nuts.'

'She was. Proper raving.'

He sneaked a look round at Maybe Mary, and saw she'd been joined by a companion: a man with broad shoulders on a stool facing her, his back to Adrian. Maybe Mary saw Adrian peeking and narrowed her eyes a little. Her lips moved as she murmured to her faceless friend. Adrian looked sharply away, telling himself to keep calm and act natural.

'She was obsessed with Russians,' Gav said, squinting at the first page.

'Yeah,' he said.

'Then there's some weird stuff,' he said, pen pointing at the next section.

Adrian leant in and reminded himself what he'd noted.

liars
horrible furniture
her waiting on him
letter there
smell [?] of the letter
gold teeth and dead inside
Clinton
Bill Billy Boy

'God knows,' he said, sitting back.

'Who had "horrible furniture"? One of the Russians? Or was she talking about the kidnapper?'

'Dunno.'

'"Smell of the letter"? Did it smell?'

'I didn't get the chance to find out.'

'Why is there a question mark after "smell"?'

'It was ambiguous.'

Gav stared at him, mystified.

'It's the way shorthand works. You miss out the vowels. The shorthand says S-M-L. The context helps it make sense. Only . . . sometimes it doesn't.'

'So, if it wasn't "smell", what else could it have been? "Small"?'

'"*Small* of the letter"?' he asked incredulously. 'I suppose it could have been "smell *off* the letter",' he said. 'But it looked pretty clean and the handwriting was nice.'

'Who had gold teeth?' Gav asked.

'Dunno,' Adrian said, picking tobacco off his lip.

'This bit's more interesting,' Gav said, reading on. '"Mother's son, Dead son, father's son, stepfather". But who's she talking about?'

He shook his head.

'And here it's like she's coming to the point.' He tapped the page. Adrian leant in to read it.

he's a killer

always said – [tn tr hds???]

not a confession

not an idiot

won't be broadcasting that will he?

Gav asked, 'What's the bit in square brackets?'

'Couldn't work it out.'

'Could be "something, something heads".'

'Oh, and the D could be a T,' he added sheepishly. 'So it might be H-T-S.'

'"Hats"?' Gav said. 'Tin tore hats? Tyre heads? Hots?'

They stared dismally at each other.

'Sorry . . .' Adrian said.

'Did she say where she got the letter from?' Gav asked. 'Was it written to her, or to someone else?'

'She said it was hers "now". As if it was someone else's originally.'

'Then how did she get hold of it? And why does she say that the letter isn't a confession? And who's "not an idiot"?'

'Look, I might have missed some stuff. Sorry.' He was exasperated now – with the conversation and with himself.

'It's okay, man,' Gav soothed. 'It was worth a try.'

'And we don't *actually* know she was killed because of what she knew,' he said.

They looked glumly at one another.

'So,' he said at last. 'What do we do now?'

'Get another drink?' Gav suggested and got to his feet.

After Gav had returned with their drinks, Adrian became conscious of some kind of high drama taking place behind the bar. The landlady Bev had arrived, and she and Damien the barman were engaged in a heated conversation involving jabbing gestures and shrugging of shoulders. Elaine had turned up for her shift collecting glasses, but was apparently keeping clear of her colleagues. Bev raised her voice and Adrian heard,

'I haven't touched it! Now, if you don't mind, I've a pub to run,' in response to which, Damien threw up his arms and marched into the room behind the bar, leaving Bev shrugging and shaking her head at the waiting customers.

'You ready?' Gav said, after lighting another rollie. He saw the look on Adrian's face. 'To make the call. That's what we agreed, isn't it?'

'What if they record it? They might play it on TV, like they did with that tape during the Ripper investigation. My mum would recognise my voice for sure, even if I did an accent.'

Gav bit his lip. 'In that case, they probably taped your call to them the other night.'

'Yeah, I realise that now, but I was so pissed . . . I tried to do an accent, but . . . I can't ring them again, Gav. I can't risk it.'

'Then I'll do it,' Gav said, sitting up. 'We can agree the script and I'll ring from one of the phone boxes outside Asda. I'll say I'm ringing on behalf of the first caller. That I'm a friend. Ade, we're being helpful, remember? We're explaining why the bag got moved, so they don't waste time on it. They can hardly complain about that.'

'We're *lying* about why the bag was moved,' Adrian corrected. 'I was looking for the letter, not her ID. They do need to know about the letter, too. They need to understand its importance.'

'You could work on your boss,' Gav suggested. 'Convince her to talk to the police about the letter. You'd just need to make her think it's her own idea.'

'Maybe,' he said, unconvinced. 'And what about the woman who rang me – Mrs Osgood?'

'Oh yeah. But we don't know who she is, or what she wants. Maybe we just have to take the risk that she's another troublemaker and . . . Gav paused, seeing Adrian's stricken expression. 'What is it?'

He'd stolen a glance at Maybe Mary and her male companion. She'd spotted him looking, and said something to her friend – who'd turned and locked eyes with Adrian.

It was Jamie Clark, the detective constable who'd interviewed him in Linda's office.

And the reason for Maybe Mary's questions at the bar earlier was suddenly, painfully, obvious.

'We're fucked,' Adrian said dismally. 'I am, anyway.'

It was twenty minutes later, and they were hunched over a greasy table in the packed upstairs of Ranchburger, beside the station.

'We're *not*,' Gav said, rolling his eyes. 'Eat your chips. You'll feel better.'

'They suspect me, don't they?' he said, pushing away the salty fries. 'Why else was she grilling me like that? The two of them were looking *right at me*. Why was he there if it wasn't for work?'

'Maybe he's gay.'

'Maybe.' What had Kev said? *PC Plod's a bumboy*—something offensive like that.

'I can still make the phone call,' Gav said.

'But they've seen us all together. They'll work it out.' Adrian put his head in his hands. 'Oh God . . .'

'Are they that bright?' Gav asked.

'Who knows? But we can't take any risks. I'm so sorry for dragging you into this.'

'It's cool, man.' Gav lit a roll-up and looked about for a foil ashtray. 'Look, here's what we'll do. I'll make the call while you're at the Jester, in full sight of that pair – perfect alibi.'

'You think?'

'Yeah. But we need to move fast. Give me some paper and we'll write out what I'm going to say.'

20

The studio lights dimmed and the cameras panned back, sighing as they relaxed on their hydraulic columns. A red light gleamed on the single camera that hung from the lighting rig and was used only once each evening, for this closing shot.

Sheila sat calmly, legs crossed at her ankles, hands resting in her lap, and smiled through the gloom at her guest. On TV screens across Yorkshire the two of them would appear in shadows, backed by a panorama of the floodlit buildings and moving traffic of Bradford city centre.

The red light winked off.

'That's us,' the director said in her earpiece, and the lights in the studio rose again.

'Thank you so much,' Sheila said to her guest as he rose from his seat. The guest, a children's writer, had been as nervous as a kitten. His relief was palpable. 'You were wonderful,' she added.

'Was I? I couldn't get the words out.'

An assistant approached to guide the guest safely away across the cable-strewn studio floor. Grace appeared and came forward.

'Happy?' Sheila asked her.

'Your friend Jeanette Dinsdale is here,' Grace said. 'They've taken her to your dressing room.'

'Thanks, Grace. Is everything OK?' There was something she didn't like in the producer's expression.

'There's another visitor for you,' Grace said. 'Down in reception.'

'Oh?'

'Security say he's very agitated. His name's Colin Joseph. He's one of the people who called after the programme last night. You told me you didn't want to speak to him, but he says he won't leave until you do.'

'I haven't changed my mind, Grace,' she said stiffly.

'In that case, you might want to go out through the back entrance.'

'That's fine.'

'I can arrange for one of the security boys to walk you to your car, if . . .'

'I'm going out for dinner with my friend,' she said. 'She'll be with me.'

'OK.' Grace looked at her, long and hard.

'Was there something else?' Sheila asked.

The producer took a breath. 'This is a consequence of last night's programme. But I think you understand that.'

'Yes, Grace,' Sheila said, squaring her shoulders. 'I understand, thank you.'

* * *

'Face him,' Jeanette said, pacing Sheila's dressing room crossly. 'I'll be with you. We can take on a grumpy bloke between us. What does he want, anyway?'

'Not sure,' she said, peering at her reflection and wiping at her make-up with cotton wool. 'I just don't have the energy for it.'

Jeanette eyed her sceptically in the mirror.

One of the security guards showed them the way through the bowels of the building, and led them along a service corridor to a fire exit.

The air outside was fresh, the sky big and dusky purple.

'You'll have seen the press,' Jeanette said over the noise of traffic, as they made their way up the hill. 'I'm not just talking about the my paper, either. It's everywhere.'

'Are you surprised?'

'People need to know. And maybe it'll make some mums and dads think twice about letting their kids play outside. That said, some of it's just salacious. Did you see *The Sun*? Front page: "The Bitch is Back", and a silhouette of Myra Hindley's face with red eyes. There'll be vigilantes on the streets before long. Innocent women getting attacked by men who "mean well". You mark my words, Sheila. Violence against women is the only possible outcome.'

They crossed Senior Way, skipping out of the path of a fast-oncoming bus.

'All right, Sheila, darlin'!' a man yelled suddenly from a passing car window, making Sheila jump.

Sheila lifted a hand and put on a smile.

'Member of the fan club?' Jeanette asked drily.

'Clearly.'

'He's got under your skin, hasn't he, this Colin Joseph?' Jeanette said now.

She looked straight ahead. 'A bit.'

'I wish you'd tell me who he is. Maybe then I can help.'

They came to a corner. 'This way,' Sheila said tersely.

A little way up the hill a woman in a short skirt stood by a car, talking through the window to an unseen driver. She nodded, the window rose, and the woman hurried round to the passenger door and climbed inside. The car crept away into the night.

'I forgot what it was like round here,' Jeanette said. 'Men like bloody predators. Those poor women.'

'Cross over,' Sheila instructed.

The owner of Amin's Tandoori met them at the door. 'I have your favourite table waiting for you,' he said with a huge grin.

'How kind,' Sheila said, and followed their host up a couple of steps to a raised area with pillars hung about with red velvet swags.

It was Friday evening, so the place was packed. A group of businessmen tucked into sizzling dishes. A young couple sat at a table in the window, holding hands. Then there were families. A birthday party for an elderly woman, her chair decked with helium balloons. Sheila was aware she'd been recognised. She kept a smile on her face and avoided eye contact.

A girl arrived with menus, then, a minute later, Amin was there for their drinks order.

'What do you recommend?' Jeanette asked, squinting at the menu.

'Everything's good,' Sheila said, 'but you can't go wrong with the balti.'

Their drinks arrived.

'Cheers, love,' Jeanette said. 'You deserve this.'

'Do I?'

'Of course.'

'You said you had something to tell me,' Sheila said, rearranging her cutlery. 'Something the police are keeping quiet about.'

'Yes, I do. But how about you cough up about Colin Joseph first.'

'Lowering yourself to extortion?'

'Extortion's an ugly word.'

'I don't want to talk about it, Jeanette.'

'Must be serious, then.' Jeanette put down her glass. She leant in and said, quietly, 'You might feel better.'

Sheila gave Jeanette one of her cooler stares.

'What did your police contact tell you?' she said, when the frost had melted a little.

'It's about the shrine,' Jeanette said. 'The newspaper cuttings weren't strung onto the cross like before. They were pinned on with drawing pins – brass ones. They're keeping it under wraps because it's different from before. The clothes, the shrine and cuttings – all that was similar, but this is new.'

'But what does it mean?'

'Well, it could indicate it's a different person doing it. Anyway, it's a detail they can use to weed out cranks making false confessions. Did you ever think we'd be living through something like this again? Whole communities in fear?'

'Maybe it's a feature of how we live,' Sheila said, eyes on her hands. 'In the Middle Ages they had wolves and cholera and suchlike. We have serial murderers. The Moors Murderers, then the Ripper, the Lollipop Man. And don't forget all the poor kids in between. That girl over in Morley – lifted off the street while buying a loaf of bread for her mum. Maybe we have to accept that there will always be evil among us.'

'I don't know, love. Sounds a lot like giving in. We have to do what we can.'

They sat in silence for a time. Then Amin was beside them, pad at the ready to take their order.

21

This is an important message. Please listen carefully. It's about the death of Mrs Edna Wormley on Wednesday 6th April.

I am the person who called you that night from a payphone in High Calder to say I'd found her dead. I found her but I did not kill her, and that's the truth. I knew she was dead because she wasn't breathing and her skin was cold. It was me that moved her handbag because I was looking for ID and that's how I knew who she was. I dropped the handbag because I thought I heard someone and got scared off.

I called you as soon as I could. I can't tell you who I am for personal reasons, and you need to respect that.

I hope you catch whoever killed the lady.

Back at the Jester, he got a drink then found a spare stool by the fruit machine, in full view of Maybe Mary. He'd seen her whisper to Jamie Clark when he'd come back in, and Clark had swivelled to take a look for himself.

Adrian met his gaze for a second, then looked nonchalantly away.

'What happened to you earlier?' a voice asked him.

He turned to find Elaine eyeballing him while balancing a tower of glasses against her shoulder.

'When?' he asked, all innocent.

'Saw you and your mate go flying out the door like the place was on fire.'

'Oh, yeah. He — er, Gav forgot he was meeting someone at the station. We'd lost track of time. He'll be back in a while.'

'Everyone's a bit jumpy just now. You know, after that old woman got coshed and killed.'

'Yeah. I guess.'

'By the way,' Elaine said now. She leant in. 'See him on the stool by the loos, facing this way? Fair hair, kinda handsome?'

Adrian pretended to take a look, though he didn't need to. He knew exactly who Elaine meant. 'Oh yeah?' He swallowed. 'What about him?'

'Asked me if you came here often.' Her smirk broadened into a cheeky grin.

'What did you tell him?'

'Said I'd seen you about. Anyway, I reckon you've got a fan.'

'Do you?' He knew he was breathing funny and tried to disguise it. 'He's too old for me,' he said. 'Tell him I'm off the market if he asks again.'

'Will do.' She winked. 'And you be careful out there on the towpath. Watch yourself, yeah?'

'I will.'

He sat on his stool another twenty grinding minutes, feeling even more awkward under Clark's steady gaze. He sipped his lager and smoked, willing Gav to reappear. When he finally did, he looked as fraught as Adrian felt.

'All right?' he asked, rising from his stool.

'Not exactly,' Gav said breathlessly, 'but it's done. I need a drink.'

They went to the bar together and Gav ordered a Guinness. Adrian managed to maintain a calm exterior but his heart was racing.

A table of men had just left so Adrian grabbed the seats. Gav joined him.

'Well?' Adrian asked quietly.

'I rang the number and read the statement.' He spoke in a whisper. 'It was a woman. She asked me to say it again, then she asked me if I was reading it off a script.'

'Well, you were.'

'She got a bit nasty. Said it was all very well wanting to be anonymous, but that they're treating the old woman's death as murder, and I could be an accessory.'

'Don't tell me you gave her your name.'

'No, of course I didn't! But then . . .'

'What?' Adrian said.

'She asked me to repeat the bit about the ID – and that that was the reason for going through the handbag. I said, yeah. And she asked if I took the ID with me, and I said, no, I left it in the bag! Then she said . . . she said there was *no ID in the handbag*. Nothing. Her purse had cash in it and that was all. So I hung up.'

'Fuck.'

'Best-laid plans, eh?'

'You did your best,' Adrian said, trying to keep the tremor out of his voice. 'It's OK.'

'The important thing was to give you an alibi,' Gav said. 'We've done that.'

An hour and two pints of Guinness later, Gav had recovered from the phone call, and was having ideas.

'We've got to get hold of that letter,' he said.

'We don't even know where it is.'

'No one knows where the old woman went after you talked to her in the square. What if she just went home? In which case it might be at her house. It could be sitting there, waiting to be discovered.'

'Wouldn't the police already have been through all her stuff?'

'They think she was the victim of a mugging – why would they think to look for evidence where she lived?'

Adrian saw it made sense. 'She lived on the High Estate. I don't know where exactly.'

'We can find out.'

'And then what? Break in?'

'We'll think of something.' Gav shrugged. 'We should talk to her daughter, the one who was on the news. Her mum might have told her about the letter. Should be easy enough to find her.'

'Her name's Sharon,' Adrian said. 'She owns a salon.'

Something occurred to him.

'What is it?'

'Mum said Mrs Wormley applied for care work with her agency. In the last week or so. Probably part of her plan to track me down. Mum turned her away, but if Mrs Wormley left her CV then it'd have her address on it. I'm going into the office with Mum tomorrow morning to help out. I can have a look through the files. It means lying to Mum, though.'

'You lie to her all the time, Ade.'

'I know.' It was brutal but true and it winded him.

He looked at his hands, clenched in his lap. Liar's hands.

'And what do we do with the letter if we find it?' he asked.

'Read it. And, if it looks important, we hand it over to the police. At which point we can step down. We've done what's required of us – ethically.'

They drank in silence.

Gav had called him a liar. It bothered him, because Gav was right. He lied to his parents every day. About where he was. About *who* he was. But what else could he do? Tell them the truth? The thought made him sick.

'Is it ever ethical to lie?' he asked now.

'Of course it is. Look at all those Germans who hid Jews. Why?'

'Because it feels . . . *uncomfortable*. How can something that makes you feel like that be right?'

'Ethical doesn't mean comfortable.'

'They lied to me,' he said.

'Who did?'

'My mum and dad. They didn't tell me what really happened the night I was nearly kidnapped. They made up a story that the man was confused about who I was. That he must have thought I was his nephew. But I knew even then they weren't telling the truth. They kept it up for so long. And . . . And . . .'

'*What?*' Gav watched Adrian's face with growing alarm.

'Something happened a week or two afterwards,' he said. 'Something big. Something . . . horrible.'

'What are you talking about, man?'

'Something to do with my dad and his mate Les.' He shut his eyes. Breathed. Opened them again. 'I've never told anybody any of this.'

Gav was frowning hard.

'The police came to the house.' His voice darkened as he recalled it. 'They took Dad away and left Mum in bits. Grandma came round and they sat in the living room and sent me upstairs. I could hear Mum sobbing through the floor.'

He wiped his eye.

'He was home again the same night. But at school a few weeks later, a boy called Stuart Briggs said something about how Dad was going to prison. The teacher dragged him out and battered him.'

'Fuck . . .'

'The teacher wouldn't tell me what it was about. Mum and Dad told me not to ask questions. I was so frightened. All this bad stuff happening to me – to *us* – and yet I wasn't allowed to understand. I stopped trusting them.'

'Did you ever find out what it was about?'

'No.'

'You could if you wanted to.'

For a moment he didn't reply. Then he said, 'I know.'

'But you don't want to?'

He took a breath. Looked hard at his friend. 'No.'

Gav sat back, eyes down. Disapproving, no doubt.

He could find out. He could go and look at the newspaper archive at the library, for one thing. But what if it was something so terrible he couldn't process it? Something worse than shameful, that put into the shade even the thing that had happened in the bathroom that night?

22

'So,' Jeanette said meaningfully, unwrapping her chocolate mint.

They'd agreed not to talk about it until coffee.

'So . . . what?'

'I'm going to help you. Do what I can, at any rate. What? Why are you looking at me like that?'

'I'm wondering what's in it for you.'

'I get the scoop,' Jeanette said. 'You know the game.'

'Is that what it is – a game?'

'I get a cracking story. You get to "do your bit for the community".'

'Don't be sarcastic.'

Jeanette bridled a little, then she shrugged, appearing to take it on the chin.

Sheila went into her bag and took out a pen and pad. She smoothed down a fresh page.

'Let's make a list,' she said, businesslike.

Jeanette talked and Sheila wrote. From time to time, Sheila chipped in with a thought or two of her own. After ten minutes they'd exhausted their ideas.

'Read them out to me,' Jeanette said.

'OK,' Sheila began. 'First, we need to find the families of the three girls who went missing in 1986 – relatives, family friends, anyone. Talk to them with a view to finding any details missed eight years ago. I'll make the approaches to the Parkers and the Sykeses, but . . . I'd prefer it if you spoke to any relatives of Samantha Joseph.'

Jeanette narrowed her eyes. 'Joseph, as in *Colin* Joseph?'

Sheila met Jeanette's searing gaze.

'Something happened between you and that family, didn't it? Did they make a complaint against you, or—'

'Something along those lines.'

'Oh?'

'Jeanette – please . . .'

Jeanette made a face. 'I'll get it out of you eventually.'

'I expect you will. Right, second task – find the two witnesses who saw Jenny Parker with the man who took her. Ask them to go over it again. There might be something the police missed.

'Third: make a list of any men – and women – recently released from prison after a period of approximately seven years.'

'Tricky,' Jeanette said, 'but I've got contacts. It'll mean talking to screws off the record. I'll need a few days.'

'Four: look into any stories – leads, gossip, anything – about female molesters or kidnappers, or attempts to take children where a woman was suspected.

'Five: my young friend Adrian Brown – formerly called Matthew Spivey. I'll try to speak to him again, though I doubt it'll be easy. I could see the fear in his eyes the other afternoon.'

'The *Calder Valley Advertiser*, is it?' Jeanette said. 'Linda Grant's the editor there. She was a trainee with us. Nice enough woman. Solid writer, but not a lot of drive. I could talk to her if you like.'

'No, don't. Not yet,' Sheila said. 'If the boy's got the wind up, that'll only make things worse. Leave him to me. I might need to go to the newspaper office and grab him as he leaves.'

'Fine.'

'Six: the girl who saw Sarah Barrett being taken away by the woman. You'll try to get her name and address. No way will Malcolm give me that kind of information. Once we have the details, we'll decide how best to approach the parents.

'Oh, and I've just remembered – there's a number seven.' She scribbled a note. 'Dee Thompson, who wrote a book about the kidnappings. She phoned the studio last night wanting to talk to me.'

'Probably looking to bring out a new edition,' Jeanette said.

'Possibly. She identified two potential suspects, and referenced a third she couldn't name for legal reasons. I'm going to ask her to meet me. She might tell me who her third suspect was.'

'We could both meet her,' Jeanette said, leaning in eagerly.

'Let me see her on my own first.'

'You sure you don't want to talk to Brian Quigley, the vigilante guy?'

'No chance. Honestly, Jeanette, can you imagine? I give them a platform, tie my reputation to theirs – next thing you know, they've attacked some poor innocent blonde woman on her way home from work.'

Jeanette frowned. 'Didn't someone get beaten up by vigilantes last time?'

'A man in Bradford,' Sheila said. 'He was a convicted child abuser. He'd served his sentence and was back living in the city. But that wasn't Quigley's gang. He was in hospital for weeks.'

'Community justice for you.'

'Community vengeance, more like.'

'People are frightened for their kids, Sheila.'

'I know that, but it's not the kind of society I want to live in.'

'Aren't we a pair of vigilantes, though?' Jeanette asked.

She thought about it. 'I don't think so. We're looking into something because we have privileged access to information and people. We're not smoking out suspects and attacking them with baseball bats. Anything we find we'll be sharing it with the police. We're *helping*.'

'"Doing our bit for the community"?'

'Yes.'

'And exorcising a personal demon or two?' Jeanette raised her eyebrows.

'That too,' she said tersely.

Amin passed nearby. 'Could we have the bill, please?' Sheila called out.

She put the notepad back in her bag, and drew out her purse.

23

Saturday 9th April, 1994

Gav collected Adrian from outside the train station in a Peugeot borrowed from one of his mums.

'Well?' Gav said, once he'd edged cautiously out into the traffic.

'Nothing,' he said. 'I looked everywhere. Waste of time.' He stared dejectedly out at the busy Saturday streets.

He'd spent a freezing morning in his mum's Huddersfield office, stuffing envelopes till his fingers stung, while his mum made calls to try to recruit carers for a new council contract. He'd finally got his chance to look in the filing cabinet while his mum made them coffees.

Frustrated at finding nothing, he'd asked her outright:

'Did that Mrs Wormley leave her details with you? Because you'll need to destroy them now, won't you? Shred them or something. I can do that for you.'

She'd gazed at him in confusion.

'Oh, yes, *her*,' she said at last. 'I don't think she left anything with me . . . No. I was quite clear that I didn't want to take her on. I'm desperate for people, but, well . . .'

'"Well" what?'

'You have to draw a line. She was quite rude to me.'

'*Rude* to you?'

'About your dad.' She bit her lip.

'What about him?'

'It doesn't matter. She was a horrible old woman, that's all.'

'Mum,' he'd asked then, grabbing the moment. 'What happened after . . . well, you know. After the man tried to take me? Did Dad *do* something?'

She stared at her hands on her desk for what seemed an eternity, then said, 'Don't ask me about that.'

'But—'

'Please, Adrian,' she said, a tremor in her voice. 'Just leave it.'

After that a tense, miserable silence had descended on them until it was time for him to go for the train.

'Which way?' Gav asked as they approached a roundabout.

'Next left,' Adrian said. 'I spend half my week driving round here.'

The road began to climb out of the town.

'Straight over at the next lights.'

Five minutes later they were passing the playing fields at the start of the High Estate. This was a bleak and windswept place. Terraces of grey houses lined the edges of the fields, tower blocks rising behind them.

Two minutes later, Adrian spotted a tatty parade of shops. 'I think this is it,' he said.

'"You-Neek Hair",' Gav said. 'That is one shit name for a salon.'

They were across the road from the shops, shovelling down

chips in a bus shelter. It was the perfect vantage point and the perfect cover: they looked like any other pair of kids with nowhere to go.

The salon's name was stencilled in pink jaggy capitals backed by blue flashes. It occupied the middle of seven units on the parade, between a chippie and a betting shop.

The door opened and a woman came out. It was the bottle-blonde, orange-faced woman who'd wept on the TV news on Thursday night, today wearing a tight black uniform.

'That's her, isn't it?' Gav asked.

'Yeah.'

Sharon Wormley lit a cigarette, then stood against the steamy window to smoke it.

'She looks way scary,' Gav said, eating another chip.

'Should have seen her mum,' Adrian said.

Sharon Wormley scowled about her, as if hating everything she saw. Her angry gaze fell on the two of them in the bus stop.

'Shit,' Gav murmured.

'Act normal,' Adrian said.

Two women had come out of the chemist's and Sharon Wormley turned her attention to them. There were greetings, nodding of heads and 'who knows?' hand gestures. One of the pair was lighting a cigarette now, and the three of them huddled in for a confab.

Five minutes later, the two women were on their way. Sharon Wormley flicked her fag end into the gutter, then brushed off her hands and disappeared back inside.

'Remind me what we're saying,' Gav said to Adrian as they crossed the road.

'Just leave it to me,' he said.

'Maybe I should stay outside,' Gav said.

'No, I need you with me.'

"Kay.'

A bell tinkled as they shuffled into the salon and its fug of steam and chemicals. There were mirrors everywhere, zigzagging ones, and blue and pink neon lights. There were three chairs, each occupied by older women, two with driers over their heads.

Stick-thin girls in black uniforms stood miserably about.

'What do you want?' an angry voice demanded.

'Are you Sharon Wormley?' Adrian asked the woman before him.

'Depends who's asking,' she said, fists on hips and top lip curled back.

'I'm Adrian Brown.'

'That supposed to mean something to me?'

Before he could answer, Sharon Wormley's attention seemed caught by Gav. She glared at him with a kind of angry disgust, and stabbed a fat pink-nailed finger at his hair. 'Don't think I'm touching *that*.'

Gav gaped in offence, and put a protective hand up to his locks.

'Bet you haven't washed that for months,' she said.

'We don't want haircuts,' Adrian said. 'We want to speak to you.'

'Oh?' She glanced behind her. 'Donna – Mrs Morris needs seeing to – *now*!' One of the stick-insect girls stepped fretfully to it. 'Want to speak to me? What about, eh?'

'It's . . . about Mrs Wormley.'

'About Mam?' Her eyes darted suspiciously between them. 'What about her?'

His face was bright red. He could feel it.

'It's for my mum, see? She wants to send her condolences.'

135

'And who's she, when she's at home?'

'Margaret Spivey, she's called.'

'Never heard of her.'

'Mrs Wormley helped when she fell over in the street. She—'

'Mam?' Sharon Wormley threw her head back and cackled. The customers were looking. Donna, too, along with her depressed-looking colleagues. 'Mam never helped no one, 'cept herself.'

'It's true,' he insisted, all wide-eyed and trying to look boyish and innocent. 'Mum fell over in the market square. Mrs Wormley helped her up and waited with her till my dad came.'

'I find that hard to believe,' Sharon Wormley said.

'Anyway, Mum wanted me to come and ask for Mrs Wormley's address so she could send flowers ahead of the funeral.'

'Won't be no funeral for weeks,' the woman said. 'Police rules.'

'Did . . . did the police say if they've got any leads?' Adrian asked, unable to help himself.

'No,' she snarled, baring her teeth. 'They did not.'

She was distracted as one of the girls helped an old lady with a fresh pink rinse out of her chair.

'So, about the address . . .' Adrian tried.

'You can whistle for it.'

'But—'

'You must think I'm bloody daft,' she said. 'God knows why you really want it, but it's not for no sodding flowers.'

'It is,' he said. But Gav had a hand on his arm and was pulling him back towards the door.

'Let's go, man,' Gav said.

'Yeah – piss off, the pair of you,' Sharon Wormley shouted after them.

* * *

136

'She's fucking horrible,' Gav said when they'd retreated, shaken, to the bus stop.

'Maybe it's the grief,' Adrian suggested.

'She didn't seem very grief-stricken. So, what do we do now?'

'God knows.'

A lady joined them in the bus shelter. 'Hello, there,' she said nicely.

'Hi,' Adrian said distractedly. Then, 'Oh, you were in the salon just now, weren't you?'

'I was,' the lady said, patting her pink-tinged white curls, a twinkle in her eye. 'Take no notice of Sharon. She's convinced the world's out to get her, so she gets in there first. Those poor lasses are terrified of her.'

'Are you about to tell us she's got a heart of gold really?' Gav said.

'No, dear. I'm afraid she's as hard as nails.' She chuckled. 'As was that mother of hers.'

'You knew Mrs Wormley?' Adrian asked.

'I did,' she said sourly.

'Do you know where she lived?'

'Yes. Why?'

'My mum wants to send some flowers.'

The lady raised her eyebrows. 'I don't know the flat number,' she said, 'but she lived there.' She pointed beyond the shops to the left-most of three looming towers of flats. 'Earnshaw Tower. One of the high floors, I think. She liked to say she could keep an eye on the whole town from up there. Lived with her brother Ken. He's still there, but he's half daft, poor fella.'

'Thank you,' Adrian said.

'Yes, thanks a lot,' Gav chipped in, beaming. 'Your hair looks great, by the way.'

Earnshaw Tower loomed grimly over them, the colour of rain clouds. Adrian counted twenty floors.

'Not exactly secure, is it?' Gav said. The entry door had a latch on it, but was banging open in the wind.

They went into the gloomy lobby.

'Mailboxes are round here,' Adrian said, following a sign to the rear of the lift shaft. 'Here. "K. Evans and E. Wormley". 16-B.'

They waited an age for the lift. When its doors had shut like a metal trap, Gav pressed the button marked 16.

The lift clanked and shook as it rose. It felt like forever before it released them onto the sixteenth floor, high above the town, and only feet from Mrs Wormley's front door.

Gav rang the bell and they heard it *driiiiiing* feebly on the other side. They waited. But nothing. Just the howl of the wind buffeting the tower.

'Try again,' Adrian said.

Gav pressed the button for longer this time, then knocked.

Still no answer.

They looked at each other, unsure what to do next.

'Maybe he's deaf as well as daft,' Adrian said.

'Or dead,' Gav suggested.

They sniggered a bit, but quickly pulled themselves together.

'Let's go,' Gav said. 'We can come back another time.'

Adrian was dimly aware of sounds from the lift shaft behind them.

'But what if the letter's in there?' he said. He lowered his voice. 'It could be evidence of murder.'

A clanking of lift doors behind them.

'I *bloody KNEW it*!' Sharon Wormley screamed, coming at them in fury down the landing. 'Donna saw you talking to that old bitch Gwen and I said, "Bet you a fiver she's blabbing where Mam lived." And here you are! Well bad luck, 'cause me Uncle Ken's at the hospital today.'

'It's a free country!' Gav said, and ducked as she swiped at him.

'That right? Bloody scarecrow. Fuck off and frighten some birds!'

'We're sorry,' Adrian said. 'We're going.'

'Not so fast, four-eyes,' she said and grabbed the collar of his green jacket with an iron fist. 'I know a ringleader when I see one. Spouting all that shit about flowers. What are you really after?'

'I don't have to tell you anything,' Adrian said. 'Please let go of me.'

'Or what?' she said, yanking his collar and twisting it so it choked him. 'What'll you do, little pansy?' She grabbed his face with her other hand, clamping his cheeks against his teeth and squeezing.

'Let him go,' Gav yelled, pulling at Sharon Wormley's fat wrists. 'This is assault! Do you want the police involved?'

That did the trick and Sharon Wormley let him go.

'Leave,' the woman spat. 'Now.'

They moved past her, to the still-open lift.

'And don't even think about coming back!' she screamed, as the lift doors clanked shut.

24

'I'm on the mobile,' Sheila said. 'Can you hear me OK?'

'Yes, fine,' Jeanette said. 'Where are you? Is that a piano?'

'I'm in the bar at the Ramada Jarvis, about to meet Dee Thompson. Tell me how you got on this morning.'

'Very well, as it happens.' Jeanette sounded pleased with herself. 'Got a few leads anyway. Let me find the page . . . Have you got a pen?'

'Ready when you are.'

Jeanette had found an address but no phone number for the parents of Jenny Parker, the second girl who'd been taken; and a phone number, but no address, for the mum of the third girl, Paula Sykes.

'The number's registered to Liz Sykes, so maybe Paula's dad's no longer on the scene,' she said. 'It's a Leeds dialling code, too, so she must have moved. I tried to find contact details for Samantha Joseph's auntie – the mum's sister – but I came up blank. Samantha's brother Colin might be the only relative left.'

'Let's put him to one side for now,' Sheila said stiffly.

'Up to you, love.'

Jeanette had found out that the retired police officer who'd seen Jenny Parker with her abductor had died, but she'd tracked down the primary school teacher who'd been the other witness. She was called Sally Gray and she was now the headmistress of a middle school. 'Holy Trinity Middle School in Toller Bridge. It'll be in the book.'

'This is excellent, Jeanette,' Sheila said.

'There's more: I've managed to find the name of the girl who saw Sarah Barrett being taken by the blonde woman. It's Zoe Trigg. The dad's put his foot down, though. Won't talk to *anyone* from the media. Anyway, that's your lot for today. I've put out feelers on the other bits and bobs: any men who've been in prison for the past seven or eight years and who've just been released; also any women who've been charged with, or suspected of, taking children, or any other kind of child molestation. I'll keep on it.'

'Marvellous, Jeanette. I really do appreciate your help. Oh – I need to go. I think Dee's here now. Talk to you soon.'

25

Extract from The Lollipop Murders *by Dee Thompson*

In conclusion, then – and in the author's view – there are three men on whom the police should be concentrating their attentions. West Yorkshire's finest have told the author that they 'have done what they are required to do'; that they have 'considered the individuals in question'. They say that they have looked at these men's files and any previous charges and/or convictions. In at least two cases, they claim to have questioned the individual about the disappearances. In relation to each, they claim that there are no grounds for further investigation.

I have covered the first two individuals, namely Raymond Clitheroe and Norman Waite. The third individual cannot be named here for legal reasons. He has never been charged with any offence, although he was questioned in 1973 in relation to the attempted abduction of a seven-year-old child from a suburb of Halifax. The method in that crime bears striking similarities to that of the Lollipop Man's, in that, while wearing a uniform of a milkman, the kidnapper took the child by the hand and walked her to a waiting vehicle, when a man intervened, stopping the abduction and calling the police.

Following Jenny Parker's abduction, and a tip-off from the author, the police questioned this third individual, but a relative provided him with an alibi for the time of Jenny's kidnap, and for that of Samantha Joseph four months earlier. Further, the police claimed the individual was unwell, suffering as he did from a debilitating illness (no details of which have been provided to the author). As has been stated above, it is the author's belief that of the three suspects she has identified, this third individual stands out as the most likely to have committed the Lollipop kidnappings.

'Sheila-bloody-Hargreaves!' the woman said, grinning all over her face. 'The one and only, eh?'

'That's me!' Sheila said, forcing good cheer as she rose to shake the woman's hand. 'It's Deirdre, isn't it? Dee?'

'Dee. That's right.'

The woman looked completely star-struck, wide-eyed and a bit mad. Dee Thompson, author of the only book to date on the Lollipop Man kidnappings, wasn't what Sheila had expected. She was sixtyish, tall and skinny, with very long, very straight, dyed-red hair, parted in the centre. Her ears were pierced multiple times, as was her nose and one of her eyebrows. She grinned at Sheila, showing lots of long teeth.

'I can't believe it's really you. Who'd've thought it?' She

started to giggle manically, and stifled it with the back of her wrist. Her fingers glittered with rings.

'Have a seat,' Sheila said nicely, waving over to a waiter to take their order. 'Another black coffee, please,' she said to the boy. 'Dee, what'll you have?'

'Oh!' Dee grinned up at him, then at Sheila, and the whole bottom half of her face seemed to be teeth. 'If you're buying, Sheila . . .'

'Of course.'

'Pint of cider, then, please!'

Sheila smiled to mask her surprise. 'Thank you for meeting me,' she said.

'I had one of those feelings,' Dee said. 'I know what you'll think, but it was like you were sending me a message through the TV screen to ring in . . . and that you'd see at once how important it was and that the two of us should get this sorted once and for all. Fate, Sheila, see?'

Sheila nodded and smiled, as if utterly delighted.

'And do you know what else I sensed?'

'No . . .'

'Your name next to mine on the cover of a new edition of my book. This time it'll be *our* book, Sheila. Imagine it. Piles and piles of shiny copies everywhere you look. Bookshops, airports.'

'Wonderful,' Sheila said, beaming away.

'My skills as a detective. Your people skills. Your network. Your *name*, Sheila. We're going to make it big!'

Dee's cider arrived just at that moment, handily knocking the woman off her trajectory.

'Dee,' Sheila said, direct but empathetic, 'let's focus on Sarah, shall we?'

'Sarah?'

'The little girl who was taken two weeks ago.'

'Oh – oh, yes! Ha ha! Of course!' She looked a bit stunned. 'Yes, yes! Why else are we here, Sheila, if not for that poor mite?'

'Do you know who took her, Dee?'

'The mystery woman, you mean? Not a Scooby.'

'Do you know who took the three little girls back in 1986? I know you named two individuals—'

'That's right.'

'Raymond Clitheroe and Norman Waite. Neither of whom – according to the police – could have been the Lollipop Man.'

'That's right. Anyway, Clitheroe's dead now, isn't he?'

'There was a third suspect, wasn't there?'

'There was,' she said, all beady-eyed now. 'Still is, in my opinion.'

'You couldn't name him because—'

'Because of legal reasons, Sheila.'

'But you did pass his name to the police.'

'I did. I had a duty, see? They told me they discounted him. Though . . .' She threw her hands up in a show of despair, and sighed.

'Can you tell me his name? As a friend?'

'I could,' Dee said slowly. 'I could tell you, Sheila – as a *co-author*.'

They watched one another like negotiators who'd found themselves at the crux faster than either expected.

'That little girl's out there, somewhere, Dee.'

Dee leant in. 'That little girl's dead, Sheila,' she said unpleasantly. 'I think we both know that.'

'Do we?'

'Whether we admit it to ourselves or not. Everyone knows it, deep down. My friend Rosa saw her, "lying there," she said.'

Sheila started. 'I'm sorry, Dee – your friend . . . ?'

The woman stared blankly back, as if she'd said nothing out of the ordinary.

'Dee,' Sheila pushed, 'what do you mean? Who's Rosa?'

'Rosa Laycock. She has second sight.'

'Ah . . .'

This was surely the same 'psychic medium' who Grace had said called the studio on Thursday evening.

'You should talk to her,' Dee said.

Sheila nodded non-committally.

'You don't look too sure, Sheila. Are you not a believer?'

'I . . . Well, I would call myself a sceptic, so – no, on the whole, I have to say I prefer verifiable facts.'

'Rosa's terribly wise. When she makes a pronouncement, you'd do well to listen. She's been proved right on more than one occasion.'

'Has she?'

'You'd be amazed. Of course,' she leant in confidentially, 'a lot of it could just be *her*, if you know what I mean – applying a lifetime's wisdom to any situation. Trusting her gut. She believes it's spiritual, but who's to say she's not just very clued in?'

'You said she saw Sarah Barrett dead. Are you saying you think she's used her common sense to work out that Sarah is *probably* dead . . . ?'

A shrug. 'Rosa listens to folk, then she puts it all together – and maybe the spirits give her a helping hand, who knows?'

Dee was smirking now. Enjoying herself, clearly.

'Dee,' Sheila said, determined to focus on what was really at stake here, 'if this is the Lollipop Man again – whether he has a woman helping him or not – then Sarah Barrett would be his fourth victim.'

'I know,' Dee said, and took a mouthful of cider.

'Whose little girl will be the fifth? And sixth?'

'Call me ghoulish if you like, Sheila, but I have to eat,' Dee said. 'I have to earn my living.' She fixed Sheila with a look. 'That book sold less than four hundred copies. All that work and I managed to pay one month's rent off the back of it.'

'What are you saying?'

'Together we could solve this thing,' Dee said. 'Sell the book to a proper publisher. Do a TV programme. Sell film rights!' She stopped, seeing Sheila's face. She said, her tone darker, 'It's all right for you, isn't it? With your big career. Nice house, I expect. Nice car. Holidays. The rest of us don't have it easy.'

'If there's a new edition,' Sheila said stiffly, 'I'll consider writing a foreword.'

Dee watched her. 'Will you interview me on your programme, too?'

Sheila swallowed. 'If my producer is willing.'

Dee thought about it, then nodded.

'Is that a deal?' Sheila asked.

'Shake,' Dee said, and put out a bony, jewelled hand.

Sheila took it and gripped it tight. 'Tell me his name, Dee.'

'His name's Edward Proctor,' she said quietly, her face dark. 'Known as Teddy. They said it couldn't be him, but I know it is. Teddy Proctor was, *is*, an evil fucking child-murdering pig.'

26

'I've never heard of an Edward Proctor,' Jeanette said when Sheila phoned her. 'Where does he live?'

'She won't say. Locally, I assume.'

'Age?'

'Don't know.'

'Come on, Christine Cagney, you're going to have to do better than this.'

'Dee doesn't want to reveal too much,' Sheila said. 'So she says.'

'In other words, she's making it up.'

'I don't think so, Jeanette. She's out for herself – of course she is – but she's convinced.'

'Leave it with me for a day or two,' Jeanette said, and they hung up.

Sheila left the hotel and turned in the direction of the car park.

She'd found the encounter with Dee Thompson wearing.

She was used to enthusiastic fans – their giddiness, their joy at meeting someone from the TV, someone they looked up to – but some people were pushy to an unhinged degree, and it was hard to bear.

Of course, it was only natural that Dee should want Sheila's name alongside her own on the cover of a new edition of her book. A famous name there, quite apart from the publicity that would accompany its release, would help sell more copies, no question; and she didn't doubt that Dee had a genuine desire to reach more readers, to tell the children's stories, to advance her theories, including about the unnameable Teddy Proctor.

But the idea of partnering with the woman made Sheila shudder. It was snobbish of her, of course. Dee was right that Sheila had so much that she didn't – a career, a nice house and car, lovely holidays. Not that that was her *fault*. Any more than it was her fault she'd been sent to a fee-paying school, that her father had earned a good income managing the Keighley branch of the Yorkshire Bank, that she'd had the chance to go to university, and meet and mix with people with talent and aspiration. But it was still unfair. Unfair on Dee, and countless others.

In one way, the idea of writing a book about the murders did appeal. It would have purpose. More meaning, certainly, than the book she was currently under contract to produce: a collection of interviews and vignettes, accompanied by uplifting photographs, provisionally called *My Kind of People: Sheila Hargreaves Meets Everyday Yorkshire Folk*. She could produce a true-crime book, and do it well. She just had no desire to do it with Dee.

A crackling shout caught her attention. Over in the square a rally was taking place. A man stood on an improvised podium, bellowing indistinctly through a sound system to the fair-sized crowd gathered before him. Sheila heard the word 'lollipop' amid the static.

Stopping to listen, she still couldn't make out the majority of the words he was shouting, but heard enough to realise this could be Brian Quigley, son of Arthur, who'd led a band of vigilantes to try to find the Lollipop Man in 1986. Brian Quigley who'd rung the studio following Thursday night's show, seeking Sheila's endorsement for his crusade.

'The police are letting us down *again!*' he bellowed, to noisy assent from the crowd. He was a short, angry-looking man in his thirties, wearing a Bradford City top and waving his arms as if he were in the stand at Valley Parade. 'Once again, we – the people of this city – are relying on . . .' More static. Then: '— to take back our streets and protect our . . .' something, something, 'before it's too late.'

There was something distasteful about the man's demeanour: the evangelical way he seemed to manipulate the crowd, and his obvious delight at their responding rage.

Anxious not to be spotted, she hurried on her way.

She'd parked in the NCP that morning, finding a spot on level seven. The single lift now appeared to be out of order, so she set about climbing the chilly, urine-smelling stairwell.

She'd reached the third landing and was turning to climb the next flight, when she heard a noise from below her. A scuffed footstep, then silence. She stopped and listened, but heard nothing more.

She started to climb – and heard it again. The ensuing silence felt . . . uncanny.

'Hello?' she called down the stairwell behind her. 'Is somebody there?'

No answer. As if whoever it was had stopped to listen, too.

'Will whoever it is please answer me?'

Her voice echoed. She turned and began to climb again, faster this time. The footsteps began again, and as her own pace quickened, so did they. Her car keys were already in her hand and she made a fist round them, so that keys stuck out of her fingers like blunt blades.

The footsteps sounded oddly spaced, as if – *oh God* – as if he was taking two at a time.

Should she turn and face him? Meet him? She'd have an advantage, being above him. Having her keys out.

But what if he was armed too? If he was, it would be with more than a set of keys.

He was running now. Gaining.

She lunged for the door on the fifth landing – *fell* against it – but it wouldn't budge. She suddenly saw herself, slumped in a corner of the stairwell, face pale, covered in blood from where she'd been stabbed. The idea of dying in this cold concrete place . . .

She let out a yelp and put both hands and all her weight on the door, desperate, nearly sobbing, when the door burst open towards her—

A woman screamed. Sheila screamed back, and understood in a flash that she'd pushed when she should have pulled – that her frightened brain had failed her.

'I'm sorry!' the woman said, hand to her mouth.

Sheila rushed forwards and the stairwell door banged shut behind her. She grabbed the woman by the shoulders, crying, 'You have to help me!'

The woman stared in amazement. 'It's *you*, isn't it?'

'There's a man following me.'

'*Following* you?'

'Is your car here? Can we go to it?'

'Oh! Yes – yes, of course. It's the blue Fiat just there. Come on. You're OK now.' She pulled Sheila by the arm.

When they were inside the car, the doors locked, Sheila turned to the woman. 'Could I ask you to do one more thing?'

'Yes,' the woman said, in alarm and amazement. 'Do you want me to take you somewhere? To a police station, perhaps.'

'I just need you to drive me up to the seventh floor. That's where my car is. Then if you could wait till I'm in it, I'd be so grateful.'

'That's no problem,' the woman said, throwing the car into reverse.

She was beaming all over her face. Sheila realised it was possibly the most exciting thing that had ever happened to her. She herself sank weakly back into the passenger seat and tried to stop shaking.

27

Monday 11th April, 1994

Nige was in the office early for once, so Adrian went through the list of appointments with him face to face in the little kitchen, Nige yawning and rubbing his eyes.

'Don't you want to make notes?' Adrian said irritably at one point. 'Don't you need to plan what lenses you'll need?'

'I'll work it out when I get there,' Nige said, shrugging. 'Like I've always done.'

Nige sloped out of the kitchen, back to his dark room. Feeling grumpy, Adrian returned to his desk.

Kev didn't look up. It was obvious something was wrong, the way he twitched and bared his teeth as he typed, as if he was having a muttered argument with himself.

'What's up with you?' Adrian asked.

'Nothing,' Kev snarled, eyes locked on his VDU.

'Sorry I asked.'

He threw himself into his desk chair as Yvonne emerged from Linda's office.

'Adrian, have you got a minute?' she said, eyeballing him.

She held the door for him. He eyed her cautiously but obeyed.

'Sit down will you, Adrian?' Linda said with what sounded like forced niceness as Yvonne closed the door.

He sat. Yvonne sat too, and the two of them faced him across Linda's desk. Yvonne looked like she was lining him up for target practice.

He waited.

'We want to know what's going on,' Yvonne said. 'Something's up, so don't pretend otherwise – we can read you like a book.'

Yvonne looked sceptical and cross; Linda merely worried.

Yvonne went on: 'You've been acting like a weirdo for days, biting people's heads off.'

'Have I?' He bridled.

'We're concerned about you,' Linda came in, clearly playing good cop. 'You're our colleague. We have a duty of care.'

'Come on, out with it!' Yvonne said.

He wondered how to answer. Whether to answer.

'Well?' said Yvonne, impatiently.

'I've been feeling anxious since Sarah Barrett went missing. I think it might be getting to me a bit, that's all.'

'Liar,' Yvonne said, and Linda shot her a disapproving look.

'Kev did a redial on your phone,' Yvonne said. 'To so-called "Mrs Osgood".'

'Oh?' His stomach flipped.

'It was childish of him,' Linda said. 'I ordered him not to but he did it anyway, so he's earned himself a verbal warning.'

Which explained Kev's foul mood . . .

Yvonne said, 'You do know who she is, don't you, Adrian? You know her real name?'

'No.' He shut his eyes. It was all going to come out now, wasn't it? Word would be out. The police would come and arrest him. He felt like crying, though oddly relieved too.

'Sheila Osgood – better known as Sheila Hargreaves,' Yvonne said. Then, when he didn't answer: 'From the TV. She's—'

'Sheila Hargreaves?' he said, opening his eyes, unable to hide his astonishment.

'Yes.'

'Why is Sheila Hargreaves telephoning you, Adrian?' Linda asked.

'In other words,' Yvonne cut in drily, 'what the *fuck* is going on?'

'I don't know,' he said, as relief rushed through him. Mrs Osgood wasn't a witness to his crime after all. 'I mean it. I don't know why she's calling me.'

'Bullshit, Ade.'

'Honest!'

'Kev said she talked to you at Gorton Lane the other day.'

'Yeah, she did. She introduced herself to me, but that's all. I never met her before.'

Another lie.

'Adrian,' Yvonne said slowly, watching him very carefully, 'we *know*.'

They looked at him. Into him. Through him.

She added, more kindly, 'We know what happened to you when you were a kid.'

Adrian froze, mouth dry as everything in his world quietly but fundamentally shifted. 'How did you find out?' he said.

'We're journalists,' Yvonne said. 'Give us some credit, kiddo. It doesn't take a genius to check dates, names, addresses . . . Your home address is on your CV. It was reported where Matthew

Spivey lived – the name of the street, anyway. Quick check of the microfiche is all it took to confirm it.'

'Does Kev know?'

'No,' Linda said.

'OK,' he said, relieved, but blushing nonetheless. 'I— I just don't talk about it, you see. Not to anyone.'

'Which is your choice and perfectly fine,' Linda said.

'Until it affects your work,' Yvonne added.

He looked at his hands.

'If you'd told us, we could have supported you,' Linda went on. 'As it is, we've now got a TV presenter ringing the office and upsetting you so that you're running out of here in a panic.'

'Sorry.'

'You don't need to apologise,' Yvonne said. 'What happened to you wasn't your fault. How could it be?'

'No.' His face still burnt. 'It's just – it's not something I want to think about. It makes me . . . feel bad. Ashamed.'

'Ashamed?' Yvonne said, incredulously.

'Oh, no!' Linda cried. 'Why on earth would you feel that way?'

'I don't know.' He shrugged, feeling wretched and sulky at the same time.

They sat in silence.

'So what's she after, kiddo?' Yvonne asked eventually. 'Sheila Hargreaves?'

'I don't know. Honestly. I didn't even know that's who she was until you told me. I thought . . . well, it doesn't matter.'

'She might want you to go on her programme,' Linda suggested.

Maybe that *was* it. To install him on her studio sofa and coo over his childhood misfortune. Unexpectedly, he started to feel a bit better.

'She interviewed me . . . back then, I mean. She worked for a newspaper and she came to the house. I got the feeling she recognised me when we were at Gorton Lane last week, even though I was only ten the last time I saw her.'

'And had a different name,' Linda said.

'My parents gave me a new one.'

'Why was that?' Yvonne asked. 'To avoid the publicity?'

He shrugged. 'I don't know, really. Maybe. Maybe they just didn't want the neighbours talking. I went from Matthew Spivey to Adrian Brown in the space of a week. You could say the experience changed me.'

'Do you want us to tell her to back off?' Linda asked. 'I could ring the TV studio and leave her a message.'

'No, don't,' he said. 'If she calls again, I'll just tell her I'm not interested.'

'Good for you, kiddo,' Yvonne said. 'She might not seem it, but Sheila Hargreaves is a dangerous woman.' She looked him hard in the eye.

'Dangerous?'

'That's what I said. Calls herself a feminist. She's no feminist.'

'What do you mean?'

Linda was listening with interest now, too.

'If you do talk to her, ask her about journalistic ethics,' Yvonne said, eyes narrow and angry. 'Specifically, ask her about a woman called Patricia Joseph.'

'I know about the phone thing,' he said to Kev when he went back into the office.

'Yeah,' Kev mumbled. 'Sorry.'

'Why did you do it?'

Kev looked genuinely miserable. 'For a laugh.'

'Do you regret it?'

'Yeah.'

'OK.' He smiled. 'I forgive you.'

'Fuck off.' Kev chucked a ball of paper at him. Adrian ducked, grabbed it and lobbed it back. It hit Kev smack bang on the nose.

28

Grace wanted to hold the production meeting half an hour later, which suited Sheila fine. She used the time to call the school where Sally Gray was headteacher. The school secretary said Miss Gray wasn't available, and took a message.

Next, she wrote a card – a nice one of Skipton Castle – to Mr and Mrs Parker, parents of Jenny, the second girl to go missing.

Then, steeling herself, she called Liz Sykes, mother of Paula, the third child, but the phone rang out. She made a note to call back that evening.

Finally, she called Malcolm Struthers.

'Anything?' she asked him.

'I'm sorry, Sheila. There's CCTV on the ground floor of the car park but – surprise, surprise – the camera's been broken for months.'

'Did you speak to Mrs Young?' This was the woman who had driven her up two floors and waited till Sheila was locked safely in her own car.

'We did. We took a statement, but she didn't actually see anybody. Neither did you.'

'I heard him.'

'You think you heard him. If it was a him.'

Of course. It could have been a woman, couldn't it?

'There's not much more we can do,' he said. 'I'm sorry, Sheila. I suggest you don't walk to your car alone in future.'

'The responsibility's mine, you mean? If I get attacked, it's down to me?'

'That's not what I said. I—'

'It's OK, Malcolm. I'm still a bit shaken up, that's all.'

'I know, love.'

She'd told hardly anyone: Malcolm – whom she'd asked to make only discreet enquiries; Alex, of course; Jeanette, who'd wanted the pair of them to stake out the car park with hammers; and Grace, who'd panicked, called a meeting and put in place a short-term security plan. Mrs Young had promised to keep the business to herself. 'I'm a very private person, really,' Sheila had said to her, asking, 'Can I rely on your friendship?' She'd taken the woman's address and sent her flowers.

'That name Dee Thompson gave me, Malcolm,' she said now. 'Teddy Proctor.'

'Yes . . .' he began gravely. 'We considered him at the time at Dee's suggestion, but I'm afraid we ruled him out of our enquiries pretty sharpish.'

'Who is he, Malcolm? Where is he now?'

'Teddy Proctor was a very unwell man, Sheila. Vulnerable, even. Lived with his mother and struggled when she went into a home. Multiple health problems. And that was over seven years ago.'

'Dee must have had good reason to consider him.'

'He was questioned about an attempted kidnap of a young girl in the early 1970s. Questioned but released. The MO was similar to the one the Lollipop Man used in 1986. I think that's what got Dee Thompson's attention.'

'Why couldn't Dee name him publicly?'

'He was never charged with anything. Unlike the other two she named.'

'And where is he now?'

'That's easy. He's dead and buried, Sheila. Died at the end of 1987. It wasn't him – then *or* now.'

'Where did he live, out of interest?'

'Between Toller Bridge and Turton, down in the valley. Water's End. Place called White Cottage, or White House. Something like that. Listen, Sheila, people like Dee . . . they mean well, but they look for evidence that fits their theory. Now, if that's—'

'There's something else I want to ask you.'

'Go on,' he said warily.

'I'd like to get a look at the file about the attempted kidnap of the boy Matthew Spivey – now called Adrian Brown.'

'Ah . . .'

'What harm can it do? I mean, there could be something in there, couldn't there? Something you didn't spot at the time, and—'

'It's not possible, Sheila.'

'Why?'

'It's lost.'

'Lost? What do you mean, "lost"?'

'Just that. I know that because I personally requested it a week ago. Note came back: "records untraceable".'

'But that's—'

'Concerning? I know. There's a chance it's part of a batch that's been sent to HQ in Leeds for putting onto the computer system, but it's a lot more likely it's been . . . mislaid.'

'Does that happen often?'

'Can do, especially when you're dealing with paper. Remember the Ripper investigation? They had to reinforce floors because of all the paperwork. There's another possibility,' he said. 'One I'm telling you in confidence.'

'Go on.'

'There's a chance the file was . . . misplaced on purpose. Or plain destroyed.'

'*What?*'

'A copper who is no longer a copper – Lester Dixon. There was a suggestion at the time that Dixon was taking an unusual amount of interest in the records.'

'Good God. What possible reason . . . ?'

He sounded deeply uncomfortable. 'I'm not going to go into it, Sheila, love. And I haven't told you that – understood?'

'OK, Malcolm.'

29

Adrian rang Gav at lunchtime to check everything was on track with the plan they'd formulated for later. It was. Gav sounded confident, giddy even. They finalised arrangements and Adrian rang off.

Linda was coming back from the kitchen with a mug in her hand.

'Can I talk to you?' he asked her.

'Of course.'

He followed her into her office and closed the door.

'I've been thinking some more about Mrs Wormley,' he said, hoping his nerves didn't show.

'What about her?' She started to arrange papers on her desk. When he didn't go on, she looked up at him.

'Remember she told me she had a letter with information about Sarah Barrett's kidnapper?'

'Yes.'

'Well . . . she said some things that made me think *she* believed it.'

'She might have been mistaken.'

'Yeah, but later the same day she was murdered. What if she did know something, and that's why she was killed?'

She frowned. 'That's a bit of a leap.'

'I wondered if she still had it on her when she was killed, that's all.'

Linda frowned and blinked, as if trying to understand. She looked tired and bewildered, and he half-expected her to start rubbing her eyes.

'If she did have it on her,' he pushed, 'then maybe the police haven't looked at it properly. They might not understand its possible significance.'

'Oh, I see what you mean.'

'And if she *didn't* have it on her, then maybe somebody took it. So the person who killed her might be the same person who took Sarah.'

Linda sat up in her chair, seeming to get his point at last.

'Maybe you could talk to the police about it,' he said gently. 'Or you could . . . ?'

'They'd just think I was a kid imagining things. And anyway, the minute they realise, well – *who I am* – they're going to think I'm nuts, aren't they?' He added, sweetly, 'You'd be much more convincing, I think.'

She nodded. 'Let me think about it.'

He went back into the main office to retrieve the car keys, ready to take Nige out and about.

He smiled, pleased with himself. Operation Linda was underway. Next: Operation Breaking and Entering.

Adrian dropped Nige at his flat outside Halifax just after half-two, then drove up to the High Estate.

He felt guilty for using one of the pool cars, but time was against him. If he got caught he'd have to own up, and hopefully Linda would go easy on him. At least he could now play up the trauma of his near-kidnap if he had to – it was about time he had some kind of payback.

He parked across the road from Earnshaw Tower, in the littered car park of neighbouring Linton Tower. He'd only just realised the theme behind the names. There was something apt about naming towers of council flats on the edge of moors after Emily Brontë's characters, solitary edifices standing between town and moorland, forever blasted by the elements.

He'd chosen this spot carefully. If he sat forward and peered up through the windscreen, he could make out the corner windows of Mrs Wormley's flat. It would make no difference, of course, but it made him feel better to know he could see the windows and imagine what was going on inside.

After a few minutes he spotted Gav crossing the road in the distance. He looked so different in his business-style suit and with his masses of hair tamed into a ponytail, but there was no mistaking his height or his loping walk.

Gav stopped and gazed about him, scanning the cars. When he was looking his way Adrian gave the headlights a double flash. Gav gave a wave and a comedy shrug, as if to say, *now or never*.

The next twenty minutes Adrian spent in tense agony, drumming his fingers on the steering wheel, and from time to time peering up at Earnshaw Tower until his neck hurt.

Eventually the phone rang, making him jump.

'Hello?'

'Oh, hello,' Gav's voice rang out, high and false. 'Is that Mr Jones?'

'Mr Jones speaking,' Adrian said, heart in his mouth.

'Oh, good. Mr Jones, it's Michael Fanshaw here. I'm with Mr Kenneth Evans just now, and he'd be very interested in finding out about the council's new scheme for tenants, as we've been discussing. Would it be convenient for you to join us in his flat in Earnshaw Tower?'

'Yes, it would,' Adrian said.

Eight minutes later, behind the disguise of an ill-fitting suit jacket, his late granddad's Homburg hat and a pair of sunglasses, he was upstairs and knocking on the door.

Gav pulled it wide, and Adrian stepped into a pink-walled hallway, dimly lit by a single shaded bulb. Gav dropped him a wink, then led the way into the living room.

'Mr Jones, this is Mr Kenneth Evans, tenant of this flat.'

'Hello, Mr Evans,' Adrian said, taking off his hat and glasses and approaching the man on the giant pink leather settee.

'I– I– I–' said Mr Evans, holding out a trembling hand.

Mrs Wormley's brother was agonisingly thin, his clothes hanging off him like rags. He had yellow, papery skin. A liver-spotted, scabby scalp showed through grey-brown tendrils of greasy hair. His yellow-stained eyes bulged and swivelled.

'It's nice to meet you,' Adrian said loudly, catching the old man's hand and shaking it. It was surprisingly strong, desperate almost, as if the old man was grasping on for dear life.

They shouldn't be doing this. It was wrong. Cruel. But it was also too late.

'Mr Evans would be interested in getting new windows, free of charge,' Gav said with a big smile.

'That's great news!' Adrian said. 'Stop these pesky draughts, eh?'

'Why don't I put the kettle on and you and me can have a

chat?' Gav was saying to the old man now. 'Maybe Mr Jones can have a look at the windows.'

'Good idea, Mr Fanshaw. I'll start in the bedrooms.'

Gav gave him another wink.

He found Mrs Wormley's bedroom no problem. It was pink, and pungent with potpourri and air freshener. Every surface was covered in dolls wearing Victorian costume, all furred with dust and cobwebs. The single bed in the centre of the room was crowded with dolls, too, like a life raft jammed with survivors.

He was jittery with adrenalin and went to look out of the window to slow himself down.

The view was spectacular. The High Estate was like a town made of grey sugar cubes. His car, at the base of neighbouring Linton Tower, was a red speck. He gazed out across High Calder, down in the valley, trying to make out his mum and dad's street, in the little estate by the woods. There were people moving below. A line of schoolchildren, with mums in tow, leaving a toytown school. It made him feel dizzy. He swayed and had to step away.

He began to open the drawers, to riffle through pants and stockings and bras and cardigans. But he found no papers.

Next, the wardrobe, which housed only clothes and folded blankets.

There was a small drawer cabinet beside the bed. The drawer contained a bible, old, leather-bound and ratty; a deck of tarot cards – a genuine deck, this one; and an address book.

He grabbed the address book and put it in the briefcase Gav had brought for the role play. Then he scouted around the rest of the room, even getting down on his knees to see under the bed and into a world of dust and hair.

When he was sure he'd looked everywhere, even feeling

under the fusty-smelling mattress while gritting his teeth, he returned to the living room.

Kenneth Evans was hunched in a corner of the settee, clutching a mug of something. Another twinge of guilt.

'How did you get on with the measuring?' Gav asked, nodding and smiling as if to jolly Adrian back into his role.

'Fine,' he said, managing a smile in return.

'You might want to look in the kitchen next,' Gav said, meaningfully. 'Mind you don't mess up the papers *on top of the microwave.*'

'Right,' he said, taking the hint.

The kitchen was filthy, with used crockery everywhere. The bin overflowed. How could the old man live like this? Surely he'd be entitled to some sort of care. Adrian wondered if he should talk to his mum . . .

Papers were piled on the microwave. Bills and other official letters, mostly unopened. He shovelled them into the briefcase before returning to the living room.

'You'll want to measure in here, too, won't you?' Gav said.

'Yeah, I'll do that now.'

The old man watched him in confusion as he acted out measuring the windows with an invisible measuring tape. 'Won't take two minutes,' he called merrily over his shoulder.

'I was just saying to Mr Evans what a lovely view he has,' Gav said, then added meaningfully, 'Mind the low table over there, won't you, Mr Jones?'

There were papers on the table, pinned under a half-dead spider plant in a plastic pot. Adrian made a show of moving the table so he could 'just get to this window', sliding the papers out and folding them inside his jacket till he could shovel them into the briefcase.

He went back to his 'measuring'. This window had the same view as the one in Mrs Wormley's bedroom. He could see kids near his car – rather, the newspaper's car. And then something else caught his eye. Even from this distance, it could only be one person: Sharon Wormley, striding this way. Within a minute she'd be inside Earnshaw Tower and summoning the lift.

'Time to go,' he said sharply.

Gav stared at him.

'*Now*.' He nodded meaningfully to the window, making a face.

'Right then,' Gav said, rising, all smiles. 'I'll just put these mugs back in the kitchen and give them a rinse, will I?' he said brightly, relieving Kenneth Evans of his.

'No time,' Adrian said.

Gav got his stuff together. 'Goodbye, Mr Evans. Lovely chatting to you.'

The old man stared, mouth open, trying to speak.

Out on the landing, Gav went straight for the lifts.

Adrian grabbed him and hissed, 'Stairs!'

'What's wrong with you?' Gav complained, as he was bundled into the stairwell.

'Sharon Wormley was crossing the car park.'

'Oh, shit.'

Briefcase safely under his arm, Adrian scurried down each flight, and out of the building. It wasn't until they were almost at the car that he realised. 'My granddad's hat,' he said. 'My sunglasses, too. I've left them in the flat.'

30

Tuesday 12th April, 1994

Rosa Laycock, the self-styled psychic medium, lived in a stone-built terrace on a steeply sloping street in Turton. She greeted Sheila at the door, a stout woman with tight curly grey hair, dressed all in black like a Victorian widow.

'I hope I haven't come at a bad time,' Sheila said, eyes on the strings of jet beads round the woman's neck.

'Any time's fine by me, lovey,' Rosa Laycock said.

It was dark inside the house.

'Mind those,' Mrs Laycock murmured, leading the way past piles of boxes and what looked like old carpet offcuts into an overheated, over-furnished living room. 'Sit anywhere,' she said. 'Only not there, that's the cat's.'

'Oh. Oh, yes, fine. Thank you.'

Suddenly aware of the odour of warm cat in the room, she put on a pleasant smile and settled gingerly into a chair by the window.

Rosa Laycock offered tea. Sheila refused gracefully, reminding

Mrs Laycock of her busy schedule.

'As you said on the phone,' the woman commented placidly.

She lowered herself into the corner seat of a longish settee with a grimace of pain, though she could only be in her mid-fifties, Sheila thought. Her face was dreadfully pale, her eyes watery grey. She wondered if the woman was ill.

'Mrs Laycock—'

'Rosa. And I'm a Miss now. Divorced fifteen years, though I kept the name' she made a sour face, 'for professional reasons.'

'Ah, and it's about that that I wanted to speak to you, Rosa,' Sheila said, glad of an opportunity to get down to business. 'You telephoned the studio, didn't you?'

'I did.'

'You said you had information. And I understand you're also friendly with Dee – Deirdre – Thompson.'

'Talked to her, have you, lovey? Wonder what she told you . . .'

'We have spoken,' Sheila said.

'Then you're interested. You are going to take me seriously.'

'I'm certainly interested to listen to anyone who thinks they might be able to help to find Sarah Barrett.'

'Poor little kiddie.' The woman dropped her eyes and contemplated her hands, fingers knitted in her lap. 'Dead and gone, I'm afraid.'

Sheila breathed.

'Do you know what happened to her, Rosa?'

'She's with the others,' the woman said, gazing into the middle distance. 'Four of them now. All together.'

'Four of them? Rosa?'

Her pale eyes fixed on Sheila's face. 'Four little girls. Lined up like dolls.'

'Where are they, Rosa?' Sheila asked, trying to ignore the chill that ran through her.

'Nearer than you'd think,' she said. 'They're above the ground.'

'"Above the ground"?'

'He keeps them,' she said. 'I can see them, pretty maids all in a row.'

Sheila felt something sag inside her. It was the oddest sensation. Not so much horror; more empty despair. She busied herself finding a tissue so she could pretend to blow her nose.

'You sure you won't have a drinkie, lovey?' the woman said, peering sideways at her guest. 'I know it's hard to hear. I've got brandy if you'd enjoy a little glass.'

'No, thank you. I'm quite all right.' A lie. 'How could you possibly know this?' she said, pulling herself together.

'How could I . . . what, lovey?'

'Did you see this?' She recalled Dee's words: that her friend had seen the girl 'lying there', as if Rosa had seen the girl with her own eyes. 'Did you see a . . . a vision? Or . . . ?'

'I have second sight, lovey. I can't help it.'

A tiny smile pursed the woman's lips. Sheila got the distinct impression she was trying to suppress a giggle.

She shouldn't have come here. This was dark and wrong. She shouldn't be humouring the woman. Shouldn't be indulging her grotesque game.

'Going so soon?' Rosa said when Sheila got up.

'I'm afraid so,' she said, moving to the door. 'Sorry to have troubled you.'

Rosa didn't come after her, but stayed in her chair, fingers still laced, plump ankles still crossed. 'There's two of them at it,' she said. 'Working together.'

Sheila took a breath. Stopped. 'Who?' she said.

'Man and wife, perhaps. Hard to tell. Hard to *see.*'

Sheila waited, hand on the door frame, glad of its solidity.

'He's in charge. She goes along with it. Sad really. She's ill, poor thing. They're saying she's like Myra Hindley, but she's not. She's weak and frightened and under his spell.'

'Can you tell me their names?' Sheila said.

'In time, perhaps.'

'Is it . . . does the name Edward Proctor mean anything to you?'

Sheila saw a light come into the woman's eyes as she registered the information, and cursed herself. This was how it worked, wasn't it? You were desperate to hear something specific, something you could call evidence. So you fed them information. Just handed it over, ready for them to reuse on someone else. How long would it be before that name was on the police's lips, mentioned at a press conference? Referred to as 'information provided'. Except the police wouldn't take it seriously, would they? Not if Teddy Proctor was, as Malcolm had said, dead and buried.

'Proctor?' the woman said slowly, frowning as her eyes travelled around the room. 'I don't think I know that name.'

'Forget I asked.' She made to go.

'My poor friend could have told you,' Rosa murmured, almost to herself.

'Your friend?'

'Passed over now . . .'

'I'm sorry, Rosa, but could you explain what you mean? This could be very important.'

'Old friend of mine,' Rosa said. 'Edna Wormley. May she rest in peace.' Rosa's eyes locked with Sheila's. 'She was murdered.'

'*Murdered?*' A bell rang somewhere. A woman had died in High Calder. It had been on the news – a mugging gone wrong . . . something like that. The same day they'd found Sarah Barrett's jacket and, later, the shrine on the moors.

'Tragic, isn't it?' Rosa said, watching her with an air of expectation.

'Yes,' Sheila said. 'I'm very sorry for your loss.'

The woman nodded, appeased.

'How did you know this . . . Edna?'

'We met at the Temple, here in Turton. The spiritualist church, you know? She had the gift, too.' Rosa nodded and smiled a little wistfully. 'She came along a couple of times, but she had no patience for it. Everyone taking their turn like that. It can go on for hours. But us two – we got talking, and we kept in touch. She'd come here for a cuppa. "Just pop by," I'd say to her. She read me my cards. A very sad person, really. Surrounded by grief. I could see dark figures all around her, bent double with pain some of them, weeping away. I didn't tell her.' She looked Sheila in the eye. 'You don't want to frighten people, do you?'

'I suppose not,' Sheila said stiffly.

It was awkward standing by the door like this, half in, half out. She stepped across the rug and perched once more on her seat by the window.

'What could Edna have told me, Rosa?' she asked carefully, leaning in. 'I'd love to know.'

'She said she knew who took those kids. Knew where he took them, too.'

'I see.' A clock on the mantelpiece ticked loudly, paring slices of silence. 'How?' she asked. 'From the spirit world?'

'Oh no, lovey, she had *worldly* proof,' Rosa said. 'Never

showed it me, but she had something. "I've got it on paper, Rosa," she said to me. "In a letter."'

'A letter? A letter from whom?'

The woman shrugged and shook her head sadly.

'Very close, Edna was. Told you only so much. She said she'd been trying to get hold of it for some time, and now she had it.'

'When was this, Rosa?'

'Just over a week ago. She lost her job over it.'

'Her job? Where did she work? Please, Rosa – this is *very* important.'

'Search me, lovey. She cleaned – for the council, I think it was. Anyway, she said she was going to use this "proof" to make her name. Show a few folk how wrong they were. Very concerned with herself, was Edna. Liked people to think highly of her. They seldom did, I have to say. I told her she should show it to the police, but she was having none of it. Said she'd take it to the newspapers instead.'

'To the newspapers?'

'Told me she was going to talk to someone at one of the local papers last Wednesday. Same day she died.'

'Did she say which newspaper?'

'No, but I took it she meant the *Advertiser*. It would be, don't you think?'

'Where did Edna live, Rosa?'

'High Calder. In one of them towers on the tops. Her "eyrie", she called it.'

'Is that the High Estate?'

'That's the one.'

'You've been very helpful, Rosa,' she said, starting to get up. 'I might need to talk to you again. Can I come back if I need to?'

'You can, lovey,' Rosa said, rising herself, with some difficulty.

Sheila waited to let the woman lead the way.

It was raining outside, but the fresh air was a relief.

'I'm sorry for you, lovey,' the woman said to her from her doorstep.

'Why?' Sheila asked, startled.

A cat had materialised from the gloom of the hallway behind Rosa. A ginger tom. He curled round the woman's ankles, flicking his stripy tail.

'You can't keep blaming yourself,' the medium said.

She tried to speak but no words came.

'He knows you didn't mean it. Honest to God he does.'

'What?' Sheila managed. 'Who do you mean?'

'Colin,' the woman said simply. 'Deep down, he knows it.'

She stared. No, *gawped*.

'How . . . how do you know that?'

The woman smiled, a little sadly. 'His mam knows it too.'

She felt winded. Shocked. She didn't believe – *couldn't* believe – that Rosa Laycock knew about Patricia Joseph and her son.

'Watch yourself, lovey,' she was saying now. 'I'm sorry to warn you, but I have to.'

Sheila swallowed. She looked up and down the steep street. There was no one about. In any case, what would they have seen? Two women in conversation, that was all.

Rosa Laycock lowered her voice. 'You're in danger.'

'What do you mean?'

Her eyes drifted over Sheila's left shoulder, focusing on something behind her. It took all Sheila's willpower not to turn and look.

'That boy will lead you places you don't want to go. He's a

176

good boy, but he doesn't understand what he's doing. Do you hear me?'

'I . . . *Yes.*'

Rosa nodded and smiled her secretive smile.

31

Sheila parked a couple of streets away and phoned Jeanette from the mobile, hands shaking as she pressed the buttons. When Jeanette answered she broke out in heavy, gasping sobs.

Jeanette was sanguine. 'She's talking shit. I've met these people before. They're bullies. Pull yourself together, d'you hear me?'

'Yes,' she sniffed. 'I know you're right. Of course you are. But how could she know about Colin Joseph? How?'

'She knows a lot of people. That's what Dee Thompson told you, isn't it? The minute you rang her she'd have been on the phone asking around.'

'And Adrian Brown? How did she know about him?'

'She didn't use his name, did she? You said she talked about "the boy".'

'Yes. Yes, she did.'

'Chances are she heard *something* about him. Look, it's bullshit. You *know* that, Sheila.'

'It was so awful. It was – it was genuinely shocking.'

'I know. I know, love. That's what they do, though. They revel in it like the parasites they are. I'd like to see her try it with me.'

'What about Edna Wormley? Do you think she's making that up?'

'No.' A pause. 'An Edna Wormley was killed in an attack last week. I know because I subbed a story for the early edition on Thursday. I remember thinking it was a horrible name.'

'It's worth investigating, isn't it? Or maybe I should just go straight to Malcolm.'

'She had a daughter,' Jeanette said. 'Name of Sharon Wormley. I saw her interviewed on the news. Owns a salon on the High Estate. Brutal-looking individual.'

'Tomorrow's Wednesday,' she said, half to herself. 'I've a free day. I could take a trip up there and speak to her.'

'Well, be careful. I can find the address for you. Do some digging.'

'Thanks so much, Jeanette. Just talking to you, I feel so much better.'

'You're welcome, love.'

'I asked Malcolm about Teddy Proctor, by the way.'

'Oh, yes?'

'He's dead. A few years back. He lived at a place called Water's End. White Cottage, something like that.'

'Water's End?' Jeanette said. 'Don't know it.'

'I found it in the *A to Z*,' Sheila said. 'Tiny place about four miles from Toller Bridge. Looks like a single-track road at the bottom of a valley. I might take a drive over there too.'

It occurred to her that she should call Dee Thompson and tell her Proctor was dead. The woman had seemed convinced

Proctor was a kidnapper and killer of children, and she was keen to understand why.

'I'd like a photo of him, if there is one,' she said now. 'According to Dee Thompson's book, he was arrested in 1973. There must be something somewhere. Maybe one of your police contacts could dig it out. I could show it to Matthew – Adrian, I mean. See if he recognises him.'

'Good idea.'

'Anything at your end, Jeanette?'

'One or two bits. I identified a couple of men recently released from jail, but neither was sent down seven years ago. One did two years, the other six. They were both arrested in Greater Manchester. I can do a bit of digging with contacts in the police there, but I wouldn't hold out much hope. Oh, and there's a woman. Beth McGee, aged thirty-eight. Kidnapped a girl for her boyfriend to rape six years ago. Who said romance was dead, eh? The boyfriend's mother found the girl in the house and rang the police. Boyfriend got fifteen years. Beth got eight, but has just been released early. This was in Hull. I know a pal who can get me a recent photo.'

'Well done, Jeanette. Right, I need to get back to Bradford before Grace has a fit.'

'You OK to drive, love?'

'I am. Thanks.'

She decided to make one more call before driving off.

'Could I speak to Adrian Brown, please?' she said.

'Adrian . . . ?' the man said. It sounded like Kevin Simpson, the unprepossessing junior reporter. He said, dubiously, 'Uh . . . one minute.'

Muffled voices.

'This is Yvonne Sharkey,' a sharp Liverpudlian voice said.

'Who is this please?'

'Oh, hello, yes,' she said, taken aback. 'I'm a member of the public, and I was wondering if I could speak to one of your colleagues. His name is—'

'You're not fooling anyone, Sheila,' the voice snapped. 'It is Sheila, isn't it? Listen, Adrian doesn't want to talk to you. And frankly this business of putting on a fake voice and giving a false name is beneath even you.'

'I beg your—'

'Don't ring here again,' the woman said. 'And leave the poor kid alone.'

32

It was lunchtime and Adrian was in Halifax. Nige had scurried off to the Golden Lion, and wouldn't reappear for at least an hour.

Adrian didn't mind. He had an egg-and-cress roll, crisps, Coke, and all of Mrs Wormley's papers to go through. He'd looked through them once the night before, but nothing had leapt out at him – certainly not the letter. He'd sorted the papers into two types: those that looked trivial, or everyday; and those that seemed worthy of further study. In the trivial wallet were bills, bank statements and a letter from a book club demanding payment. There was Mrs Wormley's birth certificate too, or rather a copy of it. It gave Edna Lillian Evans's date of birth as 3rd June 1922, and her place of birth as St Luke's Hospital, Bradford. There were lists too. Dozens of them, written in black or blue – and sometimes red – biro on scraps of paper. Shopping lists, lists of people – one of which was possibly a Christmas card list, with some names crossed out and 'RIP' written after them. There were newsletters. Mrs Wormley must have been on numerous mailing lists, including those relating to romantic fiction, dolls' houses, knitting and the supernatural. One of the last type was *Wiccan Digest*, which was printed in a gothic font. Weirdly, among the papers, there was a silver-edged business card for an architect called Andrew Allen, whose address was Sydney, Australia. There was a phone number starting +61 – which he assumed was an international dialling code. He couldn't begin to imagine why Mrs Wormley would possess such an item. On its back was another number, written in biro, starting 061.

His focus today was on the second wallet – the non-trivial papers. He emptied the contents out on the passenger seat and took out his notebook, ready to record anything that seemed important.

Most of the contents of the second wallet were A5-size school jotters, some plain, some lined. In them were Mrs Wormley's ramblings. Notes she'd made about people, and things that had happened. Things she'd seen.

Mavis Thorpe – mucky bitch, she'd written on one. *Husband left her with good reason*.

Friday 12th May. Spoke to SS again. She needs those kids taking off her. SS (Social Services, he assumed) *not interested. Rang police – same old. Told the idiot you'll be sorry when the kiddies are dead and it's you in court.*

The notes went on for pages and made for depressing reading. He tried to work out which were from this year – then at least he and others could focus on those. But there were very few signs of the year in which the notes had been made, only days and months. In some the ink was more faded than in others, that was all.

He sat back and rubbed his tired eyes, recognising the beginning of a headache.

He put the notebooks to one side for now and focused on two smaller books, both slim with black faux-leather covers.

The first of these was a personal phone book, with two pages for each letter of the alphabet. There wasn't much he could find in there. Under C, she'd listed phone numbers and extensions for several officers at the council. These were sorted under themes: *Bins, Grass, Children's Services, Social.*

He looked for his own name, under either Brown or Spivey. He wasn't there, but his mum was, under S. There was *Margaret Spivey*, and the number of her office. Next to the number were two words that made his skin crawl: THE MOTHER.

For how long had Mrs Wormley been tracking him and his family? And why? What did she think he could possibly tell her? Or was it about power? As if she'd simply wanted him and his mum to know that *she knew*.

He held the last slim book in his hands. DIARY 1994, it said in silver lettering.

Most of the annotations on the pages were banal. *Pay electric. K's prescription. Phone hosp.* However, by late March the days were filling up, used here less as a tool for planning and more as a diary. He read it twice, his skin creeping.

Friday 25th March – He's taken another kiddy. Little girl. 6 p.m. and 10 p.m. news. Sarah B.. Age 11.

Sunday 27th March – No sign of kiddy. Not talking to pol (police, he assumed).

Tuesday 29th March – Bus to W.E. I know how he did it. EVIL. A.A. knows 2.

Saturday 2nd April – Saw the evil bitch. She's denyin it but I know her and she knows I know. Am watching.

Tuesday 5th April – EDNA WORMLEY SAVED THAT KIDDY. Thats what they'll say.

Wednesday 6th April – 3. The boy. 4.30. B.A. 7. J.

Beneath this last entry – made on the day she'd died – was a second note, circled to highlight it:

Help – 0422 292 341

He stared at it, perplexed but breathlessly excited, feeling like Indiana Jones trying to understand the key to an ancient riddle.

The dialling code was local.

Did it mean that someone local had been helping Mrs Wormley?

He looked at the time, saw he still had plenty, then took out the mobile phone and turned it on, waiting until the bars materialised.

Something gave him pause, though he wasn't sure what. If it was important – and it *felt* important – then he should plan what to say. Find a way to record the call, if he could. At least have Gav with him.

For once he needed to do something that went firmly against his nature: take his time, and *think*.

33

Wednesday 13th April, 1994

'"Leave the poor kid alone!" – that's what she said to me. As if I was an abuser.'

'Blimey,' Jeanette said with a dark chuckle. 'You're not having the best week, are you?'

'You could say that.'

Sheila was in her kitchen, sitting at the breakfast bar, the phone cord stretched from the wall.

'Listen. That's just Yvonne Sharkey for you,' Jeanette said. 'She's a one-woman crusade against oppression.'

'I felt awful. That on top of Rosa Laycock and her dire warnings. Maybe I should just have been upfront. Ditched the Mrs Osgood stuff. Said who I was and why I was calling.'

'Too late, love.'

'I might have to go through his parents.'

'Is that wise?'

'I don't know. Could you help me find out their address and phone number?'

Jeanette sighed. 'I'm your personal directory enquiries, aren't I? Remind me of his name.'

'He's Adrian Brown. *Was* called Matthew Spivey. I remember at the time the father saying something about giving the boy a new identity. A way of keeping him safe, stopping people asking questions. The mum's Margaret Spivey. The dad's Peter. In 1986 they lived in High Calder, in an estate halfway up one of the hills. I can't remember where exactly.'

'Leave it with me.'

'Oh, and thanks for the information about Sharon Wormley's salon. I'm heading there shortly.'

Before setting off she rang Malcolm on his mobile number. He answered after three rings.

She told him a judiciously edited version of the story Rosa Laycock had told her the day before, about her friend Edna Wormley, and the letter she claimed to have in her possession.

'Edna Wormley was killed a week ago,' Malcolm said. 'Who gave you this information, Sheila?'

'It was a tip-off.'

'A tip-off from who?'

'The person prefers not to give her name at this point in time,' she said, pleasant but firm, and heard him sigh.

'Look, Malcolm. Take it or leave it, but a little girl is still missing. Someone has told me something, and I'm passing it on. This Mrs Wormley claimed she was going to the newspapers *the day she died*. Don't you think that's worth considering?'

'Perhaps,' he said after a moment.

'Is that it? "Perhaps"?'

'Sheila, people say things. Some of them even make things up. They think they're helping, when in fact they're not.'

It sounded like a dig. She chose to ignore it.

'You could ask, couldn't you?' she persisted. 'You could see if she went to the newspaper.'

'We could. But it's not me who's in charge of the investigation into the woman's death. Believe me, Sheila. We know what we're doing.'

'Was it the *Calder Valley Advertiser*?'

Another sigh.

'Malcolm? Tell me and I'll leave you alone.'

'And we never had this conversation?'

'We never had this conversation.'

'Then, yes, Sheila. It was the *Advertiser*. And, for what it's worth, Mrs Wormley mentioned a letter to one of their staff too.'

34

'I spoke to the police,' Linda told Adrian.

'About Mrs Wormley?'

She'd called him into her office, all secretive – guaranteed to pique Kev's interest.

'I spoke to DCI Struthers. He said they're fully aware of the letter, and of the claims Mrs Wormley made to you about it – thanks to the information you gave to DC Clark.'

'And?'

'That was that. You look disappointed.'

'I think they need to take it more seriously.'

'I suggested he check if it was still in her handbag after the attack. I think he will. Mr Struthers is a good man, Adrian.'

'OK. Thanks, Linda.'

Kev was away when he returned to his desk, so no questions, which was a relief. He was still out when Adrian's phone rang half an hour later.

'Adey?'

'Yeah. Debbie? What's the matter?' He sat up. She'd never called him at work before.

'It's Little Phil.' He could hear her anxiety.

'What about him?'

'No one knows where he is. He's disappeared.'

'*Disappeared?*' His skin tingled. 'What do you mean?'

'He was at the bar last night and went outside at about ten o'clock. He said he had to meet someone and he'd be back, except he never came back. He left his granddad's lighter behind on the bar. You know, the one he always has. He'd never leave that.'

His brain raced. 'Has anyone called the police?'

'Yeah. They've said it hasn't been long enough to mount a search. But I'm worried, Adey. The lighter . . .'

35

Sheila's sense of geography was good, and she found the salon with only a couple of glances at the map.

The bell over the door dinged and several faces, some under driers, looked her way. A mouth or two fell open in surprised recognition.

'Sheila Hargreaves,' a half-amused voice rasped. A black-clad, platinum-blonde woman with a deep orange-hued tan was standing before her, arms folded and smiling a sly cat's smile.

'That's right,' Sheila said. 'Are you Miss Sharon Wormley?'

The smile didn't budge. The woman's eyes were on Sheila's roots.

'I am. Something tells me you're not here for a cut and colour.'

So many pairs of eyes on them. She felt like a stranger in a Wild West saloon. Word of her appearance would be round the whole estate by teatime, without a doubt.

'I was sorry to hear about your mother,' she said, and glanced about her. 'I wondered . . . do you happen to have five minutes, Sharon – may I call you that?'

Sharon Wormley compressed her lips, then glanced behind her.

'I need to step outside, Mrs Walker,' she called. 'Donna, keep an eye on Mrs Walker.' She turned back to Sheila. 'All right,' she snapped and nodded at the door.

At the end of the parade, Sharon Wormley lit up.

'OK,' she said, cigarette pointing to the sky, hair flicking in the wind, 'what d'you want?'

'I was talking to a friend of your mum's,' she said.

'Mam didn't have any friends.'

'A lady called Rosa Laycock.'

'Who's she when she's at home?'

'A psychic.'

'Oh.' A smirk.

Sheila said, 'She told me your mum believed she had proof – or some kind of evidence, maybe a letter – of who took Sarah Barrett.'

'Sarah Barrett?'

'She's the little girl who—'

'I know who she is. I just don't believe it.'

'Rosa said—'

'Rosa the psychic?' Another smirk.

'Yes. She said your mum was planning to go to the papers. That she was going to a newspaper last Wednesday – the day she died.'

Sharon Wormley was momentarily silenced.

'You saying Mam was killed because she knew who took that kid?'

'No. No, I'm not saying that. But it's worth thinking about, isn't it?'

Sharon Wormley stared. 'What are you suggesting?'

'I'm suggesting, Sharon, that maybe you and I should talk to the police.'

'Piss off.'

'I beg your pardon?'

'I'm not talking to them bastards.'

'Sharon – that little girl—'

'If you want to talk to the pigs, be my guest. I'm not going anywhere near them. And don't bother sending them to me, love, because I'll just tell them the same I just told you. To *piss – right – off.*'

Something strange happened to Sharon Wormley's face. It was as though all her muscles relaxed. Her mouth slackened into a gape and her eyes glazed.

After a moment, she said slowly, 'Those little *shits* . . .'

'I'm sorry?'

The woman's eyes refocused on Sheila's face. 'Those lads. Up here on Saturday. Some story about wanting Mam's address so they could send flowers, and then ten minutes later I find them trying to get into Mam's flat, the *little bastards*. Then, two days ago I get a call here at the salon from one of my neighbours, saying there's young men in with me Uncle Ken. I shot over but they'd gone, hadn't they? Except one of them left a hat – a frigging *Homburg* – and a pair of shades like something off *Miami Vice*. Right there on Mam's coffee table. I knew it was them right away. They'd helped themselves to a load of Mam's private papers, hadn't they?'

'I have no idea what you're talking about, Sharon. Perhaps if you—'

'I'd know him a mile off,' the woman went on, teeth bared. 'The ringleader. Forget that mop-headed git. That four-eyed little bastard with the hair over his ears and the green coat, he's the one I want. And when I get him,' she made a fist and squinted at it, 'I'm going to knock his frigging head off.'

Sheila was breathless by the time she got back to the car. Not from exertion, but from bubbling panic.

What the hell was the boy doing? Because it must be him, mustn't it? Sharon Wormley's description – including of his green coat – fitted. Didn't he know he was playing with fire?

Jeanette had left a message with the Spiveys' phone number. She dialled it.

'Hello?' a man's flat voice said.

She cleared her throat and fixed a smile. 'Is that Mr Spivey?'

'Depends. Who's this?'

'It's Sheila Hargreaves here,' she said.

'Who?'

'Sheila Hargreaves. I present a television programme called—'

'Oh.' A pause. His voice darkened. 'What do *you* want?'

'I would like very much to talk to your son, Mr Spivey,' she said. 'And to you and your wife, of course. We all remember what happened to . . . Adrian.'

'Mm.'

'I don't know if you remember, but I interviewed your wife and Adrian when I was working for the *Yorkshire Press*. I feel I have a connection to you as a family.'

'You do, do you?' She heard breath whistling through his teeth.

'Now that Sarah Barrett has gone missing, well, I'm sure

you're aware of what people are saying. It's imperative that those of us who are in a position to – to make a difference – are doing everything we possibly can.'

'I don't think so,' the man said.

'Then can I leave a number? Only I'm quite worried about Adrian, and I'd really like to speak to him.'

The sound of his breathing as he thought about it. 'No,' he said, and hung up.

Five minutes later, she was passing the leisure centre when her phone started to ring in her bag.

She pulled over and retrieved it, dragging out the aerial.

'Hello?' she said, hoping it might be Peter Spivey, or even the boy himself.

'Sheila Hargreaves?' said a voice. It wasn't Mr Spivey. Or Adrian Brown. She knew – just knew – who it must be.

'Hello, Colin,' she said, and closed her eyes.

36

'I was so shaken, I just said yes – I'd meet him,' Sheila said. 'I'm seeing him tomorrow. So that's that.'

Jeanette raised her eyebrows. 'And you don't feel you can change your mind?'

'I think facing him is the only way forward.'

'Are you finally going to tell me what this is all about?'

It was three o'clock and they were in the food court of the out-of-town shopping centre at Pudsey, halfway between Bradford and Leeds. Jeanette had suggested they meet face to face once she'd finished her shift. 'All this phoning's no good,' she'd said. 'It's time to get together and plan properly.'

Sheila put her hands flat on the table in front of her, feeling its smooth coolness. 'Colin Joseph is the older brother of Samantha Joseph – who, at the age of eleven, was the Lollipop Man's first victim. She disappeared a little after five o'clock in the afternoon of Tuesday 18th March 1986, walking from her grandmother's house to her own home in Brougham Street,

Halifax – a journey of less than half a mile.

'Samantha and Colin would go direct from school to their grandmother's house because their mother worked in the evenings. Patricia was a barmaid at a pub in town. This was a newish arrangement. There'd been a boyfriend until fairly recently, who didn't work – he'd had some kind of mental breakdown after being in the army. Anyway, while Patricia went out to work, Grandma would look after the kids. All fine. Except this one evening, Samantha had to go back to the house. When she'd left for school in the morning, she'd forgotten to take with her a five-pound note for her grandma, so they could have fish and chips for their tea – Tuesdays were always fish and chips night. Only she'd left it on the kitchen counter. Grandma said it didn't matter and they'd have shepherd's pie from the fridge – but the boy kicked up a fuss. Samantha said she'd "go get the stupid fiver", and so she did. Only she never came back. Time ticked on. Grandma went out to look, taking Colin with her. No sign of the girl. They knocked on doors. Rang the mum at the pub. Eventually, towards eight, they called the police.

'Nothing. No clues. No witnesses. It was as if she'd disappeared off the face of the earth. Until, two weeks later, her cardigan and blouse were found hanging on railings at the end of the grandmother's street.'

'God . . .' Jeanette said.

'And then, two days later, a man walking his dog in Akroyd Park found a cross with newspaper cuttings attached to it.'

'And where do you come in?'

'I wrote about it for the *Press*,' she said. 'I was on leave when the girl went missing, and got roped in to write a "ten-days-on" reflection piece for the Sunday paper. Sort of taking stock of what we knew, what the police were saying, and what might happen next. I should have said no to it. I was busy. Annoyed to be asked. I certainly didn't have time to do it justice. But I did it. I wrote it, and it got printed. I didn't think anything about it at the time. And I regret it to this day. I'll regret it till the day I die.'

'What on *earth* are you talking about?' Jeanette said, leaning in and frowning hard. 'What could be so—?'

'So bad? I was lazy. I listened to gossip. I . . . I wrote a piece suggesting the police were considering charging Patricia Joseph with neglect. I hinted at a rumour that her ex might have abused Samantha, but that she was covering up for him.'

'Wow.'

'And I implied – God forgive me – that Patricia Joseph was on the game.'

Jeanette stared at her. Even she couldn't hide her horror.

Sheila met her stare full on.

'And do you remember what happened to Patricia Joseph?' she went on coolly. 'She died. Two years later. Killed herself, or as good as. She drank herself to death. They say she choked on her own vomit. The boy, Colin, found her in the living room. He went off the rails, understandably. The grandmother tried to look after him, but he ended up in care.'

Silence now. She'd said it. Spoken her shame aloud. It was a relief, but a hollow one. And still she hated herself.

'I don't even have the excuse that I was young and naive,' she said at last. 'I was thirty-eight. Experienced. Far too pleased with myself.'

'You're telling me you wrote a piece that was so bad it drove a woman to her death?' Jeanette said, frowning hard. 'I don't believe it. Who subbed it? Who approved it for print?'

'Does it matter?'

'Sheila – if you – I just . . . I don't understand how I wouldn't have heard of this. You're a journalist of some standing, now a *celebrity*. If you'd done this, and it was as bad as you say, someone would have unearthed it. One of the tabloids would have done a hit piece.'

'What are you saying?'

'I'm saying: was it as bad as you think it was? When did you last look at it?'

'Seven years ago. I don't ever want to read it again.'

'You don't think it could be worth another look?'

'I'm not reading it again, Jeanette. And I don't want you to, either.'

'You can trust me, Sheila.'

'It's not that, at all. It's what you'd think of me.'

Jeanette chuckled. 'Sheila, love . . . I'm as tough as old leather. And I'm very forgiving. You're a dear friend. Nothing's going to change that.'

'Thank you.' She swallowed.

'At worst you made a mistake. A misjudgement. One plenty of blokes would make, and not lose a wink of sleep. Look what our colleagues – and the police – used to say about Sutcliffe's victims. Had the lot of them pegged as whores. Some of them were working girls, true. But in the eyes of the police that made them lowest of the low. Don't you remember the way they referred to some of the later victims as "innocent"? As if only they didn't deserve a hammer blow to the back of the skull?'

'But that's exactly it,' Sheila hissed. 'The blokes did it. I shouldn't have.'

'Because you hold yourself to a different standard?'

'Of *course*. I caused great pain to a woman who was already in a living hell.'

'And you were sorry for it. Sheila, it was *years ago.*'

'I was sorry, yes, but . . .'

'But what?'

'I never made it right.'

More silence. Jeanette said, 'I'm going to dig out the piece –
no, hear me out! I'll read it. I bet you a tenner it's not half as bad
as you remember it. Even if it is, we're going to look at it, you
and me. And then we'll shred the thing. You'll have faced Colin
Joseph by then, too. After that you'll need to move on. Do you
hear me?'

'Maybe.'

'What do you think he's going to say to you, anyway?'

'I think he wants to tell me what he thinks of me. That he
blames me for his mother's death. For making her life hell. He
wrote to me after Patricia died. He was still only a kid. He told
me that one day he'd make me pay.'

'Jesus. Do you want me to come with you? Partners, and all
that. I could be bad cop. Make sure he doesn't get unreasonable.
I think I'd quite like that.'

'I have to do this on my own. I'm seeing Paula Sykes's mum
Elizabeth first thing in the morning. I said I'd meet Colin at
eleven.'

'Somewhere public, I hope, because—'

'*Semi*-public. I'm seeing him at the studios. I'll ask security
to stay close by.'

'Do you think he's the one who followed you in the car
park?'

'I don't know.'

'You could ask him.'

'Yes.' She took a deep breath. 'Anyway, now you know.'

'Feel better?'

'Not a lot. Well, maybe a bit.'

Jeanette smiled at her, which helped. 'Tell me about Sharon Wormley,' she said.

'You were right. She is a nasty piece of work. Told me to piss off.'

'Dear me.' Jeanette chuckled.

'But listen to this . . .'

She relayed Sharon Wormley's rant about the kids who'd taken papers from her mum's flat. 'I am *sure* she's talking about Adrian Brown,' Sheila said. 'A green coat, she said, and longish hair. He was wearing a sort of lime-green anorak the other day at Gorton Lane. If it is him, then he knows something. Sharon Wormley thinks he broke into her mum's flat. So he might well be in possession of whatever evidence Mrs Wormley had about the person who took Sarah Barrett!'

'I see.'

'He's only a kid himself, Jeanette. He's putting himself in great danger. Anyway, I spoke to his father.'

'Oh! And?'

'Hung up on me. You know, I'm seriously considering asking for my money back from that charm school. Anyway, I'm worried about him. You and me, we're old enough and ugly enough to take something like this on. He isn't. I might just have to go round to the house and try to persuade the mother her lad's in danger. Sod the dad.'

She drank some of her coffee.

'Did you speak to the headteacher?' Jeanette said.

'I'm seeing her on Friday morning.'

Jeanette rooted in her bag and brought out a photo of a woman.

'What's this?' Sheila asked.

'Beth McGee,' Jeanette said. 'Lovely looker, isn't she?' She pushed the photo across the table.

'Blimey.'

It showed a large woman in a grey tracksuit, lifting a key to open a door to a house or flat. Caught off guard by the photographer, she was looking over her shoulder and grimacing at the camera. Her brown hair was clamped in place by an Alice band. She looked tough and angry.

Jeanette said, 'She's the woman who procured a child for her paedophile boyfriend, and just out of the nick.'

'I thought the child who saw the woman taking Sarah described her as thin and blonde,' Sheila said.

'She did. I reckon Beth's a non-starter.'

'Never mind. Did you manage to check up on Teddy Proctor, by the way?'

'Yes. Malcolm was right. Dead as a doornail. I'm sorry. Spoke to my contact at the registry office in Halifax. Proctor died in December 1987.' She consulted her pad and read: 'Cause of death: myocardial infarction due to isch – ischaemic heart disease. Secondary causes were diabetes mellitus and hyper – hyper . . . hypercholestero . . . laemia? . . . I don't know if I'm saying that right. He's faxing me a copy of the death certificate.'

'I'll talk to Dee again,' Sheila said. 'I need to understand why she was so convinced it was him.'

'I have to go,' Jeanette said, reaching for her bag. She fixed Sheila with a look she hadn't seen in a long time. 'Speak to Colin Joseph, love,' she said. 'Be gentle with him, but don't throw yourself on the fire. You made a mistake, but you're sorry. And it was *a long time ago*.'

37

'Still engaged,' Adrian said, pressing the red disconnect button. 'This thing still charges even if they don't answer. I'm going to be so dead when Linda sees the bill.'

'Maybe they've taken the phone off the hook,' Gav said.

'I'll try again later.'

They were in McDonald's, upstairs, in a booth by a window – good for a signal. He'd tried the number he'd found in Mrs Wormley's diary five times now. Only once – the first time he'd dialled, about an hour ago – had someone answered: a woman, screaming over a cacophony of vacuuming, demanding to know who it was, shouting that she couldn't hear him when he spoke. He yelled into the phone, saying, 'I'm looking for "help".' 'Can't hear you!' the woman had shouted back. Then a click – and the line went dead.

Every subsequent attempt to call had failed – it was either engaged or just rang out.

'Maybe there's a way of finding out who a phone number

belongs to,' Gav said, putting down his half-consumed Filet-O-Fish and wiping gungy sauce off his chin with the back of a hand. 'Like a reverse directory enquiries or something.'

'Maybe.'

'Don't be down about it. Even if we didn't find the letter, it's a clue, isn't it?'

'Yeah,' Adrian said. 'And at least the rest of the diary entries confirm Mrs Wormley had a man *and* a woman in mind. She knew who the woman was. She was even following her. So she must be local.'

'"Help",' Gav said. 'Someone who Mrs Wormley thought could help her.' He frowned. 'It's not much, is it? We're going to have to think of something else. If we can't find the letter itself, we could try to work out who sent it and why.'

'There's so much to think about.' He told Gav about Little Phil's apparent disappearance from the Jester, and what he'd gleaned from a further phone call with Debbie.

'Are you worried about him?' Gav asked. 'I mean, if he's as chaotic as you say, then maybe he's just taken himself off for a few days.'

Adrian shrugged.

'Are you thinking there's a connection to the old woman?'

'Maybe. But probably not. I mean, Little Phil's dodgy as fuck. He's always selling knocked-off fags and CDs and stuff. He could have pissed someone off. Still, I hope he's all right.'

They sat in gloomy silence.

Gav had been shifty since they'd got here. Now he was looking at him oddly.

'What's wrong?' Adrian said.

Gav took his time before answering. 'I did something,' he said. 'I thought it was the right thing to do.'

'What are you on about?'

Gav eyed him, as if weighing up whether to say any more. 'This,' his friend said, and took a folded sheet of A4 from inside his jacket. He unfolded it and pushed it across the salt-scattered table to Adrian. 'It's from the newspaper archive.'

On the sheet was a photocopied image of a press cutting. A headline was followed by two or three hundred words of text.

He stared at it, frozen, eyes struggling to take in the words; struggling to make sense of them.

'I got it off the microfiche,' Gav said. 'I think you should read it. It's best to know.'

'Later,' Adrian said, snatching it up and folding it. He shoved it into his jacket's inside pocket.

'But—'

'I said I'll read it later.' It was nearly a snarl. 'On my own.'

'Oh God,' Gav began. 'I didn't mean to upset you. I thought . . .'

'Thought what? Thought you knew best?'

'Ade, man—'

'I've got to go.' He stood and barged his way round the table.

'Ade!'

He walked out and didn't look back.

38

Bradford Police Condemn 'Vigilante' Attack
by Staff Reporter
Yorkshire Evening Press, 29th December, 1986

West Yorkshire Police have condemned as 'utterly unacceptable' an alleged vigilante attack on a convicted child abuser in Bradford last night.

The attack on the 36-year-old male occurred at a rented property in the Manningham area of the city. Police have confirmed that two men, aged 32 and 31, are being held for questioning at Manningham Police Station. The two are believed to have forced their way into the victim's home and assaulted him with golf clubs. Police were called after a neighbour heard shouting and raised the alarm.

The victim was taken to Bradford Royal Infirmary where he was treated before being admitted for observations relating to a head injury.

The victim, who police have not yet named, is understood to be living under the supervision of probation officers following early release from a prison sentence he was serving for abusing two boys.

Police were unable to confirm rumours that one of the alleged attackers is the father of a ten-year-old High Calder boy who recently escaped a failed kidnap attempt by the so-called 'Lollipop Man'; nor that a police employee was also implicated in the attack . . .

[Continued on page 4]

The kid was there – seven-year-old Rachel from next door – silently lining up dolls in the middle of the living room carpet. Adrian threw himself onto the sofa without even taking his coat off. His dad didn't even look away from the TV.

'Where's Mum?'

'Upstairs.'

'I need to talk to you both,' he said, trying to steady his breathing, feeling his nostrils expanding and contracting, as if they were valves straining under the pressure of his fury.

'Nearly teatime,' his dad said, apropos of nothing.

Rachel watched him with her big eyes. She was a frail little thing, faded-looking, with her pale skin and gingery bowl-cut hair. Frail yet, at the same time, sly.

'Hello, baby,' his mum said, coming in and dropping a kiss on his head.

'I want to talk to you and Dad about something,' he said.

'Oh?' She glanced at his dad, then set about plumping cushions. 'What about?' she added, nervously.

'Private stuff,' he said, eyeing Rachel meaningfully.

His mouth was bone dry and his chest felt tight, but he

wasn't afraid. He was in the right. He wasn't the liar for once.

His mum smoothed her skirt with anxious hands, and looked about, as if wishing there were more cushions to arrange. She settled for closing the living room curtains.

'Maybe Rachel could go in the kitchen for a while,' he suggested.

His mum said, 'Rachel, why don't you be a good girl for your Auntie Margaret.' *Auntie Margaret?* 'You can do your colouring at the kitchen table for ten minutes, while we have a bit of a chat.'

The girl drifted silently from the room, watching him sideways as she went.

'Can we have the telly off?' he asked, glaring at his dad.

'Yes,' his mum said. 'Peter, could you . . . ?'

His dad pointed the remote and turned the TV off, huffing quietly.

'I know what happened,' he said quietly, when the door was shut and his mum was perching on the settee by his dad.

'What, baby?'

His dad still stared at the TV, as if the blank screen were merely a pause between programmes.

'I got a cutting from the library,' he said carefully. 'It's from the *Yorkshire Press* from December 1986.'

His mum put a hand to her mouth.

His dad was looking at the floor now, which meant he was listening.

'I know what Dad did.'

'Oh, Adrian. Oh, baby . . .' His mum was crying. Had a tissue out and everything.

His dad made a grunting sound.

'You never told me.'

'Adrian . . .'

'People knew, but I didn't. Kids at school, teachers – they all knew, but not me.'

'I was – we were – oh, Adrian. You have no idea. We were so . . .'

'What? Ashamed?'

She looked at his dad, her husband, as if checking to see if she was OK to speak.

'Your dad was so upset,' she sobbed. 'So frightened. So *angry*. We both were. Then he – then he heard about this *man*. This man who'd been in prison for . . . for touching boys. For *doing things* to them. That he was living in Bradford. And he and his friend Les – they wanted to do something. They thought it might be him – this Raymond Clitheroe – who'd taken you.'

'So Dad and Les went and beat him up.'

His mum nodded through the tears. His dad was impassive, his face blank, and the eyes that stared at a point on the carpet were blank as well. Empty.

'Except it wasn't Clitheroe who took me, was it? Because Raymond Clitheroe was *nothing like* the man who I described, remember? I was taken by a much older man, with grey hair. *An old man.* Raymond Clitheroe was *thirty-six.*'

His mum nodded.

'Nobody *wanted* it to happen,' she said. 'Your dad was . . . he was only trying to—'

'What? Get arrested? Go to prison? Make things a hundred times worse?'

It was insane the way he and his mum were talking about someone who was in the room with them – as if he weren't there, or couldn't hear.

'People understood,' his mum said weakly. 'The police. Even the judge. He said it was wrong, but he said there were mitigating circumstances. That's why – that's why it was . . . why it was a suspended sentence.'

Silence for a minute or two. Then Adrian said, 'You couldn't stop yourself, could you, Dad? You had to make it worse.'

'We were all so angry, baby.'

'But Dad was angry with *me*, wasn't he? Admit it. You both know it. He blamed *me*.'

'Adrian, *no* . . .' his mum pleaded.

'He was ashamed – *of me*.'

He got up. His dad had his face in his hands now. Adrian stood over him, feeling a tremor of righteous power.

'Baby, where are you—?'

'Out!' he shouted.

'Where to?'

'It doesn't matter.'

He opened the front door and was halfway down the path before he realised someone was standing at the front gate, as if waiting for him.

'Hello, Adrian.' She smiled at him as he approached. A familiar, sad but understanding, caring, famous smile. 'I'd love to talk to you,' Sheila Hargreaves said.

'Would you?'

'Yes,' she said. 'You might be the only person who can help me.'

39

Sheila steeled herself. Peter Spivey was out of the door and down the path before Adrian could even reply to her.

'Who invited you here?' he said, face contorted with rage.

'No one invited me, Mr Spivey,' Sheila told him, her heart racing. 'I wanted to talk to your son, that's all.' She remembered the man, as if it had been yesterday. Thin to the point of scrawny and galvanised by a poorly concealed anger. There was pain in his eyes. He looked angry and defeated.

'What about?' He came closer. She was glad the gate was between them. It took all her willpower not to take a step back. 'Dredging up old memories? What good will that do?'

'Mr Spivey, a little girl is missing—'

'I know that! Dead, most likely.'

'Which is why I want to help stop whoever is doing this!'

'And what d'you want him for?' Peter Spivey said, flicking a thumb at his son standing beside him. There was unmistakeable contempt in the word *him*.

'Your son saw the man, didn't he? He's one of the only people who might be able to identify him.'

'But it's not the Lollipop Man, is it?' a woman's voice said, and Margaret Spivey came down the path, as much fear in her eyes now as Sheila had seen in them over seven years ago. 'It's not!'

'We don't know that, Mrs Spivey,' Sheila said.

'They said it's a woman.'

Margaret Spivey came to the gate, hands working, fingers fretting.

'She wants to talk to him,' Peter Spivey told his wife, nodding at the boy.

'To Adrian? *Why?*'

'I think he might be able to help me to help Sarah Barrett's mum. I'm here with the best of intentions, Mrs Spivey.'

'I don't know,' the woman said, shaking her head, looking from her husband to the boy.

A child had appeared in the doorway of the house – a young girl, with a bowl haircut and a blank expression. She leant against the door jamb and listened.

'It's OK, Mum,' Adrian Brown said. He turned to Sheila. 'I'll talk to you.'

The father made a sharp choking noise, like a cough of disgust, and turned, fists on his hips and shaking his head. He spotted the child in the doorway, and shouted, 'Get back in that house!'

The child withdrew, and Peter Spivey started up the little path after her.

Margaret Spivey embraced her son, weeping. The boy looked at Sheila over his mother's shoulder, his stare unreadable.

'I came at a bad time,' Sheila said, as she released the handbrake and pulled away from the kerb. Her heart was still racing.

'I was about to walk out anyway,' the boy said. 'I've had enough.' He was sitting awkwardly in the passenger seat of the little car, hunched in towards the door, as if he were trying to get as far away from her as possible.

'I'm sorry.'

'What for?' He turned his head sharply to look at her.

'Arguing with your family – it isn't very nice.'

'I'm used to it.'

'I phoned earlier. I spoke to your dad.'

'He didn't say.' He shifted in his seat. 'Look, I only said I'd come with you as an excuse to get away. It'd be good if you could take me into town. Otherwise, just put me down on the main road and I'll get a bus.'

'I don't mind giving you a lift into town,' she said.

'OK. Thanks.'

'Are you meeting friends, or . . . ?'

'Mm.' More of a grunt than a word.

His discomfort was palpable. He seemed to her to be a coiled spring of anger. There was sadness, too; possibly even fear. She slowed the car at a tight spot, to let a small blue car pass by.

'Adrian, I want to apologise for the subterfuge with the phone calls. Osgood happens to be my married name, so I wasn't lying. I just . . . I just wanted to talk to you *quietly*.'

'Quietly?'

'Discreetly. People know me. They recognise me. Sometimes they even come over and talk to me. It's nice most of the time, but it can make things easier for everybody if I'm just Sheila Osgood now and then.'

He didn't reply.

They were at the junction with the main road now, waiting for a gap in the traffic.

'I really would like to talk to you, Adrian,' she said.

'What about?'

She knew she needed to choose her words very carefully. This might be her only chance. These next seven or eight minutes before they reached the town centre might be all she had. In TV terms, though, that would be a decent length of time for an interview with any subject.

'You saw the Lollipop Man – if it was him. You're one of only two witnesses alive who might be able to identify him.'

He turned sharply. '*Two* witnesses?'

'Yes. Two people saw him taking Jenny Parker, but one of them has since died. Neither of them gave a good description.'

'And you think I did? I know the police were disappointed by the photofit image. Besides, they didn't even believe it was the Lollipop Man who took me. He didn't have a lollipop, for a start . . . like that made all the difference. Idiots. Anyway, there's nothing I can tell you that I didn't tell the police. It's all on record. I'm sure they'd give you the file.' He looked at her and added, meanly, 'With your contacts.'

'The records are missing,' she said, eyes on the road.

Silence. Then, '*Missing*?'

'No one knows where they are.' She looked at him, and felt a moment of connection. 'They got . . . misplaced. Or taken. They think a police officer might have taken them and, well, got rid of them. That's not public knowledge, by the way.'

'"A police officer",' he quoted back to her. 'Les Dixon, by any chance?'

She glanced at him again. 'I think that was the name, yes.'

'Wow.' He sighed, then laughed, shaking his head. At the same time he seemed to relax into the seat, to come away from the door a little. 'He was my dad's friend,' he said, voice heavy with dark amusement. 'Pull in and I'll show you something.'

She parked then turned on the interior light, while he rummaged in the pocket of his jacket. He drew out a folded A4 sheet of paper and handed it to her. It was a newspaper cutting, copied from microfiche.

She read it over twice, then looked at him.

'The police employee it refers to is Lester – Les – Dixon,' he said. 'The other man was my dad.'

'Oh dear,' she said.

'They got suspended sentences for the assault. He put my mum through that, after everything else. Dixon got sacked. But not before he took my file, clearly. Dad must have asked him to do it.'

'But *why?*'

'He couldn't cope with it, that's why. With any of it.' He stared straight ahead through the windscreen as he spoke, eyes wide. 'He felt like he was the victim. Because of what people might say. He was ashamed, and angry with me.'

'With you?'

He turned and looked hard at her. 'He thought it was my fault. He'll have asked Les to take the file and destroy it as a way of eradicating what happened. Except, of course, he couldn't eradicate it. You've seen the state of him. He can't – he won't ever – forgive me.'

She let the words settle for a minute, then said, 'I'm so sorry.'

'Me too,' he said.

'Now you understand why I need to talk to you,' she said gently. 'There's nothing on record, apart from what was written up in the papers. And I've seen the photofit. You're right. It's not very good.'

'I don't know why they bothered. He looks like a potato.'

He sniggered. Then, eyes on the dashboard, he said, 'Can we drive again?'

She indicated and pulled back out into traffic.

'Have you had any help over the years? About what happened, I mean.'

'Like counselling?'

'Well, any kind of therapy.'

'No.'

'Perhaps you might consider it.'

'Mm.'

'Maybe you're like me,' she said carefully. 'You prefer to fix things yourself. Make things right in your own way.'

She kept her eyes ahead, but knew he was looking at her, wondering what she was getting at.

'What do you mean?' he said eventually.

'I'm worried about you,' she said. 'I'm worried *for* you.'

'Are you? Why?'

'I went to the High Estate today. I talked to a woman called Sharon Wormley.' His intake of breath was so slight, she couldn't be sure she'd actually heard it. 'Do you know her?'

'No.'

'She told me that some young men had been at her mother's flat and taken some papers.' She paused, waiting for him to respond. He didn't. 'She was very angry about it. Her mother was murdered a week ago here in High Calder, near the canal. Her name was Edna Wormley.' Another pause. Still nothing. He would, she realised, be good under pressure. 'I happen to know,' she went on, 'that Mrs Wormley was in possession of a letter she believed contained evidence of the identity of Sarah Barrett's killer. If my source is right, she even got herself sacked from her job because of it – whatever that job was. I also understand from a police contact of mine that Mrs Wormley was planning to talk to someone at the *Calder Valley Advertiser* the day she died. That's where you work, isn't it?'

She stopped at a set of lights and turned to find him looking at her in wide-eyed alarm.

'Adrian, Sharon believes it was you who took her mum's papers. I think Mrs Wormley spoke to you, that she searched you out because of what happened to you. I think when you heard about her death, you went to the High Estate to try to get your hands on that letter.'

'You're wrong.' He sat rigid, staring straight ahead, his eyes still wide.

'I don't think I am. She described a young man who wore glasses, had hair over his ears – and was wearing a green coat. Like the one you've got on now—'

'It wasn't me,' he said, his expression panicked, eyes darting. 'I didn't take anything.'

The lights were about to change.

'Adrian, this is my number.' She pushed a card into his hand. His fingers closed around it. 'I want to help you—'

'By going to the police?'

'I didn't mention your name! I simply enquired where Mrs Wormley had been the day she—'

'Forget it,' he yelled, and grabbed for the door handle. She jammed on the brake as he threw the door open.

'Adrian, you could be in danger—'

'Just forget it,' he shouted back into the car. 'And leave me alone.'

He slammed the door, as a lorry behind her blasted its horn.

40

'You don't seem OK,' Debbie said, in response to Adrian's bark that everything was perfectly fine, thank you, and he just wanted to drink his drink!

Then he remembered why he was at the Jester. Why they were all there. There'd been no sign of Little Phil, and now the police were taking notice.

'Sorry, I've had a bad day,' he muttered.

'It's OK. Elaine's coming in. She wasn't meant to be working tonight, but she said she'd come. I said I'd go meet her so she didn't have to walk here alone, but she said not to. It's awful, Adey. It feels sinister out there. You can't see who might be in the shadows. Bev's panicking about losing business. I mean, that old woman hadn't been in the pub, but Little Phil comes here all the time. Why would you go and drink in a place where you might get murdered or kidnapped? It's awful. Things were just coming right for him. He said he was getting some money.'

'What are the police saying?'

'Not a lot. Bev told them what she heard. She was in the back room behind the bar and reckons she heard a shout – there's a window in there, high up for ventilation. She didn't think much about it, but it could have been Little Phil, couldn't it?'

'S'pose.'

Her lip trembled. He took hold of her hand.

'Little Phil's on his own,' she sniffed. 'No family at all. He's got a social worker and then his friends, and that's it.' She wiped at her cheeks with the sleeve of her fleece. 'He really likes you, Adey,' she managed to say. 'He's mad about you.'

Adrian made a non-committal noise and shifted uncomfortably.

At that moment Elaine arrived in the pub doorway. Debbie was up and at her side in a flash.

Adrian stayed where he was. He felt wrung out and wanted time to think. He'd arrived in a stew of angry frustration, sweating from the march into town after he escaped from Sheila Hargreaves' car.

He'd been shocked at how easily she had identified him as Mrs Wormley's housebreaker. If she'd made the connection, it wouldn't be long before the police did too. How soon before DC Clark and his pal Maybe Mary wanted to interview him formally?

He did a gloomy stocktake. He'd lied to his parents about his sexuality, and about his social life. He'd found a dead body and lied about that, this time to the authorities. He'd tampered with evidence. He'd drawn his best friend into a conspiracy to conceal his earlier misdemeanour. Then, with that same friend, he'd broken into a pensioner's house and stolen his murdered sister's private papers. Since then he'd also managed to fall out with his friend, and with his parents, and had shouted at and run away from a well-loved television presenter.

He stubbed out his cigarette and lit another.

A thought: Sheila Hargreaves hadn't told the police about him. *I didn't mention your name*, she'd said. Why? Because there was something in it for her? A scoop? The inside story on a boy who survived the Lollipop Man, seven years on? Or – a remarkable thought, this – because she believed he'd done nothing wrong? She'd said that she wanted to help him. Had she meant it? And if she had, how could she? By advocating for him to the police, by talking up his character in court?

He made a poor criminal, when all was said and done. At critical points, he'd panicked, run around drunk making rash decisions, and generally failed to think ahead or take the most basic of precautions. Worse, he'd been going about his dubious business in that stupid bright green coat.

The coat . . .

A memory came to him, suddenly, and with crystal clarity: of Sheila Hargreaves, many years ago, sitting on a chair before him, asking him about a coat. Not his, but a woman's. *What colour was the lady's coat, Matthew? You said it was blue a minute ago. Are you sure it wasn't brown?*

He'd struggled to answer and she'd kept on at him. He remembered feeling confused, irritated. His mum picked up on his discomfort and suggested Sheila ask him something else.

He tried to fix on what it meant, but his mind was swimming. He wondered if there was a way he could talk to Sheila again, and ask her about it. Except even the thought of being in her presence, listening to her incessant questioning, filled him with dread.

'Finished with your glass?' a voice said. It was Damien, on collection duty.

'Not yet,' Adrian said. He lifted and swilled it about to show there was a mouthful left. Damien gave him a pissed-off look.

'What's up?' Adrian asked him.

'Her.' Damien nodded over to the bar.

'Bev?'

'How many times have I told her to leave my stuff alone – but, oh no, she has to go and "tidy up" and now my best Demi wig's gone. "Don't ask me," she says. "Well, what am I supposed to do on Sunday?" I say. "Wear your Dusty beehive," she says. I chucked it out years ago after some little shit said it made me look like Myra-Bloody-Hindley. I've got my Cilla bob but it's not the same. I told her that, and then she says, "We'll be cancelling the drag show if punters keep getting attacked," and I say, "Fine by me. I'm sure the Moon and Sixpence in Bradford'll give me an evening. One of their performers just got done for handling stolen goods." Bev says, "Fine," and I say, "Well, thanks very much. It's nice to feel wanted." Honestly, I don't know why anyone puts up with working here – quite apart from the fact you might get murdered on your way home.'

'The wig might turn up,' Adrian said, wanting to be helpful.

'Half eaten by rats, most likely. Have you been down in that cellar? Hammer House of Horrors, this place.'

He moved off, no doubt to recount his tale of woe to the next lot of customers.

There was another question he'd like to ask Sheila Hargreaves, now he came to think of it. She'd said Mrs Wormley had lost her job over the letter. He'd love to know if she knew more than that. Did it mean Mrs Wormley had stolen the letter? If he knew where Mrs Wormley had worked, then he could talk to people, couldn't he? Quiz her colleagues. Gav would know how to do that: it was the kind of ruse he'd revel in. He'd like to put it to him. Except . . .

Except he'd turned his back on his friend. Had walked out in anger. An overreaction, he now suspected, his face beginning to burn.

At that moment, the doors of the pub opened, and stayed open, framing the person standing there. He stared in amazed disbelief, and his heart leapt.

It was Gav.

41

'You had every right to be fucking furious,' Gav said. 'It wasn't on.'

'And I'm sorry for walking out.'

They sat, side by side, pints before them, sharing an ashtray.

'I had to find out some time, didn't I?' he went on. 'And it's not your fault. It's my dad's.'

'It's not, though, is it?' Gav said, gently. 'It's the fault of the creep who tried to kidnap you.'

'Yeah.' He sat back, examining the idea. 'Yeah, I suppose. I had a blazing row with him and Mum, and walked out. Only, guess who arrived at that very moment—'

The music cut, and a loud voice said: 'Good evening, ladies and gentlemen. Can I have your attention, please?'

Maybe Mary stood by the door, from where she could be seen by everyone in the pub, and she was in police uniform. Beside her, in a dark suit, was DC Jamie Clark.

'What's going on?' Gav whispered to him.

'Might be to do with Little Phil.'

'The guy who went missing?'

'Yeah.'

Maybe Mary was talking again. 'Many of you already know me to say hello to,' she said to the hushed audience. 'Not all of you know that I'm a police officer. My name's Sergeant Marion Monkton of West Yorkshire Police.'

Marion, not Mary!

'This is Detective Constable Jamie Clark,' she went on. Adrian looked away as Clark's yellow-green eyes slid round to meet his. 'We are both proud members of this community,' she went on, with emphasis on the 'proud'. 'Last night, a regular customer here, Mr Philip Daly, disappeared. While we haven't yet located Mr Daly, we have found what we believe is his jacket. The jacket shows signs that Mr Daly may have been hurt.'

'Fuck,' Gav muttered in Adrian's ear, as a murmur of dismay travelled around the pub.

In a corner, Debbie was hugging Elaine, her face buried in Elaine's shoulder. Bev, behind the bar, had her face in her hands.

'You will be aware that last week another individual was attacked and sadly died, only yards from here. We are taking Mr Daly's disappearance seriously, and we need your help.'

Clark's eyes were on him again. He pretended not to notice, and focused on Maybe Mary's face (she'd always be Maybe Mary to him). 'This evening my colleague and I will be talking to you in turn to find out if you were here either last Wednesday or yesterday evening. If you were here on either occasion, we will be asking you what time you got here, who you were with, and what time you left. We will also ask if you saw anything out of the ordinary, no matter how trivial you consider it. We might then ask you to give us a formal statement. We will also give out personal alarms to anyone who would like one. Thank you for your cooperation.'

'No mention of the phone call I made,' Gav said quietly, as people began to chat among themselves.

'They might think it was a hoax.'

'Or they're keeping it up their sleeves.'

Calm settled on the pub again. People returned to their conversations.

'It was Sheila Hargreaves,' Adrian said, picking up his earlier thread.

'What was?'

'Who turned up at my house. Sheila Hargreaves, off the TV.'

Gav stared at him.

He told him what had happened, including what she'd said about Mrs Wormley's papers – and how he'd freaked out.

'I shouldn't have run away like that,' he said. 'She said she hadn't named me to the police. Now she'll probably go and tell them everything anyway. How did I get into this mess?'

'You couldn't just leave the old woman lying there,' Gav said. 'Think how you'd feel if you had.'

They fell into a depressed silence, until Gav murmured, 'Uh-oh . . .'

'Good evening, gentlemen,' Maybe Mary said, pulling up a stool, uninvited.

'Hiya,' Adrian said, breezily.

'Adrian Brown, isn't it?' she said.

'Yep.'

'I haven't met you before,' she said, eyeing Gav. 'Seen you around, though.'

'Hi,' Gav said, looking uncomfortable.

'Won't take much of your time. We just want to take down a

few details.' She looked at Gav and smiled. 'What's your name, please?'

She took their names and contact details. Adrian gave her the number of his work mobile, explaining sheepishly that he wasn't 'out' at home. Then she asked where each had been the night before: Adrian said he'd been at home, writing an essay on Ted Hughes until nine, after which time he'd watched TV with his parents before going to bed at eleven.

'They'd confirm this, would they?'

'Yeah, but . . . you can't ask them,' he said.

'We'd be as discreet as possible,' she said. 'But we're investigating a murder and now a disappearance.'

She turned to Gav. He'd watched TV at home with Denise and Sandra from seven-thirty, till a little after midnight.

'Not Denise McArthur?' Maybe Mary said, frowning at her note of Gav's surname.

'Yeah,' Gav admitted, warily. 'D'you know her?'

'I did,' Maybe Mary said, the words heavy with meaning and a gleam in her eyes. 'We were friendly for a time in Manchester in the late seventies.'

Gav shifted awkwardly.

She asked them about last Wednesday, the night Mrs Wormley had died. She already knew Adrian had been here, but she wanted times, and names of people he'd been with.

Adrian muttered his responses, telling the truth as far as he could.

'How well do you know Philip Daly?' the policewoman asked now.

'I knew him to say "hi" to.'

'What about you?' she said to Gav.

'Never met him.'

'When did you last speak to him?' she asked Adrian.

'Erm. Friday, I think. Yeah. Only briefly, though. I got him a drink.'

'You got him a drink?'

'He never had any money, so . . .'

'Is that right?' Her eyes narrowed.

'Yeah. Why?'

'Did he say anything to you about coming into money?'

'Not to me.' He had to Debbie, hadn't he? He glanced across at her now, still sitting with Elaine. Let her tell the police what Little Phil had said about getting his hands on cash.

'Thank you for your cooperation,' Maybe Mary said. 'We'll be in touch if we need to speak to you again. Have a nice night, lads.'

And she moved on to the next table, which was round a corner and out of earshot.

'She seemed pretty cool, actually,' Gav said.

'Hmm.' A thought had occurred to him. He looked over to the seat at the end of the bar: Little Phil's favourite perch. He let the idea work its way through his mind.

'What's up?'

'Nothing.' He put it away for later.

'Maybe you should talk to that Sheila,' Gav said. 'Tell her you're sorry you did a runner and that you'd like to know where Mrs Wormley worked.'

'She'll think I might break in there as well. She already thinks I'm in danger.'

'Danger?'

'She said she was worried about me.'

'Maybe she is.'

'I don't trust her.'

'So just quiz her and give nothing away. She might be able to help you. She's a very powerful lady.'

'No she isn't.' He gave Gav a look. 'She presents a shit TV programme about boring twats from Yorkshire!'

'She's more powerful than us. She must have contacts all over. Bet you she can find out who owns that phone number.'

'Phone number?' he said, momentarily confused.

'The one no one ever answers.'

'Oh yeah.' Gav might have a point. He'd all but given up on the mystery number he'd found in Mrs Wormley's diary. It could be crucial to understanding what had happened to Mrs Wormley – and who was 'helping' her.

He retrieved his work phone from his satchel, turned it on and waited. A single bar of signal showed.

The mystery number was the last one he'd dialled. The pub was noisy with chat and music. He pressed R and put the phone hard against his ear to listen.

It started to ring. He listened, plugging his other ear. A phone was ringing in the pub now, adding to the cacophony. He looked over to the bar, where the payphone was. Bev reached over the bar and grabbed the receiver. At exactly the same time, the line he was calling was answered. He could see Bev's mouth working, and – through the phone at his ear – hear her voice. 'What d'you want?'

The words he heard matched the shapes Bev was making with her mouth.

He watched in skin-tingling amazement as she banged down the receiver, shook her head and went back to serving drinks.

'You've got to be fucking kidding me,' Gav said.

Adrian stared at the phone in his lap, dry-mouthed, heart racing.

'Mrs Wormley had the number of this place,' he said through dry lips, barely believing what he was saying. 'Someone here was "helping" her? Is that what it means?'

'I don't know.'

'We need to be careful and take our time.'

They sat in silence. Adrian looked around the busy pub. Maybe Mary was now talking to Debbie and Elaine.

Jamie Clark was sitting with three older men, who were chatting eagerly away, looking delighted at the attention from the good-looking detective.

'They're going to be on to me sooner or later, aren't they?' he said dismally to Gav.

'You thinking of owning up?'

'No,' he said. 'Not yet, anyway. I'm going to talk to Sheila Hargreaves. She said she'd help me. Maybe she can. Will you come with me?'

42

Thursday 14th April, 1994

'I'm worried about what you're going to tell me,' Liz Sykes said once Sheila was inside her terraced house in the Kirkstall suburb of Leeds. 'I don't know if I can bear it.'

'I'm here to chat, love, that's all. To ask a few questions, like I said on the phone.'

Liz Sykes nodded, but her eyes were narrow and her mouth pinched with suspicion.

'I'll put the kettle on,' she said, and led the way into the kitchen.

There was something frail about the woman. She was thin and hunched, and looked older than her forty-four years. Her face was lined, with deep creases around her mouth, as if the pain of losing her child eight years ago was etched in her face. The little house smelt strongly of cigarettes.

'Just black for me,' Sheila said, when asked. 'No sugar.'

Liz Sykes went about her task, sighing, panting almost, as if she couldn't get her breath. Sheila took a few moments to gather herself together. She'd had a bruising morning, including a run-in with Grace and her director, who were unhappy about the time she was spending away from the studios. Grace was all for Sheila taking leave and being replaced on her sofa for a week or two by a stand-in presenter. She'd stood her ground, but was now coming round to the idea.

'Is it just you, love?' Sheila asked Liz gently as the kettle started to boil.

'It is now,' Liz said. 'Me and Gary split up two years ago. We tried to make it work, but Paula was never coming back, so what was the point?' They were in the slow process of divorcing, she explained. Gary hadn't met anyone else and neither had she. She hadn't decided yet whether she'd keep his name, or revert to her maiden name of Smith. 'I always hated being a Smith. Now I think I'd quite like it. "Plain old Liz Smith". I like the idea of no one knowing what's happened to me. You can have too much pity.'

Sheila nodded.

Liz and Gary Sykes's daughter Paula, aged eleven, had been the Lollipop Man's third victim. She'd disappeared just before 5.30 p.m. on Wednesday 8th October 1986, after leaving a friend's house to walk a quarter of a mile home to her parents' in the working-class West Park suburb of High Calder. The friend's mum had walked her to the end of the street and seen her across the main road. Paula needed to walk a few hundred yards, turn left into her parents' street, and she'd be home – a three-minute walk. Sometime during those three minutes, the Lollipop Man had appeared and spirited her away. No one saw it happen. Two weeks later, to the day, Paula's purple anorak was found hooked on a railing by the side of the main road. A day after that, a shrine appeared in a corner of a High Calder park: a cross with newspaper clippings fluttering from it, tied on with bits of string. No one saw Paula again.

Liz Sykes eyed Sheila, that suspicious look back on her face, and Sheila remembered the woman's words: *I'm worried about what you're going to tell me.* It was an odd thing to say. Sheila was sure she hadn't given Liz any cause to think she was coming with news – good or bad. In time she'd ask her what she'd meant – but not yet.

Liz poured the steaming water and brought the mugs to the table.

'You must have so much strength, Liz,' Sheila said after a moment.

'I must,' she said blankly. 'But I didn't choose this, so don't give me any medals.'

'I'm so sorry.'

'I'm amazed I'm still here,' Liz Sykes said now, with a dark little laugh. 'I'm amazed I didn't drop down dead in those first few months. I was so driven to find Paula. I hardly slept. I even started selling Avon. Gary said it wasn't safe – but I needed to be out there, going to people's houses, just to get a look into their hallways. I thought . . . I thought if I kept doing it, then it might only be a matter of time before I saw *something*. I thought I'd *know* if Paula had been there. That I'd *feel* her . . . It was a kind of madness. But I had all this terrible energy. Walking and walking – that's all I wanted to do . . . in case . . . one day . . .'

Sheila put her hands over one of Liz's where it rested on the table. Liz withdrew it quickly into the safety of her lap.

'I didn't want to believe them when they said Paula was likely gone,' she said now. 'They tell me it's hard to believe, even when . . . when there's a body. Your brain won't accept that it's *real*.'

Sheila nodded. There was a photograph on the table. It was inside a protective plastic wallet, but Sheila could see it was already battered. A crease ran diagonally across one corner. 'Paula at her eighth birthday party,' Liz said. The girl sported a green dress, pigtails, and a gap-toothed grin, and was holding a new dolly. It was a picture of joy, and made Sheila smile.

'I just kept on going. Until my body wouldn't do what I wanted any more, and one day I was in the shower and my legs just *folded*, and next thing I know, I'm all crumpled, sobbing and barely able to say words. Gary got the doctor. She took one look at me and said "nervous collapse".' She smiled sadly. 'That was the end of my career as an Avon Lady. I'll put the kettle on in case we want more to drink.' She took a deep breath and added quickly, 'Then you can tell me why you're really here.'

Liz refilled the kettle then retook her seat, ready now.

'I wanted to ask you a few things, that's all,' Sheila began. 'Mention some names and places, see if any of them ring a bell.'

Liz nodded, blinking.

'There's one name in particular,' she said carefully. 'A man called Edward Proctor. Known as Teddy.'

'Teddy Proctor?' Liz frowned.

'Do you know him?'

She thought about it, frowning, her eyes looking away into a corner of the room. 'No.' She looked sharply back at Sheila. 'Was it *him*?' Her voice rose. 'Did he take Paula?'

'I don't know, love. It's a name that was mentioned to me, by someone who's . . . familiar with what happened.'

'I've never heard his name before. Who mentioned him?'

'It was Dee Thompson. She wrote a book—'

'Oh, *her*.' Liz sat back, her face twisting.

'I think she means well.'

'Like a lot of people. *Edward Proctor* . . .'

'His was one of three names Dee had in mind. She couldn't name him in her book for legal reasons.'

'And who is he? Where is he?'

'He's dead now. He died in 1987. I've spoken to the police about him and he was briefly considered a suspect, but they ruled him out. He lived at a place called Water's End, between Turton and Toller Bridge.'

'Never heard of it.'

'It's tiny. A few old houses.'

Liz shook her head. She frowned hard, as if struggling to piece her thoughts together. 'They're saying it's a woman this time, though, aren't they? It was a woman who took Sarah Barrett.'

'I don't know what they think,' Sheila said. 'Liz, have the police been to see you since Sarah Barrett went missing?'

'A family liaison officer came. Nice woman. Checking I was all right. Telling me what to say if journalists got in touch.'

'And have they?'

'A couple. I told them I don't want to talk about it.'

'I can understand that. They say talking helps, but it depends who to, doesn't it?'

Liz nodded, eyes far away again.

'Are you still in touch with the other families? The Parkers, or . . . or the Josephs?'

'Who?' She looked completely mystified.

'They're the families of the other little girls, love. Jenny Parker, Samantha Joseph.'

'Oh, no. We were never in touch,' she said. 'I was with them once, I remember. There was a press conference and we were all there. We didn't really talk to each other. It was too . . . embarrassing.'

'Embarrassing?'

'These other people who couldn't look after their kids, either.'

'Who couldn't . . . ?' Sheila tried to hide her horror. 'Is that how you felt?'

'Yes.' Liz frowned, seeming genuinely surprised at the question. 'That's what the police thought. Some of them, anyway. You could see it in their faces when they asked you questions. The newspapers, too. Some of the things they wrote. I think I got off easy.'

Sheila wondered, grimly, if she was thinking of Patricia Joseph, and about a piece written by one journalist in particular . . .

'What support have you had, Liz?'

'What do you mean?'

'Were you offered counselling, or—'

'Nothing like that. Our doctor was very kind. She gave me antidepressants. Tranquillisers, too. I still take them.'

They watched each other across the kitchen table. That suspicious look was back on Liz's face. She opened her mouth, as if to speak, then closed it again.

'Liz, you can say anything you like to me.'

Liz took her time.

'I thought . . . I thought you were going to ask me about the woman – you know, the one who took Sarah Barrett.'

'Why?'

'Not long after the policewoman left – a few hours later, she called me. Though I don't know how she . . .'

'I'm sorry, I don't know what you mean. Do you mean the

policewoman called you?'

'I've been so worried. I mean, it could be a sick joke, couldn't it? People have miserable lives, and they see you wounded, so they give the knife another twist to make themselves feel better. But . . .'

'What are you saying?' Sheila said, leaning in.

Liz took a deep breath. 'It was last Monday. Just over a week after Sarah disappeared. The policewoman came to the house, and then a journalist called, about two hours later. The *Daily Mail*. I don't like the *Mail*, and I didn't like the sound of the man. I put the phone down on him. But then, about half an hour after that, there was another call. It was a woman this time. Young-sounding.'

Sheila didn't breathe.

'She said, "I took Sarah Barrett." She said, "When he's finished with her, I'm going to put her with your little girl." And then she laughed. Laughed until she was coughing.'

Sheila felt chilled to the core.

Tears coursed down Liz Sykes's face.

'Oh, Liz,' Sheila said, and took the woman's hand in both of her own.

'I thought . . . I thought, here's one of them nutcases. We had them at the time. Horrible people. Every night. Same person at first, over and over, and then others joined in. Kids, too. The phone people monitored the line. We ended up getting a new number.'

'Did you tell anyone about this latest call?'

'I . . . I didn't want to believe it. I just told myself, it's someone being wicked. But then . . . but then I heard what they said at the end of last week – that they think a woman took Sarah Barrett . . .'

Sheila thought about it. Tried to remember dates. 'I'm sorry. Help me here. This call you received . . . was it this Monday just gone – the eleventh – or the Monday before, the fourth?'

'The one before. The fourth.'

News that a woman was suspected had become public on Thursday 7th April. She'd learnt of it from Malcolm the day before that, on the sixth. On Monday 4th April, no one apart from the police, and the girl who'd seen Sarah being taken into a car, even suspected a woman was involved.

'Liz, you must tell the police about this.'

Liz stared, pale. 'Do you think it was genuine? That she . . . ?'

'I don't know, love. But it could be very important. Did you ring the operator and ask if the call could be traced?'

'I didn't think to.'

Sheila thought for a moment.

'Malcolm Struthers is a friend of mine. He's the detective chief inspector in charge of the Sarah Barrett case. He's very dedicated. He was a sergeant at the time Paula went missing, but he's more senior now. I'd like to ask him to talk to you, personally, as a matter of urgency.'

Liz looked panicked.

'I'm so sorry to do this to you, love.' She took the woman's hand again. 'But this is so, so important.'

Liz Sykes's eyes widened. 'If she was telling the truth . . . then she knows where my Paula is,' she said.

Sheila couldn't answer that, so didn't try to.

'Tell him to phone me,' Liz Sykes said. 'I'll tell him what I know.'

Sheila was still shell-shocked as she climbed into her car, and she got a fright when her mobile phone started to ring. It was another mobile number, one she didn't recognise.

'It's Adrian Brown,' a sheepish voice said.

'Adrian!' She was momentarily lost for words.

'If you really mean it about helping me, then I'll talk to you. Only . . . something's happened.'

Concerns Grow For One Of Their Own
by Sheila Hargreaves
Yorkshire Press Sunday Magazine, 30th March, 1986

Almost two weeks after eleven-year-old Samantha Joseph's disappearance, the residents of Boothtown in Halifax are withdrawn and wary. But scratch the surface of this close community, and you will find differing views about what might have happened to 'one of their own', including some unsettling suggestions.

I spent yesterday afternoon in the suburb, talking to locals in cafes and shops, and even knocking on doors. I heard a number of opinions about what might have happened to the little girl – and about why the girl's mother, Patricia Joseph, 31, might have gone to ground.

'She knows what people are saying,' one lady tells me, over coffee in a tearoom.

Which is what, exactly? The answer is hard to get at. This is a tight-knit community, with families going back generations. People are conservative, if not in the political sense; they have values, principles, and an almost uncanny way of knowing what is going on among their neighbours.

I spoke to a shopkeeper, who told me there are rumours that members of Patricia Joseph's own family have advised her to keep a low profile. There is a feeling locally, he tells me, that she has been in denial about her 'lifestyle'.

I ask him what he means.

'She's a barmaid,' he tells me. 'But the Red Lion pub isn't the only place she's been seen serving customers.' I get the impression he wants to say more, but that modesty, or embarrassment, will not let him.

A neighbour of Joseph's tells me she often comes home at two, or even three o'clock in the morning, sometimes with 'gentlemen in tow'.

Another neighbour recalls fights between Ms Joseph and her live-in boyfriend, a Mr Neil Davison. Mr Davison had apparently argued with Ms Joseph and moved out of the house only weeks before little Samantha's disappearance. The neighbour explains that, in her view, Mr Davison did not get on with the children, particularly Samantha, who accused him of 'hurting her' when Ms Joseph was out working late at one of her many jobs . . .

[Continues . . .]

'He's already in there,' Mohammed, the security guard, told Sheila. 'He asked if he could wait somewhere private. I thought it would be OK.'

'That's OK, Mo,' she said, hoping Colin Joseph had taken the chair in the corner, furthest from the door. 'I won't be more than half an hour. Stay close, won't you?'

'I'll be here.'

She'd asked Mo specially. He was a gentle bear of a man. Any sign of trouble, he'd be through the door and Joseph would be out of there in three seconds flat.

She rapped on the door of meeting room one, and let herself in.

'Hello, Colin,' she said, coming into the room, closing the door softly behind her, and standing before him.

Sheila saw why Colin Joseph had asked to wait somewhere private. He was crying, his face a crumpled picture of wet misery. Seeing her, he let out an almighty sob and put his face in his hands, his whole body shaking as he cried.

I did this. It's my fault.

Then she heard Jeanette's voice, instead of her own: *You made a mistake, but you're sorry. And it was a long time ago.*

'Can I get you something to drink?' she said gently to the crying man.

He shook his head.

She took a seat, put down her bag and shrugged off her coat so that it folded itself over the back of the chair. She had tissues in her bag and took them out and placed them gently on the table. He didn't take one.

She waited, eyes down, ready.

It was at least two minutes before he spoke.

'Thanks for meeting me,' he said, voice choked.

She nodded, and kept her breathing as steady as she could.

The late Patricia Joseph's son would be a nice-looking young man if his features weren't contorted and blotchy. He had a fine-boned face. His hair was black and shiny, gleaming against his pale skin. His eyes, when he lifted them, were striking: almost elfin, with long dark eyelashes fringing irises of deep blue.

He's a frightened boy. And I was scared to meet him . . .

Sheila took a breath and spoke the words she'd rehearsed: 'I will regret to my dying day that I wrote and published that piece, Colin. It was cruel and lazy and I am so very sorry.'

Uncomfortable as it was, she kept her eyes on him.

He looked at her, confused. Bewildered, even.

'Why did you do it, then?' he said, and sniffed hard. He took one of the tissues.

'I don't know,' she said, when he'd blown his nose. 'I have no excuse. I think I wanted to write something quickly. I was asked to do it as a favour but I was already really busy. I resented spending the time on it. I rushed it. I should have said no, but I didn't.'

'Mum wasn't a prostitute,' he said, sniffing again, and reaching for another of Sheila's tissues. 'She wasn't. That was just people saying things. She . . . she told me herself. She was working in a bar to earn money, because . . . because . . .'

'I know, love,' she said. 'I don't think I ever used that word.'

She hadn't used it, but she had meant it, hadn't she? She'd listened to rumour, pieced together a picture of the woman, and then implied, without a care, that Patricia Joseph had had sex with men for pay.

'Would you find it in your heart to accept my apology, Colin?' she said.

He looked up, sharply. 'Mum can't, can she?'

'No,' Sheila said. 'No, love.'

He was off again, crying hard into his hands, a picture of damage.

'What is it you do, Colin?' she asked him, desperate to move him on to something happier . . . or at least something that was anchored in the present.

'What do you mean?' he said, wiping tears with the back of his hands.

'Do you work?' she said.

A big sniff. 'I work in a garage.'

'With cars?'

'I valet them after they've had work done.'

She nodded, understanding. 'Do you like it?'

''S'all right.'

'And do you have a place to live?'

'Share a flat,' he said.

'And how's that?'

He shrugged. 'Not great. We had cockroaches last month.'

'Can I help you?'

He looked at her, not understanding.

'I want to,' she said. 'I want to make it up to you – for what I did.'

'Oh.'

There was something here that wasn't being said. That was being concealed, or contained. She sensed it like a deep vibration, and knew it would be best to expose it, to find out what she was dealing with.

'You must be very angry with me,' she pushed, carefully. 'I'd understand if you were.'

Silence. He watched her, frowning, then his eyes flitted away, as if he was tracking the flight of his own loose thoughts.

'Yeah,' he said at last. 'I am. I wanted to . . . I dunno . . .'

She sat, dry-mouthed, waiting for him to say horrible things. Steeling herself. 'Maybe I can give you something,' she said. 'A letter of apology. From me to you, acknowledging what I did and that it was wrong, and saying I'm sorry – properly.'

He appeared to give it thought, then nodded.

'Maybe there's something you want to learn. A course you'd like to do, or equipment you need to help you with your work. I don't know. But if there is, maybe I could pay for it for you.'

He sat up suddenly and let out a bark of laughter.

'Is that why you think I'm here?' he shouted, face twisting in anger. 'For *money*?'

'No! No, I'm sorry. I just want to make this right. I'm trying to find a way—'

'To buy me off?'

'No. *Not* that.'

'Fuck off,' Colin Joseph said. He started to rise from his seat, his knees knocking the table. 'Fuck. Off. You fucking nosy, lying *fucking bitch*.'

She got up too, hand behind her, reaching for the door handle. But the door was already opening. Mo the security guard appeared in the crack. 'Everything all right in here?' he said, eyes locked on Colin Joseph.

'You've ruined my life,' Colin spat, as if unaware of Mo's appearance. He fell back into his seat, hands clamped on his face again, sobbing into them in loud, agonised gasps.

'We're OK,' Sheila said to Mo. 'But stay close.'

'No problem.' He retreated, closing the door softly.

She sat down again, thighs tense in case she needed to get up fast. 'Come on, Colin,' she said, trying another tack. 'This won't do.'

He let out a sighing sob. 'I'm sorry . . . Oh God . . .'

He began to calm down.

'Did you follow me into the NCP car park on Saturday?'
she asked.

He took his hands from his face, blinking miserably at her.
'The what?'

'The car park across the square, by the hotel. Somebody
followed me in the stairwell.'

He screwed up his face. 'I . . . I just . . . wanted to *talk* to you.'

'You frightened me, Colin.'

His eyes dropped. 'Sorry.'

'It was a horrible thing to do. It was frightening. You should
never do that to a woman. To anyone.'

He sniffed.

'Do you understand?'

He nodded. 'I'm not a maniac,' he said. 'There's enough of
them about.'

'No.' She let out a sigh. 'And that's why we're here, isn't it?
Because a very evil man wanted to hurt some innocent children,
and cared nothing about them or their families.'

He kept his eyes on the table.

She stole a glance at the clock. It had been twenty minutes,
but it felt like longer.

'I would like a letter,' Colin Joseph said very quietly.

She nodded. 'Give me an address and I'll write to you.'

'And an apology.'

'Yes, of course. I'll include that in the letter.'

'I don't mean that.' He looked up at her.

'Oh?'

She waited.

He said, coolly, 'I want you to apologise on TV.'

She stared.

'On your programme.' He watched her, eyebrows raised,

blue eyes shining with challenge. 'You say what you did and that you regret it, and you say sorry to me and my mum.'

'It's . . .' She thought fast, wrong-footed. 'I don't know about that, Colin. It's complicated.'

'Is it?'

The tremor of rage was back in his voice, tilting them into dangerous territory again. She held her nerve.

'It's not my programme. I present it, but there's a producer, a director, a chairman who *really* doesn't like us to stray from what viewers expect—'

'Then you're a liar.'

'Colin—'

'*Liar!*' And he was up again.

Sheila got up too, and reached for the door.

'You have to go, Colin,' she said, as Mo's frowning face appeared in the doorway.

'*Why?*'

'Because you're threatening me, and it's unacceptable!'

'Am I?' He sat heavily, so that the chair half-toppled, bashing into the wall behind him. Then he was sobbing again into his hands.

'Come in, Mo,' Sheila said, having had quite enough.

'Colin, this is my colleague Mo. He's a security guard and he's going to see you safely out of the building.'

'No!'

'Yes. You can give Mo your address and I shall write to you, but that's all.'

Mo came forwards and put a firm hand on the young man's shoulder.

'I'm sorry you're so unhappy,' Sheila said. 'Truly, I am.'

* * *

She'd held it together for long enough, but the floodgates opened once she was safely in the ground floor ladies'. Pulling herself together, she dried her eyes and redid her make-up, then headed up in the lift to her office.

'Give me five minutes,' she called to Grace. The producer had spotted her crossing the open-plan part of the office and had risen from her desk. 'Just five minutes.'

She closed the door to her room and sank into her executive's chair.

'Come on, Sheila,' she murmured to herself. 'Get a grip.'

She pressed a button on her phone and asked her PA to bring her a coffee.

She was about to call Malcolm when she saw she had a message waiting on her desk phone.

It had come yesterday – her day off – and was from a gruff man with a heavy Yorkshire accent. He sounded unsure of himself, as if he'd never left a message on an answering machine before.

'This is . . . it's a message for Miss Hargreaves . . . It's . . . *ahem*,' a rumble of throat clearing, 'it's Derek Parker here. You wrote us a letter – well, a card it was – to me and the wife.' More throat clearing. 'About our Jenny. I was minded to say "no thank you very much", what with everything, but the wife said she thinks we should, what with, well . . . Anyways, she wants to talk to you. I don't reckon it'll make much difference, but . . . you can ring us, if you like.' He gave a number. She scribbled it down then deleted the message.

She spotted movement through the little window in her office door. Grace was peering in at her.

'Later,' she mouthed more aggressively than she'd intended. She saw Grace roll her eyes. *Well, let her* . . . There were far more

247

important things at stake than the programme.

She picked up her phone and dialled.

'It's me, Malcolm. Can you talk?'

'Briefly . . .'

'I'll be quick.' And she gave him a rundown on what Liz Sykes had told her: that a woman had called her the Monday before last, and what she'd said.

'The Monday?' he said, after pausing to take it in.

'Yes, the fourth, Malcolm. So that means—'

'I know what it means.'

'I said I could help you, didn't I?' she said when she'd given him Liz Sykes's address and phone number.

'Mm.'

'And, full disclosure, Malcolm – I'm speaking to the Parkers, too,' she said. 'Tomorrow, hopefully.'

'I really wish you wouldn't, Sheila.'

'I know,' she said. 'But I can't stop now.'

44

A grumpy woman in dungarees took Adrian and Gav up in a lift and led them through a vast open-plan office area with views of the city centre. Along one wall were giant portrait photos of the stars, Sheila among them, her big face framed with silver-blonde hair, smiling with deep compassion. At desks people worked at computers, some talking on phones. It smelt of coffee and expensive perfume.

'That's Sheila's room,' the young woman said to them, pointing. 'She said just to knock. Oh – and I'm supposed to ask you if you want owt to drink.'

'I'm fine, thanks,' Adrian said, feeling suddenly very shy.

'Me, too,' Gav told her.

She shrugged and slouched off.

Gav raised his eyebrows at Adrian. 'Y'all right, man?'

'Think so.'

In truth he was a jangle of nerves.

He smiled and shrugged. 'Here goes nothing, eh?'

He knocked on Sheila Hargreaves' office door.

She called them in.

'Ah, hello. Close the door after you, would you?' She rose from behind a vast desk. She smiled but behind the smile she seemed tense. She looked a little untidy, and not at all the picture of calm, collected empathy she portrayed on telly four nights a week. 'You must be Gavin,' she said, coming forwards to shake hands.

'It's Gav.'

'Gav.' A bigger smile. 'I'm Sheila,' she said. 'It's lovely to meet you.' She looked at Adrian. 'Shall we sit on the settees?'

The room was enormous and occupied a corner of the building. Half the windows looked towards City Hall, with its Gothic tower, and the bulk of St George's Hall behind it; the rest of the windows faced west, with a view across rooftops to the moors, dark in the distance.

They sat, the leather of the settee creaking then sighing. Sheila sat opposite, knees to one side.

'Now, did Gemma ask you if you wanted anything to drink?'

'We said no,' Adrian said. 'But thanks.'

She seemed to relax a little, but it looked to Adrian as though it took conscious effort. More smiling.

She's nervous. She's as wired as I am.

'You decided to speak to me, after all,' she said nicely.

'Yeah,' he said. 'Sorry for jumping out of the car like that.'

'You were upset. I understand. Let's draw a line under it, shall we?'

'Yeah, 'kay. Thanks.'

'What's changed?' She smiled again, eyes moving easily between him and Gav.

'Well, it's hard to explain, but . . .'

'We're in the shit,' Gav chipped in.

'I see.'

'But we never meant to cause any problems,' Adrian said, voice a little higher than he'd like. 'I was—' He looked at Gav, corrected himself: '*We* were – only trying to do the right thing.'

'Tell me everything,' she said. 'From the beginning. And please . . . right now we're good friends, trusting each other, and everything is only between us.'

It was surreal, sitting there, Yorkshire's auntie smiling and egging them on.

He started with Mrs Wormley in the market square and what she'd said, the insinuations she'd made, saying she knew his mum, then about the letter and what she believed she knew.

He noticed an avid light begin to shine in Sheila's green eyes.

'You left without seeing the letter?'

'She was being rude.'

'But—'

'I know, I know. But Linda – Linda Grant, the editor – she'd told me Mrs Wormley talked a load of rubbish.'

He told her about the Jester, and getting drunk, and how, on his way home (he didn't mention the plan to go to Ste's) he'd tripped – literally – over Mrs Wormley's body.

'So it was you who called the police?' He could tell she was shocked.

'I was really drunk. I know I shouldn't have done it. It just came into my head. She was dead because of the letter. And . . . so I looked in her bag, but the letter wasn't there.'

He explained how, after calling 999, he'd called the pub to warn them. And how he'd then set about providing himself with an alibi.

'I was in a state the next day. The police turned up at the newspaper and I knew they were suspicious, but I wormed my way out of it.'

He told them how he and Gav had fixed on a plan to try to make things right: to explain to the police about the handbag being moved, but also to try to get them to take the letter seriously, and how Gav's anonymous call had gone awry.

'So we just decided to try to get hold of the letter ourselves.'

'This is just like the Hardy Boys,' Sheila Hargreaves murmured, eyes wide with bewilderment.

'Who?'

'Before your time,' she said. 'Go on.'

He explained about Sharon Wormley and how they'd located Mrs Wormley's flat, and how he and Gav had got inside.

'I regret it,' he said. 'It wasn't fair on the old man, for one thing.'

She nodded, eyes wide but apparently accepting his regret.

'And . . . did you find the letter?'

'No. But we did find something else.'

He explained what he'd pieced together from the diary: that Mrs Wormley had seemed to know *something*; that she might well have identified a woman she suspected of involvement in the kidnap. But that she'd despised the police and wasn't about to talk to them. He told her about the phone number, and how they'd found out it was for the Jester.

'That's when I realised I needed your help,' he said finally. 'This is really serious, isn't it?'

'It is,' she agreed.

'That's why Mrs Wormley was down there on the towpath, isn't it? It's something to do with the Jester. It's somebody who goes there. A woman. And a woman took Sarah Barrett.'

'Quite possibly.'

'The thing is,' he said, 'the police are suspicious, all because I didn't want to tell them I'd been at the Jester. I didn't want my mum to know, you see. About me. But now . . . I mean, things with my parents aren't great anyway. I've been staying at Gav's mums' place . . . So I don't know what to do.'

Sheila Hargreaves leant forwards, hands clasped.

'Do you want me to talk to the police with you?'

'Maybe,' he said. 'Except . . .' He looked at Gav, whose face was expressionless. 'They might just thank you and cart me off to jail. Case closed.'

'No, Adrian. They want to find Sarah. They want to find whoever's doing this. Believe me.'

'I had an idea,' he said. 'When we were in the car, you said something about Mrs Wormley getting sacked. That she'd got sacked for taking the letter – something like that.'

She was nodding.

'Do you know where she worked?' Adrian asked.

'No, I don't.'

'If we can find out, then we can maybe identify who the letter belonged to. We can work out what was in it.'

'Or the police can,' she said, tersely. '*Not* you. Any more antics could get you into serious trouble and derail the investigation even more. If this letter is, in fact, evidence, then it's vital it's protected.' She sat back. 'It could be dangerous, too.'

'Dangerous?'

'Yes, Adrian. Dangerous for you.'

'With the police?'

'With the person who's doing this. The person who took Sarah, who killed Mrs Wormley, and who's behind your friend's disappearance.'

'I'm not scared,' he said, sitting up defiantly.

'Then maybe you should be.'

'Why? Seven and a half years ago I nearly died. Except I didn't. I got away. Fate protected me. What if it's protecting me now?'

Both Gav and Sheila were looking at him in alarm.

'I don't believe in fate, Adrian,' Sheila said. 'I think what you've just said is, at best, wishful thinking.'

'You said you'd help me.'

'And I will!'

'*How?*' It was almost a shout.

'I don't know,' she said, after a moment's thought. 'Let me think about what you've told me.'

'For how long? We don't have any time!'

Someone was knocking on the office door.

'Yes?' she called.

The door opened and a woman came in. She was tall and slender, with a squarely cropped afro that made her seem taller still. 'Sorry to interrupt, Sheila,' she said, eyes taking in Adrian and Gav, her brows rising only mildly, 'but I wondered if you'd be very long . . .'

'I don't know, Grace,' Sheila said, uncertainly. She looked at her two guests, considering. 'Give me just ten more minutes, would you?'

The woman looked displeased but nodded and retreated.

'I want to think about this, but I hear what you're saying about time,' she said, eyes locked on Adrian. 'I need to know more about this letter. Can you tell me more about what Mrs Wormley said to you?'

He could do better than that, he said, and pulled from his satchel the pages of transcribed shorthand notes, along with the shorthand notes themselves. She took the sheets and pored over them, but seemed more interested in the shorthand than the longhand.

'You write Teeline!'

'Yeah. My boss is teaching me. Can you do it, too?'

'Of course. I'm a journalist by training. Did you write this down as she was speaking?'

'No, a bit later. I noted everything I remembered her saying, so it's a bit random.'

She peered at the text. 'I can see you've struggled to transcribe some of the outlines. I'll see if I can fathom them out, shall I?'

'You might want these, too,' he said, sheepish now, and handed her the two plastic wallets containing Mrs Wormley's papers, telling her what they contained.

She took them, a little gingerly, and put them beside her on the settee.

'Listen,' she said now. 'I need to meet my producer, Grace. That was her. She's less than happy with me just now, so I need to give her some time. Do you happen to be hungry, by any chance?'

45

The canteen was on the top floor of the building: a long thin room cut into sections by trellis panels adorned with plastic ivy.

Adrian and Gav sat at a table at the far end, eating the lunches Sheila's assistant had organised for them.

'I think I'm gonna be sick,' Gav said, pushing his bowl of half-eaten jam roly-poly pudding away from him. It had been preceded by macaroni and cheese with chips *and* garlic bread, and two cans of Coke.

Adrian had barely touched his cheese salad baguette.

'Imagine if you worked here every day,' Gav said. 'Man, you'd be leaving work in a wheelbarrow.'

'She's here now,' Adrian said, peering through the trellis as Sheila's pink-clad form approached through the canteen.

'Hello, boys,' she said, eyes on the devastation that was Gav's tray. 'How was your lunch?'

'Too good,' Gav said with a groan.

'Not hungry?' she said, with a glance at Adrian's plate.

'Not really. But thanks. It was nice of you to pay.'

'That's quite all right.' She was all smiles, but she looked harassed. 'I've had an idea,' she said. 'I hope you'll like it.'

'Go on,' Adrian said, sceptically.

'Malcolm Struthers is the detective in charge of the Sarah Barrett case. He happens to be a friend of mine. Do you know his name?'

Adrian nodded.

'He trusts me and I trust him,' she went on. 'I'd like to tell him about all of this, but not give your names. I'll say I believe you've acted with the very best of intentions and ask his advice. I'll suggest to him that he considers seeking your help, and listening to your thoughts with a view to overlooking any . . . missteps you might have taken. How does that sound?'

Adrian glanced at Gav, who looked distracted and ill.

'He could make you tell him our names,' Adrian said to Sheila.

'He wouldn't dare. I won't be bullied by anyone.'

'I don't know,' he said. 'It's a risk. It's my whole life, isn't it?'

'You said you want to do the right thing . . .'

'I do.' He glanced at Gav. '*We* do.'

'Well?'

He looked at the baguette in front of him, and at his hands, then at his best friend beside him, who merely shrugged again and said, 'Up to you, man.'

Adrian turned back to Sheila.

'OK,' he said.

'Thank you, Adrian,' she said, and took his hands in her own, squeezing them hard.

They were leaving the canteen a few minutes later when Gav hurried off to the loo holding his belly.

257

'No more Hardy Boys shenanigans,' Sheila Hargreaves said quietly to Adrian. 'No more anonymous calls, no more breaking and entering. Understood?'

'OK.' He was still in the dark about these Hardy Boys.

'For one thing, it's not safe,' she said. 'For another, I'm involved now . . . and I've got a lot to lose, too.'

She told him to wait by the entrance to the canteen, saying she'd send her PA up to escort him and Gav safely from the building.

'Actually, there was something else,' he said before she disappeared. 'Something I wanted to ask you. But it might sound a bit weird.'

'Go on.'

'When you interviewed me – back then – you kept asking me about the woman's coat. About the colour of it. Whether it was blue or brown?'

'Did I?' Her eyes wandered off and her brow furrowed.

'You kept on about it and I think I got upset. That's all I remember. I wondered why you kept asking.'

'It's a long time ago. I'll need to think about it.'

'I'm just . . . I'm still trying to understand some stuff.'

'Yes. Yes, of course. I'll give it some thought. I'll try to speak to Malcolm today,' she said. 'I'll also have a look at your shorthand notes. Why don't you call me at five on my number here and we can take stock?'

46

Before Sheila went up to the canteen to meet the two boys, Grace had delivered a blunt ultimatum: Sheila needed to give the show her full attention, or let David Barrow, veteran broadcaster and owner of one of the deepest tans in the business, step in for a week – two if need be.

'Fine,' Sheila had said, reasonableness itself. 'Good idea. A week should be fine but two would be better.'

Grace looked taken aback.

'What is it, Grace?'

'I didn't expect you to . . .'

'To what? To fold so easily?' She smiled wryly. 'And I'd like to thank you for finding such an excellent stand-in so quickly. Actually, Grace, you might ask him if he's free tomorrow night. I'd be more than happy to take the evening off.'

She'd left Grace sitting in a silent stew, and gone cheerily about her business.

Now, returning to her office, she half-expected to find Grace waiting for her. But there was no sign of her.

She sat at her desk and dialled Malcolm's mobile number.

'It's me again.'

'Sheila, I—'

'I need to see you. I have more information, but it's sensitive.'

'Oh?'

'I've found a firmer connection between the death of Edna Wormley and the disappearance of Sarah Barrett.'

'Tell me now.'

'Best done in person,' she said. 'It's complex. When can I see you?'

'I'm in Manchester just now, then heading to an evening meeting in Huddersfield. It'll need to be tomorrow.'

'When? Morning? I could do between, say, midday and two.'

Time and venue arranged, she rang off, then saw she had a message waiting. It was from Jeanette. She called her back.

'How was Colin Joseph?' her friend asked.

'Unhappy. Unwell, I think. I felt sorry for him, but he didn't behave so I kicked him out. Can you believe he asked me to apologise on TV?'

'Wow.'

'I said I'd write him a letter of apology and that he'll have to make do with that.'

'Feel better?'

'A bit. I'm exhausted, to tell you the truth.'

'That's the relief, love. He's not the reason I was calling, though. I got a photo of Edward Proctor. Police pal lifted it out of the records of the 1973 attempted kidnap. Want me to send it over?'

'Of course.' Heart beating faster, she read out the number of the office fax machine.

47

Adrian called Sheila from the meeting room at the newspaper office at five o'clock as they'd agreed, but she had no news for him, so he packed up and left for the day. He headed downhill from the market square towards the station to get the train to Hebden Bridge. His mum had left messages for him at work but he hadn't returned her call yet. He would, but later and from Gav's.

It was raining, windy too, and he kept his head down. He wasn't paying much attention to the traffic, so got a fright when he stepped into the road to avoid a woman with a double-buggy, and was clipped on the arm by a car's wing mirror. It screeched to a halt, then sped quickly on its way, only to stop at a set of lights. It was a small blue car. Boxy. A Fiesta, maybe, like the *Advertiser*'s pool car – except that was red. He'd only had one foot on the road, so it must have been driving very close to the pavement.

'Knobhead,' he muttered to himself, rubbing his elbow.

He passed it at the lights, and bent to peer in. The windows were tinted.

He turned left, then started to cross to the station – just as the lights changed and the little car barrelled round the corner, coming right at him. He leapt backwards, colliding with a woman, who screamed and dropped her shopping. The car disappeared with a scream of its engine.

48

Friday 15th April, 1994

TWO Witnesses Saw Bradford Schoolgirl Taken –
Locals' Disbelief
by Staff Reporter
Bradford Advertiser, 21st July, 1986

Locals have expressed shock that the abduction of schoolgirl Jenny Parker, 10, shortly after 5 p.m. on Friday, was witnessed by TWO people, neither of whom acted to prevent it.

Police confirmed today that a retired officer, unnamed at present, later reported seeing Jenny being led across Park House Road, Low Moor, apparently by a council-employed lollipop man.

A second witness, believed to be a teacher at a local primary school, also reported seeing Jenny with the man.

Neither, it is understood, realised until later that all lollipop men and women would have gone off duty by 4 p.m. at the latest. Council Head of Road Safety, Nigel Blake, has confirmed that no road patrol staff were rostered to work at that time.

Locals have expressed disbelief that two individuals of professional standing failed to . . .

[Continued on page 7]

'Phone calls?' Derek Parker, father of Jenny, asked. He frowned. 'What sort of phone calls?'

'Unpleasant ones,' Sheila said. 'Recently, I mean. Anything you might consider out of the ordinary.'

He looked at his wife, who returned his questioning gaze. They were in the Parkers' front room: a cloyingly plush space with dark curtains and cushions and silver-framed photographs – and heat, what with the radiators on full blast, as if it were the depths of winter.

'We're ex-directory,' she said. 'Have been for years now. I mean, at the time it was awful, wasn't it, Derek? If it wasn't the press, it was those . . . those spiteful, horrible people.'

'Crank calls?' Sheila asked.

'Yes, dear. Most definitely "crank calls".'

'But nothing recently? In the last couple of weeks, say?'

'No. Why?'

Sheila folded her hands in her lap.

'I saw Liz Sykes yesterday,' she explained. 'Her daughter was Paula, the little girl who . . . who went missing in the October.'

'I remember,' Nina Parker said. 'Yes. I'd forgotten her name. Liz, that's correct.'

'She received a rather unpleasant phone call last Monday. She's moved to Leeds now, but isn't ex-directory. The phone call was taunting and unpleasant.'

'We know all about those, don't we, dear?' Nina Parker asked her husband.

'Yes, indeed,' he said, shaking his head. 'Horrible, menacing calls in the weeks after Jenny was taken. Honestly, who would do such a thing?'

'You mean – the calls were all from the same person?' Sheila asked. 'Is that what you're saying? And that person was a man?'

'Yes,' the two of them said in tandem.

'Taunting us,' Mrs Parker went on. 'Telling us he had Jenny. Telling us . . . things. Horrible things. We told the police and British Telecom and they put a thing on the line – what do they call it? A trace? But then the calls stopped. We asked the police if they thought it was him.'

'They didn't think it was,' Derek Parker said. 'They said this often happens when people have had a tragedy. Unhinged people crawl out of the woodwork. But, anyway, we changed our number and kept it out of the book.'

'But nothing recently?'

'No,' they said together, very definitely.

'The police visited us last Thursday. A kind lady and her colleague,' Mrs Parker said, eyes on her husband. 'We were going to ask them to pass on our best wishes to Mrs Barrett . . . but then we thought better of it, didn't we, Derek? I mean, why would she want to hear from us who lost our own . . . Oh God . . .'

She crumpled into a fit of embarrassed weeping.

Derek Parker moved closer to his wife, and put an arm round her shoulders. 'Come on, my love. Come on, now.'

Sheila asked, very gently, if either of them had heard the name Edward, or Teddy, Proctor before. Neither had, and she chose not to push it.

'I'll leave you,' she said, rising and smoothing her skirt. 'Thank you both so very much for your time.'

She let herself out.

'I was at the head of the queue of cars,' Sally Gray said, slowly, her gaze away somewhere in the past. 'They crossed right in front of me. A lollipop man and a little girl. I didn't think anything about it. I had the radio on for the news. I stopped as they crossed, as you do. It wasn't until afterwards, when everyone was trying to piece together what had happened to Jenny, that I realised a lollipop man shouldn't have been working at that time.' She closed her eyes, wincing as if in response to physical pain.

They were in the headteacher's office, a fusty brown room that partially overlooked the playground where children tore about and playtime monitors attempted to marshal them. Miss Gray was a slight woman with colouring that was blonde heading towards white. She had on the old-fashioned unofficial uniform of a schoolmarm: cardigan and skirt in browns, and flat shoes.

'I gave the police the best description I could,' she went on. 'I said he was oldish. Somewhere between fifty and sixty. I mean, I know that's not old, but I was only twenty-six myself. His hair was grey – straggly, lying close against his neck. He had a grey face. He looked . . . ill. But that's not what's stayed with me,' she added. 'The thing I'll always remember . . . is the way Jenny was holding his hand and *skipping* across the road. As if it was a thing she'd done before, or maybe did with her own grandfather, or with . . . with the lollipop man who usually saw her across the road on the way to and from school. He must have put her straight into his van.'

Sheila listened, nodding, pen poised over her pad, still waiting for anything new.

'I still dream about it. Nightmares. I'm in the car, and the radio's on, and everything's fine . . . and they cross in front of me. Jenny's skipping. The man's leading her across, holding his lollipop. They get to the other side of the road, only before I start driving again, I see the two of them, at the back of a parked van. The door's open and he's helping Jenny inside. And then he looks back at me. His face is *hairy*. And his eyes are all bloodshot, with bright yellow irises. And he smiles at me, and shows me these sharp teeth. And I realise in that second that Jenny's being taken by a *monster*, but I can't move. That's when I wake up. You can't imagine how it's been, living with this all these years.'

'I'm sorry.'

'It's horrible. That memory's one thing. Then there are the things people said about me.'

'You came in for some very unfair criticism,' Sheila said.

'I'm not sure it was all unfair. I should have realised, shouldn't I?'

'You weren't the only one to see them. A retired policeman saw them too.'

'Yes.'

She frowned then, seeming to gather herself. Glanced at the clock. Said, 'Was there something specific you wanted to know or to ask me? I am very busy. I'm sorry, but I do have a school to run.'

This was her way, Sheila assumed, of regaining some control.

'Yes,' Sheila said. 'I've brought something to show you. It's a photograph.'

'A photograph?'

'Of a man called Edward Proctor. It's an old photo, I'm afraid, from the seventies, so he'd be maybe twelve or thirteen years younger than . . . than, well he would have been, when you saw the lollipop man with Jenny.'

Sally Gray's lips parted, but no sound came out.

'Sally . . . ?'

'You think he might be him?'

'I don't know. A friend found it. A friend who has access to archives. Proctor's name was suggested to me, and we managed to find this photograph . . .'

'Show me,' the headteacher said.

Sheila pulled out the folded A4 sheet: one of three copies she'd made of Jeanette's fax. It showed a photograph – in black and white, and a little fuzzy – of a man in his forties. He looked chubby in an unhealthy way, with cheeks that sagged. The unshaven fuzz on his chin made him look older. His hair curled lankly over his forehead and round his ears. His eyes were black points. His mouth sneered. It was a horrible face, baleful, dead.

Sally Gray stared at it blankly and without saying a word for nearly a minute. She put it on her desk and pushed it across to Sheila, then looked up.

'Sally?'

The woman said, in a wondering but shaky voice, 'It's him.' Her expression changed to one of angry disbelief. 'That's him!' She put her hands over her face. 'It's . . . it's like seeing the face of the devil. Oh, God . . .'

She started to cry. Sheila took the sheet from the desk with a shaking hand and put it back into her handbag.

She tried Malcolm from her car. She was seeing him at half past twelve, but this was too important. There was no answer so she left a message.

Then she rang Jeanette and swore her to secrecy.

'Bingo,' Jeanette whispered.

'You can't use this,' Sheila said. 'I mean it.'

'Whatever you say.'

'Can you find out *everything* you can about Teddy Proctor? Find his family – anything we know about him.'

'Leave it with me.'

Next she rang Dee Thompson.

'Oh, hiya, Sheila!' Dee's voice cooed. 'Lovely to hear from you.'

'Dee, can we meet?' Sheila asked her. 'This morning, if possible? It's very important.'

49

Dee lived in a single-storey, end of terrace cottage in a village outside Todmorden. The street was narrow, and it took Sheila seven or eight turns to get out again, while Dee gabbed non-stop in the seat beside her, wooden jewellery clanking on her arms as she gesticulated, saying things like: 'I can't believe I'm in a car with Sheila Hargreaves!' and 'No one'll believe this!', and 'Is that a CD player? Oh my God!'

She waited until they were on the moor road before explaining why she wanted them to talk so urgently. Except Dee didn't react at all the way Sheila had expected. She went very quiet, and started chewing at a finger end.

'Dee, are you all right?'

She stole a glance at her passenger, who gave a little shake of her head.

'I'll pull in,' Sheila said, spotting a layby.

'You were right, Dee,' she said. 'It sounds that way, at least.'

'Who is it, this witness?' Dee said.

'I can't say.'

'Why?'

'Because I haven't even spoken to the police yet.' It was true. She'd tried Malcolm twice more, getting the answerphone each time.

'I've got a photograph, Dee. Of Proctor. It's years old – from the seventies. Can I show it to you? I just want to be doubly sure we're all talking about the same man.'

Dee nodded but diffidently.

Sheila showed her the photograph.

'That's him,' Dee said without hesitation. 'The dirty bastard.'

'The police never took Proctor seriously as a suspect,' Sheila said. 'Yet you were sure. I'd like to know why.'

Dee said nothing, just focused on her nails, gnawing at the edge of one.

'I'll tell you,' she said, 'but I need to take you somewhere.'

'Where?'

Dee looked straight ahead. 'A place called Water's End.'

Dee directed the way without a map and before long they were zigzagging down a shady, wooded hillside and negotiating hairpin bends.

The lane emerged into a wooded valley bottom. Derelict farm buildings lay on the south side of the lane.

'Park anywhere,' Dee said. 'Nobody comes here any more.'

Sheila parked, then said, 'Shall we get out?'

Dee nodded.

Sheila locked the car – from habit rather than necessity. Dee was right. The place was deserted: the only sounds an unglimpsed stream, the breeze in the trees, and the odd bird. A busy road skirted the valley higher up, but you couldn't hear it from down in the woods.

'Is that White Cottage?' Sheila asked, pointing to an ancient-looking house further along the lane with a mottled white front.

'It is,' Dee said, appearing to wince as she said it.

'And that's where Edward Proctor lived?'

'Yes, from 1931.'

Just being here was a trial for Dee, Sheila could tell. She'd have to work carefully to get her to open up.

'Why don't we walk?' she said brightly.

Sheila led the way and Dee crept after her, eyes everywhere.

They came to the white-fronted house. Every one of its windows was smashed, and its door hung crookedly open, apparently on one remaining hinge.

'It even looks like an evil house,' Dee muttered.

'Tell me what you know about Edward Proctor,' Sheila coaxed.

Dee pulled out a gold packet of cigarettes and lit one. She held the packet out to Sheila.

'No, thank you,' Sheila said.

Dee smoked, hugging herself as if she were freezing cold.

'OK,' she said at last, seeming to get a grip. 'This is what I know. Edward Proctor was born at the beginning of 1929, to Harry and Sylvia, in Bradford. Harry was a sailor. Sylvia worked in the mills. Couple of years later, Harry inherited this place from an uncle: all these buildings and about ten acres. It was a tannery. The family moved here. God knows why they didn't just sell it. Harry let the tannery go to wrack and ruin. He was in the navy and his heart was away at sea. Him and Sylvia didn't get on. She drank, heavily by all accounts. Harry went off on his ship, leaving her with the kid. People who knew her said

Sylvia was depressive, and a mean drunk. She'd lock Teddy in the coal hole, sometimes for days at a time. No wonder he went strange.

'There were incidents at school. Fighting, attacking other kids. He tied one young girl to a tree, stripped her to her knickers and then thrashed her with nettles. Face, neck, chest, legs. She screamed till some boys came and dragged him off. The school asked why he'd done it: she was "too pretty", Teddy told them. Be a police matter now, wouldn't it? Not then. The school got rid of him, and that was that.

'Each time Harry came home from the sea he found his wife a little worse and the boy even more off the rails. He tried, but failed, to knock sense into the boy. Even took a whip to him. Then when war came, Harry went off – and who knew when he'd be back? Sylvia and Teddy were left here in the valley.

'Meantime, there were bombs dropping on all the big cities. In March 1941, three little girls from Leeds – sisters aged seven, nine and eleven – were brought to live in a cottage along there' – she pointed further along the lane – 'with an old lady called Miss Trimm. That place is half ruined now. She was kind but half blind, and she was more than happy for the girls to spend the spring out of doors, playing in the stream, climbing trees . . . and getting to know the boy who lived at White Cottage.

'Teddy – he'd have been twelve at the time – got interested in the youngest of the girls. One day he asked her if she wanted to see a kitten. She followed him into one of the outbuildings, where he clobbered her, tied her up, stuffed a cloth in her mouth, stripped all her clothes off with a knife and then spent three hours doing all manner of things to her. He sniffed her, licked her, touched her. Cut her with a little knife. The other sisters missed her and raised the alarm. They told a farmhand who was working in a field further along the valley. He and his mate seemed to know where to look, and they found Teddy and the girl. They thrashed Teddy within an inch of his life, then took the girl home to her sisters and the old lady. There was a meeting of some of the men and a decision was made. They'd tell the authorities the arrangement was no good – that Miss Trimm's health couldn't stand the strain of caring for the sisters. And the girls were sent back to Leeds, until a new place could be found for them.'

'And the little girl – the youngest of the three . . . ?' Sheila said.

'Deirdre May Dawson,' Dee said, and added, 'And, yes, I do still have the scars.'

'Oh, Dee.'

The woman gave a crackly bitter laugh. 'You can imagine how it felt when they wouldn't let me even write his name in that book . . . It was supposed to be my catharsis.'

Sheila nodded.

'The police weren't going to take any notice. I'd come to accept that. "Teddy has alibis, Teddy's too poorly." The book was going to be my way of telling the world who that man really was. That house is empty now. Has been a while, but he's still here, Sheila. I can feel him about me. It's like I can smell him.'

'He can't hurt you, Dee,' Sheila said.

'Can't he?'

'He's dead.'

'Dead?' She stared.

'Didn't you know?'

'No, I didn't,' she said after a minute. 'Mind you, it's been a while since I've set eyes on him. I came here when I was writing the book. I'd watch him from up there.' She pointed up through the trees. 'There's a place where the lane turns and you can go into the woods and see straight down through a gap. I'd watch him coming and going, in his string vest, scratching himself and spitting everywhere, the bloody pig. Sometimes he'd look up and about him, and the sun might catch those teeth of his.'

'Teeth?'

'He had these gold teeth. I came here a few times after the book came out. Just to keep an eye on him. But I haven't been back for some time.'

'I can assure you, Dee – Proctor is dead and gone. A colleague has seen the death certificate.'

'I see.' She took some time to think about it, then nodded. 'In that case, it's not him who's taken little Sarah, is it? It must be the woman they're talking about.'

They were in the car and halfway back up the twisting lane through the woods, when Dee said, 'When did he die? I'd like to know.'

'Oh, let me see. December 1987. Yes. He'd have been in his late fifties.'

Dee stared at her. Sheila slowed the car. 'What is it?'

'Your colleague's wrong,' she said. 'Tell her – she's got it wrong.'

'What do you mean?'

'I came here in 1991, Sheila. In the April. I know that because it was fifty years to the month since he assaulted me. I wanted to see him, to know he was where I could keep an eye on him. He was here three years ago, shuffling around, gobbing on the ground. I'm telling you, Teddy Proctor wasn't dead then!'

50

Malcolm was running late; Sheila was a bag of nerves.

She sat in the little room at the police station in High Calder, looking through Mrs Wormley's papers from the wallet that Adrian Brown had said was the most interesting of the two. She'd gone through the wallet carefully last night, but wanted to check for anything she might have missed before handing it over to Malcolm. She'd also looked at the contents of the 'trivial' wallet, scrutinising the lists, newsletters and other papers stuffed inside, but nothing had leapt out at her as seeming significant.

The boy was right: the diary was the most interesting item.

Next she turned to the shorthand notes he'd taken following his encounter with Mrs Wormley. She'd read through these the night before, too, and had a few ideas about some of the words he'd failed to decipher. She'd talk to Adrian about them later. They were indicative, to say the least.

'Sheila,' Malcolm said, bursting through the door without

knocking. He shut the door, threw his keys and a notebook on the table and sat.

'Hello, Malcolm,' she said, smiling, but alarmed by his briskness.

'What's so important that you had to see me in person?' he said, throwing open his notebook and clicking a pen, ready to use.

So, he was in an officious mood, and irritable with it. Fine, she'd be brisk and businesslike herself.

'Teddy Proctor,' she said, smartly.

'What about him?'

'There's a chance he's still alive. Dee Thompson saw him three years ago, despite official records saying he died in 1987.'

'Dee Thompson who wrote the book?'

'The same. Proctor raped her – or as good as – when she was a child. She's never had justice—'

'So she tried to name him a killer in her book, and when that didn't work, she roped you in to—'

'Let me finish, Malcolm! Do me that courtesy at least. Good *grief*!'

'OK . . .'

She breathed, nostrils flaring, then said steadily, 'She took me to Water's End. Clearly he doesn't live there any more. The place is a wasteland. But something isn't right about the death certificate. I think you should look into it.'

He stared at his notepad, then nodded.

'I've got this photograph of Proctor from when he was arrested in the seventies,' she said now, unfolding one of the copies she'd made of Jeanette's fax.

'Where did you get this?' He sat up.

'Never mind.'

'Sheila . . .'

'I showed it to Sally Gray, who saw Jenny Parker with the Lollipop Man in July 1986.'

'Did you?' He wasn't pleased at all.

'Your lot wrote Proctor off as a suspect, but hear this, Malcolm: *Sally Gray recognised him.* She says Teddy Proctor took Jenny Parker. And later today I'll be showing it to a young man I hope might also recognise Proctor. The boy who was taken but who escaped.'

He stared at the sheet on the table between them.

'We'll speak to Miss Gray,' he said at long last. 'But, Sheila – this has to stop. It isn't a game. And Sarah Barrett was not taken by Edward Proctor. It's not possible.'

'There's more,' she said. 'I have information. A good deal of it.'

'I see.'

'You're not going to like it, Malcolm. In fact, there's a good chance you're about to be quite cross with me. But I want you to listen to what I'm telling you.'

'Go on.'

'It concerns the death of Edna Wormley.'

'It does, does it? Then I'll stop you there, Sheila.' He got up. 'I need to leave you for a few minutes,' he said. 'I'll be back.'

'Fine,' she said, smarting.

She sat, drumming her fingers and trying to relax. Realising he was going to be more than a few minutes, she drew out Adrian Brown's shorthand notes and looked at them again, focusing her attention on those circled words.

She took out her mobile phone, checked it had a signal, then dialled the number he'd given her: the place he was staying in Hebden Bridge.

A cheerful-sounding woman answered and handed the receiver to Adrian without any fuss.

'I need to see you,' she told him. 'It's about your shorthand notes. And I've a photograph I'd like to show you. Of a man.'

'What man?'

She explained, then said, 'You'll need to prepare yourself.'

'I can take it,' he replied, breezy as anything. 'Where d'you want to meet?'

She asked him to come to the studios. Grace would be hovering, shooting daggers, no doubt, but it was tough. Sheila hoped to God she'd been able to secure David Barrow to present the evening show.

It was ten minutes before Malcolm returned. He had a colleague with him, a young man in a grey suit, with a squarish, handsome, slightly sneering face and watchful pale green eyes.

'Sheila, this is my colleague DC Jamie Clark,' Malcolm said. 'DC Clark, meet Sheila Hargreaves. No doubt you've seen her on the telly.'

Sheila glared at Malcolm but he avoided eye contact.

'Miss Hargreaves believes she has information relating to the death of Edna Wormley,' he said.

Clark watched her with his pale, unblinking eyes, and waited.

'Well,' she began, smiling to hide her juddering nerves, 'I just wanted to talk about . . . well, it's something a friend has chosen to *confide* in me. I was hoping for advice.'

'Who confided it?' DC Clark asked her bluntly.

'He'd prefer I didn't name him,' she said.

Another knock at the door. Malcolm rose.

'Come in, DS Sanders,' he said to an athletic-looking woman with a blonde bob.

'Detective Sergeant Claire Sanders,' Malcolm said, 'this is

Sheila Hargreaves. Sheila, DS Sanders is leading the investigation into Edna Wormley's death.'

He looked her full in the eye. 'I'll leave you in my colleagues' very capable hands.' He added tersely, 'I know they'll appreciate what help you can give them.'

She wanted to gape, to scream at him, possibly throw Mrs Wormley's papers at him and call him a rude shit. Instead, she nodded, fixed a smile, and tried not to look as blindsided as she felt.

'Goodbye, Sheila,' he said, and went out.

'As DCI Struthers said,' DS Sanders began, 'I am leading the investigation into the death of Edna Wormley.'

Sheila nodded to show she understood, all the while wondering how quickly she could terminate the conversation, and what excuse she might give. They couldn't keep her, could they? She'd come of her own volition. She cursed herself all the same. She'd been arrogant, sailing in on a wave of self-satisfaction.

She cleared her throat. 'I simply wished to pass on some information,' she said. 'I don't want to make a . . . a statement or go on record.'

DS Sanders eyed her blandly. She glanced at her colleague. Whatever passed between them felt like a judgement.

'Miss Hargreaves,' the DS began, 'we—'

'It's *Ms* Hargreaves, actually.'

'*Ms* Hargreaves,' Sanders corrected herself with steely courtesy. 'We are very interested to hear what you have to tell us. My team and I are working hard to find the person who murdered Edna Wormley, and we expect *all* members of the public to assist us as far as they are able to.' The emphasis on the 'all' said everything. Just because Sheila was a celebrity, didn't mean she wasn't expected – or required – to cooperate.

'An acquaintance,' Sheila began, 'has contacted me to tell me that he is the gentleman who reported Mrs Wormley's death to you, anonymously, shortly after finding her body by the side of the canal.'

'Name of this "acquaintance"?' Sanders said.

'I won't be sharing that.'

'Ms Hargreaves—'

'Don't even think about trying to bully or intimidate me,' she said. 'I shall walk right out of here and that will be that.'

Sanders sat back slightly, looked briefly at Clark, then returned her gaze to Sheila.

'We would appreciate any help you can give us,' the DS said. She raised an eyebrow, and Sheila detected an unspoken, *Let's start again, shall we?*

'My friend – my acquaintance – found Mrs Wormley's body. He was frightened but he phoned you to tell you. He didn't tell you his name for . . . personal reasons.'

The officers glanced at one another. She detected malicious amusement in Clark's greeny-yellow eyes.

'He didn't kill her,' she said, a little feebly. 'I know he didn't. He's a *good boy.*'

They were watching her with something like impatient distaste. God knows what they were thinking, or what they'd say about her afterwards . . .

'Ms Hargreaves . . . ?' DS Sanders pressed.

'I'm *thinking,*' she snapped. 'Please give me a moment.'

Change tack, she decided. Chuck everything at them and get out of there fast.

'Mrs Wormley might have been killed because she knew who took Sarah Barrett,' she said in a rush.

'Oh?' Sanders said.

'She had a letter. I don't know what was in it, but I think she might have taken it – stolen it – from someone else. She might even have got the sack because of it. Mrs Wormley believed she knew who had taken Sarah Barrett. She had a diary, and in it was the phone number of the Jester public house.' She saw them both register the significance of that. 'And she referred to a woman. She also made a note about something or somewhere that had the initials W.E., and I believe this to be Water's End.'

'Water's End?'

'That's right. And as I said to Mal – to Mr Struthers – before you came in, I think you should be thinking about a man called Edward Proctor, who once lived there. He's supposed to be dead but another . . . acquaintance . . . says that can't be true, because she saw him only three years ago – *years* after the date on the supposed death certificate.'

She knew she must sound insane, rabbiting out wild theories that verged on conspiracy. She paused for breath and considered their blank, withdrawn faces.

'Mrs Wormley's diary,' Clark said. 'Do you have it?'

'I might,' she said, made childish through a mix of irritation and shame. It was on the tip of her tongue to make him say 'please'.

'Where did you get it?' he asked.

'From a friend.'

'The same friend who . . . ?'

'Possibly.'

'You've a lot of friends, Ms Hargreaves,' Sanders said unpleasantly.

'People tell me things because they trust me. They trust me more than they trust you, clearly!'

'Please give us the diary,' Clark said.

'Happy to,' she said. She went into her bag, hoping to God this was sensible – and safe. Safe for the boy. She hesitated, and looked at them. Their eyes were avid. They wanted the diary very much. But what if they checked it for fingerprints . . . ?

'Ms Hargreaves?' Sanders said.

'Yes, yes, just a minute.'

She drew the diary from the second of the two plastic wallets then surrendered it, heart in her mouth.

Clark took it and began flicking through it.

'The very last entry,' Sheila said flatly. 'It's a note she made for what she was planning to do on Wednesday 6th April. You'll see as well that it says she was seeing someone called "B.A." at 4.30 p.m.'

'We know what that was about.'

'You do?'

'Yes.'

She waited. He looked at his colleague, who shrugged.

'She went to see Brian Quigley of the Bradford Angels – they're a vigilante group.'

'Ah. "B.A.". . .'

'Mr Quigley provided that information.'

'Oh?'

He wasn't about to let on any more than that, but it was satisfying to know the answer to that part of the riddle.

Clark had found the relevant page of the diary and was peering at the notes.

'There's a phone number, marked "help",' Sheila said. 'It's for the Jester public house.'

'Does your acquaintance have any knowledge relating to the disappearance of a young man named Philip Daly?' Clark asked.

'Is he the young man who went missing near the Jester pub?'

Clark nodded.

'I don't know anything about that.'

'This is a serious business, Ms Hargreaves,' Sanders said. 'We need the names of everyone you've been talking to.'

'I prefer not to share them.'

'*Ms Hargreaves*, may I remind you that you could be in serious trouble if you hold anything back.'

'That's very regrettable.'

'The names, Ms Hargreaves?'

The two detectives stared at her, and she stared right back.

'No,' she said. 'I'm sorry.' She stood up, lifting her bag and checking it was firmly closed.

They watched her in some surprise.

'I've finished saying what I came to say,' she said nicely, 'and I've given you what I intended to. Now, if you'll excuse me, there's a good chance I'm needed on the television!'

51

'No time,' she snapped at Grace, hand up as she marched to her office.

'But Sheila—'

'Did you get David Barrow?'

'Yes.' This through clenched teeth.

'Can he present tonight's show?'

'Yes, thankfully, because—'

'That's all I need to know!'

She slammed her door behind her before sinking into her desk chair.

She was angry with herself – and with that smug and unpleasant pair of detectives, not to mention Malcolm who'd thrown her to them, like meat to wolves. Couldn't he see that she was trying to *help*?

Would they act on anything she'd told them? Would they look into Edward Proctor's supposed death? Would they scrutinise Mrs Wormley's diary, and look for 'her', whoever 'she' might be?

She didn't have much faith.

Her desk phone rang. She looked at the display, expecting it to be Grace, but it was reception.

'A Mr Brown to see you, Ms Hargreaves.'

'Thank you. I'll be down.'

Adrian was on his own this time, waiting in the little corral where they kept visitors like obedient sheep. He looked small and crumpled, but also wired. As wired as Sheila herself.

'Let's just talk here, shall we?' she said.

'Have you got the photo?'

'Yes.'

She sat beside him. Should she say something to prepare him? She hadn't really thought this through, had she?

'Are you all right looking at it?' she said.

He shrugged and nodded, eyes down.

She went into her bag for the A4 sheet and unfolded it. 'His name's Edward Proctor,' she said. 'This photo was taken when he was arrested in 1973.'

He looked at it. Gazed at it, his eyes passing back and forth over it as if he were reading it for clues that evaded him.

After a minute or so, he folded the page and handed it back to her.

'Well?' she said, heart in her mouth.

He looked at her, lips parted, his eyes wide and wondering. 'It could be,' he said. 'It was a long time ago. I can't be sure.'

She nodded, smiling to mask her slight disappointment. 'Thank you for looking. Now, you can leave this with me. I'll make sure the right people hear about it.'

He seemed visibly to relax, sinking down in his seat.

'Did you talk to your police friend?' he said, as if he'd just remembered their deal.

'Yes,' she said airily. 'I didn't manage to . . . well, tell him everything I hoped to, but I gave him – or, rather, one of his colleagues – Mrs Wormley's diary.'

'A colleague?' he said, wary.

'Detective Sergeant Sanders and a Detective Constable Clark.'

'Oh, God.' He put a hand to his forehead. 'Clark's the one who suspects me.'

'Really?' She didn't know what to say. She could hardly set about reassuring him, could she? 'We have to try to do the right thing, Adrian,' she said. 'It's all we can do.'

He looked straight ahead, nodding. *Sanguine*, she thought to herself. *And so resilient.*

'Adrian, I've thought about what you asked me. About the coats. The different-coloured coats, and why I kept asking you about them.'

He watched her, interested.

'I think it was because you insisted that the lady who brought you back to the cinema, to your mum and dad, was wearing a blue coat.'

He nodded.

'But the lady who spotted you and brought you to where your parents were waiting – I forget her name, but I interviewed her myself – she'd worn a brown coat. You insisted it was blue – to the point where I asked your mum if you were colour-blind. She said you weren't – not that she knew, anyway. You aren't, are you?'

He blinked at her. 'I can tell the difference between blue and brown.'

'Do you . . . do you remember now?'

'I'm not sure . . .'

He stared at his hands, at the fists clenched in his lap, and she couldn't help worrying that she was overburdening him.

'Shall we talk about your shorthand?' she said, brightening her tone.

'OK.'

She took out his notes: the Teeline outlines alongside his transcriptions.

'You write it very well for a beginner,' she said, smiling, moving things on. 'Do you know how fast you are?'

'Not very. Yvonne gave me some tapes. I can do seventy words a minute, but eighty's a bit too fast. Say, seventy-five on a good day. How fast are you?'

'A hundred, I think. A hundred and twenty when I was at college.'

He looked impressed.

'It's this section,' she said, showing him the circled parts.

[tn tr hds???]
letter there
smell [?] of the letter

'Adrian, I know it's hard to recall the words someone says sometimes, but the first words there . . . could they be: *Tan their hides*?'

'"Tan their hides"?'

'Yes. Like, to hit someone – to give them a good beating?'

He frowned, then nodded sharply. 'Yes!' he said, eyes widening. 'Yes, I think that's it! How did you . . . ?'

'I'll explain in a moment,' she said. Her heart was racing, and her mouth dry. The solution to this dark mystery seemed suddenly so much closer.

'Then, this next line – *letter there* – that seems OK to me.

But look at the shorthand. You've used the shortcut for the word *letter*: an L. But here, on the third line, where you've put *smell of the letter*, you've spelt *letter* out: LTR. I wondered why you'd done that.'

He shook his head, bottom lip out, mystified.

'The outline for LTR can also stand in for another word,' she said. 'You'd write LTR the same way you'd write LTHR.'

'Leather?' he said quietly.

'That makes more sense, doesn't it? Leather can smell. It can smell quite unpleasant, really. It is animal skin, after all. Could that be what Mrs Wormley said to you, d'you think? Did she talk about the *smell of the leather*?'

His eyes were away in the middle distance. 'I think she did . . . What does it mean?'

Her lips were so dry she had to wet them. 'I think that, put together with the idea of "tanning someone's hide" and the mention of leather . . . I rather think it might have something to do with a house called White Cottage, on Tannery Lane, at a place called Water's End. And with a man who lived there. The man in that photograph.'

52

Adrian was keyed up when he left the TV studios, and needed a means of dispelling some tension.

So he rang Ste.

'Are your mum and dad still away?' he said into the payphone.

'Yeah,' Ste said. 'You free?'

'Yeah. Want me to come over?'

'If you like.'

Adrian liked.

He took the bus, tapping his feet so much that an old man barked at him to calm down. From time to time he checked the work mobile. Sheila had asked how she could contact him if she needed to. He'd given her the number of the phone. The volume was on full, but he was still paranoid about missing a call.

He'd been shaken by what Sheila had told him and had fired questions at her. She'd told him the man's name – that he was Teddy Proctor – but that he was dead. She couldn't tell him if Water's End was the place the man had taken him. He'd suggested they go there, perhaps together, to see if it jogged any kind of memory, but she'd seemed taken aback by the proposal and asked for time to think it through.

He thought about what she'd told him. About Water's End and Tannery Lane, and how the words he'd recorded in shorthand had reinforced her view that Mrs Wormley had been thinking about that place – and the man who lived there: the one in the photo.

He'd felt sick waiting to look at the image. Gazing at it, though, he'd felt surprisingly little. Here was a black-and-white grainy picture of a fat, ill-looking man, with a miserable expression and sad, empty eyes. It could be the man who took him, but it also might not be. Either way, the face didn't trouble him. It was like viewing an unpleasant exhibit in a dark museum: a foetus preserved in a jar perhaps. You didn't want to look for long and it might even give you nightmares. But it couldn't hurt you.

What she'd told him about the coats, though. That had bothered him.

He had a number of memories of what had happened to him, all of them fuzzy now, glimpsed through darkness; fragments only.

The strongest image of all was 'the reunion', so called by his mum. He remembered being pulled along the cobbles of Gorton Lane by a woman who gripped his wrist hard. In the memory the woman panted, nearly crying, almost lifting him off the pavement as she lurched towards the crowd of people by the side of the cinema. She cried out as they grew near: 'I've got him!' And the crowd shifted and opened like a single organism. Individual faces turning to them. And then he saw his mum.

In another image he was in the van, lying where he'd fallen after the hands had pushed him, but then, somehow, finding himself not in the dark cavern of the back of the vehicle, but in the footwell in front of a seat, as the woman drove him; and her hand was shoving and yanking at the gearstick, as she swore under her breath, until she brought the van to a hard stop, and was pulling him out into the night.

Where had she found him? How far had she driven him? He'd always wondered, and never known – had never asked. How had she known he'd been taken? How had she known where to take him?

He examined the memories again, scrutinising them for meaning, for clues he hadn't before noticed. He saw again that the woman who drove the van had on a blue coat. Not *dark* blue, possible in dim light to mistake for brown, but light blue, like the sky on a winter morning.

There were two possibilities: either Sheila was wrong that the woman who'd brought him back to them had worn a brown coat, or he was wrong when he remembered her coat had been blue.

Ten-year-old Matthew Spivey had, according to Sheila, insisted that the woman who brought him back had been wearing a *blue* coat. Hence all her questions at the time.

So there was a third possibility. One that was puzzling and chilling in equal measure – both obvious, and deeply alarming.

He needed to talk to Sheila about it, but it would have to wait: the bus was approaching the stop near the entrance to Ste's posh estate.

'Awright,' Ste said, meeting him at the door of his parents' huge house. He was in a Leeds United football top and grey tracksuit bottoms, with bare feet. He looked ruggedly handsome, with an untidy thatch of straw-coloured hair. 'Want a beer?'

'Yeah, OK.' He tried not to pant. It had been a hike uphill from the main road, plus he was horny and giddy with it. He kicked his trainers off at the door – a rule of the house.

'What you been doing?' Ste said, extracting a pair of cans from a pack of six in the American-size fridge in the vast kitchen. He kicked the fridge door closed with a foot and popped both cans before handing one to Adrian.

'Stuff,' Adrian said. He didn't come here for conversation. Still, Ste nodded as if it made perfect sense. 'You?'

'Not a lot.' He slurped the foam off the top of his can.

Ste worked at his dad's company on a casual basis, fitting lifts in new buildings. His parents had gone on a week's cruise and Ste never worked when they were away. Just stayed at home, drinking beer, playing video games, watching videos and – he liked to tell Adrian, to wind him up – thinking about Adrian 'doing that thing'.

'Upstairs?' Adrian asked him.

'In a bit,' Ste said, nodding towards the hallway, from where there suddenly came the sound of approaching footsteps.

'That's me away, love – oh, hiya!' It was a woman with voluminous blonde hair and a lot of make-up, wearing a tight, pink denim jacket and white tapered jeans, holding car keys with a BMW badge on the keyring. He'd half-noticed an unfamiliar car in the driveway.

'Me Auntie Jill,' Ste said. 'This is Adrian.'

'Hiya, Adrian, love.'

Adrian nodded, trying not to look embarrassed as she gave him a curious once-over.

'Tell your mum I've taken her Dior, would you, Stephen. She said to help myself. Well, that's me away. Nice to meet you, Adrian,' she said, frowning a little, possibly wondering why Adrian was so flushed.

'Didn't know anyone was here,' he grumbled to Ste as they made their way up the stairs.

It could take a good hour before Ste would initiate any action – it was always his lead to take. Adrian went to the loo, then washed himself and gargled with some mouthwash he found in the cabinet. He unfurled a good few metres of loo roll and stuffed it in his jeans pocket. Ste often just used a T-shirt or sock, then chucked it in the washing basket – something Adrian found disgusting.

Ste lay on the floor, propped on a beanbag, and reached for his Super Nintendo controller.

'Wanna play?' he asked, without looking at Adrian.

'I'll watch,' Adrian said, and climbed onto Ste's unmade single bed, making a cushion from his rolled-up duvet.

The bedroom smelt of worn sports gear and Lynx, like a men's changing room. Ste played his game and Adrian watched him with swelling lust: enjoying the way his fingers twitched as they worked the controller, and the way his broad back and shoulders moved as he jerked about, trying to keep Mario on his track.

'Ah, fuck it,' Ste said suddenly, and threw down the controller. He turned, twisting on the beanbag, and said coyly, 'What you looking at, anyway?'

Adrian smirked and shrugged. 'Dunno,' he said. 'Label fell off.'

'Cheeky fucker,' Ste said, voice a growl. And he jumped up, coming to the bed, kneeling on the edge of it so his groin was level with Adrian's face. 'Get on with it then,' he ordered.

Adrian did.

Ste's game continued to bleep on the monitor, and neither of them heard a sound. Not a door opening and closing; not footsteps on the stairs.

'*Oh my God*!' Auntie Jill screamed from Ste's bedroom doorway, face contorted in horror.

'Jesus Christ!' Ste cried, pulling up his tracksuit bottoms, and throwing himself off the bed, keeping his back to the door so she wouldn't see the massive bulge of his erection through the grey fabric.

Adrian jumped, too, but stayed on the bed, pulling his legs up to make himself into a defensive ball.

'What are you *doing to him*?' Auntie Jill screamed.

'Why are you still here?' Ste bellowed at her.

'I came back for my scarf, didn't I? What the hell's going on, Stephen? What's he doing to you? Why are you letting him?'

'I'm not! He just – he just started on me!'

Fucking liar, Adrian thought, glaring at Ste.

'You!' Auntie Jill said, a hooked finger pointing his way. 'Get out of this house, and don't ever come back. Filthy bloody animal!'

'I'm going,' Adrian said. He jumped off the bed and, with one last glance at Ste, barged past the woman, out into the landing and down the stairs.

'You're disgusting!' she screamed down at him.

He slammed the door as she shouted something about disease.

'Stupid cow,' he said to himself and hurried down the drive.

Auntie Jill's BMW was in the drive. He'd like to drag his keys down it. Teach her a lesson. Except that would be childish.

And criminal. And he may be a molester of amateur footballers, but he wasn't a yob.

As he turned out of Ste's road, he heard his phone ringing. He took it out, expecting to see Sheila's number. It wasn't hers. The LCD screen said: OFFICE.

'That you, Adrian?' Yvonne.

'Yeah.'

'Oh, thank God. Listen, Adrian, your mum's looking for you. She rang here. You need to go home, babe. Something terrible's happened.'

53

'Do they think it's her?' Sheila asked, her skin creeping at what Jeanette had just told her on the phone.

'Hard to say. They're taking it seriously, anyway. Horrible, isn't it?'

Sheila was at her desk in Bradford, Jeanette at hers in Leeds.

A woman had called in to the lunchtime phone-in on Leeds's commercial radio station, Radio Aire, claiming, with some glee, that she was about to kidnap another girl. She'd got past the researchers, saying she wanted to talk about energy prices, and had given her name as Marilyn Hyde.

On air she'd begun by saying she knew what had happened to Sarah Barrett. The presenter, brain full of facts and figures about energy meters, took a few moments to realise who she was talking about.

'I've heard the recording,' Jeanette told her. 'The woman said, "I took Sarah Barrett, and now she's dead. And today I'm going to take another one. A friend for her to play with in

Heaven." And she started laughing. Just vile.'

'They let it go out over the air?'

'The first part. They've got a six-second delay, so they cut it right after "take another one". The whole thing's on tape, though.'

'It could be fake, couldn't it?'

'It could, except this afternoon a girl went missing from the garden of a house in High Calder. We just got word. Only seven-years-old, so younger than the others.'

'Oh, Jeanette. Oh, God . . .'

'I'll have more info soon. But listen to this, Sheila – one of the boys twigged it. That caller's name. Scramble the letters of "Marilyn Hyde" – what do you think you get?'

Sheila tried to visualise the name. The clue was in the initials.

'*Myra Hindley*,' she whispered, her stomach turning over.

54

Adrian tried calling home but it was always engaged, so he started to panic. Going by what Yvonne had told him, this was no ruse to get him to come home. His mum had been in tears when she called, and when Yvonne had asked her what was wrong, his mum had said she couldn't say – that she wasn't *allowed* to say.

At the main road he looked in vain for a bus, then spotted a taxi with its light on.

He tried phoning again once they were on their way, and this time it was answered.

'Hello?' a woman's voice said sharply. 'Who is this, please?'

'It's Adrian Brown,' he said, his throat feeling as if his heart were blocking it. 'Who are you? Is my mum there? Mrs Spivey?'

'Just a moment please,' the voice said.

He knew in an instant that his dad was dead. It was probably a paramedic who'd answered the phone. She'd be bringing his mum to the phone now. A paramedic meant it had been sudden. Had he . . . ? Oh God . . . He'd killed himself, hadn't he? Destroyed himself in a final selfish act . . .

'Adrian Brown?' a new voice said. A man's.

'Yes.'

'Where are you, son?'

'I'm on my way home. I'm in a cab. What's happened?'

'My name is Detective Sergeant Chambers,' he said.

'Just tell me what's happened? Where's my mum? Is it—'

'Your parents are fine,' he said, soothing now. 'But there's been an incident, I'm afraid. Your mum was looking after a little girl this afternoon. She was playing in the garden and she's gone missing. We think she might have been taken.'

'Rachel?'

'Someone will explain when you get here.'

'OK,' he said, uselessly, and hung up, reeling with a mix of relief and horror.

There was a cordon across the end of his road, and police cars everywhere. Other cars filled the road and pavements on this side of the barrier too.

He explained to a female officer who he was, and she let him through. Along the street, people stood in little groups, watching with anxious faces.

His mum and dad's door stood open, and it looked as if every possible light in the house was on, despite it still being daylight.

For a dizzying second it was a December night in 1986 again. So many people, so many concerned faces, and dazzling lights. Except then it had been dark.

'You can't come in here,' a woman said, striding down the garden path to the gate.

'I live here,' he told her.

'Name?'

He told her. 'My mum—'

'Your mum and dad are next door.' She pointed up the street, to number 8.

Not Fiona's house, then. That was number 4.

He hurried up the path of number 8 and rang the doorbell.

The door opened. 'Can I help?' Another officer. A man this time.

'I want to see Mrs Spivey,' he said. 'I'm her son.'

The man closed the door in his face, then opened it again a few seconds later. His mum came to the door, hands out.

'My boy!' She held his face. 'My baby . . .'

Her face was bone white, gaunt, utterly stricken. She was shaking.

'Mum,' he said, and she folded him into her arms.

'Best to come back inside, madam.' The man who'd opened the door to him waved them into the living room.

The owners of number 8, Ray and Jean Frampton, were perched together on a low sofa near the window, looking ashen.

Jean Frampton mumbled a greeting.

A woman's sudden shout sounded from somewhere else in the house. It rose to a scream.

'Fiona's in the kitchen,' Ray Frampton told him.

'Beside herself,' Jean said. 'Have a seat, Adrian, love.'

He sat beside his mum.

'Where's Dad?' he said.

'Helping the police,' his mum said. 'He's showing them the back lane and the field where the children sometimes play.' She started to cry.

'What happened?' he asked her.

'She was playing outside,' she said, wiping at her eyes. 'In the garden. It was about three o'clock. I was ironing in the kitchen.

The door went and I answered it, and it was the window cleaner for his money. When I came back I looked into the garden, and I couldn't see her – and I panicked.' She said this to the room. Heads nodded, sagely. They'd heard it already. 'I looked outside. I thought she could be hiding, then I saw the gate to the lane was open. It was locked when I checked in the morning. I always lock it. I'm sure I did this time. Oh, Rachel . . .'

She took Adrian's hand and squeezed it hard, so that the bones squashed together.

'They've looked everywhere. In the house. In the attic. In all the neighbours' gardens. Houses, too.'

He looked at the clock on the mantelpiece. 5.10 p.m. Two hours since it had happened.

'Why were you at home?' he said. 'Why weren't you at work?'

'I was so worried about . . . about *you*. I called in sick yesterday and today. I wanted to be here, in case . . . in case you came home.'

He felt himself redden, with shame and pity. Then a thought occurred to him. 'But you ended up looking after Fiona's kid?'

'Yes, but . . . I said I didn't mind . . .'

'For God's sake, Mum,' he said. 'It's not your *job*.'

'I know. I wish I'd . . . I wish I'd never said I'd . . . Oh, God, how will I ever forgive myself if something's happened to her?'

An overweight, older police officer came into the room.

'Adrian Brown?' he said.

'That's right.'

'And where've you been today, young man?'

'In town,' he said, irritated. What did it matter where he'd been?

'You stayed out last night, I understand.'

'I was at a friend's. In Hebden Bridge.'

'You haven't been back here since when?'

'Since Wednesday teatime.'

He nodded, glancing at Adrian's mum. He wondered what she'd told them.

'You knew this little girl?' the man asked.

'I see her about. I mean, she lives next door. I haven't ever talked to her or anything.'

'You'd recognise her.'

'Yeah. 'Course.'

Another scream from the back of the house, followed by sobbing, and the sound of something falling or being struck. Soothing voices grew louder. He heard Fiona Miller's words rising above them: '*Where's my baby?*'

He looked round the room. At the stricken Framptons, at the fat policeman, and his mum.

'I don't know what you want me to do,' he said to his mum.

'I wanted you here, that's all. I needed to see you,' she said, crushing his hand again, then hugging him and sobbing into his shoulder. 'To know you were safe.'

'Should I be helping or something?' he asked the policeman.

'Not just now, young man,' he said. 'At some point maybe. We might recruit residents to assist us in a search, but for the time being we'd ask you to sit tight.'

'If you don't really need me,' he said, trying not to sound grumpy, 'I was supposed to be meeting people . . . only, well . . . I'm just going to be sitting here, aren't I?'

'Please don't go, baby,' his mum said.

There were new voices from the hallway, including a man's, raised in anger.

'In there, is he?'

Footsteps, then the door flew open. A thin man in a black

polo neck and black trousers glared around the room. Adrian didn't recognise him.

The Framptons looked terrified.

'Can I help you, sir?' the fat policeman said, getting up with some difficulty.

'You Adrian?' the man said, eyeballing him.

The stranger came into the room. Came right up to him.

'What you been doing to our Stephen, eh?' he demanded, a vein standing out on his forehead.

Adrian froze in horror.

'Sir,' the policeman said, 'can I ask you to—'

'No, you bloody can't!' the man said. 'I want a word with this little pervert.'

'What are you talking about?' his mum gasped, clutching his arm as if for reassurance.

'You his mother?' the man demanded.

'Yes, I—'

'You poor cow.'

'Sir, please!' the policeman began. 'This isn't the time or the place.'

The Framptons were up now, too, Mr Frampton making a desperate and utterly pointless appeasing gesture with his hands.

'Faggot for a son,' the man said to his mum.

'Wha— . . . ?'

'Tried to rape my nephew. My wife caught him at it. Poor Stephen.'

'Mum,' Adrian began, struggling for breath, 'don't listen to him. I can . . . He's mad!' He looked at the man. 'I don't know what you're—'

'Don't you, indeed? Well, my Jill's out in the car just there. Let her come in here and tell everyone what she saw! Stephen's with her, too, and he'll testify to—'

'What's going on?' Adrian's dad said from the doorway. 'Adrian?'

'*Oh, Christ . . .*' He looked at the floor. Hoped it might open up, or a comet might strike – whichever would end this sooner.

'What are you saying to my lad?' his dad said.

'Oh, right,' the man said, turning on his dad. 'And here's the fella that spawned the faggot. One yourself, are you?'

'Sir!' the fat policeman said, and put a firm hand on the man's upper arm.

'Get your hands off me!'

People were crowding into the room now, some in uniform. Adrian staggered slightly, landing against a panicky-looking Mrs Frampton. He looked at his mum, whose face was contorted with confusion.

'Baby?' she said.

'It's true, Mum,' he said. 'It's true.'

His dad stared at him.

'I'm gay.' Time juddered to a halt. Everything froze. 'I'm sorry. That's just how it is.'

The room seemed to fold in on itself. And yet they were all still staring, faces bewildered, dismayed.

Ste's uncle smirked in triumph. 'I knew it,' he said.

'I don't know what Ste's told you,' Adrian said to him, 'but you can tell him from me that I understand. I understand *completely.*'

The man stepped forwards and raised an arm, pointing a finger only inches from Adrian's face. 'You stay away from that boy, you little queer,' he said. 'Ste likes girls. He's *sporty.*'

'Fine,' Adrian said, chuckling at the weirdness of the assertion. 'Fine by me.'

'Get yourself checked as well,' the man said. '*Get tested*.' He turned to Adrian's dad, who looked ashen and exhausted, but not angry. 'Don't know why you let him stay under your roof,' he said.

'Piss off,' his dad said to the man.

The man lifted his chin. 'I beg your pardon?'

'Out of here, thank you very much,' another police officer said, and suddenly arms were around the man, drawing him slowly and firmly from the room.

'Baby?' his mum cried.

'I'm going out,' he told her, not meeting her eyes.

'But—'

'I want to be on my own,' he said.

She dropped her own eyes, and retreated. Mrs Frampton put a hand on her arm.

He passed his dad, eyes down.

'Son . . .' he began, clearing his throat. But Adrian pushed past.

The air outside was cold and wonderful. The police were escorting Ste's uncle to a waiting BMW. He spotted Auntie Jill in the passenger seat, glaring back at him. He waved then gave her a middle finger.

Down the street, through the cordon and away from the mêlée, he lit a cigarette and smoked it with abandon. *Gay abandon*, he thought to himself, and started to snigger, giggling like a loony as far as the end of the street.

Of course he hoped they'd find Rachel. He might not like the kid – might resent her feckless mother – but he didn't want her to have been *kidnapped*. But right now he had enough problems of his own to deal with. He meant to get into town and call Gav and then, perhaps, Sheila. But before that, he needed to *think*.

A car was turning the corner and pulled quickly in, bumping the kerb beside him. A man in a suit got out. He recognised him at once.

'Mr Brown?' DC Jamie Clark said, stepping up to face him.

'Oh, for fuck's sake, *what*?' Adrian barked.

'We'd like to ask you some questions,' the officer said, 'relating to the murder of Mrs Edna Wormley.'

55

Adrian wasn't under arrest, merely helping them with their enquiries. He was free to leave at any time. They explained this more than once, but in tones heavy with implication: he was in dangerous water, and would do well to cooperate.

He told himself to be careful – more careful than he'd ever been in his life. They'd sift any 'help' he gave them for the tiniest thing they could use to catch him out. And then where would he be?

In a cell, probably.

There were two of them: DC Jamie Clark, and the woman sergeant who'd accompanied Clark to the *Advertiser* the week before, DS Claire Sanders.

'Should we let anyone know you're here?' Clark said, once they were in the grey windowless room in the bowels of High Calder's police station.

Adrian thought about it. 'No,' he said. Then added, 'Unless you're planning to keep me here for days, that is.'

'We're not keeping you here, Mr Brown,' Claire Sanders said. 'You're here voluntarily, as we have explained.'

'And if I get up and walk out – what then?'

'Then we might decide it's in the interests of our investigation to detain you,' Clark said flatly. He'd taken out a notepad and pen.

'And then I can have a solicitor, right?'

'You can have a solicitor now,' Sanders said, 'if you feel you need one.'

'No,' he said carefully. 'I'm fine.'

'Noted,' Clark said, and wrote something on his pad.

Adrian didn't speak, but instead monitored his breathing, focusing hard, determined to hold himself together and remain unruffled – on the outside, at least. The truth was, he was jangled, and his brain felt like Coke when you shook the bottle. His stomach gave a giddy flip every time he remembered he'd told his parents he was gay. Not just his parents: loads of neighbours and half the police force, too.

He hadn't managed it very well, had he? In fact, he hadn't managed it at all. Just pulled out the pin and lobbed the grenade.

Well, fuck it. It had to happen sometime. Anyway, it was too late now. He wondered what his parents were saying and doing. His dad would no doubt have shut himself away, to stew in a silent rage, sobbing and rocking, as he had the night of the kidnap, while his mum . . . his mum would be holding it together – for Fiona and missing Rachel – while inside, another seam would be coming gently apart.

He felt a wobble – the kind that could culminate in tears – and swallowed, hard. He had to focus. That was everything now.

'Where were you today, Mr Brown?' DS Claire Sanders asked him, matter-of-fact.

'Today? Because of Rachel, you mean?'

She said nothing. Just waited.

'I was in Bradford in the afternoon.'

'Times,' Clark said. 'Start from when you woke up this morning.'

He told them he'd stayed at a friend's in Hebden Bridge. They asked why he was staying there. Because he'd rowed with his parents, he said, and reminded them he was eighteen and could do, and go, where he liked.

'Please try and be helpful,' Sanders warned him in a low voice. 'We'll need the name of the friend.'

'Why?'

'To check your whereabouts,' she said.

Gritting his teeth, he gave them Gav's name and Denise and Sandra's number. God knows what they'd think of him when the police called . . .

They asked about his trip to Bradford.

'I went to meet Sheila Hargreaves. She wanted to see me.'

'What about?'

'Stuff.'

Clark looked baleful, but was apparently going to let it slide – for now.

'What time did you get to the studios?' Clark asked, after several minutes of pressing.

'Can't remember. They'll know. I had to sign in.'

'Roughly,' Sanders said.

'Three.'

'And how long were you there?'

'Dunno. Half an hour.'

'And after that?'

'I went to my mate's house.' He looked at them in turn,

then, eyes on Clark, said, 'For a shag.'

Clark's eyes widened. Adrian smirked to himself.

He outlined what happened next, watching them carefully, darkly enjoying himself as he recounted Auntie Jill's reaction. Then he told them about Yvonne's call to say his mum was trying to get hold of him.

'Then the shit hit the fan,' he said, and he recounted what happened in the Framptons' front room.

Sanders was impassive, but Clark listened intently. Was there a degree of sympathy in his eyes – in the way he bit his lip – when Adrian recounted Auntie Jill's husband calling him a 'faggot'?

'I didn't take Rachel,' Adrian told them. 'Why would I?'

'But you did kill Edna Wormley, didn't you?' Sanders said.

'No, of course not.'

'You killed her because she knew you'd kidnapped Sarah Barrett—'

'*What?*'

'She accosted you but you walked off, so she went to the Jester pub to find you and you killed her. You took evidence from her handbag.'

'No, I didn't.' He shrugged. He felt calmer than he might have expected to. Cool like marble. 'Anyway, she was looking for a woman. She talked about "her" in her diary. I don't believe you think it was me,' he said. 'You have no evidence. If you did, you'd have arrested me.' He raised his eyebrows. 'Why don't you just ask me what you want to know, and then you can try to find out who's really doing this?'

She said nothing. She and Clark exchanged glances.

'I'm happy to help you,' he went on. 'If you want my help, that is. If you're not going to play stupid games where you try to bully me into admitting something I haven't done, just so you can say you're "making progress".'

'Do you think that's what this is about?' Sanders said.

'Actually, I have no idea what this is about.'

Sanders raised her eyebrows. Clark narrowed his eyes. Adrian met his gaze and held it.

Stalemate, he told himself.

'Stop the bullshit,' he said, 'and I'll talk.'

Sanders turned to her colleague. 'I need coffee,' she said.

'Me too,' Clark said, exhaling.

'Mr Brown?' she said, breezily.

'Black, please,' he said. 'Extra strong. Oh, and I'd quite like to make a phone call – if that's all right with you.'

Coffee warmed the atmosphere a little. Through its steam, he told them about the evening in December 1986 when he was taken by a man who might or might not have been the Lollipop Man. They listened intently, but without once giving away whether they already knew about it. He told them that was how he knew Sheila – that she'd interviewed him and his parents in the days after the kidnap.

Then he talked about Mrs Wormley.

'The way she talked – it was sinister,' he said. 'I felt uncomfortable about the whole thing. But, at the same time . . . she did seem to *care*. At one point she was nearly crying.'

He explained how – several hours later and extremely drunk – he'd stumbled over the old woman's body, and rooted in her bag for the letter, only to find it wasn't there.

'Next day, when you came to the office, I . . . I panicked. I thought you'd know it was me who'd called you and arrest me or something. Or that you'd think I'd killed her.'

'You conned your way into Mrs Wormley's flat,' Clark said. He told them about that.

'So you found these papers,' Clark said after a moment, 'and then you spoke to Sheila Hargreaves?'

'I realised I needed help.'

'You went to a TV presenter you'd met once before, years ago, rather than come to us?'

'Yeah, but it's a bit more complicated than that. She'd worked out what I'd been up to. She came and found me. I trusted her. I didn't trust you.'

'May we ask why?' Sanders said, sounding a little peeved.

'I thought you'd go straight to my mum and dad and tell them I'd been at the Jester. You lot don't exactly have a good reputation for discretion.'

Sanders said nothing. Adrian eyeballed Clark, who at least had the good grace to look away.

'It doesn't matter now, though,' he said dismally. 'They know everything. Ste's relatives have seen to that.'

'So you and Sheila Hargreaves are "on the case",' Clark said snidely. 'Along with your chum?'

Adrian didn't reply.

'Mr Brown . . .' Sanders pressed.

'What?' he said. 'I didn't hurt anybody. I didn't kidnap Sarah Barrett or Rachel Miller, and I didn't kill Mrs Wormley. And I don't know what's happened to Li— to Phil Daly, either. I only—' His voice cracked a little. 'I only wanted to help. To *do the right thing*. Look, I've told you what I know, and I know Sheila gave you the diary. Everything you need's in there. The phone number, the link to the pub. The fact Mrs Wormley was following a woman. I don't know what else I can tell you.'

He felt exhausted. Physically and emotionally drained. But

also, unexpectedly, untouchable. They couldn't make him feel any worse than he did already. It was oddly liberating.

'Over to you now, isn't it?' he said.

He looked at his watch and rose from his chair, zipping up his jacket. Their eyebrows went up in astonishment.

'My lift'll be arriving any minute, so I'm going to leave. If you want to keep me you'll need to arrest me.' He added quietly, 'I don't think you will, though, will you?'

56

It was dusk when he emerged from the police station. He felt a burst of relief to see Sheila was already there, her MG parked right outside when he came out of the main door. She spotted him and waved.

'All OK?' she said, as he fell into the low passenger seat and reached for the seatbelt.

'I think so.' He sighed and shut his eyes, feeling the tension leak from him.

'It wasn't me who gave them your name,' she said, starting the engine. 'They asked me, more than once, but I didn't tell them – honestly.'

'I know,' he said, believing her. 'It was only a matter of time. Clark's been after me for a week.'

'They might be watching us,' she said, peering past him, at the gloomy edifice that was the police station. 'I'll drive round the corner.'

She took a left, then a right, until they were in a quiet, elegant street of legal offices, shut up and dark at this hour on a Friday.

'I told them everything,' he said, when they were parked again. 'I also told them you were helping me. Hope you don't mind.'

'I don't,' she said. 'Adrian, when you say you told them "everything". . . '

'I've no reason not to – not now, anyway.' And he told her about Ste's uncle. 'So that's that, isn't it?' he said, dismally.

'Yes,' she said, gently. 'I suppose it is. It'll be all right, you know. It generally is.'

'Yeah, well . . . Shame it had to be in front of half the town and a load of coppers.'

She frowned. 'Coppers?'

'Yeah. Didn't you . . . don't you know what's happened?' He explained about Rachel.

She looked at him in amazement. 'I'd heard that a girl was missing, but I didn't realise it was your mum who . . .'

'Funny "coincidence", isn't it?'

They looked at each other.

'I take it they haven't found her yet,' he said.

'No. I had the news on while I was driving over here. They've got police officers from three counties and more coming from Greater Manchester. Sniffer dogs, the lot.'

'It won't make any difference.'

'We need to hope . . . Do you want me to take you somewhere? Your friend's place in Hebden Bridge, or . . . do you want to come to mine? My friend Jeanette is going to come over. She's been helping me with some research into this business. She's the one who found the photograph of Edward Proctor. I think you'd like each other. She'll probably ask you for an exclusive interview, though – just to warn you.'

'I want to go to the Jester,' he said.

She was silent.

'You think I should steer clear, don't you?' he said.

'I think you should,' she said, looking at him the way his mum did: with a face full of worry.

'I need to do *something*. And that place is at the heart of it. Mrs Wormley thought so.'

She looked ahead, thinking about it. After a while she nodded. 'OK,' she said, starting to drive. 'That doesn't mean I like it. You'll need to direct me.'

57

The ring road should have been the quickest way, but traffic was sluggish and they found themselves in a jam.

Sheila turned off the engine. Adrian began to feel cold, in spite of his thick jacket.

'I was thinking about the coats,' he told her in the ticking silence. 'About what I remember.'

'Oh?'

'The lady who found me – the one who brought me back to my mum and dad – she was wearing a brown coat.'

'That's right.'

'There was a woman in a blue coat, too,' he said, his mouth dry. '*Another* woman. She took me back into town and made sure someone else – a woman who happened to be wearing a *brown* coat – returned me to my parents. It's obvious, isn't it? Two different women. I must have tried to explain, except I couldn't articulate it.'

'Tell me more about the van.' Her voice was urgent.

'There isn't much to say. The woman in the blue coat drove me back into town in a van, and . . . I think it was the same van the man had taken me away in.'

She gaped at him. 'Adrian, this is astonishing.'

He didn't answer, but looked ahead, focused on the bumper of the car in front of them in the jam, though his mind's eye was away in the past, seeing a bony hand clutching a gearstick.

'The woman in the blue coat knew the Lollipop Man,' he said, feeling something click into place. He turned and looked at Sheila. 'She knew him, and she knew what he'd done, and . . . she wasn't having it, so she rescued me. The woman in the blue coat saved my life.'

A minute passed. The traffic jam felt like a neutral space, suspended in time.

'Could you describe her?' Sheila asked him.

'Maybe. I tried to at the time, didn't I? Except my description didn't match the description of the woman they'd all seen me with. The woman in the blue coat was thin and old. I don't know how old. Seventy, maybe. And she was poor because her tights had holes in them and her shoes were old and coming apart.'

'She wasn't with him when he took you? Is that what you're saying?'

'I think he took me somewhere, and she was there when we arrived. Then she drove me back and we left him behind.'

The traffic slowly began to move, lights coming on as engines restarted. Brake lights blinked like red eyes all around them.

'We need to talk about this properly.' She put the car in gear. 'I want Jeanette to hear it too, then we can decide what to do with the information.' She bit a knuckle. 'Are you sure you won't come back to mine? We can get something to eat and discuss it.'

'I want to be at the pub.'

He needed to be among his friends and familiar faces. To think long and hard about who it could possibly be. Who 'she' might be – although he was starting to have an idea about that . . .

Sheila had a point, though, didn't she? There were important things to consider and discuss. And time was against them, especially now another child was missing.

'Adrian . . . ?'

They were moving again, slowly.

'Come with me,' he said. 'Come to the Jester. Your friend could come, too. It's really important for me to be there. I don't know why. It just is.'

58

The Jester glowed at the far end of the dark towpath, its sandstone walls gold in the lamplight. Flickering rainbow lights played behind the frosted windows and disco music pulsed from within.

But its warm promise only made the darkness between here and there even more sinister. The towpath was no better lit than it had been the night he'd stumbled over Mrs Wormley's body. The canal gleamed blackly between the cliff faces of the derelict wharfing houses, smelling stale and unhealthy.

'Do you come down here alone?' Sheila asked in a whisper.

'Yeah. But normally there aren't murderers. Watch your step. There are big hooks on the edge of the canal – I think they used to tie the barges to them.'

'Show me where you found her.'

'Just there.' He pointed.

'You must have been terrified.' She was holding tightly on to his arm and he realised how frightened she was.

'I was drunk,' he said. 'I wasn't thinking straight. I thought I heard him – the attacker, I mean. I went for him but banged my head.'

'Someone's left flowers,' she said.

He peered through the dark. She was right. Cellophane glittered dully in the pub's reflected light.

'Have you got a torch?' he asked.

She went into her handbag, and handed him a torch that was like a pencil but shone brightly.

He illuminated two bunches of flowers in plastic cones, with Asda stickers still attached, and a bigger, nicer wreath. It was the labels he was interested in. The label on the wreath read, *To Mam (Edna), Love Sharon + Kids + Kenny + Violet + Barkly*. The label on the first of the two bunches read simply, *Love from Milly and Sid*. The third bunch bore a longer message: *For Edna*, it said, *Colleague and friend. From Cindy and the Parkview girls xxx*

'Parkview,' he said to Sheila. 'That must be where she worked. We should write it down.'

'Better than that,' Sheila said. 'Give me the torch.' She took it, and knelt, keeping the hem of her coat off the cobbles. She stood up and handed him the label, neatly torn from the plastic wrapping.

'Put it somewhere safe,' she said. She turned off her torch and dropped it back in her bag.

The pub was half empty and there was no one else waiting to be served. Damien turned and saw Sheila and his mouth fell open.

'Your Majesty!' he intoned.

'What do you want to drink?' Adrian asked her, ignoring Damien.

'No, I'm buying,' she said, and went into her bag. 'A pineapple juice and lemonade for me, please,' she said with a huge smile.

'Certainly, ma'am!' Damien cooed.

'Sweet of you,' Sheila said, matching him camp for camp.

'Adrian?' she said.

'Coke please. Full fat. No ice.'

'This isn't a temperance house, you know,' Damien said, pulling the lid off a bottle of pineapple mixer. 'You're still expected to have fun, murders or no murders.'

'And I'm sure we will,' Sheila said, demurely.

Damien took her money and handed Adrian his Coke, making a face that said, 'Get you, eh?'

'Over here's usually quieter,' he told her and led her to the nook beside the fruit machine, ignoring the craning necks and open mouths as people realised who was in their midst. 'Is this your first time?'

'First time?'

'In a gay pub.'

'Goodness, no! I've been out on the scene all over the country,' she said. 'Back in the eighties. My friend Charlie was gay. We went to all the best nightclubs – London, Manchester, Leeds.'

'Leeds?'

'Oh, yes. I even went to the Old Penny.'

'Jesus . . .'

'I know. They didn't have a ladies' loo. There wasn't even a toilet: just a sort of wall for the boys. When I needed to go I had to nip to the pub next door.'

He was laughing, but there was a fly in the ointment: a delicate use of the past tense.

'What happened to your friend?' he said, carefully.

'Charlie died.' It was almost a whisper. 'It's been eleven years.'

'Sorry.'

'He was one of the very first – in this country at least.'

He nodded, eyes down, squirming inside.

'I still miss him.' She smiled, looking around her. 'He'd love it in here,' she said. 'Anywhere bright and loud.'

A chilly prickle crept up his back and over his shoulders.

'You do take care of yourself, don't you?' she said now. 'I feel awful asking that, but I've seen it. You must be very careful.'

'Yeah,' he said, gruffly, resenting the question, but resenting his own discomfort even more. He breathed, and reminded himself she meant well.

'It's complicated with your mum and dad, isn't it?' she said, changing from one uncomfortable topic to another.

'Just a bit.' It was the understatement of the year.

'They love you very much, Adrian. I saw that when I interviewed you all those years ago. They were so frightened. They thought they'd lost their precious child.'

'Mmm . . .' He felt uncomfortable. Painfully so. He gripped his Coke glass, something solid to hang on to. Droplets of condensation squeezed between his fingers.

'When I came to your house earlier this week, you'd been arguing with them, and I could see the pain in their faces. They love you.'

'My mum does,' he admitted.

'Your dad, too.'

'I don't think so.'

She peered at him for a moment.

'You said the other night that you thought he blamed you for the kidnap. That he was ashamed of you and couldn't forgive you. I was very shocked when you said that. What did you mean?'

He rotated the glass on the mat.

'He thought it was my fault,' he said, slowly. He looked up at her and smiled ruefully. The smile became a cynical laugh. 'Because of my hair.'

'Your *hair*?' She stared, uncomprehending, as if he might be pulling her leg.

'I had long hair. Longer than it is now. I didn't like getting it cut and I said to Mum that I wanted it long. She gave in. My dad hated it. When I got kidnapped – he said the kidnapper must have made a mistake. He took girls. My dad said he took me because I had a girl's haircut.'

She looked horrified. Good. She was right to be.

'I once heard him tell Mum that if I had my hair like that I might . . . grow up "funny". I was *ten-years-old*. Can you believe it?'

'Adrian, that's . . .'

'Deranged? Sadistic? And that night, after everyone had gone – all the neighbours, the police . . . he and my mum had a screaming row about it. He said it was Mum's fault for letting me get my own way. Then he dragged me up the stairs into the bathroom and locked the door. My mum was outside, screaming to be let in. He had scissors with him. Big ones from the kitchen. He ripped my jumper and T-shirt off and set about cutting my hair. He *sheared* me.'

'My God.'

'And all the time he was doing it he was crying. Saying over and over, "What will people think?" and "What will they say?" Thinking of himself, you see: what would people say about a father who let his son go around with a girl's haircut? Do you remember when you interviewed me? I was wearing a baseball cap. They had to put that on me because by that time I was half bald.'

'Oh, Adrian . . .' She was holding his hand tight in her own. He could feel her trembling.

'It's why they changed my name too. Adrian was my middle name and Brown was my mum's surname. That was my dad's idea. He didn't want people knowing who I was. He had this idea of moving us out of the area too, but then he lost his work and we were stuck.'

'I'm so sorry,' Sheila said.

'So you see, what he found out tonight – that will be my fault too. Confirmation of what he suspected nearly eight years ago. To him it's nothing to do with "nature". It's just something else I've done on purpose, to humiliate him.' He retrieved his hand from her grip and sat up. 'I'll be OK,' he said. 'I'm pretty tough really.'

As he took a drink of his Coke, something occurred to him. Something amazing. A revelation.

'Maybe the Lollipop Man *did* think I was a girl,' he said and put down his glass. 'He wouldn't have had much time to pick a kid, would he? He took me, bundled me into his van and drove me away. And then, when we got to wherever it was, he realised that he'd made a mistake. In that case, the woman in the blue coat didn't *rescue* me. He handed me to her to . . . to "take me back to the shop".' He shook his head. 'This is such a headfuck.'

'We might never know what really happened, or why,' she said in a low voice.

Something else occurred to him now. Something so momentous his skin tingled and the hairs on his arms and neck rose.

'The fact he took *me*,' he began, carefully, 'means he didn't take a girl. If he had he'd have kept her, wouldn't he – and killed her?'

'Probably.'

'Which means I saved someone's life,' he said. 'There's someone – a girl, probably about my age – who was there at the cinema that night, walking around now, who otherwise . . .'

She was smiling at him gently. 'Have you really only just realised that? The fact he took you was nothing for you to be ashamed of. You were an accidental hero.'

59

By the time Sheila came back from the bar with more drinks the place was getting busy. Bev was there now, serving alongside Damien. Elaine darted about the pub, stacking empties into towers that she cradled against her shoulder, then nipping behind the bar to stack the dishwasher.

He spotted a face that looked familiar: pale and elfin, framed by black hair, and belonging to a man in his early twenties who was heading for the loos. He couldn't place him, but he'd seen him before.

'Oh good, you've got a table,' a mousy, sharp-faced little woman said, arriving at their table in a gale of energy. 'Traffic's a mess.'

'Jeanette,' Sheila said, and got up to embrace her. 'I'd like you to meet my friend Adrian.'

'Well, hello, Adrian,' Jeanette said, extending a narrow bony hand.

'Hi.'

Jeanette looked to be brimming with energy. She bit her lip and squinted hard at Adrian's face, as if she was trying to read his innermost thoughts, then nodded, satisfied about something.

'Tomato juice, is it?' Sheila asked her.

'Please.'

Someone stepped past them and Sheila's face – her whole demeanour, in fact – changed in an instant. It was the slight man with the pale, elfin face. Sheila stared after him, mouth open, as if unaware that shock showed so plainly on her face. He hadn't spotted her, but weaved through the customers to the cigarette machine, and began feeding it coins.

'I'm sorry,' she said, seeming to come back into the moment.

'Do you know him?' he asked her.

'Yes,' she said quietly, eyes on Elf Man's back. She gave him a bright but unconvincing smile. She seemed nervous about going to the bar but pushed through the crowd anyway.

'Any news of the little girl?' Sheila asked when she returned with Jeanette's drink. She seemed relieved to sit down, though stole a glance over her shoulder.

'Not that I've heard,' Jeanette said, sipping her tomato juice. 'But it's a bit more promising, what with the witnesses, and—'

'Witnesses?'

'Yes. Two young boys kicking a ball about at the end of the road saw a small blue car – possibly a Fiat – park round the corner, and a woman in a black coat with the hood up get out and cross the road. They didn't see her go into the street but there's an alleyway that runs up behind the gardens.'

Adrian and Sheila exchanged glances. Jeanette didn't know it, but she was describing his street. He wondered who the witnesses were. The Sullivan twins? They were always out with bikes or skateboards, or booting balls into neighbours' windows.

'They saw her return a few minutes later with a girl, dragging her by the arm. She shoved her into the back of the car and sped off towards the town.'

'A Fiat?' Sheila said.

'An E-reg, and then an eight or a three – the boys are at odds about that. One thinks there was a P in it, too. They're not naming the boys, by the way. Talking about putting them in a hotel with their parents. Right now they're in danger from whoever's doing this. Honestly, what was she thinking? Taking a child in broad daylight. It's insane. The call to the radio station was so unguarded, too. It's almost as if she wants to be caught.'

'What call to the radio station?' Adrian asked.

'A woman rang Radio Aire this lunchtime,' Jeanette said, 'saying she was about to take another little girl.'

'What?' He was aghast.

Jeanette explained.

'Did the boys describe the woman?' Sheila asked Jeanette now.

'They tried to. Not very tall, quite thin, very white hands, apparently – she wasn't wearing gloves. They didn't get a good look at her face.'

'What about her hair?'

'Had her hood up the whole time, but they thought she had brown hair. The woman who took Sarah Barrett had blonde hair, and lots of it, according to the kid who saw her. There's a chance she's dyed it since then, of course.'

Adrian nodded, thoughts whirling. He looked over to the bar, where Damien was having trouble unscrewing a giant bottle of wine. Bev watched him, hands on hips, shaking her head in mock despair. Elf Man was perched on the stool at the end, in Little Phil's favourite spot, his head in his hands – and in a flash Adrian remembered who he was. He was the man who'd been there last week, on his own then, as now, sitting sobbing in a corner – the one he'd thought might be ill.

'The police sound relatively hopeful,' Jeanette said, wiping away a moustache of tomato juice. 'Chief Constable's concentrating all resources for the next twenty-four hours.'

'I should be out there,' Sheila said. 'Jeanette – what can we do?'

'We've plenty to be doing, love,' Jeanette said, and delved into her bag for a notebook and pen.

Sheila's eyes were on Elf Man's back again.

'Who is he?' Adrian asked her quietly, unable to help himself.

She took a deep breath, and said, 'Someone from the past. His name's Colin Joseph. Best that he doesn't see me.'

An arm came past Adrian's head for his empty glass.

'All right?' It was Elaine.

'Yeah, you?'

'Kind of. Debs is in bits. You know they found Little Phil's jacket? Word is it was covered in blood.'

'Oh God!'

'It was just hooked on the corner of a bench on the main road, over towards the hospital.'

'Jesus.'

'They're looking in the canal at the other end of the tunnel. They've got divers out and everything.'

Adrian swallowed, digesting the news.

'Were you working here the night he went missing?' he asked Elaine now.

'No. Debs was in for a drink, though. She's kicking herself for not keeping an eye on him.' She glanced towards the bar. 'Better get on.'

She moved to the next table and he turned his attention back to Sheila and her friend.

'It's definitely not Beth McGee,' Jeanette was saying.

'Who's Beth McGee?' Adrian asked.

'A charming young lady who procured kids for her paedophile boyfriend. Recently released from jail. I was telling Sheila I finally managed to talk to the kid who saw Sarah Barrett being taken. I showed her the photo of this Miss McGee and she looked at me as if I was mad. She said the woman she saw was thin—'

'Which chimes with the woman the boys described today,' Sheila said.

'Exactly.'

'Right,' Jeanette said smartly, beaming at them. 'Now, are you ready for the really interesting news?'

'Go on.'

'I spent part of my afternoon at Water's End.'

Adrian sat up, eyes on Sheila.

'And?' Sheila said.

'Should be called Dead End, if you ask me. I can't believe people still live down there.'

'Do they?'

'Not at White Cottage. That's a ruin – as are most of the buildings. I had a good poke around. There's a track that runs from the road down the side of White Cottage to a bunch of old outbuildings. There's a cottage at the very end of the track. Old boy lives there. Could see him moving about in the living room, but he must be deaf. I banged on the door and shouted, but he didn't hear me.'

'What did he look like?' Sheila asked.

'Old. Thin. Bent.' She rolled her eyes. 'He's not Teddy Proctor, Sheila. Proctor's dead, whatever your nutty friend says. If you follow the road through the hamlet there's another cottage right at the end there. Old dear in the garden, putting rubbish out. Gave her the fright of her life. We got chatting. I complimented her on her cat, and she invited me in for a cuppa. Anyway, this lady – Violet Evans – turns out she's been there all her life. Born in the cottage in the 1920s and never left. Looked after her parents until they died. Her brother and sister went off and got married – more about the sister later! *Anyway* – I get to asking Violet about Edward Proctor. "Dead as a doornail," she tells me. "I know that," I say, "but I'm interested to hear about him – his family, and that." So she tells me what she knows.

'There've always been Proctors at Water's End, apparently – all very *Cold Comfort Farm*. Teddy came as a baby. His dad Harry was away at sea half the time; came home to find the boy half grown up and a whole heap of trouble.

'Harry died in 1951, leaving Sylvia and Teddy together at White Cottage. Sounds like Sylvia just got on with it. She got some hens and geese and sold their eggs and meat. Teddy was very strange. Not so much half-witted – Violet's description – as lacking a soul. "Nothing behind the eyes," she says.

'A few years later – this was in the 1950s – Sylvia got herself a new man. Chap from a local dairy – Ernie Thirkell, a few years older than her. The two of them got married, and Ernie treated Teddy as part of the package. Even got him work at the dairy, helping load the milk floats during the night.'

He caught Sheila's glance in his direction. So, she'd spotted it too . . . A dairy worker would wear a white coat – like the white coat the Lollipop Man had worn.

'Violet Evans says it was happy families until the early seventies, when Teddy tried to take a child and got arrested. It was in 1973. That's how we got the photo of him. He tried to take a seven-year-old girl, right off the street in Halifax. Chap stepped in and called the law. Teddy was interviewed under caution but no charges were pressed. "All a misunderstanding", apparently. Shocking, I know.

'After that Ernie and Sylvia kept Teddy indoors. Violet Evans says she'd see him peering out of the window, but when she asked about him, Ernie and Sylvia clammed up – or said he was unwell. Violet says she saw him outside just once, shuffling along, and that Sylvia came running out of the house and bundled him back inside. She thought he seemed *drugged*.

'Ernie died in 1985 and after that Teddy was out and about again. Sylvia began to shut herself away. Curtains stayed drawn for weeks at a time. If Violet saw her outside for any reason, she found her bewildered.

'That's how it went on. There were occasional sightings of strange Teddy, going about his business, but very few of Sylvia.

'Teddy died at the end of 1987 – he *did*, Sheila; do you know how hard it would be to fake a death certificate? Sylvia was diagnosed with dementia shortly after that and taken into a home.'

'This doesn't get us very far, though, does it?' Sheila said gloomily. 'I mean, Teddy's dead. We know that he and his mother had a miserable life.'

'The dairy's the key,' Adrian murmured. 'He'd have had a white coat, wouldn't he?'

'Like a lollipop man's uniform,' Sheila said. 'Dee Thompson wrote, without naming him, about the attempt Teddy made to take the child in 1973. According to her, he wore a "milkman's outfit". He could have held on to that coat and used it in 1986, this time disguised as a lollipop man.'

'How would he get the lollipop sign, though?' Jeanette asked.

'They keep them in the schools,' Adrian said. 'The janitors look after them. More than one lollipop, if there are a few crossings by the school.' He caught their frowns. 'I've thought a lot about it, you see.'

'But how would he have got into a school?' Jeanette said.

'Delivering the milk,' Sheila suggested with a shrug. 'If he went back to working at the dairy after Ernie died . . . It's a possibility, isn't it?'

'It's horrible.' Jeanette shook her head.

'Who's the old man that still lives there?' Sheila asked after a minute. 'Violet Evans must know – if there are only the two of them living in the valley.'

'A Mr Desmond Baxter. Some years older than Teddy would have been. Sounds like a very frail gentleman. Violet says he has carers going in from the council every day. Says she's been expecting him to pop off for years.'

'We could check his identity,' Sheila said.

'I already did.' Jeanette smiled. 'I knew you'd ask. He's on the electoral roll: Desmond Geoffrey Baxter, now aged 75. Registered at Water's End for the last nine years. He receives social care visits. Has done since he moved there.'

'OK,' Sheila said, giving a defeated look, 'but I don't see how any of this helps.'

Jeanette smiled a mischievous smile. 'That's because I haven't got to the gold yet.'

'Oh?'

'Violet Evans had an older sister. She left home as a girl, married, and moved to Huddersfield. But a few years ago she moved back to High Calder. Once a month she'd take the bus and walk down into the valley to visit Violet at Water's End.

Bring her some shopping, prescriptions, that kind of thing. She'd stay for a couple of hours.'

'Right . . .'

'Violet got quite tearful, telling me about her . . . because the sister died recently. *She was murdered.*' She watched their confused faces with barely suppressed glee. 'Violet Evans's sister was Edna Wormley.'

They stared, stunned.

'Evans was Mrs Wormley's maiden name,' Adrian murmured. 'There was a copy of her birth certificate in her private papers.'

'That explains her interest in Water's End and Teddy Proctor,' Sheila said.

'She grew up there,' Jeanette said. 'And listen to this: Mrs Wormley last visited her sister on a Tuesday at the end of March. The twenty-ninth, Violet thinks it was. She arrived all excited because she'd met a man standing about in the lane outside White Cottage, taking photos with a camera. She stopped to talk to him and he said he wanted to find out about someone who'd once lived there – Edward Proctor. They talked for some time, and Mrs Wormley was fired up about what he'd told her. She didn't share any details with Violet, but Violet could tell it was important. This man, the one taking the photographs, was an Australian. Violet thinks her sister referred to him as Alan. They'd agreed to talk on the phone. He was going to be in this country for some time.'

'An Australian?' Adrian said, frowning. 'Mrs Wormley had a business card in her papers for an architect in Australia. It seemed so weird, especially because it was an Australian address. And there was another phone number on the back. Handwritten. It started with 61. I'm trying to remember his name. It could have been Alan, but . . . Yes, that's it! *Andrew Allen.* Don't you remember, Sheila? Mrs Wormley had made a note in her diary: A.A. He looked at her, stricken. 'But you gave the folders to the police, didn't you?'

'Yes.'

'We'll need to get them back. Either that, or try to find an architect in Australia with that name. We need to talk to him as soon as possible. He might hold the key.'

A sudden hush fell over the pub. Adrian looked round. Everyone – Bev and Damien behind the bar, Elaine at the hatch, customers at tables and standing – turned to face the door. Adrian half-stood, peering round the fruit machine to see what had caught everyone's attention.

It was Maybe Mary, in uniform, DC Jamie Clark beside her in a suit. Their expressions were stony.

Adrian got up and moved to the end of the bar. Jeanette and Sheila came close behind.

'Friends, we're here with some very serious news,' Maybe Mary said to the attentive faces.

'*Oh, God!*' he heard Debbie cry through the crowd, though he couldn't see her.

'Police divers have discovered the body of a young male in the canal half a mile the other side of the tunnel.'

Cries of horror and dismay erupted in the pub. He heard someone scream, and someone else sobbing. He felt Sheila's hand on his arm.

'We believe it might be the body of Philip Daly. I'd like to ask for a volunteer to make an identification.'

60

The next half hour passed in a haze of tears and horror. An ashen-faced Bev went with the police to identify the body. Debbie sought Adrian out and cried inconsolably, so that his hair was wet. Elaine took her outside for fresh air, which he was relieved about. He simply didn't have the energy to comfort anyone.

Sheila and Jeanette spoke in hushed tones, while Adrian sat in a kind of catatonia.

Behind the bar Damien served drinks, glum-faced, handing over glasses and taking money without making eye contact. The music was off and voices were low.

Elf Man – real name Colin Joseph, the brother of the Lollipop Man's first victim, as Sheila had now explained – remained on his stool at the end of the bar, staring blankly into space. Little Phil's favourite spot: the optimum place to cadge free drinks as people ordered rounds, though Colin Joseph didn't appear interested in such a scheme.

The optimum place for other things, Adrian now realised. For hearing things, or for reading the notices on the board beside the bar.

There, behind Elf Man's head, in the middle of the noticeboard, was the poster for Damien's drag karaoke show, and beside it the police appeal for help finding Sarah Barrett. There were other notices, including items people wanted to sell. And finally a poster offering work: the one Adrian himself had pinned there, advertising for carers to register with his mum's care agency, Hardaker's in Huddersfield. He didn't need to go over and read it. He knew it off by heart.

CARE TO HELP? THEN HELP TO CARE!

Help. The word Mrs Wormley had noted in her diary alongside the phone number of the Jester.

Something clicked in his brain. Help. *Social care.*

Bev was back within thirty minutes. A single nod when she'd come through the door had confirmed everyone's worst fear. The body in the canal was Philip Daly. Adrian watched her as she lifted the hatch and stepped back behind the bar. As she put a hand on Damien's shoulder and whispered something to him. Damien nodded, then swiped a hand across his eyes – at which Bev pulled him into an embrace. At least their stand-off had thawed, and they'd overcome the contretemps about the blonde wig.

Little Phil, from his stool, would have enjoyed a ringside view of any number of staff battles. He might even have—

Adrian gasped and jerked, galvanised by a sudden, shocking realisation.

'Are you all right, Adrian?' Sheila said.

'I'm fine,' he said. 'It's just . . .'

'What?'

'She was here,' he said, his mouth dry as a bone. 'On Tuesday night.'

'Who was here?'

He licked his lips. 'I need to get out of here. Can we go somewhere else? Anywhere?'

61

Sheila's house was enormous: an elongated L-shape in old stone, with floor-to-ceiling windows, and different levels inside: wood, carpets, stone pillars, and everything beautifully lit.

'This is my husband, Alex,' Sheila said.

'Hello,' Adrian said to the thin balding man in cords who met them in the big comfy living room, holding a magazine and looking only mildly taken aback.

'Jeanette's coming too, dear,' she told her husband. 'And, if he's got any sense, Malcolm Struthers will drop by at some point. We'll stay in the kitchen and I promise we won't make a lot of noise.'

'It's close on ten, Sheila, love.'

'There's no need to be sociable,' she told him sweetly. 'Honestly, go to bed. We're trying to do what we can to find this latest little girl. I'll be up when I can.'

'You know best, dear.' Alex Osgood didn't seem in the least bit alarmed that his wife, her friend, a senior police officer and a random teenager were planning to fight crime in his house. They left him reading and went into the roomy kitchen.

Sheila filled the kettle, then they heard the sound of tyres on gravel, and headlights shone in through the window.

Jeanette wiped her feet quickly on the mat before coming in. 'Did you get hold of Malcolm?' she said.

'I did. I told him we have crucial information and evidence of a firm link between Water's End and Mrs Wormley. I asked him to bring the folders of Mrs Wormley's papers. He started asking questions so I rang off. He tried calling me back, but I didn't answer – so I expect him here any minute.'

'Ha!'

A cafetière made, they took seats around the kitchen table.

'Right, young man,' Sheila said to him, hands folded on the table before her. 'Time to spill.'

'It's the barman at the Jester,' he began, feeling inhibited by shame and disloyalty. He knew that once the words were out, there'd be no taking them back. 'Damien – the one who was serving tonight. He does the Sunday night karaoke, in drag. His drag name is Demi Whore.'

Jeanette made an expression of distaste.

'He's quite good – well, if you like that kind of thing. Well, one of Demi's wigs is this big blonde thing. The thing is, it went missing a few weeks ago. Damien was doing his nut about it. He accused Bev of moving his stuff – she's done it in the past, I think. She denied it, but there was a bust-up. Which makes me think . . .'

'What?' Jeanette said.

'What if the woman who took Sarah Barrett wore that wig, as a disguise?'

'She didn't wear a blonde wig when she took Rachel Miller

342

earlier today,' Jeanette said, glancing at Sheila as if to check if her scepticism was shared.

'Well, the wig had been put back, hadn't it?'

'It's a bit of a stretch, Adrian,' Sheila said gently, as she poured the coffee.

'I don't think it is,' he said. 'Little Phil used to sit on the stool at the end of the bar. It was *his spot*. He sat there so people would notice him and buy him drinks. But from there he'd have had a good view of anything that went on behind the bar. He could even have seen into the back room, where the bar staff keep their coats and other belongings. Look, Little Phil was dodgy. He was always selling knock-off cigarettes and DVDs. He'd do anything for money.'

'So you think—'

'He saw someone take the wig, or put it back, and he blackmailed them. He even said he was expecting to come into some money.'

'And got killed for his trouble?' Jeanette said.

'Yes. It's all centred on the Jester, isn't it? Mrs Wormley was going there. She was killed a hundred yards from the front door. The wig going missing *could* be a coincidence, but . . . but now Little Phil's dead.'

'So it's someone who works there?' Jeanette said.

'Or drinks there,' he said. 'Bev's not exactly formal about things. I've seen people go behind the bar and get crisps and leave the money by the till. We all know each other, in the main.'

'Then who?' Sheila said. 'Damien? The wig going missing might have been a bluff.'

'But Little Phil wouldn't have thought twice if he'd seen Damien with the wig, would he?'

He fell silent, his mind returning to ideas he'd begun to develop in the pub. To places he really didn't want to go.

'Then who?'

'I don't know.'

'Liar,' Jeanette said. 'I think you know full well.'

'I don't!'

'Rubbish. Spill, kiddo.'

'Jeanette . . .' Sheila said gently.

Just then, beams from headlights filled the kitchen.

'Malcolm,' Sheila said, standing and heading for the door.

62

'Edna Wormley's sister lives at Water's End?' Malcolm Struthers said, slowly.

'Yes,' Sheila said. 'Mrs Wormley was on the spot. She grew up there. She'd have known the Proctors. If Violet believed Teddy died years ago, then Mrs Wormley probably did too. But then, one day, a few weeks ago – *after* Sarah Barrett went missing – Mrs Wormley was at Water's End to see her sister and she met an Australian man there. A man who told her something. We think – don't we, Adrian? – that this chap's business card was among Mrs Wormley's papers, and we'd like to take a look.'

'Would you indeed?' Sheila judged him beyond tired. He was a husk of a man.

'I remember seeing the card,' Adrian said. 'He was an Australian, and his name was Andrew Allen. There was an address and phone number on the card, but there was also a number written on the back in pen – as though he'd asked her to call him. And Mrs Wormley had written "A.A." in her diary,

I'm sure of it. I remember thinking it was like a code. Like something from *The Famous Five*.'

'*The Famous Five* . . .' Struthers growled.

'Yeah.'

Struthers looked at the three of them in turn, his eyes staying longest on Sheila.

Sheila said softly, 'Isn't it worth a shot, Malcolm?'

'I'm at the end of my tether,' Struthers said quietly, and to no one in the particular – or perhaps to himself. 'I'm lost. I really am. That child is out there somewhere . . .'

'I know,' Sheila whispered.

'To hell with it,' he said, and rose from his seat. 'I'll be back.'

He made good on his promise, and was back from his car in a flash, throwing the two plastic wallets onto the kitchen table.

'Find it,' he said to Adrian, with a nod at the wallets.

Adrian took up the one containing the trivial papers – the papers he'd *thought* were trivial – and tipped the contents onto the table, moving the lists, newsletters and circulars about until he found, and retrieved, what he was looking for: the silver-edged oblong of white card.

Andrew Allen, Architects, RAIA
19 Hosking Place
Sydney NSW 2000
Australia
T: +61 2 9250 6781
F: +61 2 9250 6782
Design for better living

And on the back a phone number in blue biro: *061 434 5672*.
'Here,' he said, and passed it to Struthers.

'An Australian architect in West Yorkshire?' Struthers murmured. 'Why?'

'Exactly,' Adrian said. 'What did he know that Mrs Wormley would find interesting? And why would he ask her, of all people, to phone him? The number on the back must be his home number in Australia, don't you think – in case he wasn't at his office?'

Struthers turned the card and contemplated it.

'No,' he said, after a moment. 'That's not an Australian number. I can see why you'd think it, given the Australia dialling code . . . 061 is Manchester.'

Adrian stared, and reached out for the card. Struthers handed it back to him.

'Maybe he was staying there,' Struthers said. 'Manchester's only twenty miles down the road.'

'Let's call the Manchester number, Malcolm,' Jeanette said.

He hesitated, then said to Sheila, 'Can I use your phone?'

'5672,' said an elderly, middle-class woman's voice, heavy with alarm. 'Who is it, please?'

'Forgive me,' Struthers said into the phone's speaker. 'I know it's late, but this is the police.' He gave his name and rank. 'I was hoping to speak to a Mr Andrew Allen, if he's there.'

'*Andrew?*' the voice said. 'You can't, I'm afraid. He left earlier this week. He was here for the funeral, but he has work, a family, waiting for him. The *police*, did you say? Is it . . . has something happened?'

'Yes,' Struthers said, 'though it's nothing for you or him to worry about. Just something Andrew might have seen while he was here. It is somewhat urgent. You say he's gone home – to Australia?'

'Yes, that's right. Do you have his number there? It'll be Saturday morning there. You should be able to get hold of him.'

'I have an office number for him. If you could give me his home number, that would be very helpful, Mrs . . .'

'*Miss* Allen,' she said. 'I'm Andrew's aunt. My brother was Andrew's late father. Now, give me a moment, would you? I'll find my address book.'

A few minutes later they had the number – and address – of Andrew Allen's home in a suburb of Sydney. Adrian, Sheila and Jeanette watched and listened as Struthers communicated with Allen's wife, Suzie, and established that Andrew was out at the gym. He wasn't sleeping well because of the jet lag, Suzie said. And no, she couldn't say when he'd be back. Did Mr Struthers want to leave a number?

'No,' Struthers said. 'But if you would take a brief message and tell him I'll try him again, that would be very helpful.'

Malcolm hung up.

'The night you came on my programme and we did the appeal,' Sheila said, 'a number of people called the show afterwards. Dee Thompson among them. But there was a man – I'm sure Grace told me he had an Australian accent. Said he might have information but needed to check it and he'd be back in touch if he did.'

'Did he leave a name?'

'No.'

'Did he contact you again?'

'I assume not. It could be him, couldn't it?'

'It could. I need to go, Sheila.'

'But what about—'

'About Andrew Allen? He can wait.'

'Can he?'

'It's nearly midnight,' he said, eyes on the kitchen clock. 'I need to sleep. I'll try him first thing in the morning.'

'But—'

'And I'll tell you what he says,' he said. 'You'll just have to be satisfied with that.'

63

Saturday 16th April, 1994

Adrian asked if he could use Sheila's phone in private.

'Of course,' she said. 'There's an extension in my study. Is there something . . . ?'

'I want to call Gav and ask him to come and get me.'

'Why not take a taxi? I'll pay. It's no—'

'I'd prefer Gav to come. Could you write down your address for me?'

'Of course.' She led him to the study. 'You'll need to tell your friend to look out for the white gateposts. Most people drive straight past.'

Gav answered. He and his mums were still up. Adrian could hear the TV and a voice that sounded like Michael Caine's.

'Hang on a sec,' he said, and Adrian heard the TV noises fade. Then his friend hissed, 'What happened to *you* tonight?'

'Everything,' he said darkly. 'But I'm OK. I'm at Sheila's house. Can you come and get me? I know it's late, but . . . there's something I need to do.'

'Ade, man – are you all right?'

'I'm fine,' he said tersely, then gave Gav Sheila's address. 'Come as quick as you can.'

He returned from the study to find the two women having some kind of silent stand-off beside the trembling kettle. Jeanette was facing Sheila, arms folded and looking mutinous.

Sheila seemed relieved he was back.

'Ah,' she said with false cheer. 'Did you manage to get hold of your friend?'

'He's gonna come.'

'I was just making some tea and then I thought we'd try to find a news programme,' she said, then cast a cross look at her friend. 'Would you like a cup?'

'No, thanks.' More glowering.

The kettle boiled and Jeanette moved away, eyes down. Whatever had happened, or been said, they were both still pissed off about it.

'You can wait with us in the living room,' Sheila said to him, as she passed Jeanette her mug. 'Your friend'll be at least thirty minutes if he's coming from Hebden Bridge.'

''Kay.'

He mooched after them into the vast living room.

Sheila perched on the edge of a cream armchair, and clicked through TV channels, finding no news, and only sport on Sky.

She turned it back to the BBC and loaded up Ceefax.

They waited in silence for the yellow text on the local news pages to appear.

'Here we are,' Sheila said, and read aloud: 'No sign of missing child. Police are appealing for witnesses and information relating to the disappearance of a female child from Bainbridge Gardens, High Calder at around 3 p.m. on Friday. Anyone with information should contact police on the following number . . .'

The page refreshed, showing a new story, this one about an accident at a timber yard in Wakefield.

Adrian checked his watch. It was 12.30 a.m. Gav would be another ten minutes at least.

'Look at this,' Sheila said, when a new page of yellow text materialised on the TV screen. 'Police release details of killer's call.' She looked at her friend.

'That's it,' Jeanette said, sitting up. 'My God, they've gone public with it.'

Sheila read: '*Police have confirmed that they are investigating an anonymous call made to a Leeds radio station on Friday. A female caller claimed she was about to kidnap a child, then hung up. Later on Friday afternoon a seven-year-old child was taken from the garden of a house in High Calder. Witnesses claim they saw a woman leading a child towards a small blue car, possibly with an E-registration plate. Police have made the call available for* – Oh, good grief. This is page 1 of 2. Come on . . .' They waited for the page to change and the new text to load. 'Here we go: available for members of the public to hear. A recording will be played on local and national television and radio over the weekend. Members of the public can also call a special telephone number to hear the call for themselves.'

The page gave the phone number. Jeanette had a notebook out and was scratching it down.

'I can't believe it,' Sheila said, looking at each of them in turn. 'What if it turns out to be a hoax?'

'They know what they're doing,' Jeanette said. 'They're either convinced it's genuine, or they're so bloody desperate they're willing to take the risk. Let's ring it.'

Sheila looked at Adrian.

'I don't want to,' he said.

'But, what if you . . .'

'I'm too tired,' he lied. 'I'll call it tomorrow.'

She watched him uncertainly.

'Adrian . . . there was something you were going to tell us, before Malcolm came.'

'Was there?'

'Yes,' Jeanette broke in. 'You were about to tell us who else could have taken that barman's wig.'

'Oh. Yeah, that . . . No. I don't know.' He looked at his hands, feeling his cheeks burn.

'Adrian . . .' He could feel Sheila's eyes on him, 'if there's something—'

'Please, just leave it,' he said.

A noise from the front of the house.

'A car,' Sheila said, eyeing him cautiously, perhaps not wanting to let him go. 'That'll be your friend.'

'You got *arrested*?' Gav said.

'Well. "Taken in for questioning". Not quite the same thing.'

They were still on the moor road, going slow because Gav didn't like driving at night. 'Kudos for coming out to your folks, though.'

'Cheers,' he said glumly.

'I wondered if it was something like that,' Gav said now.

'What do you mean?'

'You mum phoned my place earlier. Denise talked to her for like *ages*, shut away in the dining room. Wouldn't say what it was about, just that your mum wanted to talk through some stuff.'

'Right . . .'

His feelings were a mess. The idea of his mum calling Denise and Sandra's to talk about him – her newly out son – was both unsettling and oddly reassuring. He'd caused her pain; precipitated a cry for help. But she had asked for help – and quickly. Had perhaps been ready to receive it.

It all felt suddenly, chillingly real. He looked out at the night, at the black nothingness of the moors.

'We're coming to a junction,' Gav said. 'Which way?'

'Left,' Adrian said. 'Then it's a few miles before the roundabout, and you go right.'

'Where are we going, anyway?'

'Place called Paradise Valley,' he said. 'But they were taking the piss when they named it.'

Paradise Valley was nothing like the High Estate. There were no towers here, just long terraces of two-storey 'maisonettes'. Rows and rows of them, stretching away on both sides of the main road, with grass and concrete running between them, and everything floodlit.

'We're looking for Eden Gardens,' he said, and leant forwards, peering hard for street signs, and alternately squinting hard at the *A to Z* in his lap. 'This place is a maze.'

'I thought you said you'd been here before,' Gav said.

'I have, but it was New Year and I was pissed. I think it's left here. There should be a petrol station. Yeah, there it is.'

Gav took the turning and Adrian angled the *A to Z* to catch the streetlight.

'Park anywhere on the left,' he said.

They got out and crept along Eden Gardens, keeping to the shadows and whispering like burglars. The place was dead, eerily quiet, and everything was draped in a light mist that glowed in halos round the streetlamps.

He stopped by an entrance to a stairwell. 'I think this is it,' he said. 'Let me check the name on the door.'

He crept forwards, peering through the darkness.

Gav leant in: 'Allardyce? Who's Allardyce?'

'My friend's granddad.'

'We're visiting someone's *granddad*?'

'No. That's not why I came.' He led Gav back out of the stairwell into the paved area that ran between the rows of flats and headed for a parking area at the far end.

'So what are we doing?' Gav pressed when they were standing among the parked cars.

'Looking for something,' Adrian said.

'Like what?'

'A small blue car. E-reg. I think it's a Fiat.'

Even as he spoke he spotted it.

He pointed and said quietly, 'Say hello to Debbie's Smurfette.'

64

'I left a message and gave her your number,' Jeanette said.

'In that case you'll need to stay,' Sheila said. 'I'm minded to make you sleep on the floor in the study so he wakes you up rather than all of us.'

'Sheila, this is so important . . .'

'It's sneaky. It's betraying Malcolm.'

Jeanette had the grace to look ashamed – a little, anyway.

They'd had a brief but tense set-to in the kitchen while Adrian was making his call, after Jeanette had confessed what she'd done. Peering over Malcolm's shoulder, she'd taken a mental note of Andrew Allen's home number with the intention of calling Australia herself. Sheila had pointed out the potential danger of interfering in the investigation at this stage, which only met with Jeanette's scorn.

As soon as Adrian had left with his friend, Jeanette had taken herself into Sheila's study and made the call.

'I'll sleep anywhere you want me to,' Jeanette told her now.

'So long as I'm in reach of a phone.'

'I'll get you a pillow and some sheets,' Sheila said, and headed upstairs.

She was calmer when she came back. 'Wake me up when he calls,' she said.

Jeanette gave her a small smile. 'He might not, of course. He might think it's some kind of scam. But if he does, I'll come and knock.'

'Don't worry about waking Alex. He wears earplugs. Goodnight, Jeanette.'

It was a little after 1 a.m.

65

'Ring the number, man,' Gav instructed him, for about the eighth time. 'You need to know.'

'You think?'

They were in the large kitchen of Gav's house. The place was cluttered and comforting. The two cats slept in a loose knot on a cushion by the Aga.

'Do it,' Gav said gently. He pushed the portable receiver across the crumb-covered table.

'Fuck it.' He picked up the receiver and dialled the number he'd memorised.

It rang three times, then something clicked.

'Thank you for calling West Yorkshire police,' a taped man's voice said. 'You are about to hear a recording which you may find upsetting. If you believe you know who the voice on the recording belongs to, we ask you to call us without delay on the following number.'

The voice gave a Leeds phone number, then repeated it slowly.

He watched his friend, his heart thumping in his chest. His hands were cold and his mouth bone dry.

Something clicked on the line, and a cheesy-sounding man was speaking: 'And our next caller is Marilyn Hyde calling from Saddleworth – hey, isn't that the wrong side of the Pennines?' He laughed, pleased with his joke. 'Marilyn, you're live on Radio Aire – what's your question?'

'Hello, Johnny,' a deepish female voice said, and Adrian felt a fist close round his heart. 'It was me, Johnny.'

'You, Marilyn? Ha – you'll have to help me, I'm af—'

'I took Sarah Barrett, and now she's dead. And today I'm going to take another one. A friend for her to play with in Heaven.'

He threw the receiver down. It caught the edge of his plate and skittered, spinning. He stared at it.

'Is it her?' Gav asked.

'No,' he said, rising and knocking the kitchen table with his thighs. 'No, it's not.'

He stared at Gav in growing confusion. 'It's not Debbie,' he said.

'But that's good, isn't it?' Gav said.

'Yeah, of course!' He stared at his friend, skin crawling. 'But I recognise that voice. Jesus, Gav. I know who she is.'

66

'Sheila?'

A gentle, incessant tapping at the bedroom door.

'*Sheila. Wake up.*'

Sheila padded to the door and whispered, 'Is it him?'

'He's waiting on the line.'

'What time is it?

'Just after four.'

'I'll be down in one minute.'

She came into her study to find Jeanette at her desk, hunched over the phone, its loudspeaker light on. She was making bland small talk with the person on the other end.

Sheila pulled up a chair and sat heavily, sleep still dragging down her limbs.

'Andrew, I'm here with my colleague Sheila,' Jeanette said, now, dropping Sheila a wink.

'Hello, Andrew,' Sheila said, not feeling particularly comfortable about any of this.

'I wish you'd tell me what it's about,' Andrew Allen said, his accent softly Australian but with a hint of his Mancunian roots.

'It's about an elderly lady by the name of Mrs Edna Wormley. And a man called Edward – or Teddy – Proctor. Does either of those names ring a bell?'

A very brief silence. 'Yes,' he said. 'The old lady spoke to you, too, did she?'

'Not exactly,' Jeanette said, eyes on Sheila. 'I'm afraid Mrs Wormley died over a week ago. I'm sorry to tell you, but she was murdered.'

'*Seriously?*'

'We think it might have been because she had information about a number of child abductions.'

'Oh, my God, is this for real?'

'I'm afraid so. Your business card was among Mrs Wormley's possessions. We'd love to know how it came to be there.'

He was shocked, clearly, and stammered out a number of questions, which Jeanette valiantly answered.

'Well, I met her,' he said eventually. 'Erm . . . I'm trying to remember what day. A Tuesday, I think. Yes, because – well, you see, it was my father's funeral the Friday before – that was the twenty-fifth, and I had a more few days in the country. Sorry, I'm gabbling. This is a lot to take in.'

'Take your time,' Jeanette said.

His story became clear. He'd been back in England following the death of his father. After the funeral he'd spent time visiting old friends, and one of those visits had taken him to the outskirts of Bradford. On his way back he'd found himself passing a sign to Water's End.

'It felt like fate,' he said. 'All the time I was in West Yorkshire, that place was in the back of my mind, and there I was.'

'It was in the back of your mind? Why was that?'

'Because of the stories my mother told me. And so I took the car off the main road and down into the valley to take a look for myself.'

'Tell us about your mother's stories.'

'OK, but it's . . . pretty dark.'

His mother Barbara had died two years before. She and Andrew's father had divorced several years before that, and she'd moved to be near her son in the late 1980s. For years leading up to her death, she'd told stories about her brother, and the family he'd married into. Her brother was Ernie Thirkell – Jeanette and Sheila's eyes met as they recognised the name.

'Ernie Thirkell married Sylvia Proctor, didn't he?' Jeanette said.

'Yes, that's right. In the mid-1950s.'

'And Ernie died in . . . ?'

'1985.'

'He gained a stepson – Sylvia's son from her first marriage.'

'Teddy, yes,' Andrew Allen said.

'Tell us what you know about him, Andrew,' Jeanette said, pen poised over her notepad.

'There was something wrong with Teddy. Ernie and Sylvia both knew it. He . . . wasn't right. Ernie used to tell Mum about it behind Sylvia's back. Ernie got Teddy a job but Teddy went off the rails a few times, and I mean *badly*. One time he'd tried to abduct a kid in Halifax. It freaked Ernie out. The police didn't act, so Ernie decided to take things into his own hands. They kept Teddy under a kind of medical cosh, using tranquillisers Sylvia got prescribed for herself. Unethical, but it did the trick. Teddy got fat and diabetic, and never went out.

'Ernie died in 1985, as I say. Mum went to the funeral and even stayed with Sylvia and Teddy for a night. She said Teddy lurched about the house, off his head on whatever Sylvia was giving him, doped but still aggressive. Shouting, throwing things. Mum could see Sylvia wasn't coping, and she told her so. She asked her what she'd do if Teddy took another child but Sylvia seemed to be in denial. Mum told me something else too.' His voice darkened. 'Something . . . horrible.'

'Oh?' Jeanette said.

'A couple of years ago, when Mum was dying, she told me she suspected Teddy eventually succeeded in taking a child. More than one. There'd been a spate of disappearances in 1986, the year after Ernie died. She'd called Sylvia. Sylvia hung up on her, so Mum called the police. She told them they needed to consider Teddy a suspect. They said they would, but then Mum heard nothing. *She* had to chase *them* – can you believe that? Eventually they told her he was not being considered a suspect. That he was too ill and anyway, he had alibis – ones provided by his own mother . . . *Jesus Christ.*

'Mum spoke to people. Asked for advice. She even spoke to a woman who was writing a book. This woman believed her, but she wasn't allowed to name Proctor publicly.

'Mum returned to England a couple of times to see family in Manchester. Once in 1989, then again in 1991. The second time, she went to see Sylvia. Sylvia told her where to get off. Mum saw Teddy watching her through a window. Glaring out at her, baring his teeth like an animal.'

Sheila stared at Jeanette, mouth open, shivers coursing over her skin. Dee had been right. Teddy Proctor had still been alive *years* after his supposed death.

'Go on, Mr Allen,' Sheila said.

'But on that same visit, something happened that reassured Mum a little. You see, just before she left, a carer arrived. She asked the carer, "How are the two of them getting on?", nodding to the house. And this woman said, "They're doing fine, though he can't get about at all now." Meaning Teddy was pretty much immobile. It was a relief to Mum. The carer was there to make sure he got help to stay in his own home.'

'"Help",' Sheila said quietly. 'That's what she meant. That's what Mrs Wormley meant . . .'

Jeanette shushed her with a hand.

'So you see,' Andrew Allen went on, 'it meant Mum didn't have to worry any more. Teddy was clearly disabled. In need of professional care. She'd failed to get the authorities to consider Proctor as the kidnapper, but at least she knew he wasn't going to take any more kids.'

'Why did you go there, Andrew?' Sheila asked. 'Why did you go to Water's End?'

'Mum had talked about the place, but . . . but she also asked me to keep an eye on things if I was ever over here. Also . . . well, I know this sounds a bit ghoulish, but . . . well, I kind of wanted to see the place for myself. And then . . .'

'What, Andrew?'

'The same day as Dad's funeral, a child went missing from Toller Bridge – only four miles from Water's End according to the map. I knew it couldn't have been Teddy, but . . .'

'You felt drawn,' Jeanette said.

'I did. And that's where I met the old lady – Mrs Wormley. She was walking along with a bag of shopping, and asked me what I was doing. We got to chatting. She said she was a cleaner in the care home where Sylvia Thirkell now lived. She also told me Teddy had died. That he'd died years back – in '86 or thereabouts. I told her that was rubbish, because Mum had seen him in '91. Should have seen her face. And now you're telling me she's dead? That someone killed her?'

Sheila asked, 'Did your mum ever put her concerns about Teddy to Sylvia in a letter?'

'She told me she wrote to her more than once. I don't know if Sylvia ever replied, or if she even kept the letters.'

She kept one, Sheila thought to herself grimly.

67

It was just before seven and a milky light was creeping over the moors, but as they descended into the valley they returned to night.

Gav brought the little Peugeot to a halt by the first building they came to.

'Well, this is Water's End,' he said.

Adrian got out first, looking about in the chilly, slightly misty morning air.

'Recognise it?' Gav said, joining him outside.

He peered as shapes materialised slowly from the darkness. Saw crowding trees, a broken-down stone wall, a pale-fronted house with black squares for windows – and recognised nothing.

He closed his eyes and thought hard. Tried to envision what had happened to him that night. The exchange that must have taken place between the man who took him away in his van, and the woman who drove him back to town. Where had that happened? Had he even been conscious?

'Y'OK, man?'

'I'm fine.'

'Place is fucking creepy.'

'You're telling me. Let's look around.'

They passed the white-fronted house, then an entrance to a driveway, where a wooden gate hung askew from a stone pillar. Low stone buildings ran away from the road in a line, disappearing into the gloom. Running water sounded in the distance. Along the lane from the driveway entrance, more trees; then, round a curve in the road, three more cottages, ruined and empty.

He looked at his feet, at the crumbling surface of the road under his trainers and experienced a flash of . . . *something*.

'Cobbles,' he said to Gav. 'There were cobbles.'

They looked around, then at each other.

'No cobbles round here,' Gav said.

'Let's go back to the house,' Adrian said. He led the way back along the lane. It was lighter now, and he saw that the house's windows were broken. There was glass on the sills. He stood before it, hands in his jeans pockets, and tried to force his memory to work, to fill that gap between the back of the van and being in the footwell while the woman drove him back to Toller Bridge and his mother's arms.

'Should we take a look down here?' Gav said, indicating the driveway entrance.

'You go,' he said. 'I want to be on my own for a minute.'

Gav disappeared down the side of the white house.

Adrian looked along the lane in both directions. The place had more definition now. He could distinguish trees; could pick out individual trunks. Huge bushes that he thought were rhododendrons swelled between the trees, some with big flowers, still colourless in the dawn's monochrome palette. But it was still misty in places, and he was tired, so his vision swam.

And then he saw the woman.

One moment, nobody, then she was there, a good distance away, standing at the edge of the road by the trees. She wore dark clothes and a long coat like a mac open at the front, and he could just about make out the expression on her face: one of bored truculence.

Her hair was light, piled on her head like a high helmet. That hair, and the expression on her too-familiar face . . .

She isn't real. She isn't there. You're tired. Hallucinating.

For a moment his vision shifted, and she was gone again, as if she'd been a figment of his imagination.

Or a ghost.

'Hello?' he called out.

Nothing. Only the echo of his own voice ricocheting back from the trees.

'Ade,' Gav hissed, emerging from the driveway behind him.

Adrian glanced round at his friend, then back along the road to where the woman had been. She'd vanished.

'Ade, man,' Gav was calling him. He stood at the entrance to the driveway that led away behind the white house.

'What is it?'

'There's somebody down there,' Gav said. 'There's a van and a light on in a little house right at the end. Only . . . you might want to come and look.'

'Why? Have you found cobbles?'

'Yeah, now you ask, but there's something else too.'

He followed Gav down the driveway into a yard behind the white house. Cobbles, wet with dew, gleamed all around them. Flashes of memory came to him, but unformed and incoherent. Like *déjà vu*, but with emotions too. Fear.

'Recognise it?' Gav said.

'Don't know.'

'The van's this way,' Gav said.

He followed him beyond the cobbles, along another lane, this one narrow and muddy, with low buildings down one side. The sound of water grew louder the further they went.

A light shone dully through the gloom, coming from the window of a little house at the far end of the muddy track. It illuminated a small van parked outside.

Gav slipped down one side of it and beckoned Adrian to join him.

'Brace yourself, man,' he said.

He came down the side of the van and read the logo emblazoned on the side in big black letters in a classic font, one designed to reassure:

Hardaker's Carers

'My mum's agency?' Adrian whispered. 'You're fucking kidding me.'

68

'Can I help you, ladies?' a stentorian voice called across the car park of Parkview Care Home – a modern brick-built complex surrounded by gardens on the outskirts of High Calder.

'Oh, yes! I very much hope so,' Sheila said gaily to the woman approaching from her car. 'We were hoping to speak to someone about a place in the home.'

'I see,' the woman said, slowing as she drew closer. She was a big woman in her fifties, wearing a suit and holding a set of files and a sizeable handbag. She had a key out, ready for the main door. 'Not looking on your own accounts, I take it?'

'No,' Sheila said, all smiles. 'Not yet anyway.'

'I know you,' the woman said. 'You're Sheila Hargreaves.'

'That's right. And this,' she gestured to Jeanette, 'is my sister-in-law Jeanette. It's Jeanette's mum, my mother-in-law we're enquiring for.'

'Well you're talking to the right person. I'm manager here,' the woman said. 'Valerie Mayhew. Val, if you like.'

'Nice to meet you, Val.'

'It's usual to make an appointment,' Val Mayhew said disapprovingly. 'It's only just gone eight. The residents won't be started on their breakfast . . .'

'I'm so sorry,' Sheila said, laying it on. 'We'd heard wonderful things and we're both *so* busy, we thought we might just pop by and try our luck . . .'

The woman turned the key in the lock and let herself into a lobby. She looked back their way. 'I can give you ten minutes,' she said. 'Seeing as it's you.'

'Wonderful,' Sheila cooed, and dropped Jeanette a sly wink.

'Park yourselves here,' the woman said when they reached her office. 'I'll be a few minutes.' And she went on her way.

'I wonder where they keep their files,' Jeanette said, eyes scanning the filing cabinets in the blandly decorated office.

'Don't you dare,' Sheila warned her.

Val Mayhew was soon back, and took a seat at her desk, ready to answer their questions.

'I'll give you a very quick tour in a few minutes,' she said, 'though, as I said, a lot of the residents are still getting up, so it *will* be whistle-stop. Now, what's the name of the lady you're enquiring for?'

Sheila reeled off the fiction they'd concocted in the car. Her 'mother-in-law', Jeanette's supposed mum, Gladys, was struggling to get about, though very with-it mentally.

'Age?' Val said.

'Eighty-five,' Sheila said. 'Though she could pass for seventy-five, wouldn't you say, Jeanette?'

'Oh, yes!' Jeanette chimed in.

'Gladys has a friend who moved here some time ago,' Sheila said blithely. 'I believe she still lives here.'

'Oh? Who would that be?'

'Sylvia Thirkell,' Sheila beamed.

'Sylvia . . . *Thirkell*? Oh . . . yes,' Val said. 'Thirkell was her name, wasn't it? Proctor first, then Thirkell. She's still with us, yes. She struggles, I'm afraid.'

'There was some trouble, wasn't there?' Sheila asked, head on one side, the concerned but empathetic interviewer.

'Trouble?'

'Something Gladys said . . . I think she'd been talking to a relative of Sylvia's – an item of hers that was taken . . . or,' she frowned at Jeanette, 'am I getting confused?'

Val Mayhew watched her with mild suspicion. 'What relative would that be, now?'

'Oh, goodness knows! I'm not sure Gladys herself would know, would she Jeanette?'

'Probably not,' said Jeanette.

'Any . . . incidents,' Val Mayhew began cagily, 'would be regrettable, but would be dealt with *very swiftly*.'

'That's good to hear,' Sheila said, nodding. 'The cleaner was sacked, wasn't she?'

Val Mayhew looked at her desk and seemed to take stock before answering, 'You may rest assured that I took necessary steps.' She nodded as she spoke, and Sheila knew in that moment that she herself had personally fired Mrs Wormley.

'It might be nice for Sylvia to have Gladys here,' Sheila mused aloud now, suspecting she might be pushing her luck. 'I don't expect the old lady has too many visitors, does she?'

'Not many,' Val said, frowning a little.

'Despite being married twice?' Jeanette asked. 'Wasn't there a . . . son, for instance?'

'Sadly passed away,' Val said stiffly.

'Ah, well.'

'Now,' the manager said, 'why don't you tell me a little more about Gladys?'

They played the game, spinning their fiction, to no end that Sheila could now see. They'd got what they'd come for: confirmation – or as good as – that Mrs Wormley had lost her job here after stealing something belonging to Sylvia Thirkell.

'Oh, look at the time, Jeanette,' Sheila gasped eventually.

'Are we running late?' Jeanette said, all alarmed.

'I'm so sorry, Mrs Mayhew.'

'Val, please.'

'I'm so sorry, Val. May we come again? I promise we'll phone next time.'

'Of course!' The manager stood. 'I'll show you out.'

Something occurred to Sheila as they reached the main door.

'Val, might I ask – earlier, when I mentioned Sylvia, you seemed surprised at her surname being Thirkell. Has she changed it again, or . . . ?'

'Well, yes, she has.'

'I see.'

'She reverted to her maiden name. I don't know why. People do sometimes.'

'What was her maiden name, if you don't mind my asking?'

'Not at all,' Val Mayhew said, adding, quite casually, given the tremendous import of what she was about to reveal: 'She's Sylvia Baxter.'

69

'My mum's fucking agency,' he said, for about the tenth time – this time sitting in the car.

'She must employ carers all over the county,' Gav pointed out.

'Yeah, she does, but . . . I can't believe *she's* in there now,' he said. 'With *him*.'

'Who do we tell?' Gav said.

'Police, I guess,' Adrian said. 'Except they're not going to believe us, are they?'

'Sheila, then. Tell her. She can call the rozzers. They'd listen to her.'

Adrian took out his work phone and turned it on. The battery was very low.

'You ringing her now?' Gav said.

'No.'

'Who then?'

'Ssh.'

The signal was rotten. The ringing sounded like it was

coming through a transistor radio. But she picked up and her voice was clear enough.

'Debbie?'

'Adey?' She sounded sleepy. 'What's wrong?'

'I need to be quick, but I need to ask you something.'

'Ask me something? Adey—'

'You know my mum's agency?'

'Yeah.'

'Does . . . did Elaine sign up for some shifts?'

'Yeah, she did. A couple of months ago.'

'Right.'

'She doesn't like people knowing, Adey. She's only allowed to work so many extra hours because of her course. They want her focused on that. Did your mum tell you, or . . . ?'

'Not exactly. Does she do overnight shifts? You know, where they stay with old people in their homes?'

'Yeah. Easy money, she says.'

'Right.'

'Adey, why—'

'Just one more thing. Have you ever lent her your car – your auntie's car, I mean?'

'The Smurfette?' She laughed, though nervously. 'Yeah, a few times, if she needs it. I haven't told Auntie, though. Adey, you're scaring me now. Why are you asking me all this?'

'I can't explain. I haven't got time. I've got to go.'

'Mrs Wormley worked it out,' he told Gav. '"Help" refers to Elaine, because she's Teddy Proctor's carer. Mrs Wormley had probably seen the van's logo when it was parked down here. She went to Mum's agency to find out more. Then she realised who Mum was. Mrs Wormley tracked Elaine down to the Jester and went there to meet her. Probably threatened her with her

375

knowledge. Elaine killed her. Elaine must have taken Damien's wig so she could disguise herself to kidnap Sarah Barrett. Little Phil saw her take the wig, or – more likely – put it back. Then he tried to blackmail her. He arranged to meet her outside the pub on Tuesday night, and she knifed him and pushed him into the canal.'

He looked at the phone, finger poised over the 9 – when the battery died.

70

'Malcolm, Desmond Baxter was related to Sylvia,' Sheila half-screamed into the phone. 'Baxter was her maiden name! Do you see? He might be her brother!'

'What are you talking about, Sheila?'

'Just listen!'

Jeanette put a steadying hand on her shoulder, and she settled back into the passenger seat of her friend's car.

'It's possible,' she said, trying to keep a lid on her frustration, 'that it wasn't Teddy who died but *Desmond*. I bet you anything that death certificate was signed by a locum doctor – or someone who wouldn't know Desmond from Teddy. For years Sylvia had been trying to protect Teddy, but people started asking questions, watching her and her son – Dee Thompson among them. Ernie Thirkell's sister, Andrew Allen's mother, another. It was convenient to pretend Teddy died, then to get a care package in place for him under Desmond's name.'

'Sheila, this is—'

'He's still *there*, Malcolm! Teddy Proctor is living in that valley under his dead uncle's name.'

'I interviewed Teddy Proctor in 1986, Sheila. He was a very poorly man.'

'He has *help*, Malcolm. That's the meaning of the word "help" in Mrs Wormley's notes.'

'Sheila, this is conjecture—'

'*It's not!* We've spoken to Andrew Allen,' she said and took a deep breath. 'We rang him up.'

Stunned silence down the line.

'I'm sorry, but we did. He told us horrifying things. Now, do your job, man! Meantime, I'm going to find that poor boy your lot seem so determined to persecute.'

71

'Ade, wait!' Gav cried, as he scrambled from the car and legged it down the driveway. Gav caught up with him and put a hand on his shoulder. '*Stop*. Let the police deal with it. We can drive to a station.'

'The police don't believe a fucking word I say to them! Meanwhile, Rachel might be alive in there with those two fucking monsters. I've got to *try*!'

Gav got in front of him. 'I know, man, but listen—'

'It's nice that you want to look after me,' Adrian said. 'But I can take care of myself.'

'Bullshit, man. If you go in there, I'm coming with you.'

They looked at each other in the misty gloom of the damp courtyard.

'It's your decision, then,' he said. 'Once we go in there, we don't know what we'll find. You've got to understand that.' He blinked and swallowed. 'We've got to find that kid.'

72

'Gav went out just after midnight,' Denise McArthur told Sheila when she phoned from the car. 'He didn't come home. We're a bit worried, to tell you the truth.'

'I'm sure he's perfectly fine,' Sheila said, smiling into the phone to reinforce the reassurance with her tone.

'Was there something you . . . ?'

'No, no,' Sheila said. 'It was actually Gavin's friend I'd hoped to talk to – young Adrian. I don't suppose he . . . ?'

'We haven't seen Adrian since yesterday morning,' the woman said darkly. 'Perhaps you can tell me what's going on.'

'I can't, I'm afraid, love.'

She cut the call and turned to Jeanette. 'They're there already,' she said. 'At Water's End. Don't ask me how I know. We've got to go there, Jeanette.'

73

The light was growing, and the mist had receded to reveal a ruined place: low stone buildings in poor repair, hemmed in and loomed over by trees. It felt damp, unhealthy, utterly neglected.

They edged along the driveway towards the van and the little house at the far end. Most of the buildings weren't houses and never had been. Nor were they stables, but had some kind of industrial function.

'It's half eight,' Gav whispered. 'They'll be up and about by now.'

'Fine,' Adrian whispered back grimly.

'What's the plan, exactly?' Gav asked.

'Wait till she's gone, then find a way to get in there,' Adrian said. 'Deal with the old man – incapacitate him if we need to – then find the kid and get out.'

'Sounds good in principle. Shouldn't we, like, arm ourselves in some way?'

'With what, exactly?'

'Dunno. Hammers?'

'Nah. If he's old and frail enough to need an overnight carer, we won't need hammers.'

'And what if it's not him?'

Adrian looked at Gav but didn't have an answer.

They crept down the side of the Hardaker's van, and continued along the track, where it petered out and trees grew thickly. There was a small building standing on its own here – a shed with a smashed-in door. It would be a perfect vantage point, with a clear view of the cottage and the van.

'In here,' he said, squeezing through the gap in the door.

Gav followed.

'I'm freezing, man,' Gav said.

'It won't be long now.'

Another light showed in the little cottage now, and Adrian was sure he glimpsed movement: a shadow behind a dirty-looking blind.

They waited, Gav humming Smiths tunes softly to himself all the while.

A click from inside the cottage, and its front door came open, showing a sliver of light within a brown hallway. The light in the hallway went out, and the door came wider. A slight, hooded figure slipped out, then turned and locked the door from the outside. It unlocked the van, then climbed inside. It was dark in the van's cab, but then the internal light came on, showing the figure in the driving seat, their head down, as they looked for something, in a bag, perhaps. Then a hand came up to turn off the van's interior light, and at the same time another came up to tug back the hood – and in the split second before the van cabin became dark again, he saw their face clearly. And saw that his suspicion had been right.

'Is it her?' Gav hissed in his ear.

'It's her,' he said grimly.

Elaine. Trainee paramedic. Part-time bar worker at the Jester. Casual girlfriend of Debbie. Helper to a child killer.

She reversed the van up the driveway to the courtyard behind the house, where she carried out a three-point turn then drove out onto the lane that ran through Water's End, and away.

They listened as the engine droned into the distance, and faded.

'So how do we get in?' Gav asked. 'Do we just knock on the door then push past him, or . . . ?'

'Let's take a look round the back first,' Adrian said. 'Get the lie of the place. Then we'll decide how to get in.'

He led the way from their shelter down the side of the house. The land fell away here and the slope was slippy with mud. He had a sense that water lay at the bottom. A pond, perhaps. He kept close to the building, and clambered along as far as the corner at the back.

It could only be a small place, with no upstairs. A pair of windows overlooked the woods at the back. One was curtained, the other not. He edged his way to the clear one, gesturing to Gav to follow.

He peered gingerly in and saw a rudimentary kitchen, lit by a single bare bulb hanging from the ceiling. There was an old cooker with a raised grill, and a mucky-looking worktop and metal sink. Packets of food sat on shelves. He couldn't see a fridge.

A door led out of the kitchen into a dark hallway.

'Try the window,' Gav whispered.

He did. It was locked, or jammed.

'What about the next one?'

The curtained window was jammed too.

'Break it,' Gav said. 'Fuck him. He's a killer. It's not as if anyone will hear you. I'll do it if you like. There were loose bricks in the place we were hiding.'

A sound from inside. He shushed his friend with a hand and peered closer.

An angled stick appeared beyond the doorway, then a big hand holding the top of it, followed by a second stick. A man was heaving himself along the hallway.

'Is that him?' Gav hissed.

'I don't know.' He felt as if his heart were in his mouth.

More of the man's body came into view. He was tall and thin, and his clothes looked dirty in the electric light from the kitchen. Then: a glimpse of hair. A big grey beard, and straggling grey hair on his head that framed a bony grey cheek. To move clearly took great effort. The man's face was contorted with it.

Something about the shape of him, and the greyness of his skin and hair . . .

It was as though every muscle in Adrian's body had suddenly clenched.

'I think it's him,' he whispered. 'Jesus, Gav. I think it is. But he's loads thinner. That's the man who tried to take me. He's the Lollipop Man.'

They watched, frozen, as Teddy Proctor lurched out of view.

'Let's go get that brick,' Gav said.

They hurried round to the front of the house, Gav holding a brick, ready to smash the window by the front door, when he said, 'No, let me. I want to do it. Besides, if there's any comeback, then it's on me. Cover your eyes.'

He shielded his own with an arm and swung the brick into

the window. It broke dramatically, loud cracks crazing the pane for a second, before the whole thing smashed, shards tinkling to the ground and the floor inside the house.

Gav came forwards, his jacket wrapped round his arm, and swept away the glass remaining in the bottom half of the frame, then yanked aside the grubby curtain that hung there.

'After you,' he said.

It was a low sill and he scrambled over. Gav came after.

They were in a gloomy living room, lit by a shrouded lamp. It was like a room from a horror film: ratty leather furniture was caked in dust, and cobwebs clogged the corners. It smelt of something horrible. Something *animal*.

'That's where she must sleep,' Gav said, indicating a makeshift bed, piled with blankets.

'It's Matthew Spivey, Teddy!' Adrian bellowed into the house, making Gav jump. 'Remember me? I'm the one that got away!' He grinned at Gav, feeling an unexpected rush of glee. 'Ready to see me again?'

They went into the hallway and saw into the kitchen. The old man had been here only minutes before. But there was no sign of him.

Gav kicked open a door into a filthy bathroom. It, too, was empty.

That left one room.

'In here?' Gav said, hand on the handle of a door opposite the living room.

'Go for it,' Adrian said, his heart racing.

Gav twisted the handle then booted the door. It flew open. Another grim chamber, this with a single mattress but unoccupied.

'So, where is he?' Gav asked.

'He was in here,' Adrian said, matching his incredulity.

'Is that a door?' Gav said, pointing at what looked like a cupboard at the end of the hallway.

Adrian marched up to it and tried the handle. It was locked.

'Stand aside,' Gav said, and ran at it, giving the door a powerful ninja kick. It juddered, the lock smashing, and the door came ajar towards them.

Adrian pulled it wide, and they looked into a dark passage with a floor that sloped gently down from the hallway.

'This is like fucking *Scooby-Doo*,' Gav said.

'It must connect to the other buildings,' Adrian said. 'Have you got a torch?'

'No.'

'He must be in there,' Adrian reasoned. He added quietly, 'It's probably where he keeps the kids.'

'Jesus, man.'

'Come on. Stick together.'

It was cold in the passage, and the air was damp. Whatever they'd smelt in the house was stronger here. He crept forwards, blinking in the darkness, detecting a dim light source ahead – possibly daylight.

The passage levelled out, and the floor became gritty, then he was aware of space. Shapes began to solidify in the meagre light, and he saw the place was vast.

'What is it?' Gav said. 'A factory?'

'A tannery,' he said. 'They used to tan leather here. That's what the smell is. Stinks, doesn't it?'

It was a huge, low-ceilinged room, longer than it was deep, perhaps stretching all the way up the driveway to the lane, as far as the pale-fronted house. Before them a narrow cement path ran between square pits on either side. The little light there was came in through gaps in the wooden slats that formed the room's long left-hand wall. Beams hung over the pits. Chains hung from these and from metal hooks on the sides of pillars.

'Where the fuck is he?' Gav hissed.

Adrian looked around him. At the far end of the path between the pits was a dark arch: an entryway to another building.

'The only place he can be,' he said, pointing.

'He can get about on those sticks,' Gav said.

'Let's go,' Adrian said, and set out along the path.

The first few pits were deep but dry, but the next ones had shallow water in them. The water stank. Gav retched into his sleeve and tried to muffle it. 'Sorry,' he gasped.

'Doesn't matter,' Adrian said. 'He knows we're here. Let him listen. He'll be shitting himself.' He shouted, 'Where are you, Teddy?' and his voice echoed back at them. 'You know we're going to find you, you crazy, murdering old bastard.'

He started to lead them, but stopped as a noise came from the far end of the long room. A scraping sound.

'Oh, God,' Gav whispered.

A light had come on beyond the archway. A single bulb swung gently, so that shadows danced. The archway became a proscenium, waiting for the show to start.

'Show yourself, Teddy!' Adrian shouted.

Another sound, like something hitting concrete.

'You don't think he's armed, do you?' Gav asked.

'Maybe,' he said. 'One of us should go back to raise the alarm in case anything happens.'

'I'm staying right here,' Gav said.

More sounds. More bumps on hard floor – and a stick appeared, angled into the lighted area. An actor was about to enter stage right.

Another bump. A second stick, then a pair of legs, scraping the floor as the torso heaved forwards.

And there he stood: a giant, shambling man, hair sprouting. An ogre at the gateway to its lair.

Fear coursed through Adrian, but he stood his ground, feet planted firmly, arms at his side, and faced the man who'd taken him.

'Where are they, Teddy?' he screamed. 'What have you done with them? With Sarah? With Rachel? With the other ones?'

A growl from the man with the sticks. He moved, the sticks lifting and thumping before him. He was coming towards them with surprising speed.

'Through there, are they?' Adrian yelled, and marched forwards, leaving Gav behind him.

'*You . . .*' the old man began, in a sneering snarl. '*Get out.*'

'No,' Adrian shouted, slowing as he came within metres of the old man. Something didn't feel right underfoot. 'Not without those kids. You think you *can*—'

The path under Adrian suddenly crumbled. He shifted his weight but it was too late and he plummeted into darkness, so surprised he didn't yell, but landed hard on his side, the air forced from his body.

He lay in the dark pit, on wet mud, breathless, panic rising.

'Jesus, man. Are you OK?' Gav had jumped down into the pit and was kneeling over him.

Can't breathe, he tried to gasp, but couldn't get any air.

Gav was pulling him up, *unfolding* him, till he stood, propped up by Gav.

Above them, the noise of sticks punching concrete. The old man was moving.

Gav scrambled at the side of the pit to lift himself back up onto the path.

Adrian was able to take small breaths. He felt his way along the wet wall of the pit, till he was in a corner.

Above him the old man was roaring. Gav crouched over the pit and reached down. Adrian took his hand.

Gav pulled at his arms while Adrian grappled, seizing the edge and levering himself up with his arm.

A shape loomed over the pair of them. The old man leered down, and gold teeth glinted between his drawn-back lips.

Gav, still crouching, tried to turn, then the old man's stick came down hard on his head, sending him falling backwards.

'Fucking bastard,' Adrian said. 'Don't hurt my friend.' He scrambled to his feet and thumped the old man in the chest with both fists.

The old man swayed, but righted himself. Gav was up, though holding his head. He grabbed the stick, tore it from his grasp, causing the old man to wobble.

Adrian ran at Proctor again, so that he tottered and then fell, a look of sheer astonishment on his face, and landed with a splash in the water at the bottom of the nearest pit.

He and Gav held each other up, each panting, gasping.

The old man was groaning and trying to move. The water wasn't deep, but the pit was, and there was no way he'd get out without help.

Faintly, from beyond the archway there came a new sound. Unheard till now, but unmistakeable.

The sound of a child wailing.

He and Gav looked at one another.

'Stay here,' Adrian said. 'Keep an eye on him.'

He hurried towards the archway and its slow-swinging light.

74

He was in a corridor with a door at one end and a narrow stone staircase at the other.

The wailing came again, and he lurched up the stairs, ignoring the pain in his side, the pain of breathing. The stairs twisted as they climbed, then came to a door. It was closed, but not locked.

The sound of sobbing came from beyond it. He pushed it slowly open.

An attic: long, low, with a pitched roof. It was dark, but enough light filtered through the rotting roof for him to get a sense of the layout, and of furniture in the room. Chests stood about, and boxes, the odd chair, and then the beds.

There were four beds: narrow, metal-framed and old-fashioned, like something from a barracks. Or a prison.

She was sitting on the one nearest to him, a tiny huddled shape, shivering with fear as she watched his approach.

'Hello, Rachel,' he said. 'It's Adrian from next door.'

He smiled, to show her it was OK.

And then he saw the others, sitting all in a row.

'Oh, Jesus. *Oh, God . . .*'

And in that instant an image seared itself into his brain that he knew he would never, ever be able to erase.

'You found her?' Gav cried as Adrian brought Rachel, her hand in his, slowly along the path between the pits.

'Rachel, this is my best friend, Gav,' Adrian said.

The child sniffed.

'Hi, Rachel,' Gav said. 'What about . . . ?' He gave Adrian a hard look.

'Up there,' he said. 'All of them, I think. What about . . .'

'Still down there. He isn't moving.'

'Hello, Adrian,' called a woman's voice.

They turned and looked. Adrian pulled Rachel close to him.

Back along the path, where the doorway opened from the house, stood Elaine. She was holding something. It took him a second to understand that it was a shotgun.

'You worked it out,' she called, a mocking note in her voice, and started coming towards them. 'Clever you. Always did have your nose in other people's business. Friend to everyone, buying everyone drinks.'

'I don't think you're in a position to criticise,' Adrian said.

'I wasn't criticising,' she said, coming closer still, the gun held casually across her chest. 'I was mocking you.'

'Nice,' Gav muttered.

'You'll never understand,' Elaine said to him. 'You and your fucking *empathy*. What about me? Don't you have any empathy for me?'

'Debbie does,' Adrian said, eyes on the gun. 'She likes you.'

'Debbie's an idiot.'

'Why did you help him?' he said, keeping his voice level. 'Did he make you?'

'Teddy? No. We got talking. We found we both had a thing for . . . taking things from people. Taking happiness.'

'*Jesus*,' Gav said.

'You took Debbie's car, didn't you?' Adrian said. 'And Damien's wig. Only Little Phil saw you.'

'I enjoyed putting a knife in him, greedy little pig.' She sounded so satisfied.

'It's over now, though,' Adrian said, astonished that his voice was so calm. It was as if he'd now seen and heard all the horror, and was immune to it. 'People know. Not just us. Others. Police. They're coming now. Oh, and Teddy's in a pit back there, if you're interested. I think he's dead.'

She shrugged. 'Don't care,' she said.

Rachel began to cry. He kept her close against his leg but urged her to move behind him. Gav saw what he was doing and came close, to make a shield.

'Time to say bye-bye, Adrian,' Elaine said, and positioned the gun against her shoulder.

Gav made a move.

'Not so fast,' she spat, pointing its double-barrel his way.

Adrian moved back, pushing Rachel behind him.

'Let's talk about this,' Gav said, very reasonably. 'Maybe we can help you.'

Elaine cackled. The gun wobbled off target.

He thought fast.

'I can hear sirens,' Adrian said, looking away and frowning.

'Me too,' Gav said, quick as a flash.

She looked sceptical, then cautious. Her eyes flitted aside.

'Don't move,' she said, then turned and hurried back down the path to the house, where she pushed the connecting door shut.

In the space of those seconds, Adrian lifted Rachel under her arms, said to her very quietly, 'Be a very good girl and then we can take you to your mummy,' then crouched and lowered her over the edge of the nearest pit. 'Stand against the wall here,' he hissed, then stood again.

'Keep apart,' he hissed to Gav. 'Keep her confused. She's only got two bullets max.'

Elaine was back. Gav stepped neatly away from him.

Elaine pointed the shotgun, first at him, then at Gav.

'Walk back that way,' she said.

'OK,' Adrian said, and put his hands up. He started to move.

Clearly she wanted them over the biggest pits, where the water was dark and looked deep. She'd shoot them there, so that they'd fall in.

As far as he could tell, there was one chance now – for all of them: pretend to acquiesce, then surprise her.

She'd shoot one of them, at least, but the other might make it.

Gav and he shuffled backwards. Without moving his lips, he muttered, 'I'll run at her. You crouch. She'll shoot at me, but you go for her legs, OK?'

'Fuck, man,' Gav hissed back.

'Keep moving,' Elaine said. She was coming with them, keeping pace, only a couple of metres from them now.

'Where would you like us?' Adrian said brightly, helpfully.

'Back a bit,' she said.

'This is like taking a photo,' he said now. '"Back a bit, back a bit".'

Gav laughed uproariously.

She didn't like it. It unnerved her. She crouched and waved the gun between them.

'Hey,' Gav said loudly. 'Can you hear voices?'

Her eyes flickered. It was enough of a distraction. Adrian ran, head low, barging at her, arms out. He landed on her, and the gun blasted.

'Oh, my God!' a woman's voice screamed. Not Elaine. Another woman. 'Help him!'

And everything went mercifully black.

75

Sunday 17th April, 1994

The pain woke him a few times in the night – at least he thought it was night-time; it was hard to tell in this windowless room – but apart from that he slept deeply.

Then Gav was by his bed, perched on a weirdly high armchair, rolling fags and lining them up on the arm. There were four rolled already, and he'd nearly finished a fifth.

'You're awake!' he said, in surprise.

'Time is it?' It came out in a croak.

'2 p.m.,' Gav said. 'It's Sunday, in case you were wondering.'

'I'm in hospital.'

'No fooling you.'

'What happened to me?'

'I'm not really supposed to say.'

'What? Why?'

'Police want to interview you, don't they? They want your story as you saw it. They told me not to tell you anything.'

'Fuck that, Gav. Come on. What happened to me?'

Gav sighed.

'That mad bitch shot you in the shoulder.'

'Shot me . . . ?'

'Yeah. Double-barrel shotgun, point blank. Bang. You ran at her and she shot you, but the pair of you went down.'

'The kid,' he said, sitting up with a burst of adrenalin. 'Rachel. What—?'

'Completely fine. Back home, or in a safe house or something. Honestly, man, you'd better not tell the rozzers I've told you any of this. You saved the kid's life, man.'

He sank back on the pillows and closed his eyes again, only to find himself back there, in the twilit tannery, surrounded by black pits. He opened them again.

'Drink,' he croaked.

'Here.' Gav passed him a glass of water. 'Do you want me to hold it for you?'

'I'll manage. Can you get me my specs?'

'Ah. They broke. Sorry, man. They're making new ones.'

'Did they get her? The police?'

'Yeah, they got her. She wasn't in a good way.'

'What happened?'

'Your friend Sheila turned up with that friend of hers – just as Elaine shot you. It was insane, man. That Jeanette woman sort of landed on top of her and Sheila got the gun off her. They had some idea about tying her up, but Elaine made a run for it – only Jeanette got the gun off Sheila and shot her in the arse. Said she'd never shot a single bullet before. She was pretty pleased with herself. Anyway, Elaine's in here somewhere, in a secure ward. They arrested her and there are cops on the door and everything.'

'And what about . . . him?'

'Proctor? Dead. They think he tried to get out of the pit but fell back into the water and drowned. Big shame. Not.'

'I pushed him in. I killed him.'

'He was the devil,' Gav said.

They fell into silence.

'Your mum's about here somewhere, by the way,' Gav said, as he lined up his sixth rollie. 'That's her coat on the hook. She's a bit fragile.'

'Where is she?

'Gone to ring a neighbour.'

'Were all of them there, Gav? All four of them? I saw . . . *bodies* . . . but I didn't take it all in. I didn't count them.'

'Yeah,' Gav said quietly. 'I didn't go up, but Sheila did before the police came. She said she recognised Sarah Barrett from the photos. And that there were three others too. He'd put them in a row, like dolls. And . . . well, Mrs Wormley was right. He'd tanned them. He'd preserved them.'

He closed his eyes to control a wave of nausea.

'How's Sheila?'

'All right, I think. She's really . . . *sorted*. I like her. Her friend's a pain in the arse, though. On at me to give her an exclusive interview – talking about selling it globally through a press agency. I told her where to go.' Gav saw Adrian's face. 'Man, what is it?'

Adrian hadn't even realised he was crying.

'Everything's OK, man.' Gav knelt close to the bed, holding his arm.

'I know.'

'You're a fucking hero.'

'Am I?' He coughed out a laugh.

'You're my hero, anyway. You'll be all over the papers. You'll be famous, man.'

'Oh!' A voice from the door. His mum.

Gav got up.

'Ade's a bit emotional,' he explained.

'Oh, baby,' his mum said, coming round, and taking Gav's place at his side.

'I'll be back later,' Gav said. 'Bye, Mrs Spivey.'

'It's OK, Mum. I'm OK. Everything's going to be fine.'

'My baby.' And she was sobbing into his arm again. 'Fiona's so grateful. We all are. But you shouldn't have done it. You could have been *killed*.'

'I know. I didn't think about it. And I was angry.'

'We love you so much.'

'Yeah.' He swallowed hard. 'Me too.'

'Your dad and me – you're our world.'

'Dad?' He regretted saying it the moment it was out.

'Your dad loves you like nothing else.'

'He's ashamed of me, Mum. You know that. He always will be.'

'No, baby.' She looked genuinely gobsmacked. 'No, no, *no!*'

'He was always so worried about having a gay son. You know that. Remember when he cut my hair off?'

'We're so sorry.' Eyes down. 'About everything.'

'OK.' He tried to shrug, but it sent a bolt of pain through him and made him cry out.

'We love you – we *will* love you, *whatever* happens. Whatever you are. You're our precious baby.'

He nodded, trying not to cry again.

'People have been calling the house non-stop,' she said. 'Including . . . your friend.'

'Who?'

'Stephen.'

'*Ste?*'

'He sounded embarrassed.'

'Yeah, well . . .' It was darkly satisfying.

'And Debbie rang, too. The woman – the one who did this – she was her friend. Did you know?'

'Yeah. I knew.'

'She's devastated,' she said. 'Said she wanted to come and see you.'

'Depends how long they keep me here, doesn't it?'

'Fiona wants to come too, except they've taken her and Rachel to a place – a sort of clinic. After everything that pair did to her . . . Fiona says she doesn't know how she'll ever thank you. She says you're her hero.'

He rolled his eyes.

'It's true, baby. It is. You're my hero too. You always will be. I wanted to ask you . . . if you think you'll come home now.'

'I don't know.'

'We want you to.'

'I want to go to uni, Mum. If I pass my exams. You know that. I want to go live in Leeds. I'm hoping Gav'll be there, too. That's what I want.'

'I know, baby. I know.' She was nodding, gripping his arm so that it hurt. 'You've survived so much. You can do anything now.'

76

He dreamt about the office. About Kev being a dick. Then woke up to find Kev sitting in the weirdly high armchair, biting his nails.

'Gay-boy's awake!' Kev cried.

'Who let you in?' He felt better. Less sore. His head was clearer.

'Hot nurse. Reckon she wanted to give me her number.'

'You're such a dick.'

'I was right, though, wasn't I?' Kev said now, smirking. 'You were gay after all.'

'So?'

'I could tell.' He shrugged.

'You must have a really effective gaydar, Kev,' Adrian said. 'It's like your superpower, or something.'

Kev looked horrified.

'All right, Adrian,' Yvonne said, coming into the room. She had drinks in takeaway cups with lids, balanced in a tower.

'How you feeling?'

'Like I got shot in the shoulder by a psycho,' he said.

Kev snorted with laughter.

'Give me that chair, Kev,' Yvonne said. 'Been on my feet all day.'

Kev got up and took his coffee.

'Linda won't be in to see you,' Yvonne said. 'Her eldest got arrested last night for joyriding, but she said to say hi. She said you'll get paid while you're off and we'll see you when you're better. She wants me to write up the story and put you on the front page. Nige wanted to know if he could take photos of you in the hospital. Make it more authentic.'

He wrinkled his nose. 'Maybe wait till I get my glasses fixed. I look better with glasses.'

'You're the town hero, Ade,' she said. 'Make the most of it— What? What's so funny about that?'

'Oh, oh,' Kev said suddenly, eyes on the little window in the door. 'Look who's here. The Queen of Sheba.'

'Oh, her,' Yvonne said, distastefully. 'Best make myself scarce, then.'

'She's OK, Yvonne,' Adrian said. 'Really, she is.'

Yvonne rolled her eyes.

'Bye, Gay-boy.'

'Bye, Knobhead.'

'Just don't tell me I'm a hero,' he said, as she settled onto the armchair.

'I wasn't going to,' Sheila said. 'I was going to tell you off. You could have got yourself killed. It was very foolish.'

'Yeah, well.' He tried to fold his arms and winced in pain.

'It was also very brave. You took risks for other people. I

admire you very much, Adrian.'

'Do you?' She looked like she meant it. 'Thanks.'

She smiled.

'Jeanette shot Elaine,' he said. 'Gav told me.'

'That's right. She said she didn't think about it. She just reacted.'

'I don't understand how Elaine knew we were there,' he said now. 'I mean, we watched her leave. She seemed relaxed. She reversed up the drive and drove away.'

'She saw your friend's car,' Sheila said. 'She suspected something and went back to check on Teddy. She's told all this to the police.'

'Teddy who was supposed to be dead,' he murmured. 'They fooled people all that time.'

'Sylvia's brother Desmond came to stay with her after Ernie's death. He was ill and died a little later. Sylvia reported the death as Teddy's, that's all. Teddy became Desmond and was safe from people who asked questions. Desmond had been a loner, living in a council flat in Brighton. Sylvia wrote to the council and said he'd come to live with her. Nobody batted an eyelid.'

'Have the police spoken to Sylvia?'

'They've tried but she's confused. The rest they've pieced together from Andrew Allen's stories heard from his late mum.' Her eyes dropped. 'The police aren't very happy with me, Adrian. My friend Malcolm is simply furious. They say I could have derailed the entire investigation. I think they'd like to try to find something to charge me with.'

'Can I help?'

'No,' she said, breezily. 'Just tell the truth. I'll fight my own battle. I've got Jeanette on my side. She doesn't take nonsense from anyone. Apparently they terminated their interview with her because *she* was asking all the questions.'

'You did nothing wrong,' he said. 'Either of you. None of us did . . . well, if you don't count me and Gav breaking into Mrs Wormley's. It was Proctor and Elaine. They're the wrongdoers. Can't they see that?'

'They can, but they're embarrassed we got there first.'

'Why did she do it? Elaine, I mean.'

'She told you and your friend she liked the power, didn't she? I expect that was true.'

'We'll need to go to court, won't we?'

'I expect so. It'll be unpleasant but we'll get through it.'

'I'm supposed to be doing my A level resits next month.' He looked down at his bandaged shoulder and arm. 'How am I supposed to write four essays in three hours with this thing?'

'I'm sure they'll let you dictate them. They might even give you special dispensation.'

'What do you mean?'

'There might be a way you don't have to do the exams, given everything you've been through. They might be able to award a grade on the basis of your tutor's testimony.'

'No,' he said firmly. 'No, I want to do the exams. I'm good at exams.'

'The main thing for you is to get better as quickly as possible.'

'What will you do?' he asked.

'Me? What do you mean?'

'You can't go back to celebrity interviews now, can you? You helped catch a killer. You should do a programme about crime. About cold cases.'

She smiled. 'Jeanette wants me to write a book with her.'

'About the Lollipop Man?'

'Yes. I've said I'll think about it.'

'Do it!'

'Would you help?' she said.

'What, like with interviews and things?'

'Well, yes, but . . . I was thinking you could write it with us.'

'Me?' He laughed.

'Whyever not?'

'Because . . .'

He couldn't think of a because.

'Maybe,' he said. 'But after my exams, OK?'

'Of course.'

A rap at the door.

'Another visitor,' she said, standing. 'I should go in any case. The police are coming to the house to take a formal statement.'

'Come and see me again,' he said.

'I will.'

Sheila opened the door and Adrian saw who'd come to visit.

77

'Did you talk to him about the book?'

'I did, Jeanette. But very gently.'

'And?'

'I think he'll do it.'

'And what about the interview?'

'I didn't mention that.'

'Sheila, for God's sake. I've got Geoff to hold tomorrow's front page! Where are you now?'

'I'm in the car. I'm about to leave the hospital.'

'Well go back in. Tell him he needs to do this. Tell him it'll be cathartic.'

'No, Jeanette. And don't you go bothering him. Not today. He needs space.'

'Space? Sheila—'

'Yes! And actually, so do I.'

'You? What do you need space for?'

'To write a letter,' she said.

'A *letter*?'

'Yes. To Colin Joseph.'

'Letters are dangerous things, Sheila. People keep them. Remember, it was a letter that started this whole thing . . .'

'It was a letter that caught a killer, Jeanette. I'll talk to you later.'

78

'Hello, son.'

'Hi, Dad.'

His dad closed the door behind him. Eyes down, head down, he was the picture of sheepish defeat.

'How's the . . . er . . .' He gestured towards Adrian's shoulder.

'Painful.'

'Brave lad,' his dad said, and sniffed.

'Sit down if you like,' Adrian said.

His dad nodded, and took a seat on the high armchair. He looked stiff, awkward, anything but relaxed. And, as ever, there was no eye contact.

Adrian waited.

'Fiona's singing your praises,' he said gruffly. 'We're proud of you.'

Are you? Aloud, he said, 'Thanks.'

'We love you, son.'

He nodded, eyes on his hands, folded on the bedspread.

'We want you to come home.'

'Yeah, well.'

'We miss you.'

'Do you?'

His dad nodded.

'I'll think about it.'

More awkward silence.

'Of course,' Adrian said, lifting his tone a little, 'I'm famous now, so . . .'

'You've always been famous, son.'

'No I haven't. You changed my name, remember. Why did you do that?'

'Why did we . . . ? To protect you, of course.'

He stared at his dad. 'Really?'

His dad lifted his head and looked right into Adrian's eyes. 'Yes!'

'I thought . . .'

'You thought what?'

He held his tongue, but only for a second. 'I thought you were ashamed – of what happened. Ashamed of me.'

His dad stared, mouth open. 'You thought . . . ? No! *Never that.*'

'Dad, you cut my hair off. You cut my hair off because I looked . . . because you thought I looked like a girl.'

'I . . .'

'You did! Don't deny it, Dad!'

They stared at each other across a gulf of time and disconnection.

'I thought he might come back for you,' his dad said at last, in a tiny, frightened voice. 'I wanted to change your appearance. We'd failed to protect you that night. I . . . I was so scared . . .'

And that's what you want to believe now.

Peter Spivey put his face in his hands and began to weep. The weeping became sobs. Loud, anxious, angry sobs.

Adrian listened for a minute, before speaking.

'Stop it, Dad,' he said, but gently. 'It's OK.'

'God forgive me, Adrian.'

'It's OK. Really, Dad. It's OK.'

And for now, it was.

Author's Note

Several places in the book are real, including Bradford, Halifax and Leeds, but others are made up – though they might feature elements of real places, and the roads and moors that connect them. It's all the more important to stress that none of the characters is based on any real person. I do, however, make reference to Myra Hindley, Ian Brady and Peter Sutcliffe, who were all too real, and whose crimes continue to hang over the communities of the north of England.

Acknowledgements

Thank you to Katharine Bradbury, who read the book in instalments over several months and gave ongoing feedback and suggestions. Thank you as well to Margaret Murphy, crime writer and friend, who helped me to bottom out some key problems in the early section of the book.

Dr Heather Reid OBE began her broadcasting career with BBC Scotland in 1994. Heather read a draft and gave me several very useful pointers about what it was like to broadcast live from a TV studio then.

Joanne Welding, who taught me A-Level English in the early 1990s, gave me pages of very useful feedback and asked some challenging questions. Miss, Miss! What mark did I get?

Emma Darwin gave me some very useful guidance (and reassurance) when my confidence was low and helped me think through how to structure the opening.

A big thank you to other friends who read the book at various stages and made useful comments: Alison Winch,

Gordon Munro, Astrid Reid and Laura Hamilton (to whom this book is dedicated).

My amazing agent Francesca Riccardi believed in this book and helped me to make it a better one. I'm hugely grateful to her for placing it for me. Thank you, as well, to my editor Lesley Crooks and the team at Allison & Busby for believing in this book and bringing it to readers.

DANIEL SELLERS is the author of the Kindle-bestselling Lola Harris Mysteries and is an obsessive fan of Agatha Christie. His crime thrillers are pacy and dark, with as much interest in whydunnit as who. He grew up in Yorkshire, and has lived and worked in Liverpool, Glasgow, Ireland and Finland. Sellers now lives in Argyll in Scotland.

DANIELSELLERS.CO.UK